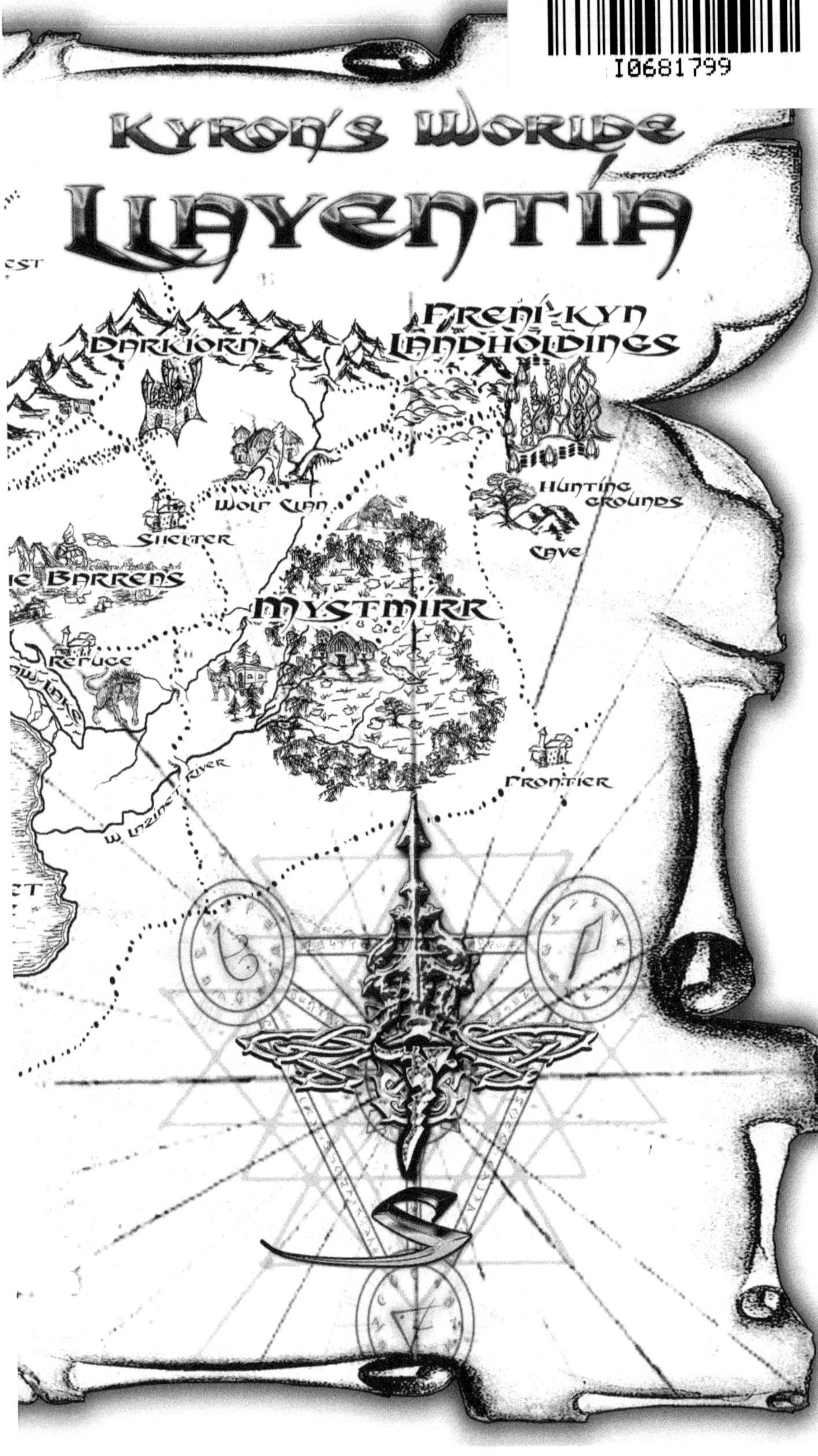
Kyron's Worlde
Llayentía
Darkiorn
Freni-kyn Landholdings
Wolf Clan
Hunting Grounds
Shelter
Cave
The Barrens
Mystmirr
Refuge
Frontier
River

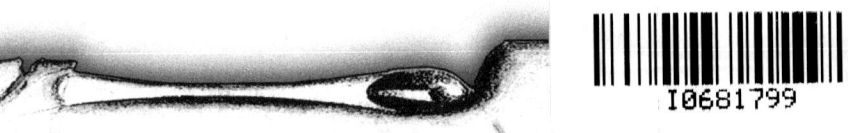

Sarenka lowered her lashes, hiding the fully dilated slits of her pupils and the rage seething just below the surface. She sought to bring the sparks in her hair to a more passive color but gave up. She was wound too tight for that kind of subtlety. The raking slashes across the baron's body, each vicious groove a testimony to what a Freni-Kyn was capable of, strengthened her resolve.

"Okay," she mumbled without lifting her head.

The metallic clink of metal against metal as he unlatched his belt filled her with dread.

"Hurry it!"

She jumped, his voice a stinging whip against her already shredded nerves.

"If I'm gonna get you outta here, we gotta make this quick-like."

Now.

Now's the time.

And there's no going back from here.

Heart pounding, avoiding eye contact, she steeled herself against what she was about to do.

I am evil itself.

Vile.

A creature of the darkest night.

Rising to her knees, she slid a hand up his leg and lowered her mouth. His muscles tensed with expectation under her hands. She risked a peek through her lashes and watched D'trav's eyes slip closed.

Oh yes… he needs this…

She tensed her fingers and the claws slid free of their nailbeds, sinking into his groin.

With a muffled shriek, his eyes flew open. He jerked backwards, causing yet more pain and another shriek.

Her grip tightened.

For a moment he was stunned, unmoving, then his hand drew back, forming a fist.

"Do it," she dared, "and I'll slice them off!"

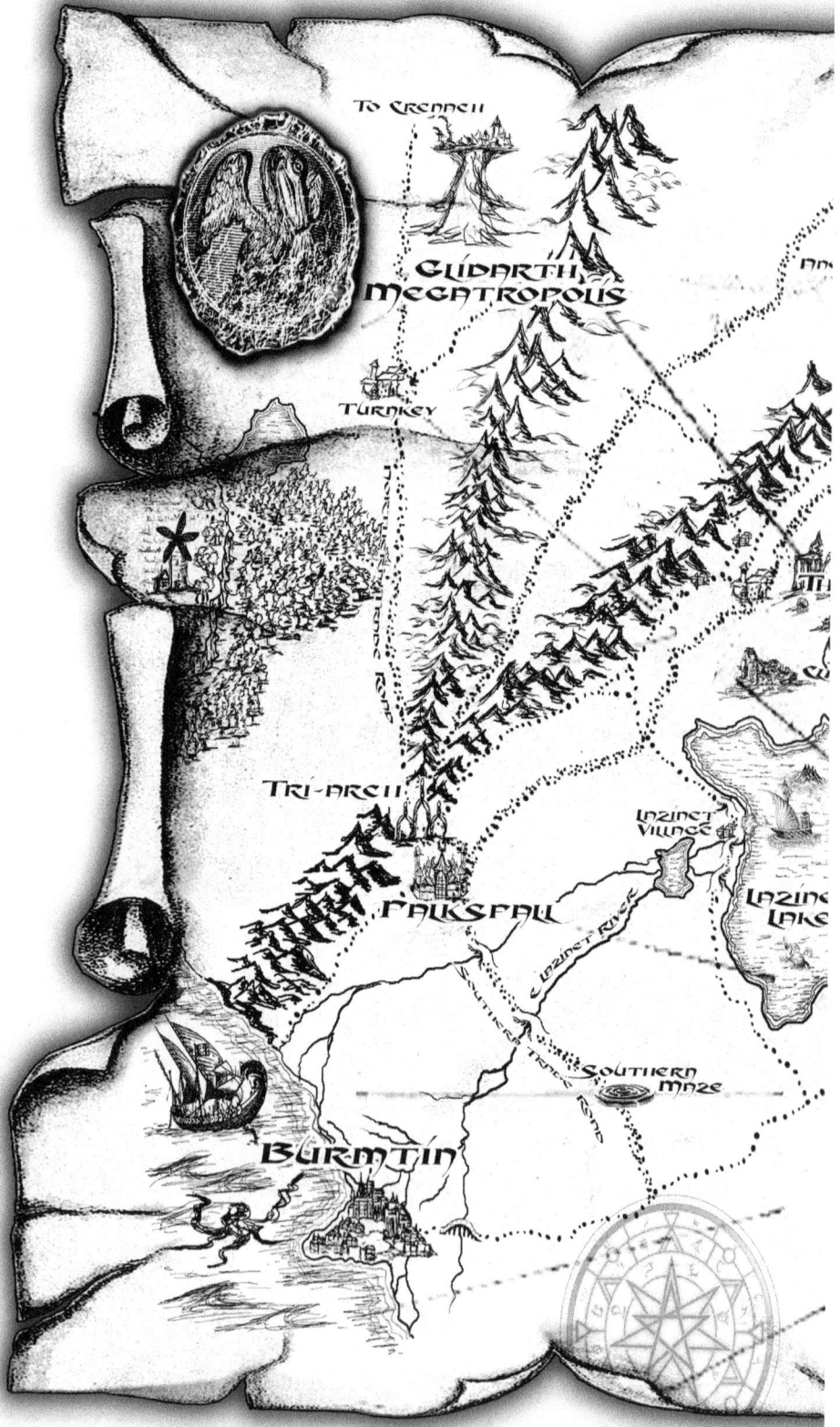

To Crennel

Gudarth Megatropolis

Turnkey

Tri-Arch

Falksfall

Lazinet Village

Lazinet Lake

Lazinet River

Southern Trail

Southern Maze

Burmtin

BURMTÍN

1 Apothecary
2 Barracks
3 Destinguished Dainties
4 Donielson Blacksmith
5 Jump Tower
6 Manor
7 Sad Town
8 Flaming Block
9 Warehouse District
10 Well
11 East Gate
12 North Gate
13 South Gate
14 West Gate

Other Kyron's Worlde books:
Foretold Betrayal
Foretold: Seduction's Blade
Foretold: Special Edition

www.kyronsworld.com
www.facebook.com/ES.Tilton.Author
www.sexyfantasyfiction.com
www.pinterest.com/ESTilton
www.twitter.com/sexyfantasybook
www.estilton.deviantart.com

Full size maps can be downloaded from:
www.kyronsworld.com/kyron-s-worlde-map

KYRON'S WORLD

TRAPPED

WITHIN ILLUSIONS

BY E.S. TILTON

A TIME STREAM ADVENTURE

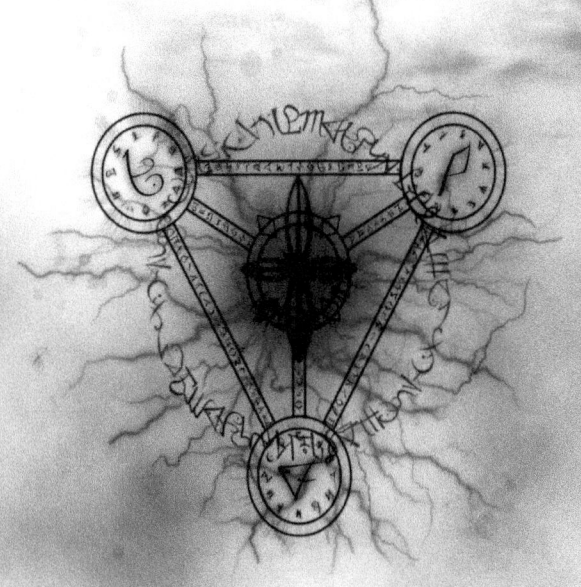

KYRON'S WORLD

Dedicated to Mark Hardman, who created the cover art I needed to launch Trapped in Burmtin years ago, and who would not let me throw Trapped in the trash during the transition from a tiny novella to a massive novel. You have been my steadfast support, shoulder to cry on, Photoshop teacher, and combat guinea pig. For that I am so filled with gratitude that thinking about it brings me to tears.

TABLE OF CONTENTS

KYRON'S WORLDE

TRAPPED

WITHIN ILLUSIONS

E.S. Tilton

Kyron's Worlde Creation

Author's Note

Kyron's Worlde

Although I have attempted to give a working idea of all new items, terms, and races as they appear in the text, I know that there are those who always want to know more. For any with that inclination I've included a glossary in the back of the book. In digital versions, click the word and it will jump to the definition, then click the word in the definition and it will jump back to the first incident of the word. You may also choose to visit www.KyronsWorld.com for a printable download of the glossary and maps.

Two specific things worthy of note:

The Preral cycle and the **Preral sickness** are afflictions suffered only by the Freni-Kyn people. Perhaps most easily thought of as a cat in heat, the Preral cycle must include a mating or it leads to the Preral sickness. Should the Preral sickness occur, the Freni-Kyn female is rendered unable to control her actions and will mate with any, and all, available males and females until the sickness runs its course and the tension is resolved.

The **Foreveron drug** was accidentally discovered by the Watrelk Pirates and rapidly taken advantage of. Like the Preral sickness, it renders the recipient sex mad. However, it may be ingested by either male or female. The drug is addictive and without the proper series of antidotes the person suffering from it will eventually die. Alcohol staves off the craving but is not a cure.

Author's Note

Kyron's Worlde

A note concerning italicized parts:

All mental thoughts are italicized. Kyron's Worlde includes psychics who deliberately, and sometimes not so deliberately, send thoughts. I've chosen to differentiate those thoughts with this symbol: ~

A psychic thought, deliberately sent, will look like this:

~Read more E.S. Tilton books, read more E.S. Tilton books, they're good for you!~

All other thoughts will look like this:

Kyron's Worlde sure does rock... I should tell people about the series.

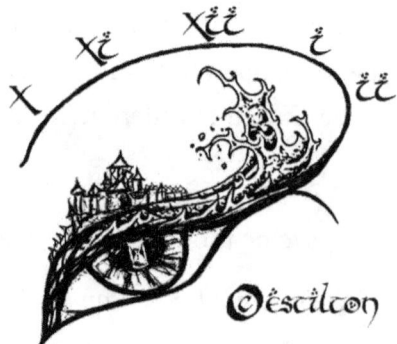

Intro to Kyron's Worlde

It is the year 2658 After Betrayal. With nearly 2500 years of Rage Wars behind them, peace rests uneasily upon the people of Llayentia. Technology has grown stagnant, devolving in most places. Desolate cities dot the land, promising treasures of mysterious magics and machinery to the few brave enough to explore their wraith-filled maws.

Seven Seers, believing that the time of foretelling has dawned, have shifted into place and are searching for signs of The One. Their goal is to return unity to Kyron's Worlde, but despite their rare psychic gifts, they cannot clearly see the future and are sometimes caught within the liquid webs of possibilities.

CHAPTER 1

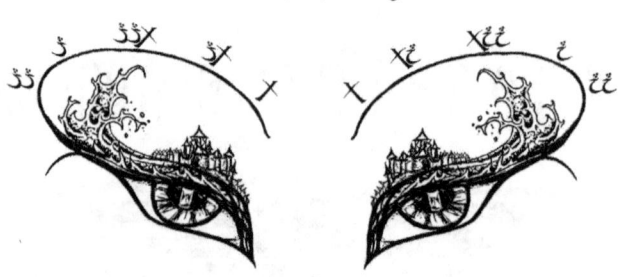

"The conscious mind is a stone skipping across the liquid fabric of reality."
Xoltern Prigseth
Frevellian Seven Mouthpiece of 711 BB

Parian plummeted through the engraved ceiling of Leanor Manor and threw his arms forward, flailing about in a vain attempt to stop. He grasped at empty air, ricocheting off stone walls before crashing to a halt midair. Horror filled him. Panting, striving not to touch the walls, the ceiling, the floor, anything, he couldn't help but whisper, "My god! So much blood!"

Looking down on the slaughter, he hovered at ceiling level and gulped for air through immaterial lungs before remembering that he wasn't really there. His body waited elsewhere, in another city, another time.

And that's where I should be.

Not here.

Not now.

He threw himself upwards but merely bounced off the ornate ceiling.

Parian turned, drifting in the air, searching the rough stone walls for answers.

Why am I here?

Where's the anchor that's keeping me from leaving?

He took in each detail of the elaborate cell with growing dread. The windowless walls gave prisoners no opportunity to cut, break, or burrow free. Blood covered everything in long sweeping sprays of red, and the cloying scent was a visible cloud to his psychic-enhanced eyesight. Obscene in their opulence, velvet cushions lay scattered across the wooden floor and a pile of embroidered sleep garments lay before the only piece of furniture, a mirrored wardrobe.

"I can't be stuck here. I've got to get away from this... this..."

Slaughter. He couldn't bring himself to say it out loud.

"It's too much."

He panted and reached for calm.

I'm a Seven...

A psychic...

Immune to death...

To brutality.

I've seen the worst, the most depraved thoughts...

I'm past shocking.

Guttering tourches threw flashes of red and yellow light across the bodies.

But this is different. This isn't a sick thought. This is...

Death.

He covered his face and realized the truth as a band of despair tightened around his chest. He was too late. They were both dead, the trail to The Foretold already dissipating, the one who would save their world, gone. A slight movement caught his attention, and he whirled back, peered closer. Strands of the Freni-Kyn's living hair lifted and swayed, dull embers dancing across the tips.

She's alive!

And if she's alive, maybe...

Eh stared at the man, searching for life.

Dead, without even his spirit lingering.

Parian turned back to the woman. A heavy chain ran from her shackled ankle, lacing a path through scattered puddles of blood before disappearing into a shadowed corner. Every useful item lay outside her reach, even the simple silver sconces whose prongs might serve as a pry bar. Yet the cost of this special chamber, even that of hauling in the ancient stone, was negligible when compared with the price of her servitude. She was the valuable commodity, the shimmering jewel in a setting of stone.

And she's teathered to this nightmare as securely as I am.

Blood seeped from shallow cuts, swaths of scarlet across indigo skin. Her nostrils widened and her eyelids twitched, fluttering long Freni-Kyn lashes. He brushed the edge of her mind and recoiled, sickened, as the haunting scent of blood joined her dreamscape.

"Kryon... no... no..." almost inaudible, she called upon their god, fingernails sheathing and unsheathing as she fought the dreams, the reality. Her hands jerked up to cover her face, revealing wrists scraped raw. Layers of mottled handprints, green and brown, covered the backsides of her arms, a silent witness to old abuse.

"I can't..." Her voice, so low, was but a whimper.

Parian feared the worst. She too was dying.

"No... please no..." she said.

He touched the edges of her mind and dared go no further. Not while *that* drug raced through her bloodstream. Not without risking sanity. Even the welcome release of sleep gave her only surreal battlefields—a residual effect of the Foreveron. He saw that, knew it, and could do nothing to aid her.

Tethered, an immaterial guardian of death, he waited.

The moments ticked off, drip, drip, drip.

Unnerved, Parian found the source of the sound and watched as blood slid down a sconce, gathering force. He held his breath, waiting, and the thoughts of the manor's inhabitants picked at the edges of his mind, demanding attention.

It fell, landing in a crimson puddle.

Drip.

A shudder worked its way up his body, an undeniable force.

The air went cold and still. And into that silence, while the half-life of dawn rose over the city of Burmtin, a whisper of the past stepped from the darkness. Crackling energy sparked against Parian's disembodied form, raising the hairs on his arms and head.

Barely chest high, feet gliding above the floor's surface, she approached the Freni-Kyn woman.

Parian's heart gave a resounding thump of fear.

Kneeling, head tilted as though curious only, the transparent figure watched the slumbering woman's struggles. Her hand lifted, reaching towards the unconscious woman's forehead.

Parian fought to surge forward. To stop her. To keep the child wraith from doing—Kyron-knew-what. He willed his limbs to move but they wouldn't budge, not even a scant hand-span. Trapped in that amberous grip, he was forced to watch.

Her transparent fingers rested against the Freni-Kyn's bloodied skin. The silence expanded, stretching forth its scream, blending past and present into a perfect pitch of knowing.

The Freni-Kyn drew a startled breath and then quieted, as though drawing solace or even, Parian dared to think, peace, from that ghastly touch.

A tiny lift of the lips, the barest suggestion of a smile, touched the child's face as she locked gazes with him and faded from view.

Searing tendrils crept through Sarenka's mind, pushing her towards consciousness, and with that came the tormenting aches of heart and body that always plagued her after a night with—

No! I won't think of that bastard!

Not yet.

Not before I'm even awake.

Fighting the drug fog, she struggled towards clarity and pushed away fragmented memories of body parts and leering faces. They whirled past, each jarring vision slashing at her brain with razor accuracy, lacerating her very soul.

How many?

How many people this time?

Sarenka curled into a protective ball, pulling against a shackle and chain, the ever-present reminder of who, and what, she was: A slave. A plaything for the wealthy and powerful. A commodity to be bought and sold.

With longing she thought of the things she'd lost, the warmth of the sun on her face, the silky velvet of a dog's ear, the rich smell of earth in her hands, the wild ride of outrunning the city guards after snatching their lunches, and the gleeful laugh of beggar children when she shared it with them. Freedom to do what she wanted, go where she pleased, and take adventure wherever it found her. Things she would never experience again, not as long as she remained trapped within the manor, chained like a dog and forced to another's bidding.

No opening the eyes.

No letting them know I'm awake.

She chanted her morning ritual and forced her mind down the familiar paths of a regimented assessment—the same survival training that had cost her freedom.

Sore, yes, but without the ache of new bruises.

Torchlight flickering red and pink through closed lids.

The scent of raw meat.

Her stomach responded with a growling protest, but she continued on.

Leather soles scuffing past the door...

And what's that?

She strained to focus past the scuff of the shoes.

The intermittent pling of dripping water.

She stopped, focused, her pleated ears unfurling.

Water?

At a cold touch to her forehead, she shivered and reached for the thin blanket. Instead, her nails scraped a hard surface. She extended her claws and pulled them back towards her body, scratching at the ground. It resisted, tearing away in a manner she recognized.

Wood.

I shouldn't be…

This is wrong.

I should be…

Her thoughts reeled, searching for answers.

On my cot, clean, bandaged, not…

Sticky…

Not hearing water…

Not smelling….

Recognition burst through her mind, creating explosive tingles throughout her body.

Blood!

CHAPTER 2

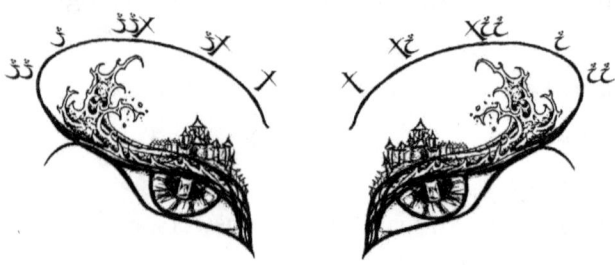

"The Seven kings finally sent in their d'yroap order today:

> Seven metals of increasing value
> Seven symbols
> Gems inset into the most costly to raise the value even further.

We've chosen these metals and symbols for the different races:

> pink copper-----------star---------------Freni-Kyn
> grey silver-------------wave-------------Watrelk
> yellow gold------------arrow-----------Sharpra
> green riseen-----------tree--------------M'hakru
> blue breyt-------------gavel--------------Frevell
> purple airnelk--------wing--------------Glidarth
> black nighshk--------map---------------H'euman

We aren't giving them rings. Our craftsmen insisted on loops so that they aren't worn on fingers. I'm sure this will not please some, but the task of engraving the rings again, after they wear down through use, is just too costly."

Jura Lennalth
Secondary Clerk
Glidarthian Tomes 4023 BB

Her Freni-Kyn hair sparked, throwing off bits of glowing color, and her scarlet eyes snapped open. She threw herself backwards, scrabbling to get away, twisting and pulling against the anchoring chain as it jerked into a straight line inches above the ground. Reason returning, she dropped her shackled ankle to the ground and squeezed her eyes closed, refusing to look.

Too close…

He's too close…

Gathering courage, she forced them back open.

The master's glazed eyes stared across the short space, cold and empty.

Her stomach wrenched into dry heaves, and she hunched forward, fighting the nausea of the Foreveron drug. Shards of pain stabbed through her head, and she pressed her palms to her temples. A single pain-tear trickled down her cheek.

She gave the baron's arm a tentative nudge. It moved flaccidly, and if not for the broken way he lay and the lacerations covering his body, she'd think him asleep. Flinching, she leaned over and peered into his eyes.

Still moist…

Not dead long.

Couple of hourglass turns…

Maybe…

It sank in.

Dead… he's… dead.

Raw emotion flooded in, overwhelming her with the desire to laugh, to cry, to scream, to jump. Instead she stared at his broken body and her lip lifted in a snarl.

He'll never touch another slave.

Relief faded into panic. She lunged for the heavy chain, sparks flying from her hair. A silent scream stuck in her throat.

No!

No-no-no-no-NO!

Heart racing, she stared at the stone door separating this room from the rest of the manor. Before long, someone would arrive.

"Please… please-please-please-please."

She strained forward, pulling the chain taut, striving to reach the key. It hung out of reach, tormenting with a promise of freedom and the ridicule of defeat.

Too far...

It's too far...

She dropped her hands to the ground, giving up. Her shoulders slumped forward, and she stared down at the blood-splattered wood without seeing it.

I've failed.

And earned death.

The torches burned low, and still Sarenka sat as picture after picture flashed past, poison, torture, hanging, gutting, beheading, pulling limb from limb, a thousand scenarios, each more gruesome than the one before. The room closed in, suffocating, and all she could see was blood and death.

A chill leached into her bones, reminding her that she still lived. Turning from the endless morbid futures, she faced the present danger. Death had not yet arrived, and when it did, she'd face it with claws unsheathed.

Damn you!

She cursed the baron for leaving her chained within this stone coffin, his last cruel act.

"Kyron damn you to his deepest hell!"

The thump of approaching footsteps came from the hall.

Without warning, Parian was jerked up through the ceiling, ricocheting back through time and space like the fruit of the rubber tree. Each jarring bounce shook free thoughts and feelings from years past. Things he didn't dwell on, some sweet, some poignant, some distasteful. Friends who had passed beyond the veil, the smell of sunshine on the meadows of the Freni-Kyn landholdings, the feel of velvet against his skin after a ride in the moonlight, the chafe of the saddle after a week-long travel, the beauty of his grandmother's face.

He threw his hands out, trying to buffer the hits, but it was futile. There was no telling what would strike next, shoulder, left foot, top of his head, right elbow, one after another, too rapid to stop. Each jarring hit sent an echo of pain through him as his mind supplied the memory.

Stop thinking that! Rule number 38. If you believe it's real, it is.

He landed back in the chalk circle and settled into his body with a thud. His physique bounced, slamming down onto the ground with enough force to bruise his whole backside. His eyes flew open, and his chest arched upwards as if he had been hit by lightning. He froze, caught in that bent position, and after what seemed forever, drew a drowning man's breath. Muscles relaxing, he settled back to the ground.

With a groan, he rolled over. "Kyron's beard…"

~Parian are you——~

The send startled him into another jump. Parian pulled himself up, balancing on hands and knees, swaying to the rhythm of his labored breath. A cold sweat broke out over his body.

~Parian?~

He gagged, heard her mental gasp, and could hold it back no longer. His breakfast spewed forth with enough violence to throw him off balance and face forward into his own mess.

"Oh dear god. Shut up. Get out of my mind." He shifted his head, trying not to breath in the viscid liquid.

Airintia withdrew, in part. *~What are you doing?~*

"I found The One," he spoke aloud, too tired to send.

~You what?~ Her mental shout echoed through his mind and brought on another round of retching.

Weakened beyond measure, Parian lay in his own filth while the room swam in and out of focus. Finally, he summoned the strength to whisper, "Go away."

~Parian I…~

Parian embraced the solace of darkness, glad for the peace, the silence.

~*You heard?*~ Airintia whispered.

~*We heard,*~ half a dozen voices whispered back.

~*He's... okay?*~ Airintia asked.

~*What he's done... dangerous...*~ the Eldest thought, and even her mental voice sounded older, wiser, more experienced, than theirs.

Airintia waited while the older woman scanned Parian's body, checking for injuries. She would have preferred to have done it, but the Seven didn't move on whims. They followed traditions, and by rights the Eldest did the healing.

When the Eldest spoke again, her projection was faint. ~*It's caused serious damage, I'm not sure we can— *~

Airintia lost control. Her fear washed over the group, causing their hearts to pound and hands to sweat. They withdrew, pulling away from Parian and that distant room which held his body.

As the fear abated the Eldest continued, ~*As I was saying... I'm not sure I can repair all the damage.*~

Airintia's cheeks heated with shame and she was glad they were not there to witness it. ~*I'm sorry.*~

Silence hung.

The seers waited.

A palpable wave of concern surrounded the aura of the Eldest while she worked to save Parian from afar.

Frantic, Sarenka gave the shackle a last twisting tug as the door swung open.

The guard stopped, half in, half out, and a roulette wheel of emotions flitted across his face, finally settling on cautious neutrality. Pushing back a stray lock of hair, he surveyed the hallway before stepping in and shutting the door.

The metal band slipped through Sarenka's fingers, forgotten. She stared at his brawny frame, frozen in uncertainty.

"Welp, the vapoor bastard finally got his comin' up, did he?"

She unfolded her ears, straining to hear the muttered words. Instead of angry accusations and the beating she expected, he sounded strangely satisfied. That he dared call the master the slang equivalent of burning lizard shit, even in death, gave her hope.

"I didn't…" She searched his face for the compassion he'd shown in the past, for the man who had slipped her rations and extra blankets.

"What to do… what to do…" D'trav rubbed his fingers back and forth across his cheek, scraping night-old bristles and creating a soft scratching noise. It meant nothing. A habitual gesture, done without thinking, one he'd made many times over the last few months.

CHAPTER 3

"Please D'trav… you know I didn't. Please…"

He looked at her as if only just remembering that she was in the room. "Nope, don't suppose you did. That Foreveron…"

"Please, just let me loose. They'll kill me."

"Right out of your mind with it, most like. Bet you don't even remember the night. Not that they'll care."

"When I woke up… he was…"

His gaze shifted to the brutally killed man and he frowned.

Her hopes came crashing down, dashed to an untimely death on the bloodied ground. He wouldn't help, not with that body right before his eyes.

"Sorry Darlin, I'll not be lettin' you go. Can't let 'em think I had my hand in it."

Sarenka lowered her head, staring at his gear-covered boots through a fringe of brown hair. Staring, but not actually seeing. She imagined lunging past, flipping the chain around his neck, bracing her feet on his back, and strangling him. Between the year spent in the acrobatic troupe and the rush of energy that always came with danger, she could do it. Muscles tensing, she looked at the extra chain, and all the fight went out of her. There wasn't enough for that maneuver, and without the key it was pointless.

It's no use.

There's only one thing left to do.

No matter what she did, no matter how far she ran, her father's despicable heritage always caught up. Even now, three years later, she still needed that childhood training. With loathing, she turned to the 'Freni-Kyn underbelly,' as her H'euman brothers had taken so much delight in naming it. She wet her lips, enhancing their fullness, and widened her eyes into pools of innocence before looking up.

"Please, I'll do anything."

"Anything?" D'trav's brows shot upwards. He ran a fingertip along his jawline, tracing the jagged edge of a scar.

"Anything."

Pupils dilated, his gaze swept over what remained of her hourglass figure, lingering long enough to make Sarenka feel vulgar and low. She knew that all-too-familiar look of hunger. Despite the garish blood, she remained enchanting to the other races.

"Anything…" he repeated, gaze traveling along the length of the chain. Aroused, breeches tightening, he shifted position. Without warning, he turned and scooped up the single key hanging from a nearby peg. He dangled the bit of green metal in front of her. "For this here key, you'll do what I say?"

"Yes," Sarenka answered so softly that it barely moved the air. She knew he'd been watching her lips when he threw the door bolt.

"Tell you what. I'll let you go, Darlin, but first you'll do for me what you done been doin' for…" He kicked the baron with enough force to cause a limb to flop, splattering more blood across Sarenka.

Horrified, she wiped at the wetness but only succeeded in creating larger smears of red. It was too much. Something within her stirred, and the shame which always simmered just below the surface turned to rage. She should have known this would happen, this shift from trustworthy guard into a man commanding her to perform. It always happened. Visions of en from her past loomed, expecting her to wait on them, obey their commands at the snap of a finger, take the punishments they doled out—every kick, every slap, her lot in life. Inevitable. As always.

He dangled the key above her head. "Well, what's it gonna be, Darlin? Me or the hangman?"

Hatred sheared through Sarenka, slicing away at her self-control. The tips of her hair, filaments swaying with a life of their own, settled into embers of red. She stared up at the lust in D'trav's face and ground her teeth.

I won't!

Not ever again…

She shook her head, throwing off tiny sparks of red.

"Don't be sayin' no so fast. I 'spect you'll be dead within the week, lessin' you choose rightly."

His words hammered a spear of fear through her heart. The key rocked back and forth, light glinting off the green riseen metal, taunting her once more with a promise of daylight. Without it, she was trapped in the twilight of a torch-lit room. Without it, she was a dead woman.

Sarenka lowered her lashes, hiding the fully dilated slits of her pupils and the rage seething just below the surface. She sought to bring the sparks in her hair to a more passive color but gave up. She was wound too tight for that kind of subtlety. The raking slashes across the baron's body, each vicious groove a testimony to what a Freni-Kyn was capable of, strengthened her resolve.

"Okay," she mumbled without lifting her head.

The metallic clink of metal against metal as he unlatched his belt filled her with dread.

"Hurry it!"

She jumped, his voice a stinging whip against her already shredded nerves.

"If I'm gonna get you outta here, we gotta make this quick-like."

Now.

Now's the time.

And there's no going back from here.

Heart pounding, avoiding eye contact, she steeled herself against what she was about to do.

I am evil itself.

Vile.

A creature of the darkest night.

Rising to her knees, she slid a hand up his leg and lowered her mouth. His muscles tensed with expectation under her hands. She risked a peek through her lashes and watched D'trav's eyes slip closed.

Oh yes... he needs this...

She tensed her fingers and the claws slid free of their nailbeds, sinking into his groin.

With a muffled shriek, his eyes flew open. He jerked backwards, causing yet more pain and another shriek.

Her grip tightened.

For a moment he was stunned, unmoving, then his hand drew back, forming a fist.

"Do it," she dared, "and I'll slice them off!"

Captain Lator, dressed in his usual pressed suit, scanned the documents for the third time. Casually, as if there were no rush and lives didn't depend on his decision, he picked up the inking shell. With the skill of long practice he dipped the red quill, wiping away excess ink.

And then he stopped.

Burk, sitting across the wide desk, pulled at his wrinkled collar and crossed his legs. He leaned further forward, uncrossed his legs, tried to smooth out the cotton, and squirmed in the leather seat, obviously finding no comfort in something that Lator considered a frivolity.

Distracted, ink laden quill hovering, Captain Lator stared at Burk with unfocused eyes, not really seeing him. Lator's face, visible in a dozen or more mirrors scattered about the room, twisted into a mask of rage. Pain shot through his clenched fist, and he peered down at the mix of blood and ink seeping between his fingers.

"Kyron-be-damned," Lator dropped the fractured inking shell and settling his features back into the emotionless mask he normally wore.

Burk's eyes grew wide. He half rose from the leather chair.

Lator leveled his gaze on him, waiting.

Burk sat down and looked at his knees.

Lator watched beads of moisture form on his underling's forehead. "How did you let this happen? This—disaster?"

"I—"

"Do not even tell me that you did everything right. Obviously you did not."

"Captain, I don't know. When our sources discovered Onglat was living in the manor—"

"Yes, I know," the captain interrupted Burk again. "You set the trap so carefully."

Burk ran a finger along the inside edge of his collar. "We did sir. We sent word out on the streets about the Freni-Kyn."

"And?"

"It should have worked, sir. We did it long before the Slave Day sale, and we made sure every inn had at least one blathering informant, yapping away at how much we wanted for her."

"Such a high sale should have lured Onglat into rescuing the slave." Lator smoothed his finger over an angular eyebrow, smoothing it.

"It's Onglat sir. He's slippery."

"How dare you flout that nickname in my face?" Lator spoke without raising his voice, face impassive.

Burk gulped. "I-I didn't mean it that way, sir. It's just... he seems impossible to catch. We thought he would show up just so he could thumb his nose at us, but even this time he..."

Reaching forth a hand, unhurried, each move precise, Lator chose an unadorned kerchief from a leather basket.

Burk stared at Lator's bleeding hand, transfixed. "The information leak should've sealed the deal. How could he resist, knowin' the Baron spent nearly a mint in gold d'yroap?"

Lator nodded. She was a huge bait, a magnificent target, worth a small fortune. Taking something that would make the local Red Pelican contingent rich should have pulled Onglat out of his lair. Meticulously, he wrapped the kerchief around his punctured hand.

"This will not do," he said, searching for the weak points of their plan.

Burk cleared his throat and sat forward expectantly.

Lator raised a brow at Burk.

"Everything went off without a catch," Burk blurted out, "except he didn't take the bait. So we put out word that she was to be paid for over time. Like a time slave, but unwilling, and till then she belonged to us. We had her secured within the manor in just a few turns of the hourglass."

"And?"

Burk flushed. "Then we sat back to wait, and wait, and wait."

Lator stared past Burk, considering.

Burk fidgeted nervously as the silence drew out. "And then we paid the baron to keep waiting, long after he lost interest in the girl."

"Months. It has been months."

"Yes, sir."

"On last report, Sarenka has lost significant weight, and there has not been even a whisper of Onglat at the manor," Lator said.

"No-sir, the bastard pulled off a bunch of stunts across Burmtin."

"He is mocking the Red Pelican, rubbing our nose in your lack of efficiency."

Burk stared at the ground. "It's a failed mission, the traitor mustn't be in the Manor."

"Have you checked the other houses?"

Burk wiped his hands nervously on the leather arms of his chair before tucking them under his legs. "No-no, sir, I—" His voice cracked and he stopped talking.

Captain Lator spared him a glance and took in the sweat beading on his underling's upper lip, the tension in his body. *Terrified, and rightly so. The idiot should not have brought me the information that led to this catastrophe. He will pay for this, one way or another.*

"You know what this means," Lator said.

"Yessir." It came out in a yelp and Burk cleared his throat.

"Buy her back."

Burk gulped and looked away, avoiding the captain's eyes.

Lator's left brow rose in an arc, "Well. You have something to say." It wasn't a question. It was a statement of the fact, and he did it on purpose. His men thought he read minds. They were wrong; he read bodies.

"The Baron told us up front, he won't sell her back."

The captain stared, unblinking.

"Sir." Burk rushed to add.

"I will have your wings for this." The captain turned to stare at the wall. "Get her back. Or face the consequences."

Burk scrambled to his feet and rushed from the room. He closed the door and leaned against it, panting for breath, shocked that he had escaped being sent to the whip master. He pressed his fingers to the hard-won pelican wings attached to his collar and gave a bittersweet sigh of relief. Instead of excruciating whipping sessions for the next week and scars to last a lifetime, he'd lose the wings he'd fought for three years to get.

Unless I get her back.

And I will get the Freni-Kyn bitch back!

Even if I have to steal her.

A cleaning boy rushed past, dirty rag and leather bucket in hand. Burk grabbed the child by the collar and brought him to a choking halt.

"Get something for ink spills and clean the captain's desk." He shook the boy for emphasis. "Now!"

The boy gasped and dropped his rag to grapple with the chokehold on his collar.

Burk released the child and waited.

The boy coughed, tears streaming down his thin cheeks.

"Well?" Burk lowered his voice into a threat that was far more frightening than the chokehold had been.

"Okay, okay, I'm going… master crap hat." The child slipped sideways past Burk's darting hand and laughed as he raced down the hall, turning once to give a mocking bow.

"Cheeky little shit."

Burk stared at the mix of people as they passed him in the hallway and focused his attention on a scar-covered female of the M'hakru race. Covered in black leather armor comprised of a multitude of straps, latches, buckles, and spikes, she was formidable, even without the body modifications. It was appalling what they did to their infants, cutting them at birth and sewing the ears so that they bent forward in a point. Every one he'd ever seen had capped those ears in metal, creating knives attached to the sides of their heads. And as if those metal sheathed ears weren't vicious enough, this one had paid for a row of spikes from forehead to the back of her neck. A head butt from her would kill a man.

"Better watch himself, or he'll end up gutted."

Not everyone's as nice as I am.

CHAPTER 4

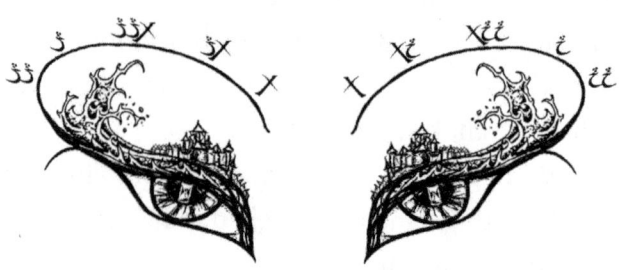

"A pack of vespra-lanirs can strip a horse of its flesh before ten drops of sand hit the bottom of an hourglass. Never use more than one creature at a time to torture prisoners."

Lieutenant Bandor of the clan Dorget
Torture Master
Third century Book of War

D'trav's guard training kicked in and a thousand strategies raced through his mind. He shifted direction, grasping the hilt of his sword instead of striking with his fist.

The movement shook her hands, needling his groin with shocks of pain.

Clumsy with fear, D'trav grappled with his weapon, fighting to pull it free.

Her nails sank deeper, shocking his brain into gear.

He froze.

She smiled. And in the sudden stillness, in a voice laced with icy sarcasm, she said, "The master *liked* my nails."

With a flex of her free hand, she unsheathed the blade-like nails. "But don't worry. You won't be a eunuch for long. Your screams will draw the guards. They'll think *you* killed him. After all, *you'll* be standing here with your pants down, taking advantage of a dead man's slave."

He darted a glance at the baron's cut-streaked body, registering the parallel claw marks for the first time. *Kyron! No wonder he's done been killed!*

She pressed a hand to her forehead. "Shut up… just shut up."

She's mind-lost. Beads of sweat broke out across D'trav's face and he swallowed. *Or still under the influence of the Foreveron.*

"I'll tell them you framed me. That's easier to believe than that a precious pleasure-slave had enough balls to actually kill one of them. They'll *want* to believe it. *You'll* be the one who hangs."

He stared at the body again. He couldn't help himself. *Must've been crazed, leavin' blade-sharp nails on a Freni-Kyn Foreveron-slave.*

"Yes, he was a fool," she said, jarring him with how close to his thoughts she'd come. "Gentle now. Move slow. Undo that chain."

"Like I have a fuckin' vespra-lanir kinda choice—" D'trav bent to grasp the shackle, wincing at even that slow movement.

His ponytail slid forward, trailing across Sarenka's arm and hiding her face from view.

She shifted position, moving enough that her face was revealed.

He glanced at her dilated eyes, and his stomach churned. She looked like a cornered animal, feral with terror. Sweat dripped from his forehead onto the shackle, and the blood slathered across the blue metal shone violet in the dim light, surreally matching her skin. Shivering, he fumbled with the breyt shackle, hesitated, pulled a little away.

She pressed her nail-tips in, applying enough pressure to remind him of his danger.

He leaned further forward with a groan

Shifting the angle of her grip, she moved with him and the blood pooling in her hand landed on the ground with a solid splat, loud in the quiet room.

He slowed, mind thundering with possibilities.

Her leg muscles, so close to his face, tensed.

He pushed the ideas aside, her threat was real. The castration would be automatic and over in a heartbeat if he fought now. *This can't… happenin'… all the sacrifices… Elsa's death… for nothin'…*

She groaned. "Please, just shut up. Why do you keep whispering?"

Her skin moistened with sweat, frightening him further. He had to keep her calm. The shackle clanked open, and the pain in his groin lessened as she sheathed her nails ever-so-little.

"See. When you're good you get less pain. My brothers taught me that, how to take torture." She jerked her chin towards the shackle and half stood. "Now put it on."

"You fuckin' vespra-lanir bitch! They'll be thinkin' I killed him." He glared up at her and adamantly shook his head. "This here's suicide of the worst sort."

"If I was as vicious as a vespra-lanir bitch, you'd be dead already. And the death those creatures gave you would make my claws in your testicles feel like a caress. By the time they were done, you'd beg for release, just like you made me beg." She gave her head a disparaging shake. "No, you fool, they'll think I killed him. As for how I got the key... devise a believable story. I'm sure you've got the imagination for that."

D'trav didn't move.

I have to talk her out of this.

There has to be something I can do.

"Put it on. Do it now! Or lose them." She sank the nails in a sliver and gave a grim smile when he flinched.

Blood dripped down her fingers in a thin stream as he moved the shackle to his own booted ankle. Awkward with pain, he bumped her arm, making her nails slip. His sight went white and muscles clenched, frozen in agony, until she released the pressure enough for him to continue. He groaned as eyesight returned.

"Get them off. Now!"

Flipping the hinged latches, he clumsily yanked the boots free and dropped them near her feet.

She glanced at the Glidarthian design and her eyebrow lifted.

He flinched, and it was all he could do not to draw attention to his d'yroap pouch by looking at it. *Now she'll be thinkin' I've got gold to burn.*

Nails fixed within his tender flesh, she scooped the boots up by their weathered straps. "Too big for my feet, and too fancy to lug around town without attracting attention."

He twisted his wrist, and the lock shut with a snap.

She smiled, tossed the boots into a far corner, and said. "Give me the key."

He held it out.

Her grip loosened as she reached for it.

He struck, slamming into her face with the back of his elbow and knocking her backwards.

Instead of letting go, she clamped her hand down tight, pressing the nails in deep.

He screamed and the key fell from his hand, bouncing on the wooden floor before landing next to her bare foot.

In a blur of motion, she retracted her nails, scooped up the key and grabbed his shoulder with the bloody hand.

At the release of pressure even more pain shot through his groin. He screamed again, doubling over.

She pressed down on his shoulder and leapt, landing on his back with bare feet and bearing him further towards the ground as she balanced there.

Rage burned through what remained of his reasoning. He surged upwards.

Using the momentum, she propelled herself into a backwards flip, landing in a clumsy face-down sprawl across the room.

Gripping his crotch, he doubled up as yet more convulsive pain shot through. "Kyron-be-damned, fuckin' monkey acrobats, every last one of you oughta be…"

As the pain abated, D'trav opened his eyes.

Sarenka was crouched in a flexed stance, one hand still on the ground, ready to spring. Her eyes bore into his.

He pulled a hand free and let out a relieved breath. It was bloodied, but thinly, and not enough to be dangerous.

She let out a sigh that echoed his, drawing his attention just as she turned away, and he glared at her blood covered back.

"Looks like you get to keep your balls after all," she threw out, bending to rub her scar-laced ankle. "You'll survive, probably not even have scars"

Alarmed at the thought of permanent damage, he scrabbled to examine himself and was relieved to discover the bleeding lessening.

A rummaging sound drew his attention back to Sarenka. She grabbed a garment from the wardrobe and rubbed it down over her body, wiping away the worst of the blood. He stared, determined to memorize everything she took. If he was to die on the gallows, he'd make sure they had a description of her too.

After hurrying through pulling on turquoise leggings, she wrestled with a chartreuse shirt, navigating the billowing fabric twice before succeeding in threading her arms through. The beaded fringe caught in her hair, provoking a yelp, and he couldn't help but smirk. Turning back to the wardrobe, she produced a cotehardie and grimaced with distaste. He held his breath, hoping she'd take it. The quilted sky-blue fabric, with its scarlet piping and a flamboyant overlay of embroidery would make her easy to find in a crowd.

Come on...

Come on...

You need it.

The leather insides'll keep you nice and warm.

"Warm enough, but how is anyone's taste this bad?" Sarenka interrupted his thoughts.

"Only a Kyn would say somethin' like that in this sorta situation."

Sarenka nodded.

He realized he'd spoken aloud and bit his tongue, determined to keep the rest of his thoughts to himself. Raised for entertaining—acrobats, actors, whores, magicians—as all Freni-Kyn were, she couldn't help worrying about frivolous things like style. Nothing broke those instincts, not even being held as a slave for months on end. Everyone knew that. The slavers banked on it.

Scarves and hats and folded shirts landed behind her as she searched through the bottom of the closet. Pink in the face, she stood back up and peered around the room. With a rush, she fell upon the Baron's discarded clothing the baron and lofted a pair of curled-toe slippers into the air, dangling them by their laces.

"Well, better than nothing I suppose." After putting them on, she tapped her heel against the ground experimentally and ran a few steps, turned, and ran back.

He noted the way her feet slid forward in the shoes with each step. *Good, that oughta slow the wench down some.*

She frowned at him, eyes narrowing as her gaze slid down his body, focusing on his waist.

He glanced down and started to close his breeches, suddenly self-conscious.

"I don't supposed that fancy hinged belt of yours would fit me?"

"Custom made, so lessen your waist grows a good bit… no."

"That figures." Wrapping a woven cord about her waist, she turned to stare in the mirror and made a face. "Ugh!"

He agreed. The hideous outfit, made of things she didn't have the station to wear, was beyond ridiculous. But it shouldn't matter, it was clothing to escape in, and running through the streets naked would draw more attention than a mismatched noble's attire.

"Take the sword off. Toss it near the door."

He scowled from under furrowed brows and threw his sheathed sword across the room before going back to gently closing his trousers.

"I'll leave the key. If you work fast, you'll be out in a few minutes. Don't bother looking for me. Just run for it. As the night guard… well, you know… the one with opportunity and all that."

She grabbed a dagger with a pelican engraved into the blade and walked several steps towards the door, then stopped.

He stared at her back. "The key?"

Turning back to the wardrobe, she shoved loose clothing onto the ground before palming the triangular Red Pelican death card and sliding it into the cotehardie pocket. "Toss me that ring he's got around his neck."

D'trav grimaced and yanked the signet ring free, breaking the chain in the process. "You don't know what you're messin' with girl."

"I've got a pretty good idea."

He tossed the ring and she caught it mid-flight.

Too adept...

Knows too damn many moves...

Bet she can even throw that Kyron-be-damned dagger.

Definitely been in some travelin' acrobat troupe 'fore they done snatched her up. That'll be the secret to trackin' her down, too, I'd wager good d'yroap on it.

Sarenka went back to frantically opening drawers and dumping the contents on the ground. In the end, she closed her eyes and lifted her chin and then abruptly ran at him with a look of rage on her face. Just out of reach, she hurled a vial. It flashed through the air, tumbling end-over-end before shattering against the ground.

D'trav threw up an arm to cover his eyes. Shards of glass bounced off his body and patterned the ground in dangerous glitter.

"Where. Are. They?"

"He never did keep more of the Foreveron in the room."

"Not the drug, you idiot. The cure. Where?"

D'trav shook his head.

Fear turned her face desperate, and her knuckles whitened around the dagger hilt. "Tell me!"

"I don't know. I... I'm not sure he keeps any."

For a moment, he thought she would throw the dagger, and after seeing her expertise with backward flips, he doubted she would miss.

Instead, she whirled around and ran back to the dresser.

"You won't find any. Trust me."

"Shut up. I know. Kyron-be-damned! There has to be some coin!" After several more minutes of fruitless searching, she turned back to D'trav. "Toss me your d'yroap pouch. And be easy, or I'll take the key with me."

"Kyron-be-damned, fucking, dung rolling, whore of a whale," flowed out from under his breath while he fumbled at his waist string.

"What's that? Did you just call me something particularly vile and smelly?" Her words were frost sharp with threat.

He stopped cursing.

Sarenka's lip quivered with pent in laughter.

Not daring to say a word, his face heated with rage. She could afford the mockery now that she had the upper hand. Lips flattening into a compressed line, he tossed the bag toward her feet. The embossed sporran landed with a muffled jingle.

Sarenka scooped up the leather pouch, weighing it in her palm before giving him a sickening-sweet smile. "Lovely, just get paid?"

"Look here, girl. I can help. Just let me go with."

She gave a jeering laugh that turned his face even hotter.

"I'll set things right. Promise."

"Yeah, like you wanted to *help* earlier? No thanks. I've had enough of that kind of help."

She stared at him and bit her lip, as if thinking.

"Come on girl. You're no cold-blooded murderer. "Don't leave me here like this."

Her gaze landed on the corpse next to D'trav. He grimaced. *Okay maybe she is a cold blooded murderer.*

"It wasn't my fault."

"I know. So let me go."

"You a time-slave?"

His heart gave an extra thump, and he pressed his lips tight.

"What's it take to sell yourself into servitude for a chunk of d'yroap?"

"Somethin' real bad, I 'spect," he answered, looking away.

She started to toss him the key but stopped, arm still in the air. "You never beat or used me. Not like the other guards. But today... today when I needed help the most... today you crossed a line."

"Sarenka, please. I'm sorry."

Her eyes narrowed with anger. "I'll give you a way out, but not one without risk, and not one that will give you a chance to catch me."

His body went cold and sweat dripped down his face while he waited for her to explain.

"Strip!"

Chapter 5

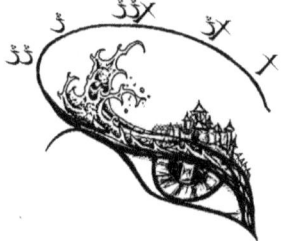

Found on a scrap of scroll aboard the The Deserter:

Darlin Yanorra.

It's the find o' the century! We'll all be rich as kings now.

Anenon was sent to scrape barnacles last week and come back so filled with the lust that damned if he wasn't humpin' the ship wheel. He got chained after tryin' to knock Captain Lanorrett to the ground and rape her. Next thing we know, he's claimin' he never done such a thing. It was quite the laugh until it happened again a few hours later with one o' the new recruits. Poor lad got himself skewered by the man he tried to fuck below decks.

The herbalist wat wrapped him up for tossin' to the fish, done noticed the green under his nails, and after some bit of hubaloo it's dun been proven. We've got us an aphrodisiac what makes oysters seem like dung. Damned if it's not addictive though. I crave the stuff day an' night and when I don't have it I feel like my guts be turned inside out. Anenon dun killed himself from the wantin' today. The captain says tis fit only for the slavers.

Your lovin' man,
Denham 'No-Fingers' Gabranth

~I've done what can be done. The rest is up to Parian.~ The elder seer's thought was faint, as if it took too much for her to hold the connection.

~But he'll live?~

~Yes.~

Airintia let out the breath she was holding.

~What of The Foretold?~ Lanion asked.

~A fabrication.~

Airintia tasted the sneer behind those words and bit back the retort she wanted to send.

~Born of too much time between times,~ another finished.

~I believe.~ Airintia's anger went with those words, stinging the listeners with shame.

~You believe he's found what we've searched for since before you were born?~ the Eldest's thought was cautiously neutral.

~He's adept at walking between times,~ Lanion sent.

~More than anyone in over a hundred years,~ Airintia added.

~True...~

~The implications...~

~This must stop!~ The sneer was gone, now the voice held only fear. *~He's got no replacement.~*

~The One...~

~If he's found...~

~No. Too dangerous.~ The Eldest's thought was soft, unfocused, as if she didn't want to send it.

They dared not lose Parian without a trained Freni-Kyn psychic ready to replace him. It was a basic truth of their seer existence.

~He must stop,~ the Eldest sent.

They retreated, and silence hung between them, a precipice of dread.

Airintia spoke first. Of all the seers, she was the closest to Parian. Though she cared for their mission, mostly she cared for her friend. *~Agreed.~*

~Agreed,~ the rest chimed in, one after another.

They felt Parian moan and roll over, smearing the vomitous mess across the chalked symbols drawn on the floor and kicking over the wooden bowl of water.

Sarenka glared at D'trav and hoped he would cooperate.

"Oh, *come* on…" D'trav's voice trailed off.

"You-you filthy, low life slug. You don't even deserve to be let free at all." She piled the insults on. *This has to work. He has to strip. I can't leave him here to die. He has to believe me.*

Face purpled with pent up rage, he unbuckled his leather cuirass and dropped it to the ground.

"All you had to do was help." Sarenka snarled out, watching through slitted eyes as he pulled his shirt over his head. She gave her shoulders a shrug, the tiny piece of her that had been hoping to find a redeemable characteristic, squelched.

Not a slave. No telling inks across his back, even if he turned white as a ghost when I mentioned time-slaves earlier. Her attention shifted to the baron. *What kind of person chooses to work for this type of man?*

"I should just let you rot here."

D'trav bent to push his trousers onto the chain.

She frowned, wanting to slice the pants to shreds and slow the pursuit further. But no. Too risky. "Further away."

D'trav's brows raised. "You're Makin' this damn near impossible. They'll kill me."

He waited for her to relent.

She stared at him.

He lifted the chain, sending the trousers sliding away.

"Throw the rest over there." She gestured toward the corner where the chain was anchored. "Everything but the belt."

Soundless, his lips moved.

Her eyes narrowed. "That's right, keep that tongue civil."

"Come on girl, have a mercy."

"This *is* mercy." She held up the key for an overhand throw.

D'trav raised his hands to catch it.

Calculating the distance, she tossed the key.

D'trav threw up his hand and jumped it as it flew over his head, landing on the far side of the room. Its slight jingle on the wooden floor was muffled by the clank of chains as D'trav flung himself around to look. "Kyron-damn-it! These chains won't let me reach that, and you know it."

"Really? Do you think I'm that cruel?" Sarenka gave him an askance stare, one brow raising.

He lowered his head and looked away.

She nodded with satisfaction and tucked the RP dagger up under the cotehardie, securing it out of view. Stepping to the door, she scooped up his sword, and dropped it almost as quickly. Though only as heavy as a jug of water, it was too long for her to wield and would slow her.

"Use the belt on the key," she threw over her shoulder and slipped out the doorway, knowing the latch would make the perfect hook. As she took a hesitant step down the unfamiliar hallway, a dizzying flush of relief overwhelmed her. She leaned against the closed door, waiting for her head to clear, and heard the frenzied clanking of chains filter out through the thick wood, a reminder of the man who would surely want revenge when he got free.

Almost free of this Kyron-forsaken hell.

The last vestiges of ruby dawn spilled through narrow doorways, creating pools of light and shadow. An early-morning hush cradled the sleeping manor, but it wouldn't last. Soon this hall, with its multitude of confusing doors and side passages, would fill with servants, guards, and nobles.

I've got to disappear...

Or die trying. That thought brought with it such a surge of terror that it threatened to overthrow her training. Her heart thudded like crashing waves in her ears, and her lungs constricted, stealing breath as she fought for reason.

She searched the hall for signs of a way out and darted forward, turning down a random side branch. She knew so little; her vision of the route to and from the chamber had been hampered by an eyeless hood, and time was slipping past faster than her racing feet. Through open doorways, rooms flashed past in blurs of brown and burgundy and blinding light from narrow windows.

She ran, breakneck, and the moments ticked past like hours.

From the corner of her eye came the flash of a vast swath of bright-green. Sighting the first window large enough to climb through, she flung out a hand and grabbed the doorframe, desperate to escape. Her feet slid forward inside the velvet shoes moments before her shoulder slammed into the adjoining wall.

Ragged panting escaped her mouth, loud in the dawn hush. She scanned the luxurious room, searching for occupants, then centered her attention on the panes of an enormous window.

Sprinting to the window, she pressed her face to the glass and gazed past a beckoning swath of garden toward the looming heart of Burmtin. The unaccustomed brightness forced her to squint as she turned the crank on the windowsill, creating just enough of an open-ing to slip through.

The soft scuff of leather slippers against wood came from the hall-way.

She glanced over her shoulder at the open door.

Damn it! Should have shut that.

She threw herself at the half opened panel and squeezed past, scraping her chest raw as she fell into the garden, landing on one outstretched hand and her feet. Panting, she dodged to the side and waited to see if she'd been sighted. Like the poison it was, the throb of Foreveron withdrawal thundered through her head, distracting her from the search.

Antidote…

I need antidote….

Tranquility surrounded her, and peace offered itself in stands of calla lilies and star roses. She pressed herself up against the building, listening. Beyond the sound of the city, she heard nothing, no hurried footsteps, no call for the guards.

She drew in several calming breaths before focusing on the Freni-Kyn illusions. Unlike earlier, when controlling the color of her hair-sparks was impossible, the illusions worked. Her face shifted into a nondescript H'euman, losing its telltale heart shape and blue coloring, while her hair fell about her shoulders in a coal-black mass, shedding the characteristic Freni-Kyn lights.

Good.

Foreveron wearing off...

A little better control...

Chosen because it blended in so well with the general populace, she wore the simple face she had been creating since childhood. It wasn't much of a disguise, and she knew it.

The spicy-sweet scent of flowers rolled through the garden, re-minding her that not everything could be covered with illusions. She sniffed her arm and grimaced. Unless she escaped through the main gates immediately ridding her body of the blood before someone smelled it was paramount.

And that *was* the best plan. Get out of the city before they even knew she was gone. Meanwhile, illusions masked red smears and spat-ters quite well.

As long as nobody touches me.

And if...

If I can hold onto this face long enough.

Sarenka raced across town for the city gates, grateful for the soft soled slippers. The beaded fringe slapped against her hands and chest in an annoying tinkle, matching tempo with her thoughts.

Now's the time

run away...

and fleee...

Find a different...

safer place…
Quickly!
Before they…
discover…
the body.

CHAPTER 6

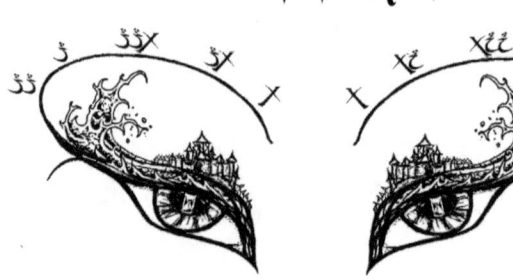

D'trav bundled a cloak under his arm before leaving the cell. He paced rapidly down the halls and called a greeting to the day guard.

"G'day."

"Quiet night?"

"Quiet enough." D'trav's heart thudded, and he was sure his face was flushed. He fought the urge to draw his blade.

"They awake?"

"Still sleepin'. Might as well grab some Banish."

The guard put his finger in his mouth and pretended to gag. "I'll not be drinking that horse piss."

"Perks me right up."

"Tastes like piss."

"Hey!" D'trav nudged his arm. "I like my horse piss. Join me?"

The guard gave the cell door a worried glance.

"Come on, nobody'll even know."

"Can't afford the docked pay." The man took another step towards the cell.

D'trav tensed, hand tightening on his sword hilt.

"Hell with it." The guard swung around and walked back towards D'trav. "Like you said, they'll never know."

They walked in silence, and with each step D'trav felt better.

"Know they make that Banish from manark shit, right?"

D'trav growled. "That's a lie."

"I've got it on good word."

"Don't care. Wakes me up. All that matters."

As they passed an open doorway, D'trav jumped sideways into welcome darkness. He listened to the guard's steps continue several paces, then the hesitant stop and returning footsteps.

"Hey! What you—" the guard said as he poked his head in the doorway.

D'trav grabbed the man's collar and yanked.

Surprised, unable to see, the guard stumbled and threw his arms out to catch himself.

With a heave, D'trav spun the man around, ending the scuffle by slamming the guard's head against the wall.

The man's body slumped to the ground.

D'trav checked for a pulse and muttered. "Serve you right, talkin' bout a man's drink like that."

After checking the hallway, he softly shut the door. Nobody had heard. They were safe until noon, when this room would fill with the lesser lords and ladies, ready for their midday meal. Working by feel, D'trav stripped the man of his shirt and ripped it into strips, then bound and gagged him. He slicked back his hair with a shaking hand, tidying it before bundling the cloak back up under his arm and reaching for the door handle.

The guard moaned.

D'trav paused, listening while the guard's soft rustles turned into panicked thumps. His shoulders slumped. "Didn't want to have to do this."

He drew his sword and advanced on the guard. Reaching out, he felt for the man's head in the dark and found a piece of soft flesh. The head jerked to the side, back out of his reach. D'trav's grip on his sword tightened and he tried again, this time grasping a hank of hair. He clung while the man bucked and shifted, throwing his weight around, trying to break free.

D'trav lifted the sword, cocked his head as if listening for where to strike. Satisfied with placement, and that he was not going to accidentally harm himself, he made a move born of much practice and flipped the sword about in midair before cuffing the man with the hilt.

The man went limp, pulling D'trav's hand downward as he slid to the floor.

D'trav tightened his grip on the guard's hair and dragged him into the darkest area of the room, a spot where no shuttered slants of light would touch, and hoped it would be a while before he awoke.

He stepped from the room and strolled towards the kitchen. A rustle came from behind, and he swung around, hand on sword. A servant girl turned the corner behind him, skirts a flutter, wooden bucket in each hand, cheeks rosy.

Did she hear? That why she's rushin' away? This is gettin' downright messy.

He took a step after her.

No. Just gotta get outta here.

He spun on his heel and pushed open the kitchen door. Steam billowed out, momentarily blinding his first few steps, and his stomach grumbled at the fish scent. His favorite cook was hunkered forward over a pot like a guard dog, stirring the wooden ladle with two hands while greasy hanks of hair came dangerously close to the gurgling liquid.

He looked up, and a smile wreathed his face. "D'trav!"

"Heya." D'trav avoided his eye and kept walking.

"Come taste this, boy."

"Not today."

"Yer passin' up food?"

D'trav glanced at the door with yearning and ground his teeth, but he let his pace falter. The cook would know something was wrong if he didn't act like food were the only thing he cared about. "Well… just a nibble."

"Now then, there's the boy I know and love."

D'trav grinned. "Baitin' me with food. Know I'll even tolerate bein' called boy for your soup."

The cook laughed, pushed a long braid over his shoulder, and ladled soup from a smaller pot into a bowl.

D'trav brought the bowl to his mouth and touched his lip to it.

"Not hot," the cook said. "Been coolin' a while. Tastes a bit off."

D'trav smiled over the edge and slurped it down, drinking the liquid before chewing on the bits of fish. "Is good."

The cook, who had returned to the other pot, looked up. His brow wrinkled with doubt. "Tis?"

"Yes, tis. Touch of garlic. That'll do it justice."

The cook grabbed a rope of cloves and began mashing them, his back to D'trav. "More?"

"Gotta chat up the blacksmith 'fore he gets busy-like."

The cook nodded and waved his mallet. "Day then."

Whistling an offbeat tune, D'trav sauntered through the manor gate and turned down the first side street. He rolled his bear-trap-tense shoulders and, without breaking stride, unfurled the cloak and spun it around his body. Then he picked up the pace, rushing through the streets, never pausing for more than a moment before hurrying forward again.

Shouts of alarm came from behind.

He tugged the hood over his head, hiding his features from all but the most observant. The steady thump of running feet caught his ear. He gripped his hilt and stepped to the side, making as if to peer into a storefront.

Panting hard, a guard ran past with scroll in hand.

As D'trav resumed walking, his foot twisted on a loose cobblestone, throwing him off balance, and he stumbled.

Pain knifed through his groin and shot down his leg. The pain became unbearable, and he bent forward, grasping his crotch, ready to fall to the ground. Grinding his teeth together, he forced himself to remain standing and resumed walking.

"Kyron-be-damned." He rubbed his hand on the inside of the cloak, leaving behind a smear of red.

"Fuckin' bitch. I'll kill her."

Chapter 7

"They rose from the Istoarm Sea like wraiths, sails pale against the night sky, carrying great spears and curved blades. The coastal town of Burmtin was taken in a day, all its leaders put to a grizzly death on public display, while the Watrelk Pirates walked free, their eyes shifting color with the wind.

Leaving us to ask, how is it that a people so shy could birth such brutal monsters?

With the waterways locked tight, we can expect supplies of common items to become rare. Hold onto your delicate laces and sweet-drinks. It might be a while before you get more."

Mannie Silvestre
Falksfall Courier
Year of Betrayal

The light was blinding. It pierced Parian's peace, ripping away at his mind and reminding him of his hunger.

The noise, the incessant banging, why will it not stop?

Parian rolled to the side and raised a hand to block the foul stench. His eyes flew open and he sat straight up. The banging at his door continued. He tried to speak but only a croak came out. He looked down at his body, covered in hardening vomit, and the smudged symbols scrawled across the floor. Forcing himself to stand, he staggered to a pitcher and gulped the cool water down in great drafts.

"Moment," he said, but it sounded more like a bark than words.

The banging continued.

He swallowed and tried again, shouting this time, "A moment!"

Finally. Quiet. He breathed a sigh of relief and stumbled around the room, hurrying to wipe away the chalked markings with the toe of a besmeared stocking, before sloshing the contents of a wine bottle into the privy and laying it on it's side in the middle of the floor. Hands on hips, he squinted at the room with a frown.

Not convincing enough.

He picked up a blanket and threw it, along with a hefty book, down next to the bottle. Surveying the room one last time, he sigh-ed and ran a hand back through his hair. Instead of feathering the strands with that habitual move, his hand stopped in mid-swipe, caught by the glue his bile had turned into. No wonder he had such a bad headache. He lowered his hand and sighed.

This is going to cost me.

He opened the door, leaned against the frame as if drunk, and slurred out. "Yesh, yesh, what?"

The innkeeper, who had been in the middle of wringing his hands, stared past Parian into the room. "Been three days. Need paying."

"K, okay, ready." Parian stumbled to his pack and pulled free more d'yroap silver than he owed. "Here. Three more days too."

The keep rubbed the silver together and smiled with relief before noticing Parian's face for the first time. His mouth dropped open. "Do… do you need anything else?"

Damn it. He's seen. "Jesh a bath, and some victuals."

The keep stared at his eyes, mesmerized. Parian tried to focus on the man's face, knowing it was impossible. His eye would look wherever it damn well pleased.

The keep glanced away and then back, as if he couldn't help himself. He raised his hand in a ward then looked away, fear written all over his face.

Parian risked touching his mind.

What's wrong with that eye? Why's it keep moving to the side like that? Now it's staring at me again. Now what's it staring at? Evil. Tis evil, tis. Gonna curse me. Need to get away for he does. And that scar, half his nose… gone, just gone.

Parian broke contact at the rise of revulsion washing off the innkeeper. He was safe, for now. The man didn't remember that he'd arrived wearing a different face. He turned away and tried to raise his illusions but failed. Too tired. Just as well, if he changed his appearance now he'd need to mess with the man's memories and that was… well, it just shouldn't be done. But it did mean he'd need to move to a different inn. It was either that or be harassed, and worse, remembered. Oh well, there was nothing to be done for it.

He turned back and raised the brow over his good eye at the keep. "Well?"

Fingers twisting over and over in a ward against evil, the keep shook his head. "I'll see to the bath… and send up some victuals."

Parian shut the door as the man hurried away.

Well, at least I'll get a bath first. Unless he decides to call the guards.

Sarenka clasped her hands over the beaded fringe on her chest and skirted the outer edge of the busy marketplace, eyes straight ahead, as though delivering an important message. In reality, she observed everything, taking in all the details and filtering them into threat categories.

The cutpurse near the gaudy tent rated low-threat, only a three.

The men with hoods pulled forward over their faces—a five.

The M'hakrus—a seven.

The guards—they were a ten: to be avoided at all cost.

She bit her lip, worried she'd be noticed, but beyond a few curious glances for her speed, she passed unseen.

The crowd intermingled like a *kaleidoscope* she had owned as a child, bits of broken glass shifting into new configurations with each turn. Jaded merchants, dressed in overdone clothing with threadbare cuffs, hawked their wares. Frevells in stiffly-structured suits marched past on official business, ready to settle legal disputes. Children with eyes too wise for their age slipped through the throng, avoiding the hands that reached for them.

Consumers from every walk of life browsed the stalls, sometimes arguing over pricing. Tarnished Freni-Kyn girls and boys, with makeup betraying the seamier underside of the city, pressed against consumers suggestively and pouted when turned away. Blue-haired Watrelk Pirates sauntered about with hands on weapons and a sneer for the merchants who cringed at their flagrant lack of peace-ties. M'hakru mercenaries—covered in a plethora of scars, body modifications, tattoos, buckles, latches, straps, and weapons—flashed through the area, appearing and disappearing faster than she could track them.

Every race, every color, every type of person cruised Burmtin, purchasing legitimate—and often not-so-legitimate—goods. Everything here had a price, even Freni-Kyn runaways. She had learned that lesson the painful way.

So many damn people. They're everywhere. Bumping your elbows and asking questions, always talking on and on. No peace and quiet. Kyron, how I hate this place. All I wanted was to be alone and have a bit of adventure. Why did I pick Burmtin?

A mistake. A terrible mistake.

She swerved to the side, avoiding the claws of a mantling hawk, and searched the crowd again, this time for dangers of the animal sort. Cockatiels and parrots perched on shoulders while yapping terriers pulled at their leashes, ready to nip the unobservant passerby. Massive guard dogs—Boxers, and Mastiffs, Dobermans and Shepherds, even Horned Shield dogs and wolf blends—flanked those wealthy enough to afford the luxury. Mounts, both of the equine and feline type, waded through, letting out a mixture of snorts and snarls for the bustling crowd. Sarenka gave the cat mounts a wide berth while watching where she stepped, ever concerned about the offal that accompanied the beasts, both man and animal.

The scent of unwashed bodies, heavy perfume, and animal feces mingled until she could taste it in the air.

It's too much! She lifted a hand to cover her nose, but scratched it instead. *Only a Freni-Kyn would do be that sensitive to smell. I won't give myself away that easily.*

Strengthening the illusions, Sarenka fought to seem like a typical Burmtin resident. She was here and would be seen, there was no stopping that. *But I'm nothing, a nobody, a courier delivering a message, no one worth looking at.* She projected the image, desperate to believe her grandmother's touted stories of how thoughts had the magic to change reality.

A clang reached her ears, and sounded again, and then again.

The tower's warning bells!

They echoed faintly off distant walls and taller buildings.

She threw herself forward in a rush for the wall.

An old woman rolled her flower cart out in front of Sarenka, blocking her path.

Sarenka dodged to the right and ran into a cart filled with spoiled fruit. Flies burst into the air, and she turned back, running in the other direction.

The massive gate began to lower, copper pelican relief flashing in the early-morning light. Her breath a wheezing gasp, she skidded to a halt, angry with herself for not moving fast enough. The polished metal dropped the last few inches with a thud that rumbled through her slippers. A cloud of dust billowed up, diffusing the red copper and causing nearby strangers to cough and cover their mouths. Dressed in pelican-emblazoned tunics, a squad of guards trooped northward at a run, heading towards the baron's estate.

Sarenka became aware of gawking strangers, all staring at her.

"Oh! Those look amazing!" She pitched her voice loud enough to be heard over the crowd and thrust her hand forward, letting it hover above the nearest cart, as if undecided at which delicacy to pick.

The vendor squinted, peering first at Sarenka's hand then her face.

Sarenka chose a random pastry. It didn't matter. All that mattered was the disguise now.

"One silver," the elderly woman barked out.

Sarenka jumped, surprised at the harshness of the demand. Nervous, fumbling with the bag at her waist, Sarenka decided the woman had reason for her gruffness. She did indeed look the part of a ne'er-do-well. Dressed in a rich man's stolen goods, rushing through the square like a common thief, not the impression she was trying to create.

I'm not a petty thief-by-trade. Not anymore. I worked hard to break free of that life.

No, I'm not that. I'm worse. I'm a murderer.

Her cheeks flushed with shame, and she was glad the illusions covered the color. Digging out a silver loop, she handed it over without a word for the extortion of the overpriced roll.

The woman accepted the loop and brought it to her mouth, licking the metal as if she could discern its legitimacy by taste alone. She raised it above her head, turning it this way and that, examining the inscription before finally pocketing it and nodding at Sarenka.

Relieved that D'trav's coin was true and not some clever fake, Sarenka took a bite, ignoring the faint scent of fish that pervaded the hearty brown texture. A bead of pink tinged sweat rolled down her face, landing on the edge of the cart.

The merchant's gaze traveled from that splattered droplet up to Sarenka's face. She smacked toothless gums together and squinted. "Not hot enough out here to make a person sweat."

What to say... what to say... Sarenka remained silent.

The merchant nodded at the next troop of guards to run past. "Hope they catch the bastards! Thieves, most like!" She raked her gaze down Sarenka's motley clothing, and a glint of greed filled her eyes.

"Wouldn't that be a sight?" Sarenka turned and dashed off at a half run, throwing over her shoulder as she went, "No time to enjoy the show. Messengers don't get paid for arriving late."

She rushed forward, peeking back until the guards rounded the corner, their Red Pelican emblems a taunting reminder of her latest failure.

I have to get out of here. They'll take me back to them. And then the torture. She broke into a sweat. *Not a quick death. Not a clean one. No, it'll be slow.*

Any other city was safer than Burmtin and its Red Pelican head-quarters. Even a M'hakru slavers city was safer, though not by much. She'd find a way out, maybe go to the Freni-Kyn landholdings and hide there for a while. *No, that's not safe either, not for a half-breed. Where then?* Her geography lessons came flooding back. *Darkiorn. H'euman city, far enough away to start a new life. I'll be H'euman. Red Pelican won't hunt that far.*

She nodded. It was perfect, far enough from Burmtin to throw off the Red Pelican and not far enough north to put her near her parent's lands.

But what'll I do? I've got no skills. Guard duty? No, too public. Clerk? Cook? No never! She raced through even more ideas but threw off that concern. *Doesn't matter. I'll figure it out later. Right now I just need to hide.*

Moving from street to street, she dodged the point of accusing fingers. The hunt was on and everyone wanted the reward, especially if it earned them recognition among the upper crust of Burmtin. She dodged into another alley and panted for breath.

This clothing. It's got to go, and soon too. Stands out too much.

She started out again, glancing down alleys for garments, freshly laundered and hung to dry. A common enough thing for the lesser classes who lived in huts built so close that they could talk to a neighbor without stepping outdoors. But here her luck failed, for all she found were children's clothing, too tiny for use.

A woman was hustled past, struggling against the guard's rough hands. The Freni-Kyn captive lost control of her illusions and the painted façade of a harlot disappeared, revealing an unadorned pale face and bright-red hair.

Sarenka gulped down guilt.

Oh... please... don't let them kill her... or torture her. She's a red head. Not a brunette. Surely someone will notice.

Sarenka touched her hair, glad nobody could see what it really looked like. The harlot's innocent pleas for mercy rang in Sarenka's ears long after she disappeared.

Sarenka hunkered down and covered her head, holding back shudders of guilt and fear. A boy lifted his hand, pointing, and she scrambled away. Slipping into an alleyway, she spent the next turn of the hourglass shifting from one darkened area to another before finally squatting behind a wooden crate to rub dirt into her clothing.

A beggar's lot. That's what I need now.

She rubbed the sleeves against the rough cobblestones, fraying the elbows and cuffs before doing the same to the leggings and peering at herself in a piece of fractured glass.

"Better. But not enough."

She turned her attention to the bead fringe and yanked savagely at it, slicing fingertips and leaving behind bloodied remnants of threads. Scooping up the scattered beads, she deposited them in her pocket with hopes of a later sale. After rolling the cotehardie in a puddle until its bright threadwork was shaded in browns, she walked to a different city gate. Merchants with loaded-down carts stood before the gilded copper, arguing for passage.

A red-faced guard shouted, "Nobody's gettin' out! Not till we find the killer!"

Sarenka's stomach lurched. She scanned the walls and estimated their height at twenty stride-measures tall, or more. Even if she managed the climb without falling to her death, she couldn't move fast enough to bypass the guards pacing along the top. For a moment she wished she'd let D'trav come with her. She could have used his help. But she knew that wouldn't have lasted, he'd have betrayed her just like any person she ever lived with. He'd already proven his nature in any case. Her gaze traveled back to the gate, and bitterness settled in the pit of her stomach.

It's too late. I'm pinned to this city, a butterfly set against velvet and left to die.

Weeks—no, months—would pass before the search died down enough to run, and she didn't dare let the Red Pelican Assassins' Guild catch her. She knew the stakes. Their muttered words about the mysterious Onglat still haunted her sleep, and she had ruined their plans, killing the very person who was supposed to help them find the traitor.

Not that it was her fault. Just last night she'd argued with the Baron over her nails. She had begged him to trim them, knowing the danger. Not that she wanted him alive, no, she was not so kind of heart as to be foolish, but she didn't want his death on her head. He'd scoffed at her caution, cuffed her across the face, pinned her head back, and forced her to swallow the drug, nails intact. What he hadn't expected was for the drug frenzy to combine with her rage at the rough treatment, triggering violence. She touched her split cheek tenderly, and her lip lifted in a partial snarl.

Well, I guess he knows now.

And I'll pay the price because of his foolishness?

No!

I won't let them catch me.

I've wrecked all their plans. I'll get antidote and deal with fixing this afterwards.

An impossible task and she knew it. The Red Pelican controlled all trade in Burmtin of both the drug and the antidote.

As she turned a corner, a hastily sketched image of her face stared back at her. She put her hand on the wanted poster with disbelief. So fast. Not even a day and already the posters were up. The temptation to give up, to let frustration and tears take over, lashed like an angry whip, but she pushed it away. Crying would draw unwanted attention and survival was all that mattered.

I've got to hide. Now!

She turned away, ignoring the matching poster with D'trav's image on it, and set out for the seamier side of Burmtin with one thought in mind.

I will survive.

No matter how detestable my life becomes.

I'll find a way to survive.

That's who I am. That's who I've always been.

A survivor.

As night settled over the city, and the outcries dwindled to an occasional yelp for attention, Sarenka crouched behind a jumbled stack of crates and took stock. She needed to ditch anything that even vaguely smacked of the baron. That was her first job.

Thanks to D'trav, she had d'yroap enough to buy whatever she needed, but the marketplace was too dangerous. The wanted posters were plastered everywhere she turned, flapping in the breeze, attracting crowds of onlookers and speculative stares from strangers. She stared boldly back when they looked at her, as if she too were sizing them up and trying to decide whether to point a finger at them. It was an effective strategy that usually made them look away. For now.

She chewed her bottom lip and considered possibilities. The washerwomen along the coastline were there at the break of dawn, working for a pittance. A few silvers would procure any goods she wanted.

And set the guards on me within moments.

No. That won't do.

Neither would buying clothing from street dwellers. Compared with the amount on her head, what were a few silvers, or even golds?

She sighed at what she knew must happen and began walking to Sad Town—an apt name given the nature of that impoverished part of Burmtin. Before approaching the borders, she removed D'trav's pouch, securing it out of sight under the cotehardie, and tucked several coins between the tight edge of the belt and the shirt. She skirted the familiar streets, searching for the best entry point, ever aware of the invisible line that separated this part of Burmtin from the rest of the city. On one side lay well-kept buildings, city guards, and as much safety as Burmtin offered. On the other side lurked squalor, unwashed bodies, and if she wasn't cautious, death.

Sarenka squinted, darting glances from the uneven ground to darkened doorways, shadowy alleyways, and back again. The narrow streets were strewn with refuse and excrement, forcing her to walk an erratic path in the scattered torchlight. Unsavory smells assaulted her sensitive Freni-Kyn nose, and she wished for the impossibility of a scented cloth. Something that would make her a target, or worse, reveal her identity.

The buildings leaned drunkenly, supporting each other with rickety frames, as though they, like their inhabitants, found solace at the bottom of a drinking horn. Bits and pieces of wood and shell and cloth were tacked to the outside, not as decoration, but at a means for holding the buildings upright.

The sound of children's laughter drew her to a side street where scrawny bodies threw dice and shouted with glee over winnings. Half-eaten biscuits, a wooden cup, threadbare shoes, and a pinch of copper shavings lay mounded in the center, ready for the winning roll. She walked past, pretending disinterest. Rounding the corner, she stopped to wait for the end of the game. A shout of triumph arose, mingling with a chorus of curses and signaling her time to act.

She held her breath at the scuffing sound of approaching feet.

A child rounded the corner, head down, walking dispiritedly.

She grasped the boy and jerked him into the shadows.

CHAPTER 8

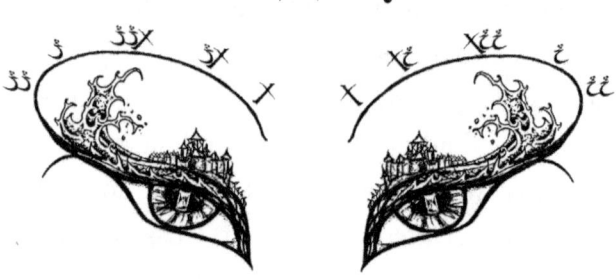

Within the hour Parian was settling his illusions into place and leading his horse from the inn, hair still damp. As he walked across town, passing buildings of stick and daub, he picked up thoughts and helped those he could. His deeds were small and mostly unimportant to any but the people he aided. They were filled with things like pointing a golden haired child in the direction of her lost kitten, reminding the elderly man of where he'd left his d'yroap pouch, helping a mumbling youth memorize the numbers he needed to get a job.

Sometimes he risked all, for to shift fate shifted everything, but how could he allow a drunk caught in the throes of rage to murder his cheating wife? Some things just had to be shifted, if not, then what was the point of having the gifts?

He passed a storefront and smiled at himself, perfect teeth, perfect eyes, perfect face. No terrible scar to frighten children with, or roving eye to bring out wards against evil. No, he was Freni-Kyn, and he was perfect, exactly as the world expected him to be.

The scent of jasmine caught his attention. He halted and closed his eyes and drew in the heavy fragrance, savoring the memories before turning, eager to find the source. And she was worth watching, a vision in rustling taffeta, all peach and roses, gray hair caught up in a tight bun, skin soft with wrinkles.

Perfect.

A perfect match to my perfect face.

Parian gulped and withdrew a square of waxy white from his pocket. He raised it to his lips and bit down, chewing the bitter mass with resolve. While he chewed, and bottle-flower oil coated his mouth, his other hand drifted to his pocket of its own accord. He withdrew the locket and shifted it back and forth between his fingers, counting out the turns.

~Parian…~

He took another bite.

~Parian, are you eating soap again?~

He flipped the locket, twenty, twenty-one, still chewing.

~You can't keep doing that.~ Airintia's mental voice was petulant.

When he reached twenty-two he stopped and turned away, as if awakening to find himself somewhere unexpected.

~I do what works.~ He smoothed a hand down his velvet waistcoat and slipped the soap back into his pocket, then he kissed the locket and tucked it away, and turned back towards the stable he'd been seeking.

~You'll make yourself sick.~

~If I can find my replacement then it won't matter anymore.~

Airintia didn't bother answering.

Parian nodded, knowing he'd won that argument. The replacements appeared when they appeared and no amount of fretting would make that happen faster. His arrival at The Dusty Stableyard was without further distraction. He ran a cautious eye over the rough exterior and understood how it had gotten its name. Despite the disrepair, the animals were all healthy and sending off waves of contented thoughts. He patted the distinctive star shaped mark on his horse's left shoulder.

"Sorry girl. Have to do this. The innkeeper might track me through you."

The horse whickered and dropped its head, ears settling into a decidedly depressed droop.

"I know, I know. I'll make sure you get a good home with someone that gives you lots of sugar."

It lifted its head and backed up until it was face to face with Parian. Gently it reached forward and nibbled Parian's collar.

"Hey! Stop it! I thought I broke you of that last year." Parian pulled his collar from its teeth and turned towards the stable. The horse pressed his face against Parian's back and gave the seer enough of a shove that he stumbled.

"Cantankerous old goat." Parian said, and stepped to the side just in time to see the horse shove empty air. He laughed and the horse whickered, as if the two were sharing a private joke.

He sold Treteana and her saddle for half her worth and planted thoughts in the stable master's mind that would see her sold to a loving family where she'd be spoiled and probably end up fat and pregnant. As he walked away he sent one final goodbye.

~I've set you up. Now you do your part and don't eat their collars.~

A high pitched whiney came from behind.

After throwing the leather bags over his shoulder, Parian cut across town, moving quickly. His stomach gurgled, unhappy with the soap, and he kept his head down, breathing through his mouth and hoping for no more distractions: no scent of flowers, no beautiful gray hair, no soft wrinkles. When he rounded the corner and saw Redohra's Barn he gave a sigh of relief, both the stable and yard were meticulously upkept, and he had made it there without incident.

The owner gave a short nod as he entered the building but made no move to intercept him. Parian eyed the mounts as he strolled past their stalls and sent out mental hellos to each creature. Absorbed in their freshly served dishes, most steadfastly ignored him, not so much as flicking an ear. But a few of the cat mounts crouched over their bloody carcasses and lifted lips and snarled.

Worried that he wind up with a mute animal, he started on the second row of stalls. The lonely life of a seer was a plague with little relief. The animals in this row were finished eating. The felines swiped massive paws across their faces, cleaning away blood, and the horses moved restlessly, ready to be let loose in the yard.

He called again, louder this time, and as he passed an empty stall finally got an answer.

~*You don't have to yell.*~

Parian backtracked to the last occupied stall.

A horse lifted its ears expectantly and thrust its head over the top of the gate.

~*Hello?*~ Parian sent, quieter this time, touching its mind and finding only thoughts of carrots.

A snort came from behind.

Parian stepped backwards and squinted at the empty stall.

Black as a velvet midnight, an Oce-fel padded from the shadowed far end and stopped, its massive cat body half revealed.

Parian took a step back.

~*What do you want, Freni-Kyn?*~ The feline's head lifted as it scented the air. ~*You smell of sweat and fear and lust.*~

Embarrassment flamed in Parian's face, and he looked away.

The cat sniffed again and cocked its head. ~*And now shame.*~

Parian glanced down the aisle at the last few stalls.

The cat made a sound that was alarmingly similar to a laugh. ~*You needn't fear being overheard. I've not met another thinker since I was taken from my littermates.*~

Parian nodded, shielding his thoughts. He hadn't been worried about being overheard, he just wasn't sure he wanted this sarcastic cat as a companion, but apparently he had no choice. Oh well. Better than a mute animal.

"You want out of here?"

The cat stretched, extending claws as long as Parian's middle finger, and left behind long rakes in the dirt. It walked the rest of the way to the gate and pressed its snout up against Parian's neck.

Parian held still, hoping it was a test.

It bared its teeth and rubbed them against his jaw in acceptance.

"I'll take that as a yes." He opened the gate and led her forth.

Shoulders brushing his, she followed him across the yard to the stable master.

The man whistled as he worked, pitchfork in hand, tossing hay to one side.

Parian cleared his throat.

The man stabbed the tool into the pile of hay and turned around. His face went pale and he took a step back. "Wha... wha..."

Parian panicked, fought the urge to run, thinking he'd somehow let his illusions slip.

The feline next to him snarled.

The stable master reached for the whip at his waist.

~Your heart's pounding like thunder. It's me he's afraid of.~ She snarled again and crouched for a spring. *~He pulls that string, he's dead.~*

A loud staccato of bangs interrupted Captain Lator's train of thought. He looked up from perusing a document and frowned at his door. It was enough that the thud of the city gates had disturbed him moments ago.

What next?

Before he could respond, the door to his underground office was pounded again, this time hard enough to make it shake. Lator gazed into a nearby mirror and pulled a speck of white off the shoulder of his tailored suit. He schooled his slim face into neutrality. As head of the local Red Pelican's Guild, self-control wasn't an option, it was a calling, one he followed with religious zeal.

"Enter!" His raised his voice only because he knew it wouldn't carry above the pounding on the door.

It was thrown open and Burk, red faced, breathing rapidly, rushed into the room carrying a scroll.

"The Baron's dead sir! Viciously murdered. They're blaming it on a guard."

Lator's pulse quickened. "Onglat?"

"Could be sir, if he caught wind of what we're up to, but we've had no sightings."

"Did he get her?"

"I... I uh..."

"Did he get her? Yes, or no!"

"It's too early to know."

Lator stared past Burk.

Burk shifted from foot to foot.

"Call back every operative. Find out what they know." Lifting the quill, Lator turned his attention back to the document and scratched out a line.

Burk stared at him a moment before realizing he'd been dismissed. "Yes, sir."

At the thud of the door shutting, Captain Lator dropped all pretense of calm. His porcelain skin reddened with rage, and his free hand clenched into a fist, crumpling the parchment beneath it. Using the desk for leverage, he thrust himself upwards and snapped the quill he was holding in half in the process.

Kyron-damn-it!

He tossed the broken pieces onto the desk and paced the room.

He was there all along. I had him.

And by now, he has long gone!

Picking up a stool, he threw it at the wall with enough force to shatter it and reached for a figurine, but stopped as he caught a glimpse of himself in a mirror. He touched his still reddened cheeks, drew several calming breaths, and returned to his desk.

Doesn't matter.

We'll find him.

And when we do, they will die.

They will all die.

CHAPTER 9

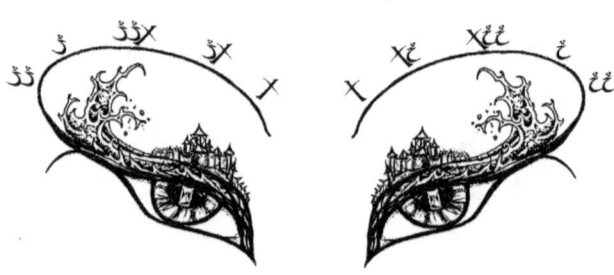

"The Freni-Kyns are the most despicable of all races. First with their supposed Preral cycle, mating like cats in heat, and now they break all natural laws with their newest corruption. How dare they offer their bodies for sexual use in order to save their cities? Have they no dignity? Like the dogs they are, the other races are embracing their conditions. Exterminate every last one of the vermin, I say."

Unsigned message sent to the Sharpra War Council
54 AB

Burk rushed down hallways, passing men and women clothed in a sundry of diverse costumes, until he reached the assignment office. He burst through the door without a knock and slammed down his paperwork on the startled clerk's desk.

"Call them in, call them all in!"

"I-I-I..." The clerk glanced nervously over his shoulder at a closed door. "You have to have an appointment."

Burk lowered his head and put his hand on the hilt of his dagger.

Eyes widening, the clerk grabbed the documents and flipped through them. His lips pursed, and he dug through the piles of scrolls on his desk and pulled one free, then held it out to Burk. "What about the Freni-Kyn?"

"I know what it says. Who do you think wrote it?" Burk sent the scroll flying from the man's hand and into the far wall. "Cancel the order. We'll get her back later."

"But I'm n—"

"No buts." Burk slammed his fist down on the desk. "Just do it."

The clerk hesitated.

Grabbing the clerk, he pulled him across the desk and glared into his eyes before snarling, "Now!"

D'trav turned down as safe a street as could be found in Burmtin and arrived at a tidy hut, three rooms, flower boxes in the windows. He stopped to look up and down the street then circled the building. Satisfied that his home hadn't yet been discovered by the guards, he took a deep breath, pulled out a sword and threw open the door. It crashed against the wall and bounced back. D'trav stuck his foot in the door to keep it from closing and waited.

Silence.

Not even a neighbor poking their head out to check.

He charged in and swung wildly.

Still nothing.

With a relieved grunt, he lowered his sword.

Crossing to a trunk, he threw open the lid and thrust his hand down past clothing and parchment and other items until his knuckles glazed across the tiny bottle at the bottom. He pulled it free and held it up to the window, peering through the miniscule liquid.

Not clouded, not spoiled, he was safe.

After shaking the bottle and uncorking it, he touched it with just the tip of his tongue, closing his eyes as a tingle went through him. It wasn't enough to take away all of the pain, but it'd keep him walking. Pushing the bottle back to the bottom of the trunk, he surveyed the cabin. It had taken a while to make it a home after Elsa died.

It had taken even longer to want a home.

Wasn't supposed to happen this way.

She's supposed to be here.

Not buried in a field under a mound of wildflowers.

He searched the room for even one thing that mattered and found nothing.

The hut doesn't matter.

It's nothing without her.

With a grunt for the weight, he hefted the trunk onto his shoulder, twitched the hood forward over his face, and marched out the door.

This is all that matters now.

His tramp across town, though less painful, left him red in the face and out of breath. When he arrived at a battered building with a steady stream of customers, he staggered and leaned against a light post, pretending exhaustion. In truth, he cased the street—scrutinizing darkened doorways, salt scoured warehouses, seedy taverns, and tiny cottages for suspicious characters and Red Pelican guards—before his gaze settled on the Distinguished Dainties sign. It hung crookedly, flapping to and fro, drawing his attention to the outside of the brothel. His gaze swept over the surface, darting from one window to the next, searching for peepers.

A gust of wind, balmy with salt, washed over him, flinging leaves and other debris as it went. His hood billowed and pulled away from his face. There was a storm coming. He grabbed the edge of his hood and started towards the building, reminded of why it looked like it hadn't seen a coat of whitewash within the last ten years.

With a thump-bang, he swung the double doors open and a shower of gilt flakes fell, littering the plush rugs. Within the darkened interior there was no hint of the disrepair that plagued the outside. Rich velvets, polished mahogany, and lush curtains muffled his footsteps in the spacious entryway. Guests, lounging about with sweet-drink or tryst in hand, peered up at him with narrowed eyes, as if expecting an attack. The merchandise, a plethora of semi-dressed men and women, started with fear and tensed, ready to run. The guard, a thin fellow leaning against the wall, startled awake, blinking rapidly before wiping drool from his chin.

D'trav ignored them and crossed the room, entering a hallway before he could be stopped. He thumped down the velvet-lined corridor, knowing that the wimp guarding the front door was no match if he decided to give chase, and turned into one of the servants' halls. Even here, in areas customers seldom saw, the gem inlaid surfaces screamed extravagance. Camille was a businesswoman, first and foremost, and the luxuries lining this gilded box helped her attract a higher class of workers.

Aware that the hourglass was draining, he rounded the next corner at a half run and nearly plowed Camille over.

She let out a shriek and threw a hand over her mouth. Then she laughed, and her tumbled mass of honey-blond hair caught the flare of lamplight, glittering with gems. "Darlin, you just about sent me to the grave."

"Get me a room."

"Well, if'n you insist." She ran ring covered fingers down her abalone encrusted corset and pressed up against him.

"No." He held out a hand, fending her off. "I'm in trouble."

Her face became a cautious mask as she turned aside. "This way."

In the role of Madame with customer, she led him around the corner. A group of Freni-Kyns burst through a doorway, their hair waving wildly and throwing off a rainbow of multi-colored sparks while they playfully pushed and shoved at each other.

D'trav stopped. "What in tarnation are *they* doin' here?"

"You like them?" Camille beamed back at him. "My newest deal. It's brilliant. I take care of their Preral cycle, and they take care of me and mine."

He grabbed her arm when she started forward again. "You've got to hide 'em. They're in danger."

She gave him a funny look. "Not if I get their cycle taken care of before it turns into the sickness."

"No. Not that. The guards… they're huntin' Kyns." He stepped towards them, thinking to hurry them off, then stopped. "Get 'em hidden, right quick like. The cellar."

"Okay, okay…" Worry lines appeared between her eyes, and she pushed at her hair with annoyance.

"Camille. You've got to take this serious." Leaning forward, D'trav half covered his mouth with a hand and hissed out, "I'm right sure the Red Pelican's involved in this here Kyn mess."

She blanched, and her gaze centered on the women. Her fingers ticked against her skirt as she counted them under her breath.

"An' get me a room. Don't care where, any room."

Camille pointed at a nearby door without looking at him.

D'trav burst into the room and dropped the trunk on the ground with a crash. He heard the door shut behind him and turned. Alone. He bent forward, cradling his throbbing crotch for long moments before daring to let go and look the unused room over. Sheets covered the ornate furniture, creating odd bumpy lumps, and a heavy blanket had been thrown over the window, blocking the coastal sunlight from ruining the turquoise velvets and brocades. Ugly but serviceable, he decided. Careful not to make any jarring movements now that he was hidden, he limped past low benches and piled pillows and stared at himself in the mirror.

"She's done ruined it all. Now I've gotta start all over again."

He dug through the trunk until he had a flask in one hand and a straight razor in the other and began the transformation.

When Camille let herself into the room, he was sitting on the edge of the bed with his cuirass next to him. Frowning, she considered the pile of hair littering the floor and sink. "Dear god, D'trav. What've you done?"

He glanced at the hair. "It's not a thing."

She raised her voice. "It's not a thing?"

He shrugged.

"How can you say that?"

"Didn't know y—"

"You've gone stark blazing mad!"

"Seriously darlin. It'll be okay. Be back 'fore you know it."

"What? What do you mean it'll be back?"

He gestured at the hair.

She glanced at the hair and then back at his face with a mix of rage and incredulity. "You think I care about that?" She picked up a hank and waved it under his nose. "You really think I care about this… this… shit?"

D'trav's brows went up. He'd never seen her so angry.

"What do you think I am, stupid?" She was screaming now, her voice causing the crystal chandelier to vibrate and hum.

"Camille I…"

She collapsed on the edge of the bed and put her hands over her face. Her voice, muffled, turned soft with despair. "You killed the Baron, and you say it's not a thing? How could you?" She dropped her hands to her lap and stared straight ahead.

He looked up from the ground and examined her kohl-smudged eyes. Now he'd find out what she was really made of. "No."

"No?"

"Wasn't me."

"Your face is plastered all over Burmtin. Everyone's looking for you. Everyone. You did it, and then you came here."

"That Kyn woman I told you 'bout did it."

"You'll rain death down on us all."

"It *wasn't* me Camille."

"They'll be here. They'll torture us all. We're doomed."

"Camille stop." He grabbed her shoulder and shook it. "You aren't listening. I didn't kill him."

"Sooo…" She squinted up at him. "You helped her escape?"

"No. I w—"

"Doesn't matter." She stood and began pacing back and forth. "You still came here. I've got illegal Freni-Kyns in my cellar. All female. You know what that means?"

"They didn't follow me. I never did tell 'em where I lived."

"You had to." Her face reddened again, as if she thought he lied.

"No. I gave 'em some innkeeper's address on the other side a town."

"So you planned this all along?"

"No! Wait. It was just a precaution, damn it."

"Even if the guild doesn't follow you here, I'll have a half dozen sex crazed bitches trying to get out of my cellar. I've got no way of taking care of their needs. Who am I going to get? They'll be clawing at the walls."

"You're right, they—"

"No, we can't wait until the Preral sickness sets in. We've got to do something. Unless…" She stopped pacing and looked at D'trav. "You'll have to take care of their needs."

At that thought D'trav bent forward and groaned.

She rushed to him.

He thrust his arms out, keeping her from making contact but that simple movement was too much. He hunched over, sliding off the bed and landing on his knees. His pants rode up as he fell, and he let out a high pitched yipe.

"D'trav!"

He groaned.

"D'trav?"

"Camille… I did somethin' bad… real bad like… but it weren't killin' that bastard."

"What's wrong with you?" She grabbed his shoulder and pulled up with more strength than he was expecting.

He clutched her arm as he stood, leaving a bloody handprint.

Her gaze traveled from that to his crotch. She gasped, and her hand flew up to cover her mouth. The blood drained from her cheeks, leaving behind a smudge of berry rouge. "Oh, Kyron. He castrated you?"

D'trav let out a rough laugh. It held no real humor. He wasn't even sure why he did it. There was nothing funny in the horror on her face or in anything else that had happened that day. "Not castrated, and not he, she. The Kyn."

"Get up on the bed. Now." She yanked him upwards, forcing him onto the bed, and proceeded to strip him down.

He grasped the coverlet and writhed when she pulled his pants free.

She bent low over him and shifted his flaccid organ out of the way.

Shamed that she saw him like this, so useless, so small, D'trav felt his face heat.

She glared up at him. "These are claw marks."

More heat came to his face. He looked away.

"There were *no* holes in your pants."

"Camille—"

"Shut up. Just you shut the hell up." She walked to the door, then half back to him. "I should turn you in. Collect the reward."

"Please, Camille. Let me—"

"No. We had a deal. You broke it."

"Camille, that weren't our deal, I—"

"You fucking bastard. First you're fucking a slave, and then you bring hell down on me."

"Camille, please, I wouldn't lead 'em here."

She opened a cabinet, grabbed a bottle, and thumped it down on his chest. "Treat your own damn wounds. You deserve this."

"I had the hood coverin' my face. Nobody followed me."

She opened the door, hesitated, and turned to glare at him, her face a mask of rage.

"And those weren't the—" he started.

She slammed the door shut.

CHAPTER 10

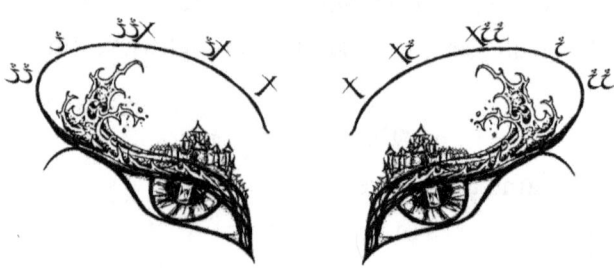

"It is with great sadness that I must report, there is no cure. Our genetic studies have brought damnation upon us. If our females do not take a mate once a month, they are doomed to give into the lust, losing their minds and taking whomever offers themselves.

The scientists have dubbed it the Preral sickness, and that seems an apt name to me. As I said from the start, we should have never tried to block the pregnancies by creating the Preral Cycle."

Cormac Forsàidh
Lead Scientist
Mamilian Genetic Studies
Freni-Kyn Landholding

Parian lifted a palm towards the cat mount, "No! Don't—"

She let forth an ear-piercing snarl.

Parian grabbed the man's wrist before he could loosen the whip. "Hold on now. Can't you see, she's afraid of it?"

"Let go of me, you idiot! That one's not fit to be ridden."

~I am NOT afraid of the string!~

Parian's grip on the man's wrist tightened, keeping him from backing away, and he turned to the cat. "Now now, shhhhh shhhhh, it's okay." *~Stop it. I can't get you out of here if you draw the guards.~*

The cat's gaze shot from its target to Parian. She snarled again for effect and lay down, muscles rippling under her sleek coat. *~Fine.~*

Parian let out a relieved breath.

The stable master quit struggling and gaped at the cat with shock.

Parian let go of the man's wrist. "How much."

"I've already got a buyer set up. She's breeding stock."

~Oh yeah?~ She snarled again, tensed her muscles.

The stable master backed up another step. "Damned if that animal don't act like it's possessed."

"I'll give you double," Parian said.

"Well… I don't know…"

The feline stretched for effect, extending claws that glinted silver in the sunlight.

"And take her off your hands today."

The stable master pulled his gaze from her claws. "Deal!"

"I'll need a saddle too."

~You stay here. No more trouble,~ Parian told her.

She brought a paw to her mouth, turning it over as she did, and began licking between the pads. *~Rosalie~*

~Rosalie? I don't know a Rosalie.~

~Name's Rosalie.~

~Okay.~

~Not cat.~

~Okay.~ He strolled across the yard behind the stable master.

~Not feline.~

"I said, okay."

The stable master gave him a strange look. "Okay to what?"

"Nothing, sorry, thinking out loud."

~Not IT either.~

Parian wondered what he'd gotten himself into.

"Well, here they are." The stable master gestured toward a row of feline saddles.

~Which one do you want?~

She didn't answer.

He peered at her. *~Rosalie?~*

She stood up and pointedly turned her back on him.

~Oh dear god. Really?~

"They'll all fit her, she's standard size, 'cept this big one on the end. That's for a warcat."

Parian reached for a teal colored saddle.

~Not that one,~ Rosalie sent.

He withdrew his hand and considered the other three. Yellow, red, and pink. The red seemed the most comfortable. He started to pick it up.

~Not that one either.~

He surveyed what was left and had a horrible feeling. She wouldn't. *~I'm not getting the pink one.~*

~But, I like it.~

~No.~

Parian set his hand on the yellow one and nodded at the stable master. It looked comfortable enough. He could live with the color, even if he didn't like yellow.

The stable master picked up the yellow saddle and turned towards the office.

~Just you try and get that on me.~

Parian watched the stable master's retreating back and tried to probe Rosalie's mind but met only a wall of determination. He groaned. "I've changed my mind. The pink one."

The stable master turned back around and threw the yellow over its stand. He gave Parian a sideways glance before picking up the pink one. "You sure?"

Parian glared at the saddle. Not only was it pink but it was embroidered with white roses. He suppressed another groan. "It suits her."

In the midst of signing the papers, she spoke again, causing him to accidentally splatter ink across the document. *~It's Rosalie. Ros-a-lie.~*

Parian drew a line through the word feline and printed her name in place. The stable master scratched his head with a look on his face that needed no mental peek to interpret; the man thought he was mind-lost.

As they approached Rosalie, the stable master lagged further and further behind, until the scuff of his footsteps in the dirt stopped.

Parian glanced back at him.

"I've… I've got some work inside to do." The stable master hurried towards the far side of the stable.

Parian grinned. "You scared him."

~*We have history.*~ She purred while he put the saddle on and waited for him to mount.

"We aren't going far. I'll walk."

She followed him from the yard, tail swishing back and forth in slow motion.

His arrival at The Mandarin Inn went without incident. Soon Rosalie was stabled, with orders for the best rabbit they could find, and he was settled in his new room. He stared out the window at the dusty streets of Falksfall with satisfaction. He was safe. He had listened to the minds downstairs for hours and there had been no inquiry for the 'evil eyed' man. Tomorrow he'd start the next phase of his plan.

The beggar boy grappled soundlessly, fighting for freedom with enough force to add more bruises to Sarenka's collection. His silence wasn't surprising; a scream for help often drew more attackers in Sad Town.

Grasping the back of his shirt collar and holding him far enough away to escape flailing arms, she gave him a shake. "Stop! Damn it. This is business, you idiot. You want coin or not?"

His arms dropped to his sides, and he stopped kicking, but the eyes staring up at her were murderous.

With a shiver she let go.

"Ought not… sneak up… on someun like that," he panted out between breaths, winded from his struggles.

The scent of fear-laden sweat and rotting fish rolled off the boy, but Sarenka resisted the urge to cover her nose. "Had to. Only wanted you, not the rest of them. You want to earn d'yroap or not?"

"I don't do the sex." He stepped backwards, closer to the street.

Sarenka's skin went cold and pale. "Kyron! No. I don't want that. I just need a pick-tool."

The boy, looking both relieved and anxious, blinked innocently. "What's a pick-tool?"

"Stop with the coy. You either sell me yours, or not. I'm sure one of the other boys'll want coin, even if you don't."

She started to turn away, and he grasped her sleeve with a filth-begrimed hand. Glancing at the small fingers, she suspected he'd been digging around near the muddier part of the coast for seaweed to eat or sell.

"Ten silvers," he said.

She laughed.

"Ten," he repeated.

"Not hardly, scoundrel. Probably aren't worth a copper."

He looked down.

She followed his gaze to a pair of filthy bare feet.

He curled his toes and pulled his pants lower on his hips, hiding his feet beneath the jagged edge of coarse fabric that had been shorn with something dull. "They get the job done. Five."

"Right. One silver."

"Ha! Three, an' those fancy shoes there." He gestured towards the velvet slippers.

"Why, you thieving son of a toad! I ought to—" She cocked her head sideways at the sound of approaching footsteps.

He grinned and turned to leave.

Reaching inside the edge of her belt, she retrieved five silvers. "Okay, you bottom dwelling little brat, let's see them."

He reached into the pocket of trousers so oversized as to almost be a dress.

Sarenka tensed. If he wanted to pull a blade, now was the time.

He fumbled about, taking too long.

Sarenka glanced up and down the street, checking her escape route. If he came at her, her only option was to run. She wasn't going to beat a child, now, or ever.

He pulled free a tangled pile of twisted wire bits and held them up for inspection.

Sarenka let out a breath of relief. No attack. Not yet anyway. She studied the mass with growing disappointment. They were the crudest possible of tools.

"Here's your three silvers." She tucked away the other two before reaching down to untie the slippers and toeing them off. "And the slippers."

He bent to pick them up.

She placed her bare foot on the ties. "Hand over the picks."

He grinned. "Smarter than you look, that you are."

She reached for the tools and gave his cheek a solid tweak before grabbing them.

"Ow! What you do that for?" Rubbing his reddened cheek, he glared up at her from under tousled hair.

"To remind you to be good. Everything has a price, especially selling tools for more than they're worth."

He snorted and bent to get the slippers.

She pressed her foot down harder on the strings, waiting until he peered up before asking, "You have parents?"

"Nope," he spoke without standing, hand still on the shoes.

"Well, get yourself a room somewhere, and find someone to apprentice to. You've got the silver for it now."

"Ummm... Sure."

Sarenka lifted her foot, disappointed and worried. He wasn't going to do it.

Clutching them to his chest like treasure, he darted out of reach.

She stared at the tools with revulsion before tucking them under the cotehardie. Using them to survive would break the vow she'd made over a year ago.

"Take care, kid." She started back towards the mercantile side of town and listened for the soft scuff of his footsteps, either walking away or following, but from behind came only the disconsolate sounds of Sad Town.

Upon reaching a safe alley, she pulled off the cotehardie, threw it over her head like a hood, and settled in, leaning against the wall to sleep. A bang startled her awake and she moved to another alley, hiding behind a crate to catch a few hours' sleep before rubbing warmth into her limbs and shifting to yet another spot.

Dawn approached at last, and Sarenka rubbed sleep from eyes as scratchy as sun-scorched sand. She lifted her head, drawing in the salty fog and wished she could use it to scour the scent of rotting meat from her body. It sickened her, the idea of the baron's blood under her clothing, a testimony to the killer within. She settled her illusions in place before moving out into the open and turned towards an area that housed the working class.

Feigning legitimate business, she marched boldly down a street filled with simple cottages and darted behind the first overgrown bush that gave a good view of the neighborhood. It was better than Sad Town, but not by much. She watched people filter out of run down cottages, some carrying baskets, some tools, others wearing uniforms that announced their professions.

Guilt plagued her as she picked her targets.

No choice in this…

Have to get rid of the master's stuff…

She thought it over and over, but it brought no comfort.

At the back door of a hut that reeked of cabbage, she fumbled with the carved wooden lock, twisting the picks this way and that until the tumblers lined up with an audible snap. Slipping past the door, she half ran through the hut and rummaged amongst their meager belongings, taking care not to leave signs of her passage. With any luck it'd be a while before they noticed things gone. She grabbed a chemise and a pair of long gloves, dropped a silver d'yroap for the owner, and fled. It was too large, but the fear of being caught red-handed surpassed the need to find something better.

I can't do this.

These people work long and hard for almost nothing.

How can I do this?

What kind of person am I?

She crept back towards the street, moving from bush to bush, and was about to step out of cover when the crisp sound of feet, all walking in unison, alerted her into staying hidden. A regiment of guards trooped past, stopping only to speak with a bystander. Sarenka grimaced when they held up a rough sketch of her face for the man to see. He shook his head, and the guards started off again, not making it far before they stopped a woman.

They grappled with the woman instead of showing her the sketch and knocked her basket to the ground, scattering her goods. A man clung to each arm, holding her thrashing body between them. She cried out with distress as a third soldier stepped forward and ran his hands over her face. He grasped her left ear, tugging it forcefully. She yelped in pain, and he let go, stepping back. The soldiers withdrew, leaving the sobbing woman to retrieve her goods from the ground alone. With a shudder, Sarenka sank farther into the shadows.

So they're checking for illusions.

How am I supposed to survive?

The guards turned at the end of the street and started back her way. Sarenka froze, thinking she'd been seen, but their pace remained measured. She closed her eyes and held her breath as they passed, listening to the thud of their perfectly matched steps. Afterwards she lingered behind the bush, waiting to see if they would return, before working her way towards the busier part of town. She dared not target the other houses now. Her thefts needed to be scattered randomly, not clustered on a single street, lest it become obvious that she was the one stealing and they compile a sketch of her with descriptions of the new-ly stolen clothing. She clasped the wadded chemise close and rushed to leave that part of town behind, hoping nobody noticed.

Upon ducking into a darkened alley, she rushed to exchange it for the billowing shirt she was wearing and pulled the gloves up past her elbows. Though the necessity of stealing galled her, pulling the clean chemise over dried and flaking blood was worse. But in that, like so many other things, she had no choice. Her inability to hold an illusion for a reasonable length of time made bathing at one of the few public baths impossible. She had no pail to draw water from the wells, and an ill-equipped woman checking into an inn, without baggage or even eating utensils, was sure to draw unwanted notice.

Nervous tension stiffening her back into an ache, she stuffed the old shirt behind a barrel and set out in search of something to break her fast with. The sun hovered on the horizon, painting the world in golden streaks as she ambled towards the food corridor.

A troop of guards entered.

Sarenka froze.

The corridor went still and quiet as people stopped to stare.

The guards spread out in twos and threes.

Trying to appear casual, Sarenka flexed her legs and prepared to run while focusing on the pair of guards coming straight at her. With a weapon she stood a chance, but retrieving the dagger from beneath the cotehardie would take too long. She eyed the sword of a nearby man and wondered if she could yank it free in time.

A woman lifted her hand, pointing at Sarenka.

Chapter 11

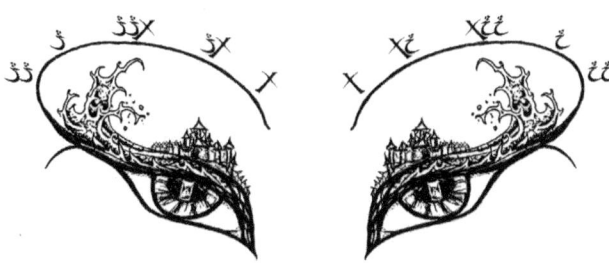

Tiny glistening beads of nervous sweat banded Parian's brow in a wet circlet. Upon the tre-points of a hand-drawn sigil, he carefully placed the elementals: a brazier stacked with oil-soaked kindling, a small stone bowl of spring water, and an empty wooden plate which held only air.

His hair floated in a random pattern around his head, each filament swaying to its own internal beat. Impatient with the distraction, he pushed it aside and paced out the distance around the elements.

Satisfied, he smiled. It was perfect and could be erased with a simple sweep of his hand, leaving no hefty repair bill with the Falksfall Inn.

Unless things go awry. And then it won't matter because I'll be dead.

Wiping away the sweat, he carefully shut off his psychic connection with The Seven and their ongoing discussion about saving the world. Right now he needed to act, not talk about what will happen when they find The One. The quarrels between himself and the others had raged back and forth for several turns of the hourglass, bouncing from one angry mind to another. Left in the aftermath was a fragile mental link, one he feared the mere act of touching would destroy. With success in finding The One would come reluctant acceptance. He was positive of that.

Friendship was one thing, their mission another, and recently his only friends, his fellow seers, hadn't agreed with the plan.

Probably because it's my plan. Not theirs.

He shrugged. It definitely put a strain on things but there was no helping it. He was not going to Burmtin in person, as some of them recommended. The thought of a real live trip to Burmtin, in the flesh, brought such a hammer of fear that he just stood there, frozen, unable to move.

No. I won't do it. I can't. Not in person. Only a foolish Freni-Kyn would visit that city, with its roiling cloud of lust, and for a psychic... Torture, pure torture. I wouldn't be able to resist, and once I lost control, I'd no longer be a Seven.

~Do you have to think so much?~ Rosalie asked.

With a shudder, he broke free of the paralyzing thoughts and turned back to the symbols. For once, her sarcasm had helped him.

~I'm sorry.~

~I'm trying to sleep and you're just blathering away,~ Rosalie sent.

~I can't help it. I've tuned down as far as possible already.~

~I know... worse this way. This annoying buzz buzz buzzzz. Like a gnat.~

~Try humming,~ he sent, exasperated. She was far more difficult to tune out than the rest of the Seven, and block them out he had. Despite what they thought, sometimes sacrifices must be made. Especially when the alternative was a trip to Burmtin in person. Jeopardizing his friendships, and even his life, was a small price to pay when the alternative was visiting that horrifying city.

Distressful thoughts of Burmtin and the coming danger turned the tips of his living hair into orange embers. Despite that almost overwhelming fear, he'd ride the tides of time alone, without the rest of The Seven, and that was what they hated, really.

Too bad. I'm not waiting for them. By then it'll be too late.

~Doing it again.~ Rosalie sent.

He checked the symbols one final time and stepped to the center of the triangle, taking care not to smudge the chalked out sigils.

Yes, perfect placement…

And better be.

His life, and the future of Llayentia, depended on that precision. Normally the support of the others would make these trinkets just that, trinkets of little worth. Unnecessary. Symbols only. Normally the combined psychic energies of The Seven, their psynergy, would be enough to take all of them into the time stream. Normally the Seven would anchor each other, making the risk of being cast astray, a body with no soul, far less likely. But not today. Today would be anything but normal. Today he must rely on external symbols, instead of living flesh, to support his seeing. Today he risked his sanity to save a sullied world.

Kyron's Worlde, Llayentia. A worlde which had once thrived, living in peace and unity, but now beat out its dying breath, destroyed by treachery from within. Like a lover he was wedded to this worlde, to Llayentia and her people, their sworn protector. Though they continued their petty lives, planning their wars, their murders, their rape of the land that birthed them, still, he was theirs. Consumed with the need to protect and nurture the land and the people, his life of celibacy was all that mattered.

He lit the brazier with a trembling hand and drew one last comforting breath, then closed his eyes and willed himself to relax. The flame leapt upwards, and a matching opaline light flickered into existence, rising from the plate. Moments later a waterspout burst from the bowl, rising towards the ceiling. Parian's breathing deepened. The elemental flames of fire, water, and air spiraled upwards and inwards, cocooning him in supernatural force. The energies twisted about his body, wrapping him in a matching sheath of fabric and almost smothering him with his own hair.

Letting go of his physical body, he slipped into the time stream, seeking The One who had been disturbing his sleep.

The city of Burmtin loomed, its squat ugliness a blemish on the coastal countryside. He shuddered to a stop, unwilling to draw closer. The call came again, faint, desperate, luring him into jumping forward. His mind zoomed through the outer gates, slowing above a Glidarthian family. The parents' leathern wings betrayed nervous tension, shifting uneasily as they strode down crowded merchant streets. Oblivious to the danger, their wingless children followed, mouths small circles of wonder.

How can he do this? Gasping in horror, Parian stared at the overweight Glidarthian. *How can he be so addicted to exotic foods... so addicted that he brings his family here... to a city that trades in sex and drugs.*

He picked at the family's psychic scents.

The little one... some ability, but not enough to send thought.

Pulling away, he took in the armored M'hakru guards surrounding them and grimaced.

The fool! He's hired M'hakru. Parian fluttered across the edge of the guard's minds and saw them signing scrolls at the mercenary guild. He watched as they received their insignias and felt the satisfaction that came with that.

Good, so they aren't just faking. But did he pay them well?

If not, there'd be nothing but a blur of motion streaking away from a pile of mutilated bodies. He pressed in further, checking the guard's intentions. His sight blurred, shifting angles, and a head flew clear of a body, spraying his face with blood. He shuddered and withdrew, blinking his eyes, trying to clear his vision.

Not my memory... his... not mine.

He turned away. He couldn't do everything, be everywhere. He was one man in a terrible and foul city.

His mind expanded, searching for the psychic scent of his soon to be replacement, or perhaps even The Foretold. He hesitated above an emaciated Frevell. The man's dark blue hair and long pointed ears marked him as a member of that dignified race.

He has a psychic flavor of...

Parian touched his thoughts. The man had come to Burmtin searching for employment as an arbitrator, but his employers had tired of his rigid mentality and turned him out on the streets. Murderous thoughts and plans stalked through his thoughts like the undead, ready to scavenge for souls.

No, the One can't be that manipulative, that cruel.

Parian moved forward with a jerk.

Somewhere...

He sent forth a tendril, hoping.

Somewhere in this locked-down city is The One, and I'm going to find him, or her. Even if it risks my own life.

~Parian?~ The familiar mind brushed against his in a faint tickle.

He blocked the inquiry.

Too dangerous to talk right now.

I've got to finish my search.

Tendrils of thought streamed in from all directions.

He paused for just long enough to get his bearings and began sifting through them, probing for the trail of one specific brain, that honey-scented mind whose presence was a promise of life after a long winter of searching. His incorporeal being floated upwards, following the mind currents towards the coast, and he turned to systematically scanning the city.

At a simple directed thought, a grid of blue light flickered into being, overlaying the landscape and helping him to keep track of where he'd already searched. He began skimming past the wave-shaped ships lining the harbor and wasn't surprised to find a complete lack of honest fishing boats. Nobody came or went from within the barricaded walls of Burmtin without the knowledge of either the Watrelk Pirates or the Red Pelican Assassins' Guild. And therein lay the problem; The mind which plagued his dreams, begging for help—that mind— seemed trapped, longing to flee, yet somehow restrained.

Why?

Why'd you come here?

Surely with the sight, you knew better than to come to this Kyron-forsaken city.

He flew upwards, turning away from the city.

I shouldn't be here…

But how can I help myself?

How can I not answer?

The yearning for answers filled him and he turned back, determined to see this through.

Reaching the end of the ships without catching the elusive scent, he turned inwards to skim over the tops of the warehouses lining the waterfront, and hesitated above an ordinary building, its simple frame sun scorched and scoured free of paint by the coastal breeze. It looked unworthy of notice, but foulness crouched over it like a misshapen umbrella of deceit, its putrid stench so evil that it buffeted his psychic body, knocking him back and forth.

He lost control, spun off track, and almost missed the pure scent that evil masked. Dread filled him, and he shuddered, but steeled himself to move in closer. Determined, he skimmed the surface thoughts of the people entering and exiting the building: Red Pelican Assassins and Watrelk Pirates. Of course. That explained the foul air, the stench of death.

He pulled up, turned, floated, considered the implications. Somewhere in the midst of that corrupt hall was his quarry; the one whose soul was tainted, yes, shadowed by darkness, yes, but whose spirit was pure.

It made sense. Anyone held by the Red Pelican would be tainted, But Parian was unconcerned, an unwilling victim could be cleansed.

Finally.

I've found you.

Parian spiraled down towards the building.

Abruptly, with a hard crash, he landed on the ground between his symbols. For a moment he lay, breath crushed from his lungs, unable to move. Finally air came, raw, painful, ragged, but he'd live.

With a shaking hand, he pulled a chunk of honey-soaked kaseloaf from his pocket and pushed it into his mouth. He fought to keep his jaw from falling open and waited for the sugar to dissolve. The sweetened saliva slid down his throat, giving him the strength to chew the rest of the cheese and take in that much needed energy.

The shaking in his limbs became more manageable, and he rolled over. He stared at the symbolic bowl, plate, and brazier with understanding. Within the brazier lay merely ash, and the water bowl held only a dusting of trace minerals. He stared at his emaciated hand. The required fuel had been devoured far faster than he expected, and without that artificial boost, his own body had been consumed.

CHAPTER 12

Without acknowledging the people he passed, Lator paced down the hallway of the Red Pelican's underground labyrinth. His high collar suit, like his demeanor, was strict but neutral. Next to him, wearing wrinkled cotton, Burk rattled through page after page of reports.

"...which basically means nobody saw anything. Not one person saw either the guard or the Freni-Kyn... Sarenka I mean... leave. But all the injuries point to murder. By her, not him. We think he coerced her into doing it and then left with her. It's been over a day. By now he's probably killed her and dumped the body."

Narrow face unreadable, like any self-respecting pure blooded Frevell's should be, Captain Lator halted.

Still talking, Burk continued walking. After several paces his face flushed with embarrassment and he halted and swung around. The corner of his eye gave a nervous twitch. "So sorry, sir. I wasn't paying atten—" He gulped several times, swallowing what he'd been about to say, and stared at Lator's pointed ear rather than look him in the eye.

Without a trace of emotion, Lator raised one brow and asked, "You really believe that he talked her into killing the Baron, and then killed her?"

Burk stared at the impeccable Frevellian with an alarmed expression on his face that quickly turned to one of fear. "Y-yes, sir."

"Very good. Send in R'kiax." Lator walked into his office, shutting the door in Burk's face.

Idiots.

This looks like nothing Onglat has ever done.

He wouldn't have left the dirty work to the Freni-Kyn.

Lator paced around his office, picking up items and resisting the urge to throw them and setting them back down. A firm knock at the door interrupted his angry thoughts. He sat behind his desk before saying, "Enter."

R'kiax paused in the doorway, taking in the details of the room.

Lator half-smiled. He enjoyed working with Sharpras. They were cautious by nature, their warrior training starting in youth. "Sit."

The shape-shifter took the chair like an animal, muscles tense, ready to spring.

"There is a slave I want back. Find her."

"A slave?" The man's tension was replaced with boredom. "You've dozens of agents, why me?"

"She is Freni-Kyn."

R'kiax nodded and bared his teeth in a grim smile. "I could just kill her for you."

"No. Locate her. Let me know where she is. Speak of this to no one."

"Yes, sir." R'kiax stood to leave.

"Go as H'euman. I do *not* want her alerted to our interest."

"But of course." R'kiax shifted: shortening and narrowing in height and stature, ears rounding into semi-points, eyes losing their slitted pupils, body hair reducing to normal H'euman standards while the hair of his head turned dirty blond and lay in soft waves upon his shoulders.

"That is a Half-Frevell."

"I don't wear H'euman."

Lator frowned, unsure of whether the man didn't want to wear H'euman or was not capable of pulling it off.

"This will work better. People confide in the illegal half-breeds," R'kiax said.

"That will do nicely." Lator nodded. "With the Sharpra sense of smell, finding a Freni-Kyn should be simple. Remember, we do not want her forewarned. And do not kill her, even if Freni-Kyns are the Sharpra's sworn enemy. Understood?"

The Half-Frevell smiled as an answer.

Captain Lator waited.

"Understood," R'kiax finally said.

The man next to Sarenka turned and ran into the busy corridor, trying to lose himself in the crowd.

The guards sprinted after him, knocking her aside in their rush to catch up.

She stumbled and banged up against a merchant.

The merchant reached out to steady her.

She fake stumbled even further away, narrowly avoiding the merchants touch, and turned back to watch the guards.

In a last burst of speed, the guards threw themselves forward, bearing the man to the ground. He writhed under their bodies, struggling to break free, until a loud crack came from the arm they were twisting behind his back.

"Please. Please. No more."

"Stop fighting, you dim witted piece of dung!"

He sobbed and lay still.

The guards stood and dusted themselves down while watching the man warily.

He shifted position.

One of the guards lashed out with a kick, catching the man full in the face.

Blood spurted from the man's nose, washing the cobblestones in red. Stunned, he lay unmoving.

Before the man could recover the guard pressed his foot down on the man's throat, pinning him to the ground.

The man coughed and spat out a tooth.

The guard pressed his foot down harder.

The man's eyes widened and his face purpled. He clawed at the shoe, desperate for air.

With a sadistic smile, the guard let up enough for the man to draw in a breath, then pressed down again, cutting off his air.

The woman who had turned him in rubbed her hands together.

One of the guards gave her an annoyed glare. "Hold onto your cats."

She rubbed her hands more, waiting.

"Greedier by the day," another soldier said.

"Yeah but we need them," the first said and held up a pouch of coins as if he were going to throw it at her, hard.

She raised her hands defensively.

He tossed it with so little power that it barely left his hand and fell to the ground half-way between them.

The woman threw herself forward, landing atop the pouch with a screech.

The soldiers guffawed and slapped each other on the shoulder, enjoying the sport. Turning their attention back to the prisoner, they dragged him to his feet, punched him twice in the stomach, and pulled him over to where the rest of the garrison had already reassembled. Sarenka counted. Three women and two men captive, all as bloodied as the one she'd seen taken down. They left, taking their prisoners with them. One of the captive women lifted her voice in a wail that echoed through the area.

Sarenka looked at the food, the ground, the people, anywhere but at the departing backs. Passing a meat vendor who was scrubbing the walk in front of his cart with a bristle brush, she stopped.

"Looks like hard work."

Still kneeling, he glared up at her. "Stupid brat pissed all over me wheel."

Well that just figures. Sarenka frowned.

"I'll do the cleanin'... for that piece of cooked sausage there." She faked the accent, hoping he wouldn't realize she was the one the guards were searching for.

He squinted, shrewd eyes taking in the mismatched outfit.

"Please. They done fired me. I be needin' a job."

Chewing over the idea, he scrutinized the yellow stain for a long moment and then stood and rubbed his hands down a blood spattered apron. "Jest the one job. One sausage. If you do it good."

Sarenka squatted to dip the brush into a bucket of sudsy water before scrubbing at the mess.

The man arranged his wares and shared good-natured chitchat with customers, stopping occasionally to shout out, "Fresh salted pork! Cooked sausages, good 'nuff for royalty!"

As promised, the butcher paid her with sausage when she finished.

Glad to have meat after weeks of gruel, she stuffed a bite in her mouth and turned to stare out at the milling crowd with grease dribbling down her chin.

"What happened to your shoes?"

"Stolen. That's what lost me job." After wiping the grease from her face with the sleeve of her shirt, she rubbed her gloved hands down over her clothing and hoped the oils didn't ruin the glove's grip.

He gave an understanding nod, thievery was an everyday Burmtin occurrence, and most jobs required shoes. "Well, off with you. Don't need vagrants runnin' off me customers. Ya do smell somethin' awful, almost bad as that piss."

Sarenka sighed and moved on. She did, indeed, stink.

She needed a place to hide and get cleaned up, but in a city of spies and cut-throats, where? There was nowhere for a Freni-Kyn murderess. Instead of a room and a bath, she moved from spot-to-spot, sleeping in several places each night. The need to hide her identity, to hide her true Freni-Kyn nature, was more important than comfort.

She glanced at the poster of her face as she neared it. Already the guards had scratched out the original d'yroap number and replaced it with a higher reward, attracting a small crowd. Shifting her path, she drew near enough to listen in. Rumors flew the streets of Burmtin like horseflies seeking blood, and she needed that knowledge to survive.

"Did you hear? Some of the... you know... secret... pleasure houses are offering an even higher price for bringin' them a Freni-Kyn pleasure slave," the man next to her said, rubbing his hands together.

"Really?" his companion answered, speculative gaze settling on Sarenka.

"Red Pelican's got a higher number on her too."

He struck like lightning, grasping Sarenka's arm and yanking her close.

Chapter 13

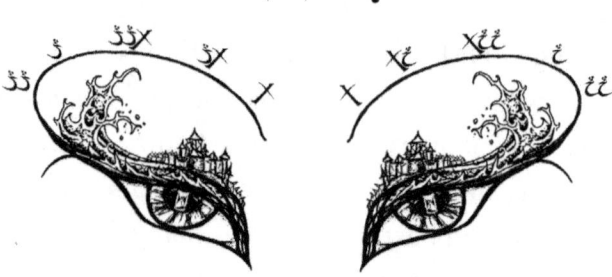

"A more apt name for the wood of the Tant tree would've been iron wood. With fibers so dense that special weapons must be created to cut the massive trees down, many craftsmen have taken to growing the trees into the shapes they want from seed. Far easier to make two cuts and have a table than to labor day and night trying to create planks. Of course, the hand sized thorns must still be removed."

Naiara De Sena
Herbmistress of Goldash
H'euman settlement dedicated to plant mastery

She kicked, catching the man in the groin and twisting free.

The other man made a grab for her but Sarenka shoved him backwards. He hit the wanted poster with a loud crack and slid down the wall, taking the parchment to the ground with him.

Sarenka ran, ducking through a series of alleys and streets to throw off pursuit. Finally she stopped and leaned forward, panting for breath. But she didn't quit watching the street, the alleys, the doorways, for more pointing fingers. She shuddered to think what the pleasure traders would do with the Freni-Kyns they caught and sold. Always a dangerous city, Burmtin had become a living nightmare for her people. No sane Freni-Kyn woman would dare enter the city right now, not with a witch hunt roaring out-of-control.

Parian felt himself pulled through time, twisting and bumping out of control along paths he hadn't journeyed before. As if the very essence of time were narrowing, pressing him flat, air was pushed from his body until, like a cork from a bottle, he landed on a green expanse of lawn. Bewildered, he sat on grass with his vision so enhanced that each blade stood out from the others. Above him massive overlapping balls of white cotton drifted across a periwinkle sky.

The air... it smells of earth and... He covered his nose.

Dung? Dirty bodies?

Kyron, what is that stench?

The background came zooming into focus: a filthy city, with its darker, filthier thoughts. Overwhelmed, he blocked the thoughts, closing off his connection with the city's inhabitants.

Where am I?

When am I?

~Hello?~ He sent out the questioning thought but no answer came.

He stood and brushed down his trousers before remembering that it didn't matter. Nobody would be able to see him here. His body was in a different place, lying within a circle, surrounded by protective symbols.

A man's voice interrupted his thoughts. "Elsa stop, I told you we can't go there."

A young girl circled a man, bouncing around him as he walked, forcing him to slow down. Her satin blond hair bounced with her in a tumbled mass of curls. She was not a beautiful child, but she was well kempt, and the joy she exuded more than made up for her simple features.

Parian skimmed their minds lightly, scooping up surface thoughts as they talked.

"Please!" the girl said.

"No."

"Please. Just for a sweet. Just one."

"They might recognize you. It's too dangerous."

"None 'cept that one beggar saw me. I was hid out behind the box."

"No, Elsa." He knelt and grasped the sides of her face, trying to keep her attention long enough to get through. "They'll kill you dead, sure as they did that man, just for seein' it happen. So, no. And that's the final word. I'll not be a riskin' you. We've lost enough already."

She sighed, smoothed down her cream dress, and gazed up at him with large grey eyes.

"Now, don't you be lookin' at me like that. You know I can't stand the puppy dog eyes."

She giggled and made some yapping noises, imitating a begging puppy.

He cocked his head sideways and whined back at her, then let out a howl that made her squeal.

Turning, she darted away, and the chase was on.

He let her win the race for a while then scooped her up in his arms and spun around until he was red in the face and out of breath.

When he set her free she staggered, then plopped down in front of him and clapped her tiny hands together and laughed.

He laughed along, joining in the delight of the moment.

"Again, do it again."

He leaned over and tied the laces of her loosened sandals. "Not today darlin. I've gotta go to work."

With a pout she stood. "You're always a workin'... always... and wearin' that funny name."

"You 'member it, right?"

"Yes."

"Say it."

"D'trag."

"No. D'trav. You have to learn it, Elsa. So as they don't find us."

"I don't like it. Sounds weird. And it's hard to say."

"That's because it's Sharpra."

"It is?" She leaned closer and her eyes widened.

"Yes, means mighty warrior." He thumped his chest for effect.

That's a lie. It means vengeance. Parian looked at the child and shrugged. *I'd have told her mighty warrior too. What does a child know of vengeance?*

"Ohhh. I like that. Can I just call you warrior?"

He laughed. "Okay. I see no harm in that. But people be thinkin' you're daft."

"Warrior," she said solemnly. "It's a good name."

He half turned towards the city. "I've gotta go. Late already."

"I don't want you to."

"I know, sweet one. But how else you 'spect me to bring home treats an' such like?"

"What will you bring me today?"

"A beetle."

She gasped with delight. "Promise?"

"What? No. How about a snake?"

"A really big un?"

"Giant." He spread his arms wide.

"Big 'nough to eat the house?"

"Big 'nough to eat all of Burmtin," he said.

She laughed. "You funny."

"Only to you, little 'un. You go on in now. I'll not leave till I do be hearin' that door lock tight."

She sighed and turned towards Parian, and as if she saw him, she stopped. Her form blurred and her spirit stepped free, no longer the joyful child. Parian's heart was pierced at the transformation, and his limbs turned to lead as her dark mouth, lined with unnatural grief, began to move.

"Now you see me," the wraith child said.

Parian's body slammed backwards, and he landed in his bed with a thump. He gasped, and his gaze darted about, jumping from one surface to another, trying to find something he recognized. Alighting on his leather bags, he realized it was a dream and rolled over with a groan.

~Parian?~

~It's nothing Airintia. A nightmare. Go back to sleep.~

D'trav awoke to darkness and shivered. He patted the surface of the side table but found neither candle nor lantern. Rolling to a stand, he regretted it immediately and bent double with a groan.

He breathed.

That was all he could do for a while, and when he could bear to move again, he found angry, misshapen swelling where once his balls had been. The M'hakru whiskey from the toy cabinet had stopped the pain and given him some welcome sleep, but it hadn't fixed his problems, and now he had a matching headache.

He grabbed the edge of the side table and forced himself to stand straight. The room was blacker than black. He put his hands out and rubbed along the papered wall, searching for the window. At last his fingers touched the blanket that served as a heavy curtain. Relieved, he fumbled to get under it and felt along the shutters. When he reached the bottom he grabbed the edges and pulled. They didn't open so he ran his hand up the center until he found the stone latch. He felt it carefully and was surprised to find it unfastened. He tried again, prying his fingertips under the lip of a shutter and pulling as hard as he could. It didn't budge.

"Are you fuckin' kiddin' me?"

He pressed his fingers between the slats and found them thicker than normal and fixed in place. Storm shutters. She had put up the storm shutters, and he knew what that meant. They were nailed shut, probably with tant wood spikes. No amount of pulling would break tant wood.

Turning back to the room, he squinted his eyes and peered about but could see nothing. He worked his way back towards the bed and cried out when he accidentally brushed against the end table. He covered his crotch and fell forward, knocking his head against Kyron-knew-what.

"Kyron fuckin', horse lickin', manure eatin'…" He felt his forehead and found a gash and wetness. "What now?"

He patted around until he found the edge of the bed and clambered back into it. As he pulled the blankets up, his elbow bumped against something cold and smooth. He reached for it, and a light flickered in the far corner.

He peered.

He drew in a breath and held it.

What is that?

He squinted his eyes.

H'euman… maybe.

"Who's there?" he called.

The person shifted slightly closer.

"Better fuckin' stop playin' with me or suffer the wrath of…" He ran out of words. "Hell, I don't know what, but I'll kill you bare handed if'n I gotta."

The person flickered and disappeared.

D'trav rubbed his eyes and searched the room for where he, or she, had gone. He held his breath and listened.

Nothing.

Nobody.

Musta been a trick of the light comin' through the shutters.

He ignored the voice in the back of his head that wondered, *What light?*

Laying back, relieved, his elbow bumped against the cold item. He fumbled about before bringing the whiskey bottle to his lips and drawing a long swallow.

"Hell with ya." He toasted the far corner and—for less time than it takes for a grain of sand to fall through a time glass—thought that he once more saw the outline of person. Small, it was true, but a person nonetheless.

And then the figure was gone.

He shuddered, took a long pull of the bottle, and tugged the blanket over his head.

Hours later he awoke covered in sweat, with light slanting through the shutters.

"Oh dear god." His hand went first to his head and then to his groin, unsure which hurt worse. He clambered to his feet and pissed into the chamber pot with great satisfaction.

"Well, least she didn't break me."

Searching the room produced a lantern, flint, and tinder, which he placed next to his bed. Hands on hips, he surveyed the room and considered stripping it of dust covers, but then decided he wouldn't be there long enough to bother. His stomach let out a gurgling growl, making him wonder how early it was. He staggered to the mirror and decided that he looked different enough to fetch food from the kitchen. Camille was obviously still mad and not about to bring him anything.

Digging through the trunk unearthed a single pair of too-small pants. He stared at them in disbelief before wadding them into a ball and throwing them at the door with as much force as he could manage. They landed softly, thwarting his need to vent. Leaning against the trunk, he considered his options. All the rest of his clothing was back in his hut, undoubtedly tossed by the guards and looted by vagrants already. The closet he had searched earlier held only women's skirts, corsets, stockings, and shoes. That left only one choice.

He wrapped the sheet around his hips before treading a painful path to the door.

The handle wouldn't turn.

She wouldn't.

Incredulous, he shook the handle.

She couldn't.

Dropping his sheet, he used both hands to try the handle.

"Camille!"

He rattled the door and let out a snarl.

"You can't do this to me. Not after all we've…"

He beat the door, shaking it within its frame and filling the room with echoing bangs, until his fists were bruised and bloody.

Sinking to the floor, he pressed his forehead against the door.

"Please Camille…" he whispered.

Sarenka tugged at a new shawl and paused near the entrance to a darkened alley. She gave her shoulders a quick shrug, acknowledging that the faded blue wrap wasn't really 'new'. Newly acquired was more accurate. Just like her frayed corset, stained skirt, and coarse chemise—the shawl was stolen. It had taken a whole week of looking over her shoulders for pointing fingers to gather an outfit as unremarkable as the face she wore.

Her nights of jerking awake at the slightest sound were catching up, as was the desperate craving for Foreveron which burned through her veins, shrieked through her mind. She couldn't continue this way forever. She needed somewhere to live, or at least a cloak with a deep enough hood to hide her face while she slept.

She approached a vendor, hoping to purchase a bruised apple. Fruit flies flew up in a cloud as she raised her hand to choose.

The merchant covered his nose, and reaching under his cart, produced a heavy stick and brandished it at her.

Her shoulders drooped as she was turned away for the third time in one day. Last night she'd been thrown out of the pub before she could get a sweet-drink, but she had to survive. She had to live long enough for the Foreveron withdrawals to stop. If she replaced one addiction with another, so be it. At least grog didn't make her mind-lost with lust.

I won't turn into my father.

I won't get addicted to the sweet-drink.

I just need it, for now.

It's the only thing that keeps away the Foreveron cravings.

She looked up and found that she'd returned to the gallows, her feet taking her there of their own accord. Guilt-laden nightmares, of men with D'trav's face and red-headed Freni-Kyn women being tortured to death, drove her there daily.

She stopped, dreading the worst. Just around this corner would be a grizzly sight.

Lator had even had a child mutilated there one day, its poor little body torn to shreds for all of Burmtin to see. She'd cried that day, tears running down her cheeks and adding to the stains of her chemise. She hadn't been the only mourner, and the guards hadn't seemed to care, or even notice.

Fearing the worst, she turned to leave, then turned back and rushed around the corner. A larger crowd than normal had gathered in the small viewing area, filling her with even more dread. She kept her eyes on the ground, avoiding the unavoidable.

She didn't want to look at the gallows, couldn't look.

Yet she had to know.

She lifted her eyes, and her heart dropped into her stomach.

D'trav...

No...

CHAPTER 14

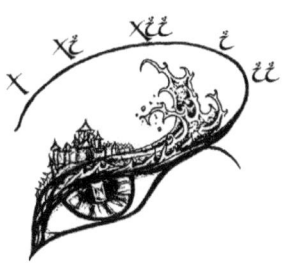

"Vengeance with a price.
Let that be our motto.
They bring us poison.
We leave them a bloody dagger."

Kasper von Putten
Founder of the Red Pelican Assassins' Guild
Journal of Death

Written the year his father, King Jasper, was poisoned.
It is unknown whether this was before, or after, he tore
down his Red Pelican Trading Post sign.

She stared with horror at what remained of a bear of a man. The prisoner's gaunt and mangled form hung from shackles, spread-eagled, gutted, entrails falling from a diagonal slit through his belly. His skin, stripped back in more places than she could count, was raw and red, meat for the butcher, and slivers of flesh dangled from a face beaten so badly that the features were swollen beyond recognition.

It has to be him, the same build, the same height. She stared at the pile of long hair laying near his feet, some still wrapped in a leather tie.

The same hair.

A Red Pelican dagger protruded from his broad chest, but not in a place that would give a quick death. No, he'd been left to a slow painful death.

Who else would they treat this badly but the man that thwarted their plans to catch Onglat?

"You old fool…"

The whisper drew Sarenka's attention to a sniffling woman whose swollen eyes were red with grief, and whose ornate corset and silk blouse were a wrinkled, sweat-stained mess.

"Everyone knows you don't cross the Red Pelican and live," came a man's voice from behind.

With a look of horror, the woman moved her hands in a ward against evil.

Sarenka swayed as the world turned black, but just as she began to fall the area swam back into focus.

Alerted by that small movement, a guard peered at her.

Her muscles tensed, readied for flight, yet she plastered a false smirk across her face and pretended to studiously examine the corpse. In reality, she stared beyond, counting the tiny cracks in the stone wall, and waited the long moments for the guard's gaze to settle elsewhere.

The other message was subtle but equally clear and didn't have to be put on display; the Burmtin authorities worked hand-in-hand with the Assassins' Guild. Any visitor to Burmtin got that message as soon as they saw the guards' black uniforms emblazoned with Red Pelicans. Nobody in Llayentia would dare use a Pelican for an emblem without direct approval of the Assassins' Guild. That would be a death wish.

A gruff mumble came from behind. "Heard they tortured him for three solid days before offing him."

The voice in her ear startled her, but she didn't dare turn to see the speaker.

The woman next to her lost control and sobbed, covering the action with a cough into an embroidered handkerchief.

As if the smell were too much, Sarenka covered her nose and mouth before whispering in a peasant's dialect, "He that one what helped murder the Baron?"

Mortified, not really wanting to hear the answer, she held stock still. The silence drew out. Her heart hammered with guilty fear, knowing they were deciding if they could safely speak in front of her.

Finally, the gruff voice spoke, "Could be. What do we know? They tell us nothing."

Sarenka's knees started to buckle, and she fought for control. Her elbow was grasped in a large rough hand, steadying her.

"It's the way of Burmtin," came the gruff voice again, much closer.

The grieving woman turned to leave, and the man withdrew his hand. The rest of the onlookers became silent, but for garbled whispers.

The guard peered at her again with a suspicious squint.

Unable to leave without drawing more attention, Sarenka was forced to stare at the tortured man. She stared past his body and counted cracks once more, but motion caught her eye. Scavenger birds swooped through the air, circling, their sleek black feathers glinting iridescent gold in the sunlight. They settled in a row on D'trav's outstretched arms, dancing back and forth from leg to leg with feathers ruffled, before calming down and staring out at the onlookers.

One burnt-orange raven shimmied sideways up D'trav's arm, head jerking at each new sound. Balanced on his shoulder, bloated body swaying with each breath, its head turned this way and that, staring at the observers as though curious at why they were there. Lightning fast, it lurched into motion, plucking the man's eye from his socket.

The crowd gasped, enthralled.

Sarenka recoiled in horror.

With another quick jerk, it cocked its head upwards and tossed the sphere into its gullet.

The sight—worsened by the stench of rotting entrails—sickened her, and she turned to the side, gulping back the gorge that rose in her throat.

Dusty heat mantled over the area, an even larger bird of prey, while rivulets of sweat ran an itching, crawling path under her clothing.

Nearby a wanted poster fluttered in a mocking salute. She stared at the sketch of her face and the numbers underneath.

Will I be next?

Several hours later, she looked around, not remembering when or how she'd left the mockery Lator had made of D'trav. The sight still plagued, a haunting reminder of what her fate would be if she were caught, and of what she had caused. She'd murdered a man, and D'trav had paid the price.

He was scum, he deserved to be hurt..., but did he deserve to die like that?

No, he wasn't total scum. He...

All the times that he'd brought her pieces of fish and tucked blankets around her, while she shook with Foreveron symptoms, paraded through her mind, one after another, until she felt she'd go mad. More than once unbidden sobs escaped, attracting curious stares from strangers.

At last she could stand no more. He was gone. She couldn't change what she had done. She had to stop or she'd attract attention and get herself caught. Pushing the memory away with determination, she turned her attention to finding a safe harbor for the night and paused at the edge of an alleyway. An overwhelming dog scent pervaded the tight space between two-story buildings, the musky odor so strong that it masked even the smell of fish, and that was a relief in Burmtin, especially near the docks where the scent of fish was everywhere. She slipped into the welcoming coolness. Where there were dog keepers, there'd be food and an ample supply of water.

Cat-like eyes adjusting to the dim light, she crept through the cobblestone-paved area and picked her way past wooden crates, barrels, scraps of rotting fabric, and other foul smelling debris. Nestled at the far end, she found what she was searching for: a rough animal pen, protected with a simple lock, one she could have picked at six winters old. She pulled off her gloves and fingered the lock that was the only thing standing between her and the animals' food.

A shadow fell across the cage.

She spun around, ready to run. Her heart pounded, drowning out the sounds of the alley, while her gaze traversed the space, but she found nothing. She looked up, searching for seagulls or pelicans or anything that might have caused the shadow.

A chorused rumbling of snarls and provoked her into making the calming shush-noises that had always worked in the past. The growls swelling in the animals' throats quieted into muffled whimpers, and their tails gave hopeful wags. Kneeling to pet them through the massive bones that made up the bars of their pen, she frowned at the matted fur and ran her hands over their sides, expecting gaunt animals. Instead she found them well-muscled and healthy, though not well loved. A long tongue swiped over her face and laughter came bubbling up, but she put her hand over her mouth, penning it in.

"It's been a long time since someone accepted me like that," she whispered to the Shepherd, grabbing its white head and rubbing behind its ears with both hands. Her thoughts turned to D'trav's death, souring the moment. "And I don't really deserve it."

As she withdrew her hands, the roughened bars scraped her wrist, drawing blood. She held the wound to her mouth and grimaced. Long before the dogs managed to chew through, the bone cage would become jagged, snaring clothing and skin. It wouldn't stop her from entering, but she didn't envy the person who had to clean these pens. The owners must not be able to afford the luxury of metal bars or stone blocks.

She pulled the lock-picks from within her ragged cloak and examined them. The tools were crude but had already provided the clothing she wore and one invaluable utensil: a large shell for drawing drink at the well. As always, they reminded her of the urchin who had sold them to her and how much he had wanted the silly slippers.

She smiled with both humor and gratitude.

I just hope he spent the loops to better his life.

She squinted and unbent one of the wires.

Instead of squandering it all on a game of chance.

Sarenka glanced down the alleyway, searching for observers before turning her attention to the common stone lock. With a flick of her wrist, once, twice, thrice, the lock snapped open.

"How mother would've beat me for that trick, if she'd ever cared enough to know." She told the dogs, knowing she sounded mind-lost.

The dogs whined and tilted their heads, trying to figure out what she was telling them.

"Not father, though. No, he treated me like precious cargo, teaching me the Freni-Kyn ways." She continued talking aloud, a recent habit that helped push back the loneliness.

Slipping into the pen, Sarenka indulged in the simple pleasure of petting the love-starved animals before working her way to their feed area.

"But mother, she was a wild woman, never knew what would set her off. She beat me daily, most times."

She reached for the bowl.

From the darkened corner of the pen came a low growl.

Sarenka froze with her hand out-stretched.

A Pit Bull crouched, ready to spring, lips curled back over pointed teeth.

With the hand that was out of it's view, Sarenka reached under her skirt and pulled free the Red Pelican Dagger.

Eyes going black and growl intensifying, its muscles bunched, readying for attack.

Sarenka stared at it, transfixed. She wanted to look behind, edge toward the door, but didn't dare.

To her left came the growl of another dog, lower, dangerous.

Other growls sprang up, joining the first.

She was surrounded and didn't dare turn even her eyes towards the second attacker. Knowing she must run, she gripped the knife in a palm gone slick with sweat.

As if Sarenka was the meat it hungered for, the pit bull's mouth dripped with slaver.

Sarenka shifted one foot backwards.

It sprang, heavy mouth aiming for her throat.

CHAPTER 15

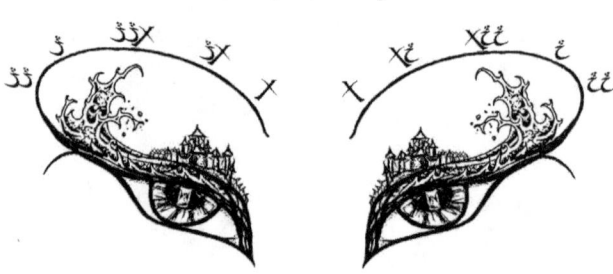

Sarenka threw an arm up between them and stepped backwards. Her foot landed in a bowl, and meaty bones scattered across the floor. She skidded, foot flying out from beneath her, and fell onto her back.

The pit bull landed on her chest, mouth wide, ready to snap closed on her throat.

She threw up her forearm and pressed it against the animal's throat.

Its jaw snapped closed, narrowly missing her face. Frothing with rage, it snapped again and scrabbled to get closer.

She was dead, she knew it.

A tan body knocked the beast aside.

Sarenka scrabbled backwards, crablike, as the two dogs became a rolling ball of tan and grey snarls.

The Pit Bull lashed out, mouth closing on the Shepherd's flank.

The Shepherd thrust sideways, throwing off the pit bull with a shrug. Grabbing the smaller dog by the throat, he threw it across the pen.

Determined to reach the cage door, yet not daring to turn her back, Sarenka kept moving.

The Shepherd landed atop the grey dog, mouth semi-closed over its face.

The pit bull stopped moving and tucked its tail.

The Shepherd let go, and the pit bull slunk away, returning to its corner. Sarenka felt a cold wet touch on her cheek and jumped before realizing that it was just another dog smelling her. It nudged her, as if to say get up, and went to stand next to the pack leader.

Sarenka stood up slowly and grimaced with distaste when she realized that she'd scooted through excrement. She stared at the two dogs, nearly identical, and wondered if they were pack mates or littermates.

Doesn't matter.

I'm leaving.

This was a colossal bad idea.

She backed towards the door and into the body of a third dog. She gulped and glanced behind. It stood between her and the door.

The dog that had touched its nose to her cheek circled around behind Sarenka and used its body to push her towards the leader.

Holding the dagger out defensively, Sarenka went. She dared not defy it with the animals this stirred up. Drawing close, she hesitated.

The body pushed against her back, corralling her ever forward.

As she stepped near the food dishes, the pressure against her backside stopped. Sarenka looked down at the only food bowl that remained upright. Her mouth watered.

The leader stepped forward, and she tensed. Extending his head, he pushed the food bowl forward until it touched her toes.

Sarenka let out a relieved breath and knelt. The pit bull cowering in the corner sifted position, and she decided to keep her blade free. The leader might have accepted her, but that animal was a menace. She rubbed the leader behind the ears before picking through scraps and settling on a piece that smelled fresh. After taking a bite, she started talking to the dogs, picking up where she'd left off before the attack, as much to calm her nerves as to calm them.

"What was I saying? Oh yes… then was that terrible row. The one that changed everything. Their angry voices echoing down the hallways, the servants hiding… I couldn't bear it. I left, running as fast as I could through pouring down rain, until I reached the pens."

She shrugged.

"I thought I was part of the pack back then, part dog, part girl. And that's where I sat, with my hands over my ears. I must have fallen asleep because, next I knew, it was day time."

Hands shaking with hunger, she gnawed the half cooked flesh from a bone.

"After that, it was all different. Overnight I became a commodity, fit for selling to the highest bidder, with not even mother daring to mar my skin. And that's when I learned the biggest lesson of all. People are no damn good. They'll stab you in the back, sure as spitting at you. I'm better off here, with you, than with a roomful of supposed friends. And fuck family. They are the worst."

She chewed some more and smiled at the nearest dog.

"I think he knew about us. The baron. It's supposed to be a secret, how a Freni-Kyn needs animal flesh. But I think he knew, and that's why he kept meat from me. To keep me weak."

She moved on towards the water trough and leaned over to smell it before grabbing an empty dog dish and frowning.

"Here I sit, eating like an animal and drinking dog water. With D'trav's coin I could be at the best of inns, eating fresh caught lobster and drinking fine Frevellian wine."

The water in the trough was fresh, though the bowl felt slimy and smelled of dog. She filled it anyway. There were days when the only drink she got was a glass of cheap wine at the most mean of pubs. Gulping the liquid down, she waved the empty bowl at the dogs.

"But no. No, I'm saving every damn loop, trying to get out of this damn city. Trying to find someone desperate enough to bribe. And that's damn near impossible."

She examined the trough again and decided that the waterlines meant it was never allowed to run dry.

Finally, enough water to…

Thought I'd never get clean.

She peered at the inner door of the pen, a door that led into the building behind it, and considered her options.

Not yet, later, after dark.

With reluctance, she left the pen and its promise of a bath and looked towards the coast with longing.

Thoughts of the coast and its cleansing waters were an impossible fantasy. The heavy patrols, which trooped randomly through, running people back from the water, posed a threat she dare not face. And even if she cracked the guard's schedules and managed to sneak past, the Watrelk Pirates that swaggered along the coastline were sure to accost or capture her.

No... not even a quick dip.

Too dangerous... illusions too weak... they'll slip for sure.

I'll be caught.

No...

Can't happen.

Have to take care of things first. Can't live waiting for a knife in the back, though I deserve death... for what I did to D'trav. Hopeless despair filled her, but she pushed it aside and turned to what it took to survive.

Sarenka waited in the shadows that evening while the sun set. The owners came and went, leaving fresh scraps and water, but taking no time to pet the animals. When she slipped back into the pen, the animals greeted her with wagging tails and happy licks instead of threatening growls. The leader sat between her and the dog which had attacked, as if to say she was safe. She peered long and hard at the pit bull, waiting to see if it would attack. It lowered its head, but she felt sure the submission would evaporate without the leader standing guard. Satisfied that her throat would not be ripped out when her attention was elsewhere, she fell upon their meat, sating her appetite before filling a bowl with water and slaking her thirst.

With satisfaction, Sarenka turned to fulfilling a much different kind of craving. She stripped away the filthy clothing and stretched, rejoicing in the freedom, naked in the moonlight. The balmy air caressed her skin, a welcome relief after days of wearing filth. Dipping the shirt into the bowl, she sloshed water over her lithe form, and reveled in relief as it streamed down in dirty brown rivulets.

She scrubbed, scouring away all remnants of the murder. Remnants that had clung to her sweating body, wailing out the death like bits of shrieking confetti. Each fleck, each silent proclamation of her guilt, turning to nothing but an obscene brown dust that could not be shed but worked its foul way into everything, including her food.

At last, satisfied, she turned to the clothing, sloshing them about in the wooden bowl until they too shed the stench of decay. Stray rays of the double moons slanted into the recesses of the bone cage, creating such a macabre atmosphere that Sarenka shivered, chilled by both the thought and the cooling air on her damp skin.

With an odd mix of reluctance and relief, she lay down on the rough cobblestones and let the Shepherds crowd in close. For the first time that week, she regretted the loss of each garish piece of the Baron's ostentatious outfit. Her wet clothing hung from the sides of the pen, blocking some of the breeze, each drip landing with a lulling plink. The night song of Burmtin wafted through, voices crying out with lust and rage, she didn't care as long as they didn't draw near. Beneath it all, barely to be heard, even by her sensitive Freni-Kyn ears, the waves crashed against the shore, chanting out a promise of safety and freedom. She rubbed her arms and shivered again.

"I'd be snug and warm if I could've kept those clothes," she told the lead dog. "Or had enough meat. The meat brings warmth too, you know."

It tilted its head to the side and its tongue rolled out.

"Couldn't risk it though, getting captured with that stuff. Way above the likes of me now."

The dog tipped its head back and forth, as if trying to figure out what she was saying.

"Nope, got rid of it all. Stuffed them behind barrels and crates."

The dog whined, lowered its head, and pawed at the ground in front of her.

She smiled and wished she had a treat to give it. "Some workers will think they hit the jackpot when they find them."

He leaned forward and licked her face.

"I'm going to call you Beast. Why? Cause you're just that huge." He started to lick her, and she grabbed his head, pulling it away to stare into its eyes. "That's why."

"You like it?" She pulled his head playfully side-to-side. "You like it, Beast? Huh? You like it?"

He bumped and licked at her face, enjoying the attention.

She stopped, suddenly tired, and patted the ground next to her.

With a grunt of muffled happiness, Beast flopped.

Another shiver broke free, and she pulled him close enough to absorb his body heat. "Sure am glad I have you to keep me warm, Beast."

Despite the odor, maybe because of the odor, the pen felt almost like home. Not the home of stifling luxuries, where belongings were more important than people. No, not that home. Rather the home of stolen moments in the guard-dog's pen, hidden from searchers, waiting out the days and sometimes nights.

Burying her face in his shaggy fur, she sighed, content for the first time in over a year. Her eyes drifted closed.

Across the alley a shadow separated from the wall, moving closer.

The dogs bristled and showed their teeth and moved to surround Sarenka.

CHAPTER 16

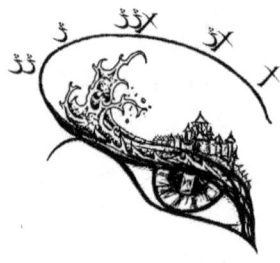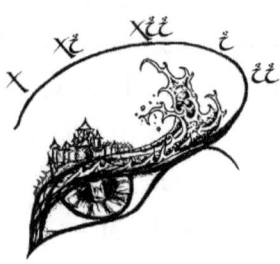

~Parian! You must stop!~

He shook his head.

~Stop shaking your head.~

~Get out of my head, and you won't feel me shake my head.~

~You have to stop.~

~Not going to.~

~We can't lose you.~ Airintia straightened the rose on her table, pricking her finger in the process.

~I'm too close. I can feel it.~

She sucked the bleeding tip and checked to be sure there were no other seers listening. *~They'll do whatever it takes.~*

Parian stopped what he was doing and rubbed his reddening fingertip. *~As in?~*

~You know.~

~They wouldn't!~

~They will.~

Silence hung between them. Uncomfortable.

~Parian?~

~I'm still here.~

~You'll stop?~

He stared out the window, searching for observers, and wanted to lie; to tell her he'd stop with the nonsense of skipping along the time stream. But he couldn't lie, not to her.

~I'll do what I need to.~

~Parian, I—"

He cut the connection. There was no point in dragging her into the same kind of trouble he was in.

Sparks flickered from a darkened doorway, and a pipe bowl glowed cherry red before darkening. Parian sent forth a tentative thread towards the shadows and met only blankness. He frowned. The man was either one of those with a natural defense, or he was being shielded by a seer. He turned back to the room and surveyed the contents. If he was forced to run, everything would be left behind.

So be it.

His broken dreams that night were riddled with visions of snakes and chains.

"Parian!"

He sat straight up, looking through blurred eyes at his empty room. He flopped back onto his bed, and tiny feathers flew free of the pillow and drifted away.

Nothing and nobody.

~Parian!~

~Noooooo…~ Parian covered his head with his pillow.

~Hate to do this, buddy, but they've called a meeting and you're late.~ He felt Lanion stretch, leaning back in his chair.

Parian yawned. *~I'm sleeping.~*

Lanion's answering yawn echoed back through the connection. *~No. You're not.~*

~I already know what they're going to say.~ Parian yawned again, exhausted beyond measure.

~Open your window, wake yourself up—~ Lanion yawned again— *~and for Kyron's sake, stop yawning.~*

Parian stumbled over to the window and pulled it open. A cool breeze brushed his skin, and the connection between himself and Lanion dropped. After visiting the chamber pot, he opened the wine bottle on his desk and took a swig, swishing it around his mouth.

Finally he sent, ~*Okay. I'm here.*~

He felt his thought picked up as the others opened their minds to him. He blinked. Instead of the expected six other minds there were far more. They'd brought in retired seers and the trainees as well. Too many thoughts. He put up buffering shields.

~*Parian, we're sorry to wake you. This was the only time everyone could attend.*~

~*Everyone could attend?*~ he asked.

~*Some of us have jobs and family you know.*~

~*So this was planned without me?*~

For a micro moment all thoughts went silent.

~*You just keep endangering yourself.*~ Lanion spoke up.

Parian paced across to the window. He closed it with a thump and heard the occupants in the room next door stir.

~*Lanion,*~ Parian sent, ~*you, of all people, have no right to...*~

~*Well, for once this isn't about me,*~ Lanion drawled out the thought.

Parian couldn't help but wonder if he had a woman in bed with him again, if he was stroking her breast while he talked. The thought both aroused and disgusted him. He shut off the arousal, knowing that to give in might lead to a sexual liaison. And that, in turn, might lead to being mind-lost within another's mind. He wasn't Lanion. He wouldn't risk his life, or his mission, that way.

~*Boys,*~ the Eldest interrupted, ~*we all have our problems. Let's not let this slide down into stave pointing.*~

Parian sighed. She was right about that. There was no point in fighting with someone he'd never meet face to face. Lanion could glut himself with women all he wanted, for now. There was nothing he could do about it, but once he found his replacement, then he'd see to it that the foolishness with Lanion was dealt with once and for all.

Airintia sent a soothing balm of peace.

He accepted the gesture. It helped, but it wouldn't stop his determination.

~Parian, we're just concerned.~

~Wasting your thoughts,~ he sent.

~Parian, see reason.~

~I'm not stopping.~

~Don't force us to this!~

~Please Parian, if not for you, for us.~ Airintia's thoughts brushed across him, feather-soft with concern.

Of all the seers, she could ask him to stop and have it hold meaning. The time he'd spent teaching her to use illusions had bonded them, perhaps forever, as friends. There could never be more than that. Not for a seer.

~I. Can. Not.~ Parian pushed each word through with a thump. ~This will be followed through to the end! Even if it means my end.~

He felt them cringe and immediately regretted the extra force he'd put behind the sending. Some of the younger ones would have bruising headaches for sure. But he had to make his point, and he was not the one that had opened this up before all the living seers. They'd need to deal with their pupils on their own. If nothing else, it was a good excuse to teach some advanced shielding techniques.

~We can not convince you otherwise, Parian, seer for the Freni-Kyn?~ the Eldest asked.

~Respectfully, Eldest, you can not. I, Parian, seer of the Freni-Kyn, have spoken.~ Parian gave the answer as formally as the question had been given and withdrew. He wouldn't discuss this further. They were wasting his energy. Energy he'd need tomorrow.

Within the turn of the hourglass, he had gathered his belongings and fitted Rosalie with her saddle.

Head low and tail dragging the ground, she padded from the stall swaybacked, as if the saddle were too heavy.

"Come on girl." Parian said as he mounted.

She snorted and took a slow step forward, grumpy at the abrupt awakening.

"I'll buy you a steak."

She took another step and lifted her head. ~*Promise?*~

"A nice big plump steak, dripping with blood."

Lifting her head higher still, she scented the night air and crouched backwards in a manner that could mean only one thing. Instead of a nice amble, she was preparing to spring.

He grabbed the saddle horn, "No Rosali—"

She bounded ahead, and the force of the leap threw him back and then forward as she took the first corner, leaping into a different direction midair.

"Oooh—my—go—"

She leapt around the next corner and down the street at breakneck speed, muscles bunching with each bounding jump as she zig-zagging through the city. Parian grasped the skin of her neck in a strangling grip, knowing that to let go would mean to hit a wall with enough speed to break his neck. Finally, she vaulted through the east gate while the guards shook their fists at them and yelled words he couldn't really hear.

~*Rosalie stop, I'm going to...*~

She stopped.

His body flew forward, and he grabbed her ears and hung on as the momentum carried him onto her head. For a moment he lay, draped over her face, afraid to move.

She reared up, bucking him off her head and onto her shoulders, and still he clung for dear life, pulling her ears downwards. She let out a snort and gave her great head such a powerful shake that her ears flapped, knocking his hands free.

He slid down onto her back, then leaned to one side and threw up.

She stepped daintily sideways. *~Well, that was dignified.~*

~Dignified? You have the nerve to talk to me about dignified?~

~What?~

~You talk to me about dignified after we almost hit the side of a building, jumped over a housewolf, rebounded off the walls of an alley, not once but twice, and scared a beggar into pissing himself.~ Parian pulled a kerchief from his pocket and wiped his face.

~I took the trajectory with the greatest degree of likely success.~

~And nearly killed me.~

~Hardly.~ She blew air out in a snort. *~Can we go now or do you want to soil yourself too?~*

Parian gripped the saddle in a death hold. *~Slowly.~*

She started off at a gentle trot, head raised, sniffing the air. *~Have you never ridden a cat before?~*

Parian stared straight ahead.

She gave a small leap over a stick.

Parian squeaked.

She let out several snorts and went back to the gentle trot. *~You're a young one.~*

~In this. Yes.~ Parian pressed his lips together, angry with the amusement that was rolling off her.

~Well then, wee one, where are we off to?~

Parian took a deep breath, started to say something, then changed his mind. Defending himself would only give her more pleasure. *~I don't know. Claw Lake maybe.~*

She sat down so abruptly that he overcompensated and smashed his face against her shoulder, before starting to slide towards the ground.

"What the—" He scrabbled to stay in the saddle, wrapping his arms around her neck, and tightening his legs around her back. "Why are you sitting?"

~I'm not going there.~

"And why not?" He stood in the stirrups to keep from falling off.

~Claw Lake.~

"Yes?"

~Claaaaw Lake.~

He laughed. "It's just a name."

~A name with 'claw' in it. Does that not suggest there might be danger there?~

A whistle came from the side of the road, and a man walked out of the bushes next to them. His fingers were busy knotting the waist tie of his breaches. He gave Parian a nod as he passed.

It was all Parian could do not to groan again.

Rosalie, eyes shining pale blue in the moonlight, watched as he passed.

~Great, now I've got peasants thinking I'm mind-lost.~

~I'd be more worried about the wards against evil he's making. You dropped your illusions.~

Parian glanced back at the man and caught glimpses of the gestures. He grabbed the hood of his cloak and pulled it forward over his face. "Let's go."

She started off at a trot. ~That's a really nice battle wound. Why do you hide it?~

Still standing in the stirrups, Parian swayed crazily from side-to-side before collapsing onto the saddle with a bounce that made him wince. He finally gasped out, "It frightens people."

~I'd wear it with pride.~

"I'm not a cat."

~Let them shake in their fur. They'd know that I was fierce. I would— ~

He cut her off. "It's too easily remembered. I have to blend in."

They continued a while in silence.

~I'm not going to Claw Lake.~

"Oh yes you are."

She let out a snarl that echoed off the nearby hills.

CHAPTER 17

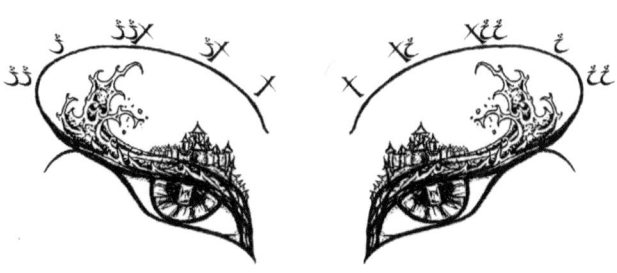

"If it please the council, they are animals, bent on destroying us all. We have pled with them, offered bonding even, and still the Sharpra refuse to parlay. They are not to be reasoned with and should be avoided at all cost.

Yes, I know it's impossible. They can be anyone, anywhere, and their shape-shifting abilities make our illusions look like child's play. Their weakness lies in the bonding. We must find some way to turn it to our advantage. I'm told of a drug, Foreveron, which might be slipped into their food. Once the lust has done its work, they'll be bonded. An effective weapon, don't you agree?"

Catotje Van Schreeven
Racial Mitigation Liaison
Freni-Kyn War Tomes
After Betrayal

Clang, clang-thump, clang, clang-thump.

Sarenka awoke with a start, disoriented. One moment she'd been trying to outrun a wagon as it barreled towards her, and the next—

She surged up, alarmed by the first soft rays of daylight slanting through the bars. Clang thump, came the sound again, and she was glad. If not for the fishermen loading their boats, the dogs' owners might have discovered her.

Beast pawed at the door leading into the owner's house, adding yet more claw marks to its rough wood, and she wondered how long before they came to feed their animals.

Grabbing the now dry clothing, she scurried from the pen and locked it. Half way down the alley, partially hidden from view behind a rotted crate, she struggled into her stiff outfit. The scent of dog had replaced that of rotted blood, but she didn't care, not if the merchants stopped treating her like a disease carrier.

She stopped to check her face in a broken pane of glass and pushed the memories aside. Satisfied that the illusions had held despite the lack of focus, and that she still looked H'euman, she gritted her teeth with determination.

Time to scavenge.

R'kiax, in Sharpra form once more, walked past Burk's small desk and rapped on Captain Lator's door.

Burk glared at him. "He's busy."

"He'll see me."

"Don't think so."

R'kiax knocked again and spoke through the wood. "R'kiax here, Captain."

Burk smirked at the steady thumping sound coming from the other side. "Told you. He's busy."

R'kiax smiled at Burk, revealing teeth long and pointed.

Burk shuddered.

Nothing like elongating my teeth to frighten the H'eumans. Unhinges the cowards every time.

The door opened, and a flush-faced man left the room, buttoning his shirt as he passed them.

R'kiax raised an eyebrow at Burk as if to say 'told you so' and walked into the office. He pushed the door closed with his foot and looked at the man across the desk. The scent of sex was heavy in the room, though he doubted any but a Sharpra would smell it.

Captain Lator, perfectly composed, gestured towards a chair.

R'kiax sat, suddenly uncomfortable. There was something unnerving about a man that could take pleasure and then be so calm, so damn neutral, that you'd think he had just finished threading a needle or some other boring task.

Lator waited.

R'kiax cleared his throat. "You asked for a report."

"It's been over a week."

"There's nothing. She's gone."

"Nothing?"

He shrugged. "I thought last night that I'd found her. Caught a scent near some dog pens, but it was a false alarm."

"False alarm?"

R'kiax wanted to growl, to tear the man's throat out. *How dare he mock me like that, repeating my words with that false neutrality, forcing me into admitting deficiency?* "I lost the trail."

Lator walked around the desk. "You lost her."

Before R'kiax could answer Lator backhanded him. "You lost her."

R'kiax dug his hands into the arms of the chair, piercing the undersides with his nails. He gritted his teeth snf brought himself back under control. "Yes sir."

"How dare you interrupt me with your incompetence? Leave." Lator said it all, did it all, without a trace of emotion.

As R'kiax stepped through the doorway, he caught the smirk on Burk's face.

"Find her," came from behind.

The door swung shut and R'kiax struck, slamming Burk square in the middle of the face. He heard the sound of a body hitting the ground as he stalked away. Upon reaching the end of the hall, he paused long enough to turn his hair satin blond, his face Half-Frevell.

The days slipped past, one much like another, and Sarenka lost track of time. Had it been a week, two, did it even matter anymore? Time seemed of little worth now that her life was filled with blinding headaches, growing worse each day. She suffered through the pain, begging for leavings from refuse heaps and laboring at the types of jobs nobody wanted. All for minute scraps of food that didn't come from a dog's picked-over bowl and castoffs that could be sold for a few paltry d'yroap. No, the days no longer mattered. The nights, those were what mattered, when she could buy enough watered down wine to sleep for a few hours without the ache, without the blinding headaches, without her guts feeling like they were being twisted around a chain.

And through it all the Istoarm Sea, with its luring promise of freedom, called to her. Waves whispered hypnotically as they crashed against the shore, offering to cradle her in their vast womb and deliver her to a life free under the stars. A life without danger lurking on every doorstep. A life where she no longer had to hide who, and what, she was.

Sleep brought no relief from the sea's promising caresses, for she wakened always with the seduction of salt scented mists, clean and wholesome, offering to hide her in their cool white folds. The possibilities picked at her resolve, eating at it like the waves did a sandcastle left too close to the shore. In the end it was too much; her resistance crumbled as surely as that sandcastle would have under the ever advancing tide.

She knew better, it was too dangerous, and yet she went. The sea called and she must answer.

Sarenka crept through drifting whiteness, sliding one cautious step after another over the slickened ground. She tugged her hood forward until her face lay draped in shadow. The fog spilled over the area in a thickening blanket, turning it into an ever-shifting reality, one that left her nerves on such a sharp edge that the slightest sound made her heart race. For an eternity, using only enough illusion to hide the lights of her hair, she moved forward. Solid ground gave way to powdery sand, and relief washed over her.

Soon, the cleansing water. Soon, the calming waves.

The taste of salt on her lips, the feel of sand brushing her ankles, and the sound of the waves crashing against the shore drew her onwards, towards freedom. Despite having her keen eyesight disabled by the fog, she moved with more confidence, using her ears as a guide. Muffled voices drifted past, speech too fragmented to make sense, ebbing and flowing like the water she so desperately sought.

Two dark shadows loomed into view.

Sarenka hesitated.

They rushed towards her.

She gasped, spun around, and ran.

A soft thumping came from behind.

She threw herself forward, running faster.

The thumping grew closer.

Her feet slid sideways on the shifting sand, unable to gain purchase. At a tug on her cloak, she jumped to the side. The world became a tumbling blur as her feet flew out from under her, and the bone clasp of her cloak sawed into her neck, choking off her air. She landed face up in the sand, and she twisted, trying to roll over.

The assailant held onto the edge of her cloak and gave an abrupt jerk, yanking her across the ground towards him.

Aiming for his kneecap, she lashed out with her foot but merely grazed his shin.

He dropped the cloak hem and threw himself on top of her.

"Stop! Let go!" Sarenka pushed against the man with desperation born of fear, and the struggles pulled the hood forward over her face, blinding her more than the fog.

"Hold her mouth, you idiot," a man hissed, grappling with her arms.

With his words came a breath of fetid air, and Sarenka imagined rotting teeth, a gangrenous body, and pox infested loins. He smelled of death. The kind of death that took its time, drawing out the pain over long months, even years, rotting away from the inside out.

Hands about her waist, he yanked her further beneath him.

The sliding movement rucked up the back of the hood, pushing it even further forward over her face. She flailed her arms, thumping against flesh, landing blind blows.

A hand grasped her chin before moving upwards, clamping her mouth and nose shut.

The second man leaned in close, grasping at the edge of her hood.

Sarenka twisted and writhed, desperate to keep her identity secret.

He stopped tugging at the hood and shifted direction, lowering his hand to paw at her breast, pinching her through corset and chemise.

The first man captured her gloved wrists in one huge paw and yanked Sarenka's skirt upwards, tearing the threadbare fabric in his urgency.

With savage kicks, she threw her lower body about but landed only glancing blows.

The attacker's hand touched her bare thigh.

She bucked and gyrated, biting the hand covering her mouth.

It was jerked away. "Ow, son of a bitch!"

"Knock her out!" said the other.

A band of iron clamped around her throat, squeezing until her ears rang and her vision narrowed, going dark.

Parian arrived at Claw Lake without incident, though Rosalie deliberately took them in the wrong direction more than twice. Parian was forced to lure her with promises of fresh meat and warm milk. Still, Rosalie's hackles went up as they rode into a tiny village that nestled between Claw Lake and her big sister, Lazanet Lake.

He looked down at her and smiled, she wasn't the well-groomed animal of a week ago, but she was still a beauty to behold. The travel had been rough on both of them, leaving her sleek black fur thick with dust and his fine clothing besmeared with grass stains and sweat. Arriving at the inn, he took time to massage her broad shoulders, trying to calm her before tying her to the hitching post.

"You behave yourself."

~Of course. What do you think I am, a common beast?~

Graphic scenes of blood spurting everywhere as Rosalie tore her prey apart with a single bite, and the almost feral look she had in her eyes while hunting, paraded through his mind. But he didn't say anything. He needed her to be there when he got back.

He returned a half an hourglass turn later with two packages wrapped in paper.

Eye's watering, she stopped bathing. ~What is that?~

He held one of the packages out to her. "I bought you a nice big trout."

She sneezed, spraying him with moisture.

"Must be something in the air." He grimaced and wiped his face with his elbow. "Come on, let's get you out of here."

~Please. And fast.~ She rubbed at her nose with a paw.

Parian reached to untie the rein and stopped with his hand outstretched. The post was whittled down, its top ragged. He examined the other ones. They were fine. Only this one was so dangerously splintered. He needed to be more careful, she might have been injured.

~Thought we were staying here,~ she sent as they walked away.

"They don't stable cats."

He was positive he felt her smile.

She sneezed again.

Upon reaching an area that was clear of debris, but for the remains of an old campfire, they stopped. Parian walked the clearing, searching for signs of other travelers.

~*You can stop looking. There's nobody here. I would smell them if there— if there—* ~ She sneezed and threw herself down, eyes streaming. ~*was. I told you we shouldn't come here.*~

"There's another place close by. They'll have a dry stable for you, and a safe place for me to… travel from."

~*I told you this was a bad place.*~ She rubbed a paw across her nose.

"I heard you already." He opened the butcher paper and tossed the fish down next to her head. "That should make you feel better."

~*It smells so… so lovely and… so delicious.*~ She pawed at the meat, flipping it over in the dirt. Her eyes streamed, and she backed away from it with an even louder sneeze. ~*No. It's…*~

Parian stared at her. "You can't be."

She circled the fish, pacing, head down, lip lifted threateningly. Suddenly she slapped it and jumped back before slapping again.

He laughed.

She turned her head towards him, and her ears flattened, and her lips peeled back over her teeth, exposing wicked fangs. ~*You tried to poison me.*~

Parian raised his hands, palm out. "Allergies. It's just allergies."

~*So the poison is named allergies.*~ She let out a low snarling growl.

Parian paled and took a step back.

She crouched, prepared to pounce.

His heart leapt in his chest as he backed away. "Rosalie. No. Not poison."

She dug her claws into the ground, breaking up the hardened soil, and bounded forward.

He threw an arm up to protect himself.

She smashed into his chest, bearing him backwards.

Landing flat on his back with all breath knocked from his lungs, he stared up into her huge face and fought for air.

She opened her mouth, exposing long wicked teeth, and snarled.

He tried to speak but she grabbed his neck.

D'trav dropped his boots and a pile of tallow candles onto the bed before sitting down, weak in the knees. He stared across the room at the door, then back down at his pile. It wasn't real food but it'd keep him alive.

He wouldn't starve.

Not yet anyway.

A week, two weeks, how long's it been since she locked me in?

He swatted at the fly that tried to land on his cheek. The chamber pot had overflown the fourth day, forcing him to use vases and the water pitcher. The flies had started the second day, swelling into great droves, buzzing about, feasting on the piles he left them.

He held a candle up to the lantern and scraped away several embedded bugs with a dirty fingernail and hoped it hadn't been made with something poisonous. Grimacing, he bit down on the candle and rocked it back and forth in his mouth, gradually drawing the wick out from between his teeth. Holding the remains of the candle, with its wax-encrusted wick dangling loosely, he chewed.

The rancid oil coated his mouth as he ground the candle into a pulp, determined to get everything he could from it, and he considered the room. It reeked of excrement and body odor. The sweet-drink was nearly gone, the linens soiled, and the pile of nuts and chocolate had been eaten the first week. Banging at the door brought no response, though he occasionally heard muffled voices. He supposed she'd cleared the hall of residents, leaving just him. It'd be easy enough to block off one hallway within the maze of corridors that made up the brothel.

No, he wouldn't starve. Water was the real issue. Yesterday the water apparatus for the tub had stopped working. That was when he began to despair. Until then, he'd been positive she'd come to him and forgive him. Now, he couldn't help but wonder if he was doomed.

Maybe she's done turned me in to the Red Pelican. Is this the first level of torture?

He looked around the room with resolve. There was no help for it. He had to get out of here or start drinking his own piss. And there was no helping what he was going to do next, either. He picked up his sword, bared the blade, and kissed it.

"Sorry for this darlin. I'll make it up to you. I promise."

He held still, listening to the silence. This was the best time to do what he was about to do. Now, before the cock crowed. He tiptoed to the window and used his blade to saw at the bottom shutter. His forehead beaded with sweat and he licked dry lips before thinking to wipe his face and lick the moisture from his hand.

"Damnation. Waste of time. I'll die of thirst 'fore I get this open."

Sheathing his sword, he peered at an excrement-filled vase.

It'll do.

Flies burst upwards as he grasped the vase, darting towards his eyes, ears, and nose. Careful not to slosh the container, he waved them away and made his way to the closet. Within lay dozens of shoes: black leather that laced to the thigh, pink satin with tiny bows, red velvet with tassels at the ankles, purple snakeskin with pointed toes, yellow leather embossed with fern fronds, more varieties than he had known existed.

Downright shame to do this, but in dire times a man's gotta make sacrifices.

He imagined the expression on Camille's face when she found them. And for the first time in more than a week, he smiled.

Here you go, darlin. Enjoy.

Tipping the vase above the red shoes, he watched as the sludge ran out, fouling the air.

Kyron's balls! Damn near 'nuff to make a man hurl.

He pinched his nose closed but kept pouring, one way or another, the task had to be done. When it began to overflow he moved on to the next shoe, taking a peculiar delight in ruining something he knew

Camille spent hours choosing in person. After every drop that could be shaken free was nestled in a shoe, or nearby, as luck would have it, he wrapped the container in a confection of pink lace.

Placing it on the ground, he gently rapped it with the hilt of his sword. Nothing happened. He rapped harder and heard it crack. A third rap collapsed the container. Covering his nose again, he opened the dress and examined the shards before choosing the one with the roughest serrated edges. He went back to the window with a new weapon, one that reeked of shit and had to be wrapped in fabric to keep from slicing his hand. Several vases later, he had three of the slats cut half way through and most of the shoes filled.

He turned back to the room and considered. The chest couldn't come with him. Pushing it into a corner, he piled it high with folded linens and made it appear to belonged in the room. Then he loaded down his pockets with candles and pulled on the boots.

He looked at the door, worried.

Now fer the tricky part.

Getting' the damn slats off without makin' too much fuckin' noise?

He turned back to the window.

Least ways, if'n I get myself caught, I'll know whose prisoner I am, Camille's or the Red Pelicans'.

Wedging his sword between two of the damaged slats, he threw his body against the flat of the blade. With a splintered crack, the first slat shattered. He kept working, shifting his sword from place to place, and the next two followed quickly.

After dragging the mattress under the window, D'trav pulled himself up by the next slat and braced his legs on either side of the window. He yanked and fell backwards, landing on the mattress with the slat still in hand.

Panting, listening, he lay still.

From the hallway came the thump of walking feet.

Chapter 18

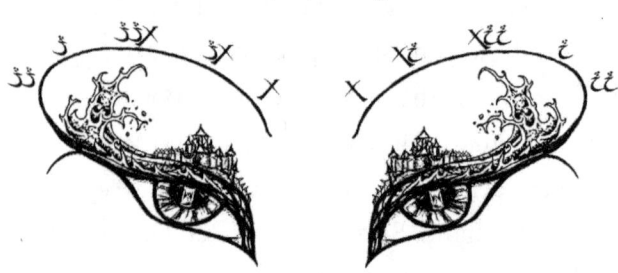

A soft voice pierced the fog, interrupting Sarenka's silent struggle for life.

"I suggest you unhand her."

The men froze for a scant heartbeat before letting go and standing, though they did not move away.

Sarenka was so startled at the change of fate that she didn't rise, but lay, staring up through a tiny fold of her threadbare cloak at the person who had spoken.

The woman's hair fell softly about her shoulders in long dark curls, but her face drew, and held, Sarenka's attention. Chin lifted high, she stared at the men with such command that no one moved. A stray ray of the moon fell across her pale face, illuminating its regal lines. Even nature was forced to acknowledge her.

The woman gaze lingered over Sarenka's raised skirt and exposed leggings before returning to the attackers faces.

Spell broken, Sarenka pulled her gaze from the woman's face and took in the rest of her attire. A corset of indeterminate design overlay a simple, off-white shirt, and about her waist an odd lump of fabric wound, like a travel bed-roll, secured by leather straps set at uniform intervals. Below the waist she was skirtless—wearing only simple leggings the color of wet sand and thick-soled leather boots—a freedom Sarenka envied. On the ground next to her lay a large bumpy fabric ball, wrapped about by intercrossing straps and rope.

Spread out behind the dark haired woman were at least ten other women, and though she couldn't see fine details in the fog, they all wore similar outfits, complete with bedroll about the waist and leggings: some striped, some light, some dark. A woman stood at an angle next to the leader, crossbow cocked and aimed at the nearest man's chest, and faintly, in the soft fog-filled light, she caught the glint of metal in the other women's hands.

Understanding why the men had stopped accosting her brought a grim sort of smile to Sarenka's lips.

"Now now, washer-woman. We don't want no trouble with your kind, and we know you don't want no trouble with us."

She remained silent. Waiting.

"Just leave us here with the whore and go to your work, none the wiser." He placed a hand on his sword hilt in an unmistakable threat.

"Leave her here." The dark haired woman spoke without emotion, neither agreeing nor denying.

Sarenka tensed and prepared to fight for her life again.

"She's ours. We caught her fair an' square."

The other held up a hand, as if to sooth his partner. "Now then, you be a knowin' the trouble that'll fall on you and youruns if'n word gets out you stopped us."

"Do you really think anyone will know it was us when they find your bodies in the morning filled with holes and beaten to a pulp?" she asked.

"Let me castrate them," someone who sounded far younger than the leader hissed out.

Sarenka focused her illusions before struggling to a sitting position, hand held to her throat. She gave a rough cough and pushed back the hood, uncovering a moon pale face with a scattering of freckles and long black tresses. And then she waited, hoping that her youthful copy of their leader had the right effect.

One of the men coughed and nudged his companion, pointing at Sarenka.

The man licked his lips nervously. "Okay, twas an honest mistake. How was we to know she was one of youruns in this here fog? Couldn't even see her face."

There was a 'twang' and the speaker went down, mouth moving futilely, hands clutching at the arrow protruding from his throat. Blood seeped through his fingertips, darkening the front of his cream colored shirt. The other man turned and ran, throwing up plumes of sand from his feet. Sarenka glanced from his fading back to the leader and opened her mouth to speak, but another 'twang' drew her eyes back to the man. Pale gray against the fog, he dropped to his knees and wavered for a long moment before falling forward onto his face.

Sarenka went cold with fear. If they so readily killed these men, what would they do with a Freni-Kyn who deceived them?

The leader held out a hand, and despite a shiver of dread Sarenka grasped it, allowing the woman to help her stand.

"Thank you."

"Make sure the scumbags are dead." She gestured towards the bodies, and the women rushed forward. "Strip them, split up the goods, and make it look like a robbery, then get them out to sea."

She turned her attention to Sarenka. "Names Tamika. And you're a fool to be down here by the docks all alone, it's past night fall."

Sarenka forced an illusion of a blush, though she wasn't sure it would be noticed in the fog. "I just wanted a swim."

"More the fool then. Or are you one of those crazies what wants to die?"

"Why? Would it kill me?"

A soft thumping started from just behind, making Sarenka jump. She turned to see the women kicking the now naked bodies and supposed that it was part of making it look like a robbery, though some of them were doing it with more enthusiasm than necessary.

"Don't have time, you want to know, you'll come with us." With a grunt, Tamika hefted the ball of fabric over one shoulder and took off for the shore. "I've got to get this stuff washed and dried before morning."

As a group, the women turned towards the sea, dragging the two naked bodies with grim determination. Sarenka watched the odd sight for a moment before hurrying to get in step next to the leader. Already over-loaded with balls of clothing, the sand made the work slow, and they took frequent turns at pulling the men. Anxious to ask questions, and grateful for being rescued, Sarenka grasped one of the men by the wrist and strained forward. Her feet slid about, searching for purchase on the shifting sand. The women, who had only given her blank stares, now threw her grateful smiles.

"Uncanny how much you look like me." Face still impassive, the leader darted another glance at her. "Probably got those men killed."

"How so?"

"Set off Lydia's protective tendencies when you sat up like you did. Should've kept his mouth shut, he should. Pushed her right over the edge."

"Then the resemblance was a fortunate circumstance, at least for me."

"I wouldn't have let them touch you." Her voice was clipped and sharp, and she stared straight ahead with her lips compressed into an angry line, obviously offended.

Sarenka struggled for the right words but could think of nothing to say. Instead, she pretended that the weight was slowing her and dropped behind. Upon reaching the sea, Sarenka let go of the man's wrist and rubbed her sore arms.

The women tossed their shoes into a pile and pulled the men into the water. As soon as they let go, the undercurrent carried the bodies away. Wading back to the shore, the women undid their bundles and hauled one item after another into the water, where they beat and twisted and scrubbed, using sand and salt to clean away the grime of everyday life.

Tamika joined them, shedding all mysticism and turning from leader into a simple washerwoman, set on finishing her chores. Between scrubbing, when she had her breath, Tamika started explaining. "Okay, this is why you would've died. There's nothing safe out here."

"No not one," a nearby woman said.

"Either the sailors'll rape you dead, or the Watrelk Pirates'll capture and sell you—they might rape you dead too, if they're in a mood—or the guards'll sell you to the pirates, or, if you make it past all of them and end up in the water..."

"In the water," the woman echoed.

"You see down there?" Tamika pointed past massive wave-shaped boats towards a distant pier. "That's where the current would've taken you. And that's where you would've died."

"You would've died." The woman slapped down a piece of clothing especially hard.

Sarenka was so relieved that she blurted out, "What? Surely you don't believe that old tale?"

"I don't believe it. I know it. I've seen them drag men out there and throw them in. They don't come back," Tamika said.

"It's not a tale. I was but a wee one when it started," said a woman, crisp and clear.

It was not the mindless echo of the nearby woman, and Sarenka turned to see who had spoken.

A gray haired woman, her wrinkled face silent witness to years of harsh winters scrubbing clothing in bitter-cold waters, held Sarenka's gaze. "There was a brawl down at the docks."

She slammed an item down in the water, making a sound like a man being slapped.

Sarenka jumped.

The other women slammed what they were holding into the water, echoing the elderly woman, as if this were a play being enacted for Sarenka's benefit.

"A sailor got cut, an' they pushed him in. An outta the water came this arm," the old woman said, lifting the clothing from the water so fast that it created a slurp.

The other women did the same.

Sarenka shuddered.

"Like a great octopus, but there weren't no rounded saucers on its underside, not that I would've known 'bout octopus back then…" She shook her head and looked away, remembering.

Sarenka opened her mouth to speak.

"No, there were blades," the elder woman continued, "glinting in the light of the moon… like lines of the guards pikes all laid out in overlapping rows… and they sliced that man, shzzths, shzzths, shzzths."

CHAPTER 19

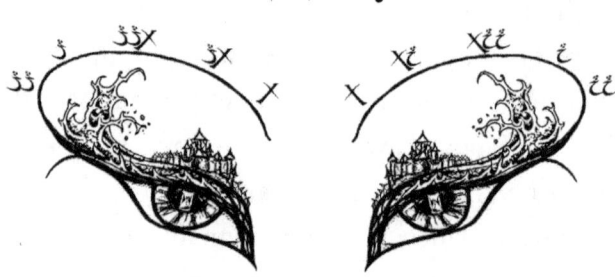

She moved her hands like she held a sword, and the rest of the women followed suit, echoing the strange blade like sound. "...till he weren't nothing more than tiny bits of floating meat, like vegetables in the soup bowl."

The women all stopped long enough to make signs of warding.

"I weren't alone in the seeing. People all along the shore cried out. I ran and I ran and I lost my stomach all over the sand. I weren't alone in that, neither." She turned back to her chores, and her stooped form curled in around itself as if seeking to hide from view.

When she spoke again, it was with her back to Sarenka. "Never a day passes that I've not seen that creature in me head. I go to sleep thinking of it, and I wake hoping that today is not the day I meet it face to face."

With a nervous shudder Sarenka glanced about, wishing she wasn't standing knee-high in the cold water.

The leader said, "They feed it now, the Red Pelican. I think they find it amusing. Sick bastards. Whenever they find some poor hapless soul lying dead on the streets, they give it a day, no more. If none come to claim him, they slash the body to draw the beast and throw it in."

Another of the women, grey in the fog, spoke up. "That's when the d'yroap starts flying, bets on which limb will be shorn first, and whether it will shred the head, or eat the head, and how long it'll take."

"I've not seen it myself, but plenty others have, including our youngest." The leader gestured at a small figure, faint in the fog. "She won't talk to you about it though. They caught her watching and hauled her out and held her over the water, till she wet herself with fear. Now she hardly talks at all. Twas days before we got what happened out of her."

Tucking her gloves into the top of her corset for safety, Sarenka aided the women with the rest of their chores, but she was forced to turn towards shore when she could hold the illusions no longer. Knowing that H'eumans didn't hold their heat well, she chattered her teeth for exaggerated effect. "I've got to get out. I'm freezing."

"Wet clothing in these waters'll do that to you, makes me envy the Freni-kyn and Sharpra their inbuilt heat. You've good and willing hands, get yourself a washer-woman's belt from a blacksmith and join us. That'll keep you from getting soaked through like you are."

"Where would I find those willing to pay me to wash clothing?"

"Now that's a wee bit trickier. You'd just have to work for me a while, least till you prove yourself. Then I'll give my recommendation. That'll get you some jobs."

I think not. I'm surviving just fine without having to be around other people every single day. All I need is the antidote and a way out of this Kyron forsaken hole of a city.

Sarenka moved through the billowing fog until she was out of sight. Sitting on the loose sand, she drew her knees under her chin and wrapped her arms around her legs and wished she had the meat that rebuilt her strength. "I'll consider it. Thanks for saving me."

"How could we do less?"

Silent, she dropped her illusions and only spent enough energy to keep her hair lights extinguished. And now the cold embraced her in truth. Shivers wracked her body while she listened to them discuss their mundane lives and the customers they worked for. A longing for that life filled her. How she wished to shed her Freni-Kyn side and be H'euman—able to go and do as she pleased and lead a simple life filled with ordinary chores—without the challenge and deceit of being a half-breed.

The women trudged towards her, splashing.

She pushed away the daydreams and raised her illusions before stepping from the fog, ready to join their walk back towards the city.

"I thought you left," Tamika said.

"No, I've learned my lesson. No more walking out here alone."

"That's good, sister." She winked at Sarenka and turned for home.

Wet skirt slapping against her legs, Sarenka fell in beside her and shifted the conversation back to swimming. "So, there's no place safe to swim?"

"No. You can bathe in it. You can wash your clothing in it. But swimming's dangerous. If the tide doesn't pull you out to sea, then the creature'll slice you to pieces."

"What about outside of Burmtin?"

"Well, of course, but why would anyone in their right mind walk all the way to another town to swim? Lessen you're visiting family, but who has that kinda leisure?"

"Can't you get around the creature and let the current take you to the nicer swimming areas?"

"They net the area off, under the water. No way around. You could probably cut the net, but by the time you did, it'd kill you. Why do you want to swim so much?"

Sarenka threw out the first lie that sprang into her head. "I'm looking to get with child. Herbalist told me it's good for the womanly parts."

A couple of the women snorted and several giggled, but the more polite ones coughed to cover their laughs.

"Best way to get with child is in a bed girl, not in the water," said Tamika.

This brought another round of laughter and several knowing nudges before they fell silent.

"Children come in their own time. You're young, they'll find you soon enough," the older woman added before the group split up, each heading towards her own home.

Alone. At last. Thank Kyron for that.

Sarenka pulled on her gloves and turned to finding an alley to hunker down in for the night.

Parian froze, flat on his back and breathless, afraid to move.

Paws crushing his chest, mouth around his throat, Rosalie waited an eternity, and then she let go. She shifted her weight, taking most of the pressure off his chest. *~Not poison?~*

He gasped, drawing in a breath that hurt. *~No. Not poison.~*

~I'm not eating it.~ Her nose ran, dripping on his face.

~You can have my food. Just get off my chest.~

She leapt to the side, grabbed the other package, and bounded away, leaving him alone in the clearing.

He stared up at the clear lavender sky for a long time, glad to be alive. As the sun inched towards the horizon and a chill crept into his back, he finally sat up and dusted himself off and grabbed the dirt-encrusted fish by the tail.

"I hate fish," he said, tossing it as far from the clearing as possible.

When Rosalie didn't return, he set camp and dozed off next to the fire with a growling stomach.

A warm rumble against his back awoke him, and he knew that Rosalie had returned. He sat up and rubbed his neck, still sore from the fall, and stared at the glowing embers where their fire had been. The warmth might help with the ache, but they needed to leave, and stirring the coals to life would take too much time.

Rosalie stretched in her sleep, paws kneading the air.

I've got a psychic cat that has to have a pink saddle, thinks it's an expert at calculating angles and trajectories on the fly, and is allergic to fish. What next?

He nudged her. "Time to go."

She rolled and twisted until her belly was exposed and looked at him upside down. Her eyes blinked slowly. He reached forward to rub her belly.

~Don't you dare.~

"You're one cantankerous son-of-a—" He snapped his mouth shut. A replay of yesterday was the last thing he needed.

~I'm not a son of anything. Cat. I'm a daughter of a cat.~

"Okay. Cat. Let's go." For once, he was glad for the gaps in her knowledge and that the nuances of cursing still escaped her.

She twisted back and forth on the ground, covering herself in loose dirt before standing.

Rolling his eyes, he grabbed the saddle and soon they were heading northwest.

Fear yammered at D'trav's heart. He sprang to his feet and grabbed the next slat, pulling and yanking until he fell to the mattress again. Pain shot through his hand. He pressed it to his side and cursed before standing up again and listening.

The steps scuffed slowly nearer.

Did they hear me?

He held his hand up to the moonlight and examined the cut.

Might just be a guard makin' the rounds.

Dare I wait a bit and...

Blood ran down his wrist, soaking into the cuff of his shirt. It was bad but he'd live.

Hell no! Can't risk it, made too Kyron-be-damned much noise.

The electric feeling he got before a fight sang through his veins. He lundged for the next slat.

The door rattled, metal on metal as a key was put in the keyhole.

He yanked again, landed on his back, and jumped to his feet as the doorknob started to turn. Grabbing the last bottle of whiskey, he threw himself out the window and sprinted off down the alley.

After running a few blocks, his legs turned to jelly, forcing him to stop. He breathed in the fresh air with gratitude and stared back at the brothel, relieved to hear no pursuers. Camille would be dealt with later, on his terms and not as a prisoner. Right now he was concerned with finding real food. The rancid tallow candles, short term energy at best, did little to stave off hunger pangs and were sure to give him the runs.

He stopped at the first vendor. "Dozen sausage buns."

The vendor covered his nose and squinted at D'trav coins dubiously, as if fearful of catching something.

"It's clean enough for the likes of you."

The man grunted and slid the loops onto his chain before handing over the bag of sausage rolls.

D'trav wolfed down a roll and stepped into the first pub he passed. When he sat down, the people nearby got up and moved. He dropped a silver d'yroap on the counter. "Ale. And make it fast."

The barkeep stared past him.

Before he could turn to see what the keep was looking at, he was grasped under the arms, dragged across the room, and tossed out the door. His silver landed nearby.

"Stay out beggar! None of your kinds welcome in here!"

D'trav sighed and stood up. "Water it is."

He pulled the M'hakru whiskey from inside of his cloak and tipped it back, drinking the last few inches of it before taking off for the well. After filling the bottle, he lifted it in a silent toast to his freedom and slugged back half of it before refilling it again.

He gnawed another roll, eating it slower as he turned down the first alley. Sheltered by those forgiving shadows, he hunkered down and ate, glad for the welcome relief of a full belly. His stomach gurgled and cramped and he knew he wouldn't hold onto the food long but it was a start. He finished the night in the alley and awoke feeling better than he had in days. As expected, he soon found himself hurrying to get his britches down without soiling them in the process. But even with that discomfort, he was glad to be free.

He considered his options. He had a bit of d'yroap to find a place to rent, and he was strong enough to hire out for menial work. He'd kept himself shaved, despite the captivity, so, as long as he was cautious—

The sight of a poster flapping in the breeze stopped him cold.

Who am I kidding? A simple shave's not gonna be enough to hide me. Not with my face plastered all over town. I need help, and goin' back to Camille is not an option.

He headed for the only safety he could think of, a blacksmith that owed him a life.

The next day dawned fine and clear, the sun burning off the fog before she could rub the sleep from her eyes. Throwing off the concealing cloak, Sarenka yawned and stretched out the cramps from sleeping curled into a protective ball. She stared at the rising sun, grateful for that little bit of freedom. Last night's answer to the lure of the Istoarm Sea had almost cost everything, even her life.

Today she would renew the search for a way out. And though every day in Burmtin brought with it new dangers, new risks, new obstacles to overcome, she decided to take them gladly. The lead to an escape route from Burmtin, or clearing her name with the Red Pelican, might be found around any corner.

Despite her optimism that morning, the day was long and unfruitful, offering up no solutions, and that evening promised to be like any other. While sipping ale from a tankard at a run-down pub, easing the symptoms of the Foreveron drug, the magical solution to all her problems arrived, almost planting himself right into her hand. While knocking back tankard after tankard of the cheapest ale, a well-dressed man with an abundance of d'yroaps and astounding dare began to publically spout hate for the Red Pelican. If he wasn't Onglat, he had to be one of his compatriots. Onglat was the only one brave enough to do what this man was doing.

Her chance for freedom had finally arrived. With Onglat turned in, the Red Pelican would pardon her of everything, even murder. Sarenka watched the other patrons edge away and waited until he quieted before befriending him.

Now, hours later, they were drinking companions. She matched his chugs with messy sips, dribbling it over her clothing like a common drunk, and slapped down the tankard after each round, sloshing most of her ale onto the countertop. Mimicking the drunks she'd grown up with, she rocked back and forth on her seat.

Her illusions—that of a pock marked whore, complete with painted lips and cheeks—wore at her energy, tearing it away strip by strip. Still, she stayed. The progress warranted the risk, and if the illusions slipped a little perhaps that was for the better, as it lent credence to her plan.

"Tell you secret Jacob," she slurred into his ear, "I never did abide by those ball sucking Red Pelican pansies."

Jacob chortled, turning red in the face.

She clapped him on the back and laughed.

"Nor did I, m'lady, nor did I."

"They cheat you out of house and home."

"That they do."

"Steal milk from a wee babe." She slammed down the tankard for emphasis and sent up a golden plume. It sloshed over the edge and spread across the driftwood countertop in a widening circle.

"Evil sots!"

"They'd even take a man's own wife from him."

Jacob nodded solemn agreement.

"But I know something secret."

"Do you now?" He leaned in close, eager to hear.

"I know a way to get 'hem back good."

The door behind her opened, banging against the wall before crashing closed again.

Drunkenly, Sarenka swung around in her chair to see who had arrived. She stared up into the eyes of two Burmtin guards and all the joy seeped out of her body, leaving her cold to the marrow.

They tugged the bottom edge of their Red Pelican tunics with self-importance before sitting on either side of Sarenka and Jacob.

She glanced around the room, wondering who in the motley crowd was more faithful to the Red Pelican than they were to their fellows in misery.

Choking on his beer and half dropping the tankard to the countertop, Jacob leaned close enough for his eyelashes to brush the rim of the vessel. He blinked his eyes slowly, struggling to focus. "Hey!" he shouted, making everyone nearby jump. "There's a fly in here!"

The pub owner hurried over and peered into it. "No, there isn't."

"Yes, tis, and dung too!"

Sarenka played along by leaning over to peer into her cup.

"Keep your voice down. There's nothing wrong with your ale, you sorry drunk," the owner growled out under his breath.

"Look, I started smelling dung soon as this gent here sat down."

Sarenka froze.

The soldier next to Jacob sprang to his feet, and the one sitting next to her slammed down his goblet, sloshing the counter with golden liquid.

"Hey now, we don't need no trouble. Get out," the owner told Jacob.

"You dare talk about me like that?" yelled the guard, throwing spittle over them. Face purpling with rage, he leaned forward until his nose was only a few fingers-spans from Jacob's.

"What?" Befuddled, Jacob blinked up at the man. He put his finger on the soldier's tunic and began tracing the edge of the Red Pelican emblem with his fingertip. "Isn't this the most interesting shape?"

The guard's brows rose in disbelief as he watched.

Jacob's finger stroked over the neck of the pelican. "I do believe thas a man's cock right there. Hey! What you wearing a cock on your shirt for? Thas just plain rude, tis."

The soldier stared at Jacob with disbelief, too surprised to move.

Sarenka went cold. *He's going to get us both killed.*

The soldier's hands fisted.

This can't be Onglat, he's too stupid.

She wrapped an arm around Jacob and stood, pulling him up with her. "Obviously my father's had too much sweet-drink. Let me buy you two *fine* young men a beverage and get him home for the night."

Caught off guard, the soldier glanced from her painted face back to Jacob's. His eyes narrowed.

Sarenka slapped down some silver onto the countertop and nodded at the owner. "Give 'em whatever they be hankerin' for."

The soldier's gaze traveled from the d'yroap to the man and back, no doubt weighing whether the bribe was large enough. With that much silver they could buy ten ales or any sweet-drink the house carried. Much to her relief, the guard's shoulders relaxed. He pushed the loops towards the pub keeper. "Two M'hakru Whiskeys."

The pub keep threw her a grateful look.

She grabbed Jacob's elbow, turning him away from the soldiers, and dragging him towards the door.

"What? What?" the older man muttered.

"Shut up," she whispered.

"I didn't say anything, and I don't want to go to bed. Are you propositioning me? I'm not sure you're my type."

She raised her voice, speaking loud enough for the whole bar to hear, "Shut up father, you're shaming yourself,"

"Am not. Bet tha one back there with tha cock on his shirt would bed you, though," he yelled.

She jerked him out the door. It slammed shut behind them, adding to her shaky nerves.

"An' I don't have a daughter."

At a running stumble, Sarenka dragged Jacob three buildings down and pulled him behind it. The door to the bar slammed open with a bang, and then back shut.

"Where'd they go?" The shout shattered the peace of the quiet street, and a trio of seagulls broke into flight.

Sarenka shuddered at the palpable anger in the guard's voice.

⊂HAPTER 20

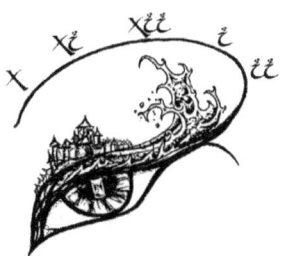

Parian fell off of Rosalie, landing on the ground with a thud.

She threw herself down beside him.

He groaned and rolled over, and despite their long discussion about the bears she scented in the area, he couldn't stay awake one moment longer. If a bear ate him, he'd never know it.

Rosalie put a paw over him and pulled him closer before pillowing her massive head on his back and closing her eyes.

Parian opened his eyes to the sound of gentle pattering. A large drop of water struck his cheek. He blinked, trying to remember where he was. Green tossed and turned overhead, and beyond that fluttering canopy, ominous clouds roiled and billowed.

He sat up.

Rain!

Lightning arced across the sky and struck with a crack. A strange smell filled the air. He gazed about. Rosalie was nowhere to be found. Water cascaded down as he ran for the nearest evergreen and crawled under, soaked to the skin. He looked back.

"Ohhh no."

His pack lay where he had left it, in a low spot that was sure to turn into a pond by morning. He crawled to the edge and stood, half sheltered by thick boughs.

Drawing a deep breath, he took off at a run. As he broke from cover, a shadow crossed in front of him, grabbing the handles of his bags as it passed. Parian tried to stop but his feet slid. Arms whirling, he went down, landing face first in the mud. Stunned, he lay immobile while the rain drummed against his back and water filled his mouth and nostrils. Gasping for breath, he slid his hands forward and began to push upwards.

Before he could stand, he was seized by the back of the shirt and dragged away.

"No! Nooooo…" He grabbed for his weapon, but with the rough passage—face first over dips in grass and brush and puddle and stone—he couldn't free it. Finally he was dropped in a pile of pinching pine needles. He lay, expecting a maw to close around his neck at any moment, eyes squinched shut.

~You look a mess. Should clean your fur.~ Rosalie snorted, blowing hot air that smelled of blood across his face.

Parian rolled onto his back and stared up at the dark branches of a pine tree. "I thought I was dead."

~Do I have to do it for you?~

Pushing her head away, he began picking off the pine needles. "No, rabbit breath. I'll do it."

~Not rabbit.~

His stomach grumbled. "Just rub my face in it, why don't you."

She turned away as if offended.

He started to apologize.

With a thump, something wet landed next to his face.

He turned his head towards the object and then jerked away from it. "Rosalie, no! You can't do that."

~You don't like it?~

He sat up and looked at the dead turkey.

~It's a present. Meat. Fresh. And I brought it to you.~

Now she really was hurt. He tried to think of a way to explain but gave up. "I can't eat it raw. It'll make me sick."

~You need fire?~

"Yes."

She turned to stare at the rain and laid her head on her paws. *~Freni-Kyn's are weak.~*

He sighed. As usual their conversations had moved from hurt misunderstanding to insults. Living with a cat had been far harder than living with a horse. She was cantankerous and ornery and determined to get her way. He wouldn't be surprised to wake up in the morning and find her gone, or that she'd led them the wrong way on purpose, yet again.

"Yes." It was easier to agree.

~You should just go there. They're right.~

"What? Where?"

~To Burmtin.~

"No." He peered out through the branches, alarmed. "You didn't already start going that way did you?"

~I should have. Can't find a quarry without getting near its nest.~

"You don't understand."

~Nope. Don't.~

"The people there are evil."

~And they weren't in that town we passed on the way to Claw Lake? I heard what that man planned to do to that little girl.~

"That was no excuse for ripping his throat out."

~It worked.~

"I could have fixed him."

~Maybe.~

He turned away, silent. She was right. His fix held no guarantee.

"It's just that… there's just too many willing females in Burmtin." She made some whuffing sounds and nudged his back.

"It's not funny."

~What's wrong with a bit of play?~

"I can't. It can backlash and mess up my abilities, or worse, I can lose my sense of self."

~*So none of the voices has ever had sex?*~

"None."

~*You lie.*~

"How do you do that? I had my thoughts blocked, and I made sure not to move."

~*Your heart sped up and breathing quickened.*~

"Okay fine, one of us does. But he's a sweet-drink addict. It's the only way he can do it."

She thumped her head down on the ground next to him with a grunt. ~*Well that's out then.*~

"Agree."

~*Why can't you just resist?*~

"I'm a Freni-Kyn. That means I'm in a perpetual state of heat. Can you resist the wild call when you're in heat?"

She was silent, and when he turned to look at her, she turned her back on him.

For once he had won an argument.

Jacob opened his mouth to speak, but Sarenka slapped a gloved hand over it. He widened his eyes innocently and snuggled up while she listened to a low murmur, followed by the sound of the pub door slamming once more. The silence drew out. She waited, listening. Only the muffled sound of voices in nearby buildings came to her ears. She could stand the suspense no longer and peered around the edge of the building. The street was empty of everything but a stray housewolf.

It turned to stare at her and bared its teeth.

She pulled back and let out a relieved sigh.

Jacob took the opportunity to nuzzle her neck.

Disgusted, she pushed him away. "That was the stupidest, most idiotic, thing I ever saw anyone do."

He laughed and all the drunkenness left his voice. "I found it highly amusing. You should have seen your face."

"I didn't need to. I saw *their* faces. You do know what they do to people they don't like, don't you?"

He tugged down the edge of his jacket. "Of course I do. I have good reason to hate them, and I could have taken both of them."

She appraised his body and doubted it. He looked a dandy, barely able to lift a butter knife, even less survive a brawl against trained guards. Taking in his cocky half-smile, her eyes narrowed. By all appearances, he wasn't even tipsy. Their game was over. It was time to get her answers and go.

"I know how to take down the Red Pelican once and for all and I'm searching for Onglat. He'll be interested in what I have to say."

One brow inched upwards. "You don't play easy, do you?"

"Nope. I don't. Not when it comes to them. Can you help me find him, or not?"

He frowned and lashed out with his fist, catching her off guard with such a heavy blow that it sent her sprawling to her knees. Her illusions faltered, flickering out, and faster than she could dodge, his hand snaked out to grasp her hair.

Pain so severe that her eyesight went white shot through Sarenka's head.

"That's right, Freni-Kyn. I know your little hair secret. I know it's alive, and if you move I'll cut it off."

D'trav's evening in the blacksmith's loft left him itching with fleas, and his bath in the trough did little more than make him cold. Without special herbs, he was stuck with the creatures. With regret, he left his filth-encrusted leathers behind and pulled on the blacksmith's rough clothing: an overlarge shirt, too snug pants, and a cloak that smelled of horse. They wouldn't protect him in a fight, but they were clean. His blade was a whole other matter. The blacksmith had sharpened it, smoothing out all the nicks and giving it an edge keen enough to shave the nether regions.

He peered through the blacksmith's window at the setting sun. It dipped incrementally lower while he paced back and forth, anxious to leave the cottage. Darkness settled over the city and, like a cantankerous child given a sweet, it quieted.

Without saying goodbye, he rushed from the building and began cutting across town. Hook-Hand Ruby would cost a fortune, but she'd help him secure papers for a new identity, and maybe even find him a disguise. She owed him that, and more, after he rescued her son last year. Muscles still weak from the days locked in a room with no real food and no exercise, he stopped often to rest.

With his mind once more clear, questions surged. If Camille would lock him in a room, where else could he turn? Who wouldn't sell him out for the price that was listed on his wanted poster? Were any of his compatriots to be trusted? The only thing left was to leave Burmtin. But not without his trunk. Not without out Elsa's keepsakes and the tools of his trade. He'd be damned if he let Camille take that from him. Thoughts running in a never-ending circle, he shifted from shadowed alley to shadowed alley without really seeing what he passed.

A whirring noise came from behind.

D'trav realized that he'd been hearing it for a few minutes and halted.

It whistled, high pitched, and then stopped with a crack.

Drawing his sword, D'trav swung around.

Outlined against the night sky was a mountain of a man. His arm flew forward and a black snake flipped with it, whipping through the sky and snapping the space between them.

CHAPTER 24

R'kiax stalked towards Burk, taking in details as he approached. The eye he had punched was still blackened, his hair rumpled and his nightshirt hastily tucked into a pair of breeches.

I see I wasn't the only one pulled out of bed in the middle of the night.

Burk gestured R'kiax into the office without saying a word.

R'kiax wanted to smile at him and frighten the man some more but he held back. This couldn't be good. He entered the office and the Captain turned away from a mirror he'd been looking in.

"Have a seat." Lator moved his hand languidly towards a chair as if this were a casual call.

R'kiax sat on the edge of the seat, muscles bunched, ready to fight.

"We have an antidote shipment arriving several days from now. I need you to accept the delivery, make the payment, and bring the drug here without frightening anyone. No fights. Nothing messy. No city guards involved. It is imperative that things stay calm. Can you do that? Or do I need to send Burk?"

R'kiax nodded, Burk had just earned another black eye. "I can do it."

"I mean it. Even if Onglat shows up and tries to steal them, this *can not* go wrong."

"It's him I should be tracking."

"Are you, a man who can not even catch a simple slave, telling me how I should run this office? What makes you think you can catch him?"

Knowing better than to say anything, R'kiax ground his teeth together.

"Just what I thought."

"Where's the trade off?"

"Near one of the wells. Get the scroll from Burk, go disguised."

He nodded.

Lator stared at him.

He stared back, waiting.

"Go."

R'kiax walked out the door, and Burk hurried to back away from his desk.

"Scroll." R'kiax held out his hand.

Burk pointed at the desk.

R'kiax picked it up and turned to leave. Lightning fast, he swung back, grabbed the edge of the desk, and flipped his feet around in a swing that caught Burk in the stomach.

Burk hunched forward, left eye landing on R'kiax's outstretched fist as R'kiax's feet landed on the ground.

Burk groaned.

"You earned that," R'kiax said, and sauntered away.

Sarenka gasped for breath, unable to speak through the pain lancing through her head and down her neck.

"So, you think you can take out the Red Pelican, do you?" Jacob's fingers tightened in her hair, and he punctuated his words with jerks of her head. "We shall see about that."

The agony mounted, turning into an unbearable, white-hot knife. Sarenka's body went cold as she went into shock, paralyzed by a torture that was forbidden amongst the Freni-Kyn.

He gave her head one last jerk and let go.

She sagged to the ground, unable to do more than breathe.

"I've got a far better use for you, girl. There are people who will pay for the use of your body, far more than the reward on your head will ever pay."

Horrified, she tried to speak, but only a moan came out.

Reaching under his vest, he pulled free a long thin reed and snapped the end off. It flared up, casting a red tint over his face before settling into a dull red glow. He stared at the burning ember a moment and lowered it towards her forehead.

She gasped, felt her pupils dilate, tried to move but couldn't; the shock still screamed through every living hair strand.

With a satisfied nod, he brought the reed to his mouth and drew in the smoke, holding it for a moment before blowing the sickly sweet fragrance up into the air. "We'll need to be careful with the billing. I may have to pass you off as Sharpra. Yes, that will do quite nicely." Though he seemed to be talking to himself, he turned to stare into her eyes.

"Are you paying attention?" He struck out with his fist, stopping just short of her face, and smiled when she flinched. "Now that I have your attention, how does this sound?"

"From the wilds of the Wolf Clan," he threw out in a sing song stage voice, "comes the delicious Sharpra..."

He snapped his fingers. "A name, we need a name..."

"Come on girl, speak up." He flicked ashes at her and took another draw. "M'lernitia. That'll do."

He dropped back into the singsong. "Willing to do the bidding of any brave enough to bear her claws."

"Those will have to be trimmed, of course. No more stupid unfortunate accidents, like that baron you sliced to pieces."

She closed her eyes, waiting while the pain abated and strength flowed back into her limbs, but she didn't move. Slavery had taught her a few tricks.

He leaned down to blow smoke into her face. "Get up. I didn't hurt you that bad."

Lashing out with a foot, she knocked his feet out from under him and rolled over, pinning him to the ground.

He grappled, freed his arms, and reached for her hair.

Twisting aside, she chopped the edge of her hand down on his throat.

Eyes widening, he struggled to draw breath and grabbed for her hair again.

She extended the claws through her gloves and pressed them against his jugular. "Don't move, you bastard, or I'll slice your throat here and now."

He froze.

"Are you Red Pelican?"

He let out a strangled sound that told her nothing.

She grasped his other hand and yanked it above his head. "Tap your hand once for yes. Are you Red Pelican?"

He slapped the ground three times, movements almost frantic in their speed.

So no.

"Do you know who Onglat is?"

He started to slap the ground but stopped with his hand wavering above it.

"The real identity of Onglat," she clarified.

With less enthusiasm, he slapped the ground twice.

Didn't think so.

"Do you know where I can find him?"

He tapped the ground twice more.

"So, you just thought to sell my body for the coin then?"

He didn't move, but she didn't need him to tap once, the truth was obvious.

"You're useless." Placing her fingers on a spot that would render him unconscious, she waited, counting out the moments before his body went slack. "A complete waste of time."

She riffled through his coat and grabbed his d'yroap pouch before standing. Hatred sheared through her as she stared down at him, and she couldn't resist a hard kick to the ribs. "That hurt like hell, too, you piece of useless dung. You're lucky I don't…"

Sarenka turned and walked away, pulling on an illusion of a young brunette woman with a huge mole on her left cheek before stepping from the alley. Upon arrival at one of her favorite sleeping spots, she settled down on her haunches and tenderly touched the back of her head. She winced at the stiffness of the hair in that area and the ache that still lingered, knowing that it'd be days before the hair healed, or died.

How'd he know our hair's alive? Father said only Freni-Kyn know about that.

Realizing how easily he could have slaughtered her while grasping her hair, she went back over the encounter and wondered which pleasure house he owned. Fortunately he hadn't known enough. His underestimation of Freni-Kyn recovery had given her enough time to fight back, and led her to believe he hadn't used hair to immobilize a Freni-Kyn before. For that she was glad.

She gave her head a small negating shake.

Regardless, he's dangerous, and not just to me.

Cold with fear, she shivered.

Probably tell the guards, or worse, Captain Lator. Just when the search was dying down. I'll never get out of Burmtin alive now. Should've just killed him—

No! I'm not that person.

Sarenka pressed her fingers to her head as the headache started up again.

But I should have.

Drink is never enough anymore.

Oh Kyron—

Shut up!

Mind-lost…

I'm going mind-lost.

Crouching into a defensive position, D'trav loosened the ties of his cloak and dropped it to the ground.

A whip. That's a Kyron-be-damned whip. Never fought against that 'fore... doesn't matter... I'll win. I always win.

The man strode closer. "Throw down the sword, and I'll take it easy on you."

"I'd sooner die than give up my d'yroap that easy."

The man grabbed his crotch and thrust his hips forward. "I'm wanting a little more than a few paltry coppers, beggar."

"Then you best be lookin' elsewhere. I'm no beggar."

The man laughed. "Hear that boys? He's no beggar."

Laughter came from behind.

D'trav whirled in a circle. Three—no four—other men surrounded him, each as burly as the first.

"Still want to fight, beggar?"

D'trav growled, low and guttural. He didn't stand a chance, but he'd die fighting, not with his throat slit after they took him.

"You know the rules of Burmtin. Give it away easy, or get it taken hard."

One of the men drew near, and D'trav swung.

The man threw up his sword, easily knocking D'trav's weapon aside.

D'trav dived left and spun back, slashing down as he moved.

The whip wrapped around his arm midair, breaking his spin and stopping his sword a hand-span from the man's neck.

D'trav stared at his arm, astounded. He lunged, pressing forward, trying to finish the swing.

The man in front of him gave a mocking smile.

The whip jerked, yanking D'trav into a backwards stumble.

Catching his balance, D'trav spun towards the whip master and pulled free his dagger with the other hand. He sliced downwards in a whir towards the whip. Again his arm was stopped, caught by another lashing whip. It yanked him in the other direction, pulling him spread-eagle between them.

D'trav fought, twisted, kicked, but the whips wouldn't release his arms. Finally, he dropped to his knees, exhausted.

"Well now, let's see what he's got under there," the first man said.

Footsteps came from behind, and he felt a blade, cold against his neck. "You'll behave yourself now. Won't you?"

Like prey caught in a web, D'trav dangled between the whips and refused to speak.

"Answer him."

They pulled the whips outwards, stretching his arms painfully.

"Yes," he whispered.

The knife traveled downwards, slicing through fabric until he was clothed in only strips. He felt himself harden and grimaced.

"Well, well, well, would you look at that? I think the beggar likes us."

They pulled him backwards, lashing him to the nearby wall by means of whips and wooden laundry hooks. His cock was caught in an iron fist and twisted until he cried out, and still it betrayed him, staying rock hard.

"Should we let him—"

"Fuck us? Not hardly. It's us what do the givin' here." The voice that spoke was sweet and high. A man with cheekbones like chiseled ice picked up D'trav's belt. He folded it in half and slapped it against his hand as he advanced.

"Come on beggar, ask us to fuck you." He slapped it across D'trav's chest and the stone bits cut, leaving behind red streaks. Lightning fast, he struck again.

D'trav's body bent backwards as pain seared his chest, then dropped, sagging.

The man raised the belt, waiting, drawing out the moment.

D'trav pinched his lips shut.

The belt came down, slapping hard against his thigh.

He glared at the man, murder in his eyes, but couldn't even hold himself up.

The belt struck again and again, the blows coming faster, a rain of pain.

D'trav's vision blurred and Elsa stood before him, beautiful curls laying like spun honey on her shoulders, doe eyes large with innocence.

Run Elsa!

Run!

Don't let 'em catch you!

He dared not say the words aloud for fear they'd notice her.

"You gotta live, D'trav." Tears slipped down her face. She fell to the street, broken, laying as he'd found her after the Red Pelican had run her down with a wagon.

He shuddered.

Yes, I've gotta live.

I'll make 'em pay for what they did.

He struggled back up, sucking in air through split lips as he stood.

They laughed.

"Well, he's one tough bastard. I'll give him that."

"The sweeter to fuck," said a woman's voice, one he recognized.

He turned his head towards the voice.

Camille walked towards him, hips swaying, a goddess in black leather.

He tried to smile at her but his face wouldn't obey.

She raised her whip. "Tell me what I want to hear."

She had won their game, and he was glad for that, though he had never held out this long before. "Just do it. Fuck me. Get it over with."

He was released from the wall so suddenly that he staggered forward. She'd take him now with her special toy, his reward for being good. His arms were grasped and twisted behind, and he remained compliant, eager to please her.

The illusion broke.

Camille was gone.

Men surrounded him with looks of hate on their faces, and it was too late to struggle. Knowing that to fight would bring only torture, he gritted his teeth and waited. He let them push him forward, bend him over, and their thrusts were not gentle, but he bit his tongue until it bled and took it without crying out.

You'd be proud of me, Camille.

When it was done, they laughed and untied him and left him with only shame for company.

He crawled to the side of the alley and wrapped his arms around himself. He supposed he should be grateful that they had not killed him, but instead he imprinted their faces on his mind forever.

I'll be back for them, even if it's the last thing I do.

They'll die wishin' they never met me, but not 'fore they know what it is to be helpless.

CHAPTER 22

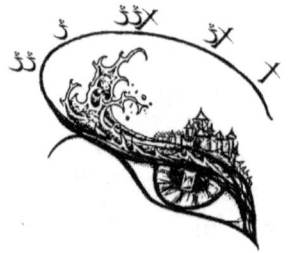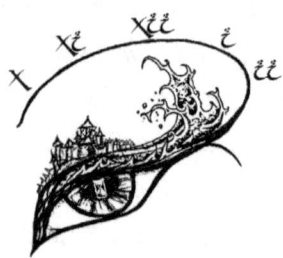

"I, Ygrainne Keerla, leave this as my last will and testimony.

Since the wars started the price of rinol-hide has quadrupled. At the rate I'm selling it, I should be able to buy a night with a Kyn within the week. I won't tell him, of course, but while he pleasures me, looking like poor Henry, I'll already be dying. The poison shouldn't take but a few hours, and then I'll join my Henry in the afterworld.

Who knew that the thing we grew for food would be turned into armor for war. I can't live with myself. Nor can I stand this land, with its fires and killings and mutilations. What have we become?

I dedicate all my lands to science. Use the rinol beasts to help clear it, they're strong enough to pull free the greatest trees. Build a fortress for those who do not war, but only work for the betterment of all the races."

Eastern Uplands
Land Rights and Development

Splash! Liquid splattered, filling the air with the scent of rotted vegetables and fermented urine.

Not again!

Sarenka's eyes sprang open.

She peered through concealing cloak folds at the retreating back of a woman, skirts swishing, refuse pot dangling from one hand.

Sarenka looked at the ground, and her eyes widened.

Nearby, oily liquid crept around cobblestones, working its way towards her sleeping spot.

Why do they always throw it down right next to me?

Covering her nose, Sarenka rushed to create short wiry hair and skin the color of dirt before rolling to her feet. With an impatient shrug, she stepped away from the liquid and pushed off the sweltering hood, revealing the face of a matron, plain and unlikely to attract attention. Another day loomed. She needed to get going or be forced to dip into her precious cache of d'yroap. She skirted the slop again and relieved her bladder behind an empty crate before starting towards her first target.

At the marketplace, she strolled from booth to booth; offering to shine stone, dump honey pots, scrub the pavers under merchant's feet—anything that would earn her a copper or two. After dumping three pots into the refuse trench running along the edge of the street, and carrying so many buckets of water from the well that her back and shoulders ached, she had enough coin to buy a meal.

She stared at the cheese, laid out on display like the finest of wares, and licked her lips. A whole round would feed her for days, but the scent would also draw rodents while she slept, and she had already learned how sick a bite could make you. Instead, she purchased a meager loaf of sandy bread and a wedge of greening cheese and nibbled the meal as she cruised the market, searching for one more job.

Rounding a tent, she came upon a butcher brandishing a knife at two snarling, Horned Shield dogs. She halted to assess the danger.

"Guards! Guards!" the H'euman shouted.

The people around him continued with their business, simply taking a different path. None lent a hand or ran to summon the guards. He drew less attention than the horseflies swarming the area in search of fresh blood. She alone lingered, fascinated with the drama playing out before her and the thought of all that meat, free for the taking if the dogs managed to drive off the butcher.

She couldn't help but admire the large boned animals' cunning as they worked in concert. One light, one dark, they were well-bred beasts, probably escaped from some wealthy manor. Starvation had made rows of ripened wheat from their ribs; covered tight by skin and fur, each detail of their bone structure into stark relief.

Desperate enough to battle an armed H'euman, the light colored one reared back, fur bristling in an angry ruff along its back. It bared its teeth in a snarl and dashed forward, distracting the butcher.

The butcher advanced, slicing the air with his blade in rapid swishes.

Shoulders hunched, the dark blue dog circled around and grabbed for the meat lying near the counter edge.

The man spun, blade making an audible hum as it cut down towards the animal's neck.

Darting backwards, it dodged under the knife.

Sarenka sighed, recognizing the combat moves the man made from her training. Clumsy though he was, the butcher would kill them. All the poor creatures wanted was a meal, a feeling she knew only too well. She stepped forward, yelling over the fray. "I'll get them out of here, and you'll never see them again, *if* you give me five sausages."

The butcher gaped at her like she was mad. "Five sausages?"

"Yes five, two up front, three more after I capture them."

The darker dog took that opportunity to nip at the man's calves, ripping the leggings but doing no real harm. The butcher whirled again and caught the darker beast across the shoulder before it could dart out of reach. It bristled even more, lips curling back over long fangs in a drawn out snarl.

"How's an old woman like you going to stop beasts like this?" he grunted out between swings.

Sarenka almost turned to see who he was addressing before remembering that her illusions were of an elderly woman. Once set, she seldom thought on the specifics of an illusion. Instead, she focused on trickling a steady stream of energy to keep them going.

"I've had some experience training dogs like these."

He shook his head.

Sarenka shrugged her shoulders, turning to leave. There were easier ways to earn food. She'd acted out of pity for the animals and stood no chance without the first part of the bribe.

"Ahhhh!" The butcher screeched. "Wait! Wait!"

She turned back.

The man alternated between wrapping a rag around his bitten calf, and waving the knife wildly about. "Five it is! Just get them away from me."

The dogs growled at him, darting in to take more nips with haunches raised. Blood ran in a thin stream down the shoulder of the darker animal.

Sarenka hurried forward, careful to move behind the butcher rather than get between him and the dogs. Snagging two large sausages on the point of her knife, she lopped them in half and tucked two pieces under her belt before moving forward, holding the other two halves out to the dogs.

"Hey!" She shouted and waved the food.

As expected, they swung around to face her, low growls rolling out of their throats at this new threat.

While they were distracted, the Butcher charged one of the animals, knife held out in front of him for a killing blow.

Sarenka's heart leapt into her throat.

The dog snapped at the man.

He jumped away, but not before receiving a slashing bite across the forearm for his foolishness.

"You idiot! Keep out of this if you value your life." *Or mine.* She knew better than to add that last. This was Burmtin, the man would step over her body if she fell to the ground right in front of him.

He backed away, placing himself flush up against the edge of the table. Blood seeped around the hand clutching his arm, streaking the rent fabric red.

She returned her attention to the animals and waved the meat in the air again.

They lifted their heads, scenting the freshly cut sausage.

"Is this what you want?" She dropped her voice into the soothing tone that most animals responded well to.

Ears perking, they cocked their heads and looked from her to the angry butcher.

The knife slipped through his bloodied fingers, landing on the ground.

The dogs growled and advanced.

His fear filled eyes darted from the meat, to the dogs, to Sarenka.

"Come on. Come on." She stepped forward and waved the meat in front of them again.

Growling, they advanced on her.

Waving the meat to keep their attention, Sarenka moved back a step, and then another, luring the dogs farther away.

Their ears came forward, and the fur along their back settled down as they realized she was offering food instead of a fight.

At last she dropped the meat at her feet and cooed to them.

"Here you go. Come on. It's all yours."

All the fight went out of the animals, and they moved forward, tails giving small wags of acknowledgment. After swallowing the sausage almost whole, they started to grab at the sausage tucked into her belt, but instead of a vicious yank at the meat, they moved slowly, drawing their lips back and trying to touch only the meat.

She held up a finger and said no with enough snap to revive their former training.

They ducked their heads with shame.

She wrestled the piece they'd tried to grab in half—coating her gloves with the greasy fat in the process—and hand fed the dogs, careful to keep her fingers clear of their teeth. After letting them lick the grease from her gloves, she rubbed their heads, giving them affection and building trust before daring to lean in close enough to examine their leather collars. Both were of the same make, fine tooled leather with expensive metal latches. She handed the rest of the sausage to the dogs, commanded them to heel, and strolled back to the butcher.

He frowned, gaze shifting from her face, to where her hands rested lightly on the dog's heads, then back up to her face.

"I'll have those other three sausages now," Sarenka stated.

"They aren't gone yet." The butcher used his chin to motion to the dog on her left, crossed his arms, squinted his eyes, and stuck his jaw forward stubbornly. "And I'm of a mind to think they belonged to you from the start."

"Suit yourself." She shrugged and turned to the dogs. "Stay."

Ears held at alert, they sat down and watched her walk away with a whine.

She heard the butcher's feet shuffle against cobblestone as he started towards the counter.

A double chorus of growls sprang up.

"Wait!" he shouted.

She turned around. The dogs were staring at the butcher with lips peeled back over their teeth and hair rising on their shoulders in a ruff.

"Here, take the sausage. Just get those beasts out of here, and make sure they don't ever come back."

Sarenka gave a short whistle.

The dogs turned their heads towards her, and their ears went up as their heads tilted.

She whistled again and both dogs raced to her.

"I'll do my best." She walked back with the dogs once more at her side and, taking the proffered sausages, couldn't help but add. "I might not be so fast to help next time I see you in need. A man who can't keep his word isn't worth saving."

She turned on her heel and strolled towards the nearest blacksmith, slicing off pieces of meat to toss the animals as she went. Upon arrival at the smoking building, she stopped to watch from across the street. The blacksmith, bare-chested and gleaming with sweat, moved from task to task, ignoring her. He seemed ordinary enough and she moved forward, hoping for a truthful answer in a city of lies.

The muscle bound man glanced up from sharpening a blade against a stone and paused in the middle of creating an ear deafening screech. "Help you, grandma?"

Sarenka removed one of the collars and passed it to the man. "I'm searching for the smith who made these."

He turned the collar over several times. "That's Danielson's work. Three streets over that way." He pointed north. "Stop when you see the house with the giant shell in the yard. Then turn right and go until you see the green house that looks like it puked its insides out, and from there you need to go three more houses and turn left... or is it right... no it's left. Should be right around the corner from there."

"Thank you." Sarenka retrieved the collar and put it on the dog before starting north. She talked to the dogs as she walked. "That made about as much sense as spitting at the double moons. House that looks like it puked its insides out... what's that supposed to mean anyway?"

They stared up at her and whined.

"I agree, people are no damn good. Go with the hot Falksfall Poodle every time."

After numerous stops for more directions, and blank stares when she asked about the vomit green house, she finally found it. She stood across the street, staring with amazement. It had more broken furniture sitting outside than she thought could have ever fit inside.

"Well, I guess that's what he meant." She rubbed the darker dog's head without thinking.

The dogs looked from her to the house with quizzical expressions on their faces.

"And that just proves my point. People are mind-lost too."

She searched the skies and set off again in the direction of a column of smoke. "Come on, it has to be close."

The smithy, when she finally found it, was a building made from the ribs of some mammoth animal, topped with a large blue hammer.

Billows of smoke gusted into her face, forcing her to cough. She looked about, searching for the owner, and found it surprisingly tidy for Burmtin, though cobwebs lay in the corners and surfaces were dusted with a light coating of ash. In the central area a fire roared, next to a trough of water and a great slab of polished tant wood.

She nodded, unsurprised. In Burmtin metal would be stolen unless carefully guarded. The tant wood was tough enough for smithing almost anything and nearly impervious to heat. And even then, the smith had probably buried the forge so deep that it would take a great rinol beast to pull it free.

Nearby, a white haired elder sat on a three legged stool, chewing on a haunch of meat.

She walked forward with a nod.

He dropped the meat into a bucket and hobbled forward, rubbing hands down his leather apron. "How might I help the missus?"

She took in his brawny arms. Despite his age, he was still virile enough to work his own smithy. "Are you Danielson?"

"That I am."

She knelt to remove a collar from one of the dogs then held it out to the blacksmith. "Did you make these?"

"Aye, I know this collar. Made up six of 'em for the sentries on the west gate. Guessin' these dogs belong to them."

One of the dogs bumped his hand, begging for attention.

With a fond smile, he rubbed behind its ears. "Beautiful creatures, aren't they?"

"That they are. Thank you." Sarenka smiled, turning to leave.

"Hey..."

She turned back and found him staring downwards, with hat in hand, scuffing the ground with his toe.

"The misses, she passed away last year, and I've got a mighty nice house that's become real empty like, and I thought, maybe..." He coughed. "Maybe you might care to come over for a friendly sweet-drink or some dinner sometime."

Sarenka gave a sympathetic smile, but she couldn't bring herself to lie, even to save his feelings. "I'm sorry. I can't."

Danielson's face fell.

"There's a woman who visits the Burmtin Inn on midweek night for a brandy. She seems a bit lonely. If you happened to be there having your sweet-drink at the same time…"

He just stared at her, uncomprehending.

"Well, who knows—" Sarenka tipped her head and lifted one shoulder—"she might take a shine to you."

Suddenly understanding, he flushed and remained silent as Sarenka turned away. When the sound of a hammer beating against metal started, Sarenka sighed, picking up her pace. Poor dear was old enough to be her grandfather. She ducked into the nearest alley and sat on the hard packed dirt, pulling her concealing cloak about her shoulders and face before letting go of the illusions.

"Stay," she told the dogs, eyes drifting closed.

Their warm bodies settled down on either side of her, and one great head landed in her lap. Scratching lazily at his ears, she rested, glad to have eaten before dealing with the Butcher. She'd need all her energy for what lay ahead.

She started awake and was pleased to find the dogs still with her. Settling the illusions back into place, she glanced at the sky. Midday. With luck, she could get these dogs back to their owners, earn a bit of d'yroap, and have the rest of her day free.

But they weren't going to the west garrison. This was an opportunity too perfect to pass up. The dogs would help her meet the guard that her tavern sources said could be bribed. She strode towards the east gate with the dogs at her side drawing an uncomfortable amount of attention. Upon reaching the east garrison, she drew back into the shadows and stared across the open ground with a shudder.

"Sure hope I'm not turning myself in with this mind-lost idea."

The lighter dog bumped his head up under her hand.

Absentmindedly, she rubbed its ear and wished she could feel its silky fur through the gloves.

This part of her plan was tricky. If she ended up behind bars for thievery, it would only be a matter of time before her illusions dropped and they realized she was the Freni-Kyn from the posters. Acting like she had nothing to hide Sarenka marched forward and was relieved to find none of the soldiers lingering outside. Upon reaching the garrison door, she lifted her hand to knock, and stopped. From behind the door came a low garble. She tilted her head and unfurled her ears, lifting them to hear better, positive someone had said 'Freni-Kyn.'

The dogs next to her mimicked the movement.

Silence.

Surely her overactive imagination was at work.

She lifted her hand to knock again, but stayed it as the voices rose and 'Freni-Kyn' drifted out, this time distinctly.

Darting glances around the area and finding no observers, Sarenka stole to a side window and peered through the glass. Her heart soared. Talking within the room was the same man she had trailed twice that week, watching his habits and learning his weaknesses and strengths. Rumored to be bribable, he was her key out of the city, and today she'd make her connection.

Another man stood with his back to her, gray of head and lean of body.

"I'm telling you, if I caught that Freni-Kyn bitch murderer, I'd be so rich that I'd buy a new hut. No, I'd buy me a mansion and get me some slaves to lick my ass after I took a shit."

Sarenka's heart plummeted into a painful flip-flop, and she put a hand over her mouth.

The gray head laughed gruffly. "Good luck finding someone willing to do that for your sorry self. But a Kyn woman, what I wouldn't give to hire a night with one of those."

The younger man snorted. "Forget that. My fun'll be watching them rip the skin from her murdering face. Bet they pull her nails out one by one too. Her screams'll be what I think of every time I spend one of those loops, get me hard as a rail, it will."

The gray haired man turned away. "Gah! You're a sick bastard, Brandon. Need to get your head checked."

Despair clutched Sarenka's heart.

She sank to her heels and covered her ears, not wanting to hear more.

Brandon's voice rose, loud with excitement. "I wonder if they'd let me have her nails. Or better yet, her ears. No! Her breasts. I'd make pouches for my d'yroap coin, big floppy boob pouches."

"Okay, that's enough. That's not funny. You're turning my stomach."

"You're a wimp, Carlton. Bet your momma had you tied to her garters. You should take the bribes like everyone else. Captain Lator's paying tons for that girl. Could set yourself up fine and dandy with it. Get that fishing shack you're always on about."

The sound of wood scraping against wood came.

"It's time for the noon meal. You coming with me?"

Sarenka scrambled to her feet at the sound of approaching footsteps. It was too late to run. She had to finish this. Her gloved hand was poised to knock as the door swung open. Pretending to be startled, she backed away.

"What you want, old woman?" Brandon asked.

"Got a couple of dogs I'm trying to sell. Trained them for guard duty myself."

"Get out of here, you filthy whore. We don't need those mangy mutts." He kicked at the dog which had dared to sniff his shiny boots. Used to life on the streets, the darker dog dodged the man's foot and exposed its teeth in a snarl.

The other man's grasped Brandon's shoulder. "Hold a moment. I happen to be in need of a dog or two. How much you want for them?"

"For you, one gold. For him—" she nodded towards Brandon— "one hundred."

"Why you fuckin' little..." Brandon raised his hand and stepped towards Sarenka.

Parian threw his arms out, trying to ward off sticks as they flew past, and landed on his face in the mud. He listened to the sounds of Rosalie's thunder through the undergrowth grow distant and hurled himself over onto his back. Through an opening in the trees, clouds drifted across the surface of the double moons.

Twigs broke as something large approached.

"How many times? How many times are you going to take off after prey without warning?"

Rosalie nudged his head with her nose. *~I couldn't help myself. It jumped.~*

He sat up and scrutinized his mud-encrusted body. "For a psychic cat..."

~I'm not retarded.~

"I didn't say that."

~You thought it.~

"I didn't."

~Well, then finish the thought.~ She nuzzled his head and began to lick the hair.

"Stop. Damn it. That hurts and I've told you before. I don't need help getting clean." Running his hands over his face and hair, he scooped up masses

~You're deflecting.~

"A throwback. Okay. You're a throwback."

Rosalie began cleaning her fur. *~And what, pray tell, led you to that conclusion?~*

"Really? You just threw me off to chase... what? A bat? Or was that a tiny owl? Does it even matter?"

~It matters to me. A seabat.~

"A seabat? An inland seabat?"

~And this is why I do not tell you what I'm chasing.~

"Fine!" He threw up his hands. "I give up. An inland seabat. The point is, you threw me off to chase it, and you tell me you can't help it. Which is why I say you're a throwback. All of that's supposed to be bred out of you."

~Well,~ she snorted, *~where's the fun in that?~*

"It's not a matter of fun, it's about safe transportation."

~Is that all I am? Your pack horse?~

"No, of course not. But Rosalie, please, have a heart. I'd like to live to see twenty-five."

She pounced, running at him full speed.

He yelped and threw out his hands.

At the last moment, she veered off, grabbing the back of his shirt as she passed. With a jolt, she tossed him into the air and kept running.

He landed on his stomach across her back. "Rosalieeee!"

CHAPTER 23

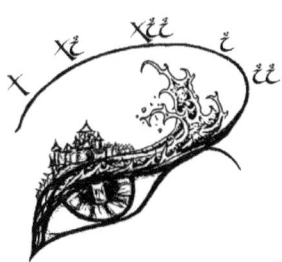

"Found along the Southern Coastline, the small trading city of Burmtin was overrun in the great Watrelk Invasion of 01 AB. After clearing out the leaders of the city, the Watrelks soon tired of living on land and struck a deal with the Red Pelican Assassins' Guild. In exchange for free run of the city, the guild would replace the city's leaders.

The rest of the tale, forbidden to discuss in most places, is one of corruption and greed. While the originator of the Red Pelican was intent on vengeance only, his followers were soon entranced by the lure of d'yroap for death. Today the city is known for its booming slave and Foreveron trade."

Szeto Meili

Upland Steep's Record of Histories

It is interesting to note that shortly after writing this, Szeto's dead body was found with a Red Pelican Death Card in her mouth.

The moons crossed, and the sun crept half way across the sky before D'trav staggered to his feet. His cloak lay where he'd dropped it, a forgotten pile of rough brown cloth, and the only belonging they hadn't shredded. He hid his nakedness within its folds and limped towards the only place in Burmtin he'd ever found comfort.

When he staggered in the back door of the Distinguished Dainties, a gigolo shrieked and ran away.

D'trav snorted. "I'm sure as cotton I do look a sight, but that's just downright ridiculous."

Unable to walk a straight line, he drifted from wall to wall down the corridor, calling for Camille.

She arrived, flanked by guards, face filled with wrath. Two strides away she placed her hands on her hips and stopped.

She'll lock me up again for sure. I oughta run. Glancing over his shoulder brought a wave of dizziness, and he found himself leaning against the wall instead of running.

"Now you listen here, you low-life drunk, you just can't come barging in the back door like that, this isn't some cheap, pay-by-favor-place you know, you take your…" Her eyes widened and she took a step forward.

He tried to smile but only one side of his lip lifted.

"D'trav? Oh my god. What have they done to you?"

He took a step forward, and staggered.

She rushed to keep him from falling over. "Help him you idiots! Now!"

The guards grabbed him by both arms.

Pain lanced through where the whip cuts into his arms, and he screamed, "No, don't touch me!"

Startled, they let go.

D'trav staggered forward and fell to his knees.

Camille pulled back the cloak and gasped. "Pick him up. Get him into the room next to mine. Don't touch his arms."

After he'd been laid out on her velvet covered bed, she moved over his body, examining each cut and rubbing sweet smelling balms onto them. "Red Pelican?"

"I'd be dead."

"Who then?"

D'trav licked his split lip. How much did he dare tell her? Too much and she'd go seeking revenge, a risk he wasn't willing to take. "Not sure."

"Roll him over," she told the guards.

"No!" D'trav gripped the bedding, determined to fight.

"D'trav, we have to treat all the cuts."

"They didn't hurt my back."

Camille regarded him with narrowing eyes. "Did you do this to yourself?"

"Not this time."

"Better not have, you can't go back down that path."

"I didn't. I Promise."

Camille nodded at the guards, "You can go. He's in no shape to hurt me."

He waited for the door to shut before saying, "I wouldn't hurt you."

"I know."

"Camille, I'm sorry."

"Wait until you're better."

"No, this needs be said."

"That's not fair, you're a mess." She sighed and sat down on the edge of the bed. "How can we have a proper fight right now?"

"Not gonna fight you, darlin. Done had my fill of that already."

"We had an agreement."

"Yes, that we'd tell each other. And I would've, in juicy detail."

She glanced away. "That was before."

"'Fore what? 'Fore you slept with that blond god, what looked like he was fit to be king? Or 'fore the Frevell with the pink hair?"

"Still…"

"Still what? I kept that agreement to the Kyron-be-damned letter. I told you every damn time I took another woman, and you did the same for me."

"She was in chains. And that's our thing."

"So, chains? That's why you got all riled up?"

She met his eyes, finally. "Yes, because of the chains."

"I couldn't resist." He stroked her arm. "She was kneelin' there, tellin' me she'd do anything. Anything. And that damnable chain hooked to her ankle, I nearly came just lookin' at her."

Camille pinched her lips together and stared pointedly at his hardening member. "You're not helping your case."

"Camille, you know me. I can't resist the chains."

She stood up and stepped to the window, her back to him.

"Please Camille."

"New agreement. No chains with anyone but me."

D'trav didn't answer. It was a promise he wasn't sure he could keep.

She walked back and stood over him, chin held high. "It won't happen again, D'trav. I won't have it."

"Okay, Camille, agreed."

"The rest of the agreement stands as is. You sleep with whoever you want, male or female, and I do likewise. And we tell each other, same as before. No secrets."

"Agreed."

"I'll be back in a while."

"Don't lock me in."

She frowned and her eyes turned sad. "You idiot, I did that to protect you. If nobody saw you, nobody could report you."

"I ran outta water and had no food."

"The tub."

"Stopped working."

"Oh." Her mouth rounded and brows rose. "Oh dear, I'd never have done that on purpose. Surely you know."

"I do now."

"There was food in the pantry." She gestured at a corner of her room.

"Weren't no pantry."

"How can you not know that every one of our rooms has a pantry?" Camille walked to the far corner and pushed a gilded flower that was a part of the carved décor. A click sounded and a small door popped open. Reaching in, she retrieved a jar of peaches and brought them to him.

His mouth watered as he took them from her. "Don't mind if'n I do."

"There's always a couple of week's worth of preserved food in there. Never know when a client will want an extended visit."

"Never took to dinin' here, darlin. Can't know somthin' I never did see."

He struggled with the lid, but his muscles were still sore and weak.

She took it from him, opened it, and handed it over along with a small knife. "I'll be back in a while, you rest."

Mouth full, D'trav mumbled an okay.

Hours later, D'trav wearily opened his eyes at the sound of the door clicking closed.

"We've got problems." Camille burst out. "Your face has been plastered across town. Wanted posters everywhere. And that Freni-Kyn still hasn't been caught. Shaving your head's good, but you've got to do more."

"Like what?"

She opened a drawer and withdrew a needle and a bottle.

D'trav scrambled to sit up despite the pain.

She placed her hand on his chest and pushed him back down. "Oh stop. I'm just going to ink you."

"No!"

"Yes I am." She walked across the room and poured water into a bowl, along with a dab of soap powder, before returning to his side carrying it. "But first we need to clean you up."

"You already done cleaned me up."

"That was just some ointments. You need a thorough cleaning, or you'll end up infected." With gentle strokes, she rubbed away the filth of the last two weeks. "About that girl…"

"Sarenka."

"Yes, she's not going to forget you."

"She's a Foreveron addict."

Camille grimaced. "So she's dying."

"Nobody's gonna sell her antidote."

"How long's she got?"

"Few months at most. Never heard of anyone lastin' longer."

Camille dabbed at his wounds, silent for a while.

"You need the inking, D'trav. It'll save your life."

"I'm not doin' it."

"No. You aren't. I am."

"You can't."

"I've been trained. I'm really quite good."

"That's not what I meant. You can't do this to me."

"What?"

"Poke me with that—that needle."

She giggled. "I forgot. You're afraid of them."

"Not afraid. It's normal caution. And you aren't doin' it."

"Yes, I am. And if I have to have the guards hold you down for this, I will."

Reminded, D'trav turned his head away. His heart banged in his chest. He gulped and considered telling her what had happened the night before. Color rose in his cheeks as shame washed over him. "Not that."

"Dear god, you're frightened half to death." Camille stood up and went to the cabinet. "Fine, take this. It'll knock you out for a few hours while I get it done."

He drank the potion, grateful for the woozy drowsiness that drove away the memory.

Unwilling to back away and angered by what she'd heard Brandon say through the walls, Sarenka flinched but stood her ground. Her training kicked in, and she shifted her weight to one leg, flexed her knee, and prepared for a kick to Brandon's groin.

Brandon slammed his fist towards Sarenka's eye.

Carlton caught Brandon's hand and knocked him backwards.

Struggling against the grip, Brandon tried to jerk his hand loose.

Letting go, Carlton snagged the front of Brandon's tunic and balled his other hand into a fist. He pulled Carlton forward, glaring into his eyes with their noses a hair width apart. "She obviously knows which of us will treat them right. You *will not* touch her on *my* shift. I'm not going to be punished for another one of your stupid childish rages."

Brandon growled and shoved himself free before turning back to the hut, entering it, and slamming the door behind him.

Carlton brushed down the front of his uniform and turned back to Sarenka.

"Thank you," she said.

"Now, one gold…" He pulled two gold d'yroap free of a pouch and reached down to rub at the darker dog's bare neck, scratching along the flattened line where his collar had been. Pinching the gold oval between forefinger and thumb he held it out to her and palmed the other metal loop. "I'll give you another gold if you sell me a pair of collars."

Sarenka snatched the gold from the man's hand before he could change his mind and stooped to pet the dogs. "You two be good, he'll take care of you. I know a good dog man when I see one."

They licked her face, nuzzling under her chin like puppies, and she considered the guard's offer of the second gold. He might think she'd stolen the dogs if she gave him the collars. On the other hand, she had no use for the collars, and selling them to a fence would earn only a few silvers. One gold bought a lot to drink and eat in a town like Burmtin. She licked her lips at the thought.

He's a dog-man, can't be that bad. Risking everything, she opened her pouch and produced the animal's collars. She pressed the collars to her chest, concealing the makers-mark behind the palm of her hand.

"Hand me the gold first."

He flipped the coin, sending it spinning end over end into the air.

She snatched it from the air and deftly tucked it into her corset before holding out the collars.

He grabbed her arm.

Startled, she pulled back.

He let her arm slide through his grip until it reached her wrist and encircled it in an iron grip that pinched, even through the glove.

She looked from her captive wrist to his face with trepidation.

He peered into her eyes, searching for truth.

She tensed, hoping that a sudden jerk would free her arm and allow her to outrun him.

"You be sure and bring me any more dogs you... raise." Giving a curt nod, he loosened his grip and slid his hand down to the grasp the collars.

"I'll do that." She let the collars go and strolled away with a prickle between her shoulder blades.

From behind, the dogs whined a dejected farewell.

With the danger past, depression settled in a heavy cloak over her shoulders. Though elated at the earning of two gold d'yroap, the loss of her ticket out of Burmtin was devastating. Just as she'd been promised, Brandon was bribable and would help anyone out of the city, except a Freni-Kyn. She dared not trust him with her life. If her illusions slipped, he'd turn on her as surely as a vespra-lanir would rip the flesh from bone in seconds.

Carlton, on the other hand...

She stopped.

No, he's too honest, too good hearted to help a murderess escape.

Her shoulders slumped as she started walking again.

She tucked herself into the nearest quiet alley and rested, wearied at the thought of yet more time in the dreaded city that had become her prison. Time and again, her mind circled back to Brandon's harsh words, and the torturous pictures he had put into her mind.

A tear trickled down her cheek.

I'm doomed, trapped forever.

Everywhere she turned dead ends loomed, blocking her path.

No... Survival is what really matters.

She pushed the pain, along with her hopes for freedom, into the darkened recesses of her heart, and turned to the matter of earning her evening meal. Though she was two golds richer, she'd save those loops for a bribe, if she ever found someone who *could* be bribed.

D'trav stared at the swirling pinks, blues, greens, and greys, trying to figure out what they were as they gradually swam into focus. When he realized that he'd been staring at the abalone inlaid ceiling for a long time, he moved and groaned and gazed down at his bare body.

"Kyron-damn-it, Camille! I didn't ask to be lookin' like some handmade doll."

He started to touch the stitches above his left nipple but instantly regretted moving so fast. With effort, he rolled to the side and forced himself to stand and immediately hunched over. Moving handhold by handhold along the edge of the bed, he reached the mirror, and stared at a new man. She was right. He looked a lot different with his head shaved and the inking.

He peered closer.

"And a crap ton of piercings."

With disbelief, he touched one of the rows over his eyebrow then turned his head to examine his ear and finished the examination by touching the ones sticking out of his nose.

"Look like I done joined a M'hakru war campaign. Even I wouldn't know me from the dog next door, if'n I saw me on the streets."

He snarled at himself in the mirror and flinched when it pulled the new piercings.

From the other side of the door came the sound of heavy footsteps and loud voices.

D'trav whirled around, gasped, and almost fell over. He grabbed a stone candlestick and waited. The Red Pelican wouldn't take him without a fight.

Camille threw open the door and glared at him. She slammed it behind her and stalked across the room. "What are you doing up?"

"They here for me?"

CHAPTER 24

"Get back in bed."

"Camille. Answer me. Who's here?"

"This is all your fault."

He stared at her flushed cheeks and half lowered the candlestick. She looked angry, not afraid.

"They wouldn't be here at all if you hadn't made such a terrible mess." She sounded on the verge of crying.

"Camille. Who?" He lifted the candlestick and turned towards the door.

"And how could you have done that to all those shoes? How could you?"

D'trav was so relieved that his knees collapsed, and he landed on the edge of the bed. He cried out as a million different places screamed at him to stop moving all at the same time.

Camille turned pale. "Lay down, you dumb ox."

"Camille I had no choice, I done thought you…"

"I what?"

"Never mind."

Her lips thinned, and she began to push him back towards the bed. "Lay down. Now."

"Don't be mad, please."

"I'd never give anyone to them. No matter what they did."

"Everyone has a breaking point."

"You don't know me at all."

"I was wrong."

The thumping outside the door resumed, and D'trav reached for the candlestick.

Camille snatched it from his hand and slammed it down on the tabletop hard enough to snap it in half. "Well, that's just one more thing broken because of you. Those--those stomping, mud covered feet—are the workers come to fix things. I won't have water for the next week due to the mess you made of that room."

"How's it my fault the water's not workin' right?"

"The Glidarths are refusing to work on the water stuff until the room's been cleaned and sanitized and smells like it should. And you know they're the only ones with enough skill to work mechanics."

"Oh." His face heated as he remembered what he'd done to that room.

"I've got to feed my people every night." She grabbed half the broken candlestick and threw it across the room. "With no water!

"I've got to give them water to wash away the sex at the end of the day." She picked the other half up and threw it too. "With no water!"

She flounced over to the door and threw it open before turning to glare at him.

Embarrassed, he looked away and saw his face turn a deeper shade of red in the mirror.

"And on top of all that, in six days I've got a famous Watrelk diplomat coming into town who wants his women in the water. Now you tell me. What am I going to do?" She stomped out, slamming the door behind her.

D'trav stared at the ceiling. He couldn't fix this week's problems with the state his body was in, but he'd see that the Watrelk had his water, even if he had to lug it home from the well himself.

Other than the occasional leaps after prey, and Rosalie's continued upset over the Claw Lake incident, their arrival in Refuge a few days later was without incident. Parian peered at the whitewashed Inn askance, and even Rosalie stopped walking to stare. It leaned crookedly, looking like it needed shoring up on one side, and what little remained of the paint was blistered and peeling as if the wood itself had leprosy.

~*You're going to sleep in that?*~

He sighed. "I'm afraid so."

He dismounted and walked forward, tugging at the reins until she followed.

Rosalie lifted her head and sniffed as they passed the adjoining stable but said nothing.

Parian tied her off out front and went in without warning her to behave. Her mouth around his neck had convinced him that treating her as a companion instead of a beast of burden was wiser. When he returned she was washing herself down, licking dust from black fur that shone sleek in the daylight.

He reached for the reins and stopped, gaze jumping from post to post. They were all destroyed, whittled into ragged splinters. He peered at Rosalie. ~*What did you do?*~

~*I had to.*~

Glancing around to make sure nobody was watching, he quickly untied her and led her towards the stable. ~*You had to tear them up?*~

~*They were pointy.*~

~*You can't just chew people's things up.*~

~*But they were pointy.*~

~*Look, you——*~ He was pulled up short and realized that she'd stopped walking. He turned around. She was sitting on her haunches in a manner that he knew only too well. She was not going to budge unless he could talk some sense into her. ~*What now?*~

~*I'm not staying here.*~

~*Yes you are.*~

~They have fleas.~

~And you know this how?~

~I can hear them.~

Parian groaned. ~Rosalie, please, this is hard enough without— ~

~Can you whistle?~

~What?~

~Like that man near Falksfall? The one who didn't like your scars.~

~Yes, of course. But what does that have to do with— ~

~Look, Freni-Kyn, you can stay in that flea infested building, but I'm not going to. So let me run. I'll come back when you whistle.~

Parian scratched his head, unsure.

~I promise.~

~What will you eat?~

She lifted her paw, extended the nails, and licked them. ~I'll make do.~

Parian paled. ~You can't eat people.~

~There's plenty else to appease my appetite."

~You can't eat their sheep either.~

~Could you not smell the hare that darted alongside the road as we entered town? The birds? The mice?~

~The mice?~

~Okay. I admit, that's a snack at most, but I can manage for however long you need.~

Nodding, he returned to her side.

She rubbed her teeth across the side of his cheekbone.

He scrubbed the thick fur under her chin and unsaddled her.

With a shake that sent fur flying, she bounded away. ~Just whistle.~

Parian lugged the bags back to the inn and went to his room. After clearing the space by pushing all the furniture to the edges, he laid down for the night.

Dawn arrived with a wash of grey. Rain fell in silver sheets, hitting the window panes and seeping in around the edges. He examined puddles under the window and decided that the inn's upkeep wasn't his problem and that Rosalie would find a place to hole up. Pulling forth a hank of jerky and some chalk, he started drawing.

A week after selling the dogs, Sarenka hunched further forward and walked towards the well, one shoulder lower than the other, rags wrapped around her feet, imitating the shuffle of the homeless elderly. She leaned wearily against a rough stone wall, only half acting. Though desperate to rest, she must wait for the sun to set before returning to the pen.

"Need a new place to sleep," she mumbled.

A man turned to look at her and shuffled sideways, creating a larger space between them.

Sarenka smiled grimly, acting insane was a proven strategy for warding off strangers.

Her thoughts returned to the problem. The pen was too dangerous now. At dawn she'd been forced to pretend at petting the animals through the cage, while actually locking it. The owner had snarled and thrust his staff at her, and she had barely missed catching it full in the face.

She pushed a fingertip under the edge of her belt and scratched, wincing at skin made raw by too many days in unwashed clothing. A rivulet of sweat ran down the small of her back, and the pungency of her stained clothing was so strong that she shifted positions, but there was no avoiding her own stench. She sighed and thought longingly of the infrequent baths in the animal's water trough. The day had been long and without a breeze, and her hood had been up for hours. The odor, the discomfort, those were the price of anonymity. Licking dry lips, Sarenka limped away, heading for an area frequented primarily by servants and the *ne'er-do-well*.

Dressed in clothing barely better than her own, a passing couple began singing a duet, their voices a lovely mix of high and low notes.

Ears lifting beneath her illusions, Sarenka paused to savor the melody. She closed her eyes while the tension drained from her shoulders, and the corner of her lips began to lift.

A loud screeching sprang up.

Sarenka's eyes flew open, and she cringed and dropped her ears, trying to muffle the sound.

Nearby a red-faced toddler, dressed in silks and fine leather, threw himself to the ground and kicked his legs. His parents stood over him arguing about whose fault it was for spoiling the child.

"Please don't let them stay," she whispered, gazing past them at the well. "Please, please, please."

The mother finally scooped the child up, all the while snapping at the father with a high pitched voice. To Sarenka's relief, they left, working their way northwards across the square. As the wail faded, she picked up the harmony of the singing couple again.

Sarenka grimaced, "Just like the rest of my day."

Her life had established a rhythm of its own, each day carrying on the tempo of the day before with percussional differences: the unwitting drop of a silver loop by a stranger, the find of a scarf which could be traded for sweet-drink, the discarded crusts of bread behind taverns. Each event adding to the song of desperation her life had become. And beneath it all, underscoring that desperate melody, the steady thud of her heart, crying out for freedom from the corruption that was Burmtin.

Today there was no rhythm; there was just the discordance of broken shells and lustrous pearls, clanking and grating against each other, disappointing and seducing all at the same time; the gnawing ache of foreveron addiction screeching against the satisfying nourishment of a pilfered hunk of meat; pleasant strolls down cobblestone streets crashing against watching every safe passage out of Burmtin crumble into abandoned sandcastles.

Sheltered within the shadows of an overhanging ledge, she stared across the cobblestoned clearing towards the well. A throbbing band of pain settled across her temples at the necessity of wearing a stranger's face, day in, day out. She was tired. So tired. Her last attempt to hold an illusion had been an abysmal failure, dispelling within the turn of an hourglass. Her eyes started to drift closed. She stifled a yawn and shifted to her other foot, fighting off the urge to sleep. This would be her last opportunity to get water before dark, and every youngling knew better than to visit the well after the sun set.

Tapping fingertips, she counted out the days of the week and considered her options. Tonight would be too busy to sleep behind the taverns by the wharf. New ships had arrived earlier, and the pirates would be letting off steam and spending their ill-begotten loot. Her best bet was an alley behind a tailor that she'd dubbed 'the weasel' for the way his nose twitched every time his beady eyes turned in her direction. The exterior wall near his chimney stayed warm on chilly nights, giving some little comfort. That settled, she turned her attention back to the drifting crowds of people, half of them with hoods pulled forward to cover their faces.

Burmtin was a city of secrets.

Noting the path of the shadows across the square, she gauged the angle of the sun and decided that she had been watching for dangers long enough to be sure nobody was checking faces. She leaned over and pulled the rags from her feet and dropped the old woman imitation. After coughing pointedly and scratching at her ankles, she straightened, darting glances about to be sure nobody had seen.

Now, while the sun danced on the edge of the world, flirting with darkness, and coolness drifted in, she was grateful for the pilfered cloak and ragged scarf. She just hoped the stench of her unwashed body didn't draw unnecessary attention.

D'trav checked the flat bed wagon again. He had every clean pail he could find loaded up and ready for the trip to the well. He gestured to a ragtag group of gigolos, harlots, and maids, and they leapt onto the edge of the wagon. He twisted around and flinched. Damned if he didn't still hurt in way too many places, but he could dress himself now. Soon he'd be well enough to exact the revenge his name promised.

He lifted his reins and shouted, "Yeih!"

The cats flicked their ears back and started forward. He frowned. Cats were terrible for pulling wagons. If they were to heat the water before the Watrelk arrived, this needed to be quick. At this rate it'd be a week before they arrived, and snapping the reins could lead to some pretty volatile results.

"Come on you old goats, speed it up. Yeih! Yeih!"

They picked up the pace, steadily moving faster, and were soon swinging wildly around corners. He held on with whitened fists as the wagon tilted up onto two wheels. It seemed the trip would get finished this year after all.

Scanning the cobblestoned area one last time, Sarenka's gaze traveled down the line of people who had come to draw from the moss speckled well. She shifted uneasily, lingering over the dandy standing at the end. His velvet trousers, bleached linen shirt, and brocade doublet were a stark contrast to the humble cottons worn by everyone else.

He'd make a good mark—no—he shouldn't be here. Not in that manicured outfit. Not twitching nervously and looking over his shoulder.

The impatient foot tapping and anxious glances were such obvious signs of frayed nerves that the people in front of him pushed forward, trying to create distance between themselves and him.

What's he here for, a duel? She studied his ornate sheath and decided it probably contained a show sword.

So not a duel.

Then what?

He retrieved a beribboned box from his pocket.

Her eyes narrowed with increasing interest as he placed the box back in his pocket then drew it forth again. While he repeated the gesture several times, she wavered on the edge of the square, hoping his hand would slip and the precious contents spill to the ground.

She licked cracked lips and her gaze shifted past him to the well. Thirst was an ever present companion on the streets of Burmtin, one that tormented with salt-laden breezes and sandy streets and would not be denied its due. Despite the unknown dangers he represented, she turned her features H'euman, darkened both hair and skin, and took a step towards the promise of fresh water. Using the pretense of dodging fresh animal excrement, she kept her head down.

A cloud of cologne engulfed her as she stepped behind the dandy, its spicy sweetness reminding her of the refined Freni-Kyn society. She drew a deep breath, savoring the scent with longing. *If only that could be stolen.* She stared at his back and considered what valuables he might be carrying. The temptation to pick-pocket was almost strong enough to push her into a pretend stumble, but she held back. Her illusions were tenuous at best.

He drew from the well, filling his etched silver cup to overflowing, and then lingered while taking tentative sips. Peering past the edge of the cup, he searched up and down the street, eyes widening with expectation at the sight of a female figure. A smile formed, only to fade into disappointment moments later. Sarenka almost pitied him by the time her turn to attach a drinking-shell to the hook arrived, and as she reached a gloved hand for the hook a loud laugh rang out, causing her to dart a glance in that direction.

D'trav!

She'd never forget that face, not after believing she'd condemned him to death in order to save her own neck.

No! It can't be. I saw him, disemboweled, eyes plucked out...

Or did I?

No, I saw a face mauled beyond recognition and a pile of hair. D'trav's hair...

Is it him?

Is it really him?

She stared at the man, unable to pull her gaze away.

Shaved head, beard, tribal inks, piercings and one bar fight too many...

She shook her head.

Can't be him.

He reached up to scratch back and forth along his jawline in a move she had seen D'trav make every time he was making a decision.

Oh my god... it is him.

He's alive!

A barrage of raw emotion slammed through; relief, guilt, elation, fear; and her illusions faltered, crumbling away.

He marched across the crowded square towards her with a leather bucket in each hand and a string of men and women following.

She dropped her head and, with fingers gone suddenly numb, fumbled through pulling the cloak hood further forward.

A refined voice came from behind. "Don't I know you?"

Sarenka's cheeks went cold with fear.

She shook her head.

Don't say it. Please don't say it.

"Hey, you're that—"

CHAPTER 25

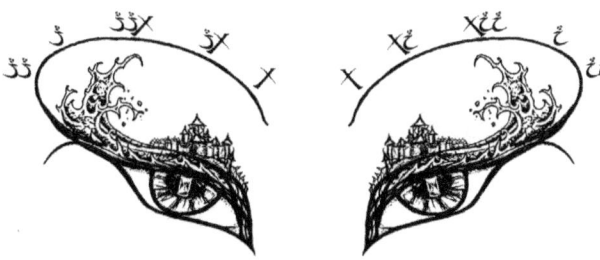

"It is said, in tomes leading back to The Betrayal, that Sad Town was named by the Watrelk Pirates after their leader was slain by a resident's arrow. Supposedly overcome by grief, the pirates sacked that area and took everything of value from it, leaving the residents destitute."

Ngai Xiaosi
Professor of Anthropology

Before the dandy could speak another word, she spun and threw an arm around his waist, hugging him close. The claws of her other hand pressed through the tips of her gloves, and into his shirt, piercing skin and drawing tiny spots of red against the white linen.

Grasping her wrist, he tried to pull it free.

Sarenka drove the nail-blades deeper.

Shock turned his face pale as he stared into her eyes.

"Say another word, and I'll make sure you need a surgeon. A good one." Her low hiss carried only so far as his ears. Taking in the H'euman wed-band on the hand clutching at her wrist, she smiled.

Perfect.

Pretending intimacy, Sarenka stepped closer and ran the hand on his back downwards in a blatant caress, ending it by clasping his butt for long enough to be noticed by onlookers.

He gulped and stared down at the growing blots of red.

The urge to run screamed through her head, telling her that creating such an embarrassing spectacle of the man was dangerous. Instead, she used her body to shield his bloodied chest from view.

D'trav voice came from behind the man's tall shoulders, jesting with the people in line about how long it was taking to get to the well.

"Darling, I told you we can't keep meeting here..." Her plaintive words rang out across the square. "Your wife will find out about us."

In a sarcastic undertone, she whispered, "I'll find out where she lives and tell her *all* about the two of us if you take this story to anyone."

The blood drained from his face, proof that her guess was correct. He was too well dressed to be loitering about the common well, and the small gift certainly had nothing to do with dueling. He'd come here for a liaison, and his mistress was late.

"Oooh, what's this? For me?" She held up the tiny beribboned box. "Thank you!"

His mouth opened but he snapped it shut at the look on her face. "Kiss me."

He hesitated, opening his mouth again as if to speak.

She pressed his head down to hers using the hand she'd been grasping his ass with, and by the time she finished the kiss, the man's cheeks had gone from death-pale to scarlet. His raised brows, and the expression of alarm on his face caused Sarenka to release his chest and pull him about.

"Hey! Bed her at the inn, lover-boy! And do be movin' your sorry ass outta the way," D'trav shouted.

An alarmed tingle went through Sarenka.

He's too close.

She locked her elbow through the man's, steering him towards a side street. "Walk away. Now. Don't turn around. Don't even look back. Go home to your wife and child and stay there."

When they reached the edge of the square, she pressed the sweetstick—which she had pilfered from his pocket during the fake caress—into his hand. "Here, your baby might want this."

"Know this, I'll be watching. If you tell anyone, I *will* come after you, your mistress, and your family. I've killed already. You know that from the posters. I'll do it again. Is that clear?"

He jerked his head in a stiff nod and started down the street, picking up speed until he was moving at a semi-run. Making sure he noticed, Sarenka trailed the frightened man before falling back and heading in the opposite direction. Her lies should buy a couple of hours.

Within the folds of her cloak, her fingers explored the edges of the tiny box, unable to tell much through the gloves. Undoubtedly a worthless trinket meant to keep a woman on the side, but possibly worth a copper or two when fenced. If she got lucky, he'd stay silent about the wanted murderess at the common well. She rolled her eyes at the thought. More likely, he was already running to the guards with a description. Better to pick a new well and steal new clothing.

"It's impossible. It's all impossible. How am I going to get out? Even getting water is…" her whisper trailed off as a man passed her going in the opposite direction. When his footsteps faded, she continued, "Every time I think I'll survive, something happens."

Shaking the coin pouch she'd taken from the man, she passed a storefront and grimaced at the sketch plastered there. In almost perfect detail, the newest rendition of her Freni-Kyn face stared back at her. A breeze picked at the edges of the parchment, and she regretted her decision not to study the forbidden magics.

How easy it'd be to create a wind and shred to pieces every wanted poster in this Kyron forsaken city.

R'kiax's eyes narrowed in on the Freni-Kyn woman walking away from the well. Without looking at the Watrelk Pirate, he held out the leather bag of d'yroap.

She's getting away!

The pirate shouldered the bag and glanced around before opening the canvas satchel on his hip. He peered into it, revealing the natural lines and dots that outlined his Watrelk eyes.

Rkiax's gaze shifted back and forth between the woman and the Watrelk.

At last the pirate plunged a beringed hand into the satchel and fumbled about. The clink of glass against stone arose.

"Come on, I need to go," R'kiax said.

The man froze and the black lines around his eyes turned a pale yellow.

R'kiax shifted from foot to foot, wanting to give chase.

"What's your hurry?" The pirate pulled out a handkerchief and shook it out with an affected genteel mannerism. Hand flashing stone rings of every shape and type, he dabbed his temples, and his hand lingered above his double pointed ears, tapping the tips in what R'kiax recognized as code.

R'kiax darted glances about, searching for the person he might be signaling. Finding no one, he returned his attention to the woman just as she rounded a corner and disappeared.

I'm losing her. His breath sped up and he placed a hand on his hilt.

The pirate took a step back.

He turned his full attention back to the pirate and fought for calm. "Just needing a sweet-drink is all."

The pirate's eye-lines moved from yellow to red, and he darted glances from R'kiax's hand to the surrounding area, as if expecting an ambush.

Knowing he'd made a mistake, R'kiax removed his hand from his weapon and held both hands out, palm up in a show of peace. "Look, I've done my part. You have the d'yroap, now pass over the antidote."

The man looked at R'kiax, and then up and down the street.

R'kiax lifted his head smelled the air. Her scent was fading. If he didn't hurry he wouldn't be able to find her.

Without stepping closer, the pirate pulled out a small box and set it on the ground in front of him. He backed away.

R'kiax sprang forward.

The man's brows went up as he spun around and fled, feet throwing up debris.

Tucked back into the shadows, Sarenka jiggled her coin pouch and watched the outside of a merchant class pub. The day had turned out doubly profitable despite the scare at the well, and soon as the sun set she was getting her sweet-drink.

The tiny box had contained a simple ring of the sort H'eumans used to show devotion. The script on the inside edge, and the poignant note folded beneath, had made her hope the man somehow found a way to be with his mistress. He too had been given no choice in his wedded spouse but he hadn't had the sense or the bravery to run.

After pounding the ring into a flattened mass, she'd sold it to the elderly blacksmith for far less than it was worth. Danielson hadn't blinked an eye at the stolen item and had told her that if she ever needed anything, anything, he'd consider it a small price for helping him find the love of his life. Assured that there was no trail for the guards to follow, she was almost jubilant. With her d'yroap pouch replenished she could afford a small celebration at a better class pub than what she typically frequented.

Scalp itching incessantly, Sarenka raised a gloved hand and extended her claws beyond the tips of the gloves. With disgust, she stared at her nails, each wicked point underscored in blackened dirt. Giving them a reluctant sniff, she shrugged her shoulders and dug into the itch, deciding they smelled of earth and not other unsavory things.

Being filthy had turned out to be useful. Even the guard's eyes traveled past, like she didn't exist. But tomorrow, if all went well, she'd have another stolen bath in the dog pen. She could only go so long before her skin rotted and the stench drove her mad.

A stray ray of the lowering sun lanced past the buildings and into her eyes. Blinking back tears, she shifted to the right and a swarm of red flies sprang upwards. She glanced down. A little further over and she'd be standing in a pile of offal. A fly lit on her cheek, drawing blood. She slapped at it and moved farther away before turning her attention back to the building.

Shingles hung at odd angles from the roof, windows were cracked in places, and the stoop had been replaced with scavenged driftwood. Sitting between the merchant class and Sad Town, she'd hoped for fewer customers and a better sweet-drink. But now that harlots were streaming through the front door, ready to relieve merchants of their hard earned d'yroap, that was doubtful. Like every other pub or tavern in Burmtin, this one did a hopping business.

After the sun had set, and she had suffered through an intolerable amount of fly bites, Sarenka crossed the street, pushed open the doors, and strolled in. People looked up expectantly before just as quickly looking away. She covered a small triumphant smile with a gloved hand. It seemed she had chosen the right face.

Pausing just inside the door, she surveyed the room with a cultivated expression of boredom. *Three exits. Harlots. Merchants. And a few of the seamier sort like me… the rest, just ordinary workers.*

The stool she chose had a clear view of the entire bar, but when she sat it creaked and listed to one side. She grimaced and remained sitting rather than draw attention by switching to a sturdier seat. The brewman peered at her from under bushy eyebrows. Taking in her measure, he squinted, and then he frowned, distrust etched into every line of his face. She let him worry and stared at the mirror behind him, gazing at her own face, the face of a middle-aged woman. Through the reflection she saw him gesture for the bouncers.

Pulling free a copper, she tossed it down. "Whatever that'll get me."

He glanced at it and raised a brow but didn't move to pick it up.

She looked from the copper link to his face, worried that it was not worth his effort.

He waited.

She pressed her lips into a stubborn line and refused to add more loops. If the sweet-drinks were that expensive, she couldn't afford to be here.

At last, he forced his nail against the edge and flipped it into the air. Catching the loop in his other hand, he clipped it to the line of copper d'yroaps at his waist, where smaller rows of silver, gold, and riseen loops jingled.

The Frevellian next to her gave a clap of delight, encouraging him to continue. To the accompaniment of jingling d'yroaps, he sashayed towards a keg, which looked like it had been haphazardly brushed free of lichen only moments before. While he walked, copper d'yroaps began flipping through the air above his head in a steady stream, and another round of clapping erupted.

With a cringe, Sarenka peered about and was relieved to discover only the man next to her watching the show. An attentive crowd was the last thing she needed. Producing a stein with a magician's flourish, the barkeep twisted the bone tap, spilling forth a liquid so pale it barely held color. Creamy foam dripped over the side of the tankard, adding wet splats to the sticky mess they called a floor. He returned, free hand flipping one coin after another into the ceramic tankard. With a thud, he sloshed it down and turned to more lucrative customers, cutting off any complaints about the amount that landed on the wooden countertop.

Sarenka gave a sigh for the waste and sipped away the foam before peering into the vessel. None of the copper loops he'd tossed into the tankard were there. Disappointed, she repressed another sigh and went back to watching the barkeep.

He filled a spiral shell with plum wine and handed it to the merchant two seats down, then he flipped the man's silver through the air, magicing it into three coppers. The merchant waved away the change, and the brew master turned to entertaining other customers with more flips of d'yroap.

She shrugged, sipped the pale brew, and relaxed. It was salty and sour, but better than her usual fare, despite its color.

Two hourglass turns later, Sarenka leaned her elbows against the counter, peered into her tankard, and wondered how much longer she could nurse it. The pub had long since filled, and the brewman had stopped his antics; too busy to do more than throw down sweet-drinks as soon as they were ordered. After three ales and two runs outside to renew illusions, she relaxed into the double bang of the front door opening and closing, only looking at the door when it stopped banging. It was a wonder what sweet-drink did for grated nerves.

Her choice of a middle aged woman's face and long dishwater blond braid worked well in deflecting attention. Neither patron nor worker chatted with her beyond asking if she wanted another ale. Youthful harlots, decked out in provocative gowns and shining tresses, wandered the milling crowd, drawing all the attention and giving her none.

She swirled the cup and watched the foamy liquid form a whirlpool. A hand brushed casually across her back and alarm quickened Sarenka's heart. She stiffened and turned her head.

A man stood with arm still outstretched, wearing clothing so loose that it draped from his frame in sloppy folds and shoulder length hair a greasy tangled mess.

Readying to run, Sarenka placed her feet on the ground.

He stumbled forward, bumping and brushing against everyone on his way.

Tension drained from her shoulders. *A drunk, no doubt needing the touch to keep from falling over.* Reaching the end of the counter, he slid onto an empty stool and called for a M'hakru whiskey.

A burst of laughter from the opposite direction pulled her attention towards the front door. An elderly patron, dressed in a dapper merchant's coat, laughed at some unheard joke and passed a redhead woman a handful of d'yroap. She giggled and leaned forward to lick playfully at his thick fingers before taking the coin. Looping her arm through the crook of his elbow, she guided him towards the door.

With a sigh, Sarenka turned back to her tankard. The windfall that afternoon had paid for her night, and her head felt better than it had in a long time, but she couldn't afford the luxury of staying. Every loop mattered. She gave her stein another swirl, lingering over the last sip.

"Mind if'n I sit 'ere, m'lady?" The question was loud and close.

Sarenka jumped, startled at being spoken to. Next to her, rocking back and forth on his heels, stood the drunkard who had brushed against her back. She started to tell him the seat was taken, but he was already sliding into it. He was loose-limbed and flopped about like he'd had far too many sweet-drinks. The stench rolling off him rivaled her own unwashed body, so much so that the man on the other side held his nose and waved his hand with disdain.

She tipped back her tankard, finishing off the last drop, then slapped it down on the counter and started to stand. "I was just…"

"M'hakru whiskey for m'lady!" The stranger shouted, thumping down his d'yroap pouch in front of them.

Sarenka sat back down. She'd tolerate the drunk for long enough to enjoy that treat.

"'Nother fer me stoo," he slurred out.

Her mouth watered.

His begrimed hands fumbled at the strings of his pouch, and he leaned forward until his nose almost touched the leather, peering at it. Finally, he opened it wider than was wise in a crowded tavern.

Alarmed at the attention it might draw, Sarenka glanced around before eyeing the loops, mesmerized by the abundance. Realizing she'd stared too long, her gaze shot to his face, but he was so focused on picking out a few d'yroap that he didn't notice her infatuation.

Surely he won't miss a few—

He interrupted her thought by tossing several silver loops on the wooden countertop and shouting, "Start me a tab!"

The loops tinkled and rolled as they landed, and the pubkeep snatched them up, lightning fast. She wasn't the only one watching the drunk's antics. After fumbling through closing the embossed pouch and tying it to his belt, the man gave it a rough shove, slinging it far back on his hip.

She shook her head. *He's a drunken fool.*

The whiskeys arrived in thick cream shells half the size of her fist, and he slid one over. Gingerly picking it up, she took a sip and closed her eyes, enjoying the smooth-as-silk way it slid over her tongue, then burned its way down to her stomach. It was a wicked drink.

"Name's Tahrek." He smiled at her with teeth straight and fine, not the blackened rot of someone who had been a drunk for years.

For the first time she noticed the man under the dirt, and he was handsome. His sun-warmed skin was unblemished, and the soulful amber eyes, set above pronounced cheekbones, were crinkled at the corners. Despite those smile lines, he was young, a few years older than her sixteen years of age, at most.

That he was flirting with a woman who appeared twice his age didn't surprise Sarenka, there seemed to be a man who preferred older women in every crowd. That he chose her now, when she reeked of gutter filth and looked like she'd rolled in the dirt, raised an alarming amount of questions. He was after something besides a friendly conversation.

"What's a pretty-boy like you doing in a place like this, Tahrek?" She leaned towards him flirtatiously. He could fish all he wanted, but he wasn't getting her name, not even a fake one.

His smile disappeared, but the anger that washed over his countenance was gone so fast that she wondered if she'd seen true. His head dipped forward, throwing greasy hanks of hair over his face and revealing the slight point of a Half-Frevell ear. When he looked back up again he was smiling, but not with his eyes. In them only sadness shone.

"Buyin' sweet-drinks fer pretty-girls." He threw out with a wink. "An savin' peoples."

She glanced about to make sure nobody was listening before leaning forward to say, "You should buy a hat."

"Ha!" He laughed and pushed his hair behind his ears, drawing more attention to the semi-points. "Hate hats."

"Hide those ears, you fool—" she leaned forward to whisper— "half-breeds aren't legal in Burmtin. It's a death sentence."

A glint caught the light, and her gaze dropped to the exposed blade in his hand.

D'trav laid back on the bed, propped his hands behind his head, and crossed his feet. He'd saved the day. The Watrelk diplomat's needs were being taken care of, and he'd brought back enough water to carry them over for several days. He'd even visited every shoe merchant in Burmtin to replace the shoes he'd fouled. That entire day, parcel after parcel had been given to Camille, until she'd complained about being out of room and told him to stop. That hadn't happened, of course, she'd be receiving exotic new shoes for the next month, some of them in her size. He gave a half laugh and closed his eyes.

His door creaked, and he peered at it in time to see Camille poke her head around the corner.

"Still awake?"

He patted the bed next to him.

She entered the room, golden ringlets bouncing and jiggling in the candlelight as she approached the bed. "You didn't need to replace all the shoes."

"I'm needin' to do a lot more than that, but first I gotta get me a job."

"That's why I'm here."

He raised a brow in question.

"Work here."

He burst out laughing and couldn't stop.

Hands on hips, Camille waited.

Red in the face, he finally gasped out, "Sorry, darlin, I'm thinkin' satin trousers just aren't to my hankering."

Her lips rounded with surprise, and she giggled. Placing a hand on her chest, she said, "Oh, dear Kyron, no. You… as a gigolo…" She laughed some more.

"Hey now. I'm all right."

"No, no. Not that. Just you catering to the men and women we get in. I can't see it."

"So what then?"

"My guard quit today. I need a new one, and you're just the man."

"Okay. Deal. Pay?"

"Same as you made for the baron."

"That works for me." He grabbed her hand and pulled her down on top of him. His gaze dropped from her kohl-lined eyes to the luscious breasts pressed against his chest, lingering over how full and ripe they were. He stared into her green eyes and licked his lips, hungry for more. "Do I get… *benefits*?"

"Oooh, definitely." She nibbled along the side of his neck, just where he loved it best.

"Camille," he let out in a low groan, "you know me too damn well."

"Makes it a lot more fun, doesn't it?"

He ran his hand down her back and cupped her ass in answer.

She wriggled her hips, grinding against his hardening member.

He winced.

"Oh!" She jumped up from the bed. "I'm so sorry."

"No. It's okay. Really."

"I didn't mean to hurt you."

D'trav felt himself soften and reached for her hand. "Just caught on the stitchin'. It's okay."

"You need to heal up before you work."

He tugged her towards him.

She pulled even further away from the bed and shook his hand free.

He dropped his hand to the bed with a thump. "Come on, Camille, one night won't hurt."

"Might pull the stitches."

"So."

"So, no." She bent over, kissed him on the lips softly, bit his lower lip in a tease, and left.

He put his arms back behind his head and stared at the abalone ceiling. "Damn it."

CHAPTER 26

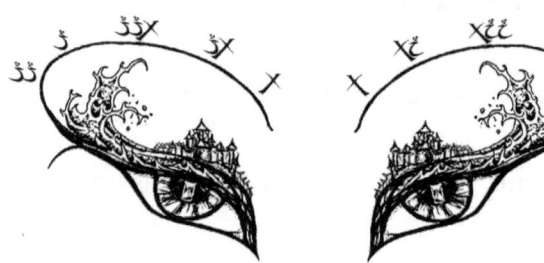

"Our studies continue. Soon we will have defined the gene that makes us the fiercest warriors of the land and debunked the myths about it being linked to our sixth finger, the barbs on our penis, or how many piercings and tattoos we have. Though I dare say, it is linked to our supernatural speed. Without that we would have been sheep for the slaughter when Rage Wars started."

Drark Agrok'nktar
M'hakru Geneticist
56 AB

Heart racing, Sarenka stared with horror at the blade in Tahrek's hand. "I'm sorry! I didn't mean to insult you."

Tahrek jerked the blade down and back, swinging in a fast under-arm jab. It sank into the abdomen of the man behind him. He pulled it free and spun around, drunken looseness replaced with fluid poise.

Sarenka jumped into a sideways turn, spinning her stool to the ground with a crash, and landed in a defensive stance facing Tahrek.

The man in front of Tahrek hunched forward, one hand covering a gaping wound in his abdomen, the other leather-wrapped fist held out defensively.

In a blur, Tahrek shoved the man's right shoulder backwards with his free hand, shifted the dagger to a forward grip and brought it up diagonally, slicing through the man's jugular. He ended the motion with a double wipe over the man's breeches, cleaning the blade.

The stranger listed into a sideways fall, deflecting most of the spraying blood away from them.

Tahrek raised his dagger and inspected it before sheathing the blade.

Sarenka blinked, trying to process what had happened.

Tahrek flipped the dead man over with his foot and pried an embossed pouch from the man's clenched fingers.

Sarenka gaped at the man who had mistaken Tahrek for an easy mark and tried to rob him. She wiped the beaded sweat from her forehead and licked suddenly dry lips. Tahrek was not the fool she'd taken him for. No, he was fast and well trained, maybe Red Pelican. The only person she'd ever seen move faster was a M'hakru. Which meant she was in trouble.

With a cock of his head, Tahrek examined the surface of the pouch. His thumb wiped across it, removing flecks of imaginary dirt before returning it to his belt. He sliced free the dead man's pouch and scooped it up, but he froze at the sound of a scuffing foot. Staring up through a mop of dirty hair, he dared any to dispute his claim.

The crowd stood transfixed, unmoving.

He gave the onlookers a curt nod before retrieving Sarenka's fallen stool. It landed next to his with a thunk, and he gave a nonchalant wave of his hand, directing her towards it.

Shaken to the core and leery of getting too close, she sat.

He leaned on the bar and swirled his shell before tossing back the whiskey. When he slammed it down on the countertop the people around her jumped. For the first time, Sarenka was aware that the pub had gone stock still.

"I hate thieves." He slapped the man's pouch down on the countertop and pulled the strings, exposing primarily coppers before pushing it towards her. "Here, you take it. I've got enough weight on my waist already."

"Get that body out of here! Caleth! Clean up that mess!" The barkeep's shouted orders returned the activity of the room to normal.

Several of the patrons jumped at the opportunity for free plunder and helped drag the man into the street.

Noting how little attention the killing received once the danger was past, Sarenka decided never to return to this pub. She stared straight ahead, afraid to move. The mirror on the other side of the bar reflected back her middle-aged lie. The illusions had held, but in the face of what she'd just witnessed, that victory seemed minor.

Would he have stabbed me if I'd tried to lift a few d'yroap?

Her skin when cold, and she gulped down a mouthful of whiskey. "Aren't you afraid the authorities will come for you?"

"For doing their job? Nope." The slur was gone from his voice, as well as the accent.

She shuddered. He wasn't drunk. Probably never had been. The dagger hadn't been Red Pelican, but that meant nothing.

"They were after you. And not just the one that stole my bag. He's got a pal back there." Tahrek nodded towards the other side of the room. "Soon as you left, they'd have cut your throat and taken your coin. I figure you deserve *their* coin instead."

"What? No." Sarenka raised a hand to her throat and shook her head. "I would've seen them."

"If you hadn't been so busy trying to read the future in the bottom of a cup, yes, you might have."

"So you... saved me?"

Why's he telling me this?

What does he want?

"Nothing so noble. I simply removed some vermin."

Now he was talking language she understood. Picking up the small pouch, she shoved it down between her breasts.

A thump came from behind, followed by rustling. She turned to see a wiry boy, dressed in clothing scarcely better than her own, drop a mop onto the splattered blood and begin smearing it around.

Her attention returned to Tahrek. "So what's a Half-Frevell pretty-boy doing in a place like this?"

The smile fled his face once more. He leaned over to wrap his arm around her shoulder in a comradely manner. Lips brushing her ear, he whispered, "Same thing a Freni-Kyn murderess is. Hiding."

Parian paced around the triangular sigil, checking the elements. After a week of trial and error on the road, scratching out the symbols in the dirt each night, he'd perfected the ritual. Or at least he hoped he had. The larger brazier, bowl, and plate were balanced within a larger triangle and etched with stronger runes, in hopes of giving him enough fuel to complete his search.

His belt slipped down around his hips as he walked. He glanced at the mirror across the room and grimaced, noting dark circles under the quiet desperation of his eyes, and other aspects of his disheveled appearance: tangled hair, grimed skin, and wrinkled clothing. The toll on his body had been great, and though he was the last to worry about a little weight loss, at this rate he'd need new clothing. If his Freni-Kyn relatives could see him now, he'd be sent to a healer to have his mental acuity checked, of that he was certain.

~I have to do this.~

~Why?~ Rosalie asked.

He groaned. Of course she had heard him talking to himself. He never knew when she'd be close enough to listen in and never grew used to the interruptions. ~It's our life mission and important enough to break all the rules.~

She sent a sound that sounded like a snort.

~We've been seeing the signs. The time is drawing near, and I've been hearing the call. The one is out there, desperate to be found.~

He didn't tell her that it was just a tiny wisp of a drifting thought, tickling and teasing at his mind. She'd have scoffed if he'd told her it was a promise of peace for all the races. It was enough that he knew the truth.

He cinched the belt tighter and checked the pockets, making sure the vials of honey, nuts, and dried meat were in place before continuing with the ritual. Walking out the pattern, he checked the placement of each rune before stepping to the center and slipping into the time stream.

Drifting over the city of Burmtin, he searched for The One with his thoughts blanketed in a fog of mundane falsities, concerned that the Seven would move to stop him if they discovered what he was doing.

He sent forth a slender thread, a lure of hope, but all he caught were faint echoes of thought, untraceable. He'd returned to Burmtin each day that week, despite the danger of losing himself in the time stream, despite the risk of never finding the way back to his body or of burning through all his reserves and killing himself with starvation, despite the fit Airintia would throw when she found out he was doing it again. Parian glided to a stop above a pub, positive he'd caught up with his quarry.

~*I've caught…*~ he started sending but stopped as fear gripped his heart.

He squinted at the blinding glow rising from the building. Sizzling tendrils flashed out, stretching towards him in an alarming manner. Caution held him frozen in uncertainty, unable to gauge whether the light was safe to touch, much less pass into. He sent forth a wisp of thought and met no animosity, no resistance, only terror.

Raw emotions washed over him, adding to his already palpable fear. He shuddered. Anyone putting out this much power was dangerous.

To themselves. And to others.

In a moment, one solitary blink of time, an errant thought could blast someone's mind, leaving them little more than empty husks. If he didn't get The One into training, something serious was sure to happen. He stretched forth a tentative hand and was surprised to find the energy pleasantly warm instead of the stinging blast he expected.

Catching a whiff of a feminine mind, Parian surged through the outer resistance and dropped through the roof. A masculine mind slammed against him, bouncing him back through the energy field. The blow, powerful enough to send him tumbling head-over-heels, ended with a floundering midair sprawl above the neighboring building. Confusion reigned while he sorted through both the dizzying vertigo and his meeting of not one mind, but two.

One person with both a male and female psychic footprint?

Or two people, working in concert to keep me away?

The improbability of both scenarios was so high that he had to steady his nerves before pushing into the building again. Engaged in harmless pub activity, multitudes of people were outlined in radiating energy, all blurring and bumping into each other. Eyes watering, he struggled to figure out where The One was, but all the energy patterns seemed equal in strength.

The One is deliberately masking himself... herself?

A man whirled, stabbing the thief behind him.

Parian reached out to save the wounded man but pulled back.

No! I mustn't.

It's forbidden.

As the man bled out, another moved forward to strike.

Parian intervened to change the thief's mind. The Seven would understand. If not, then surely Kyron would. A full blown tavern brawl might injure, or kill, his quarry.

The man who had killed the murderer drew the woman next to him into an intimate embrace.

A surge of energy roared up, blinding Parian and throwing him backwards. Helpless to do more than thrash against the power, his mind soared backwards past all the time streams, not stopping until it reached his own time. Unable to stop the mental push, he plummeted into his body.

I didn't have time to withdraw the threads I put in place.

They'll dispel on their own...

But the energy…

It's too great…

The room swayed into the depths of a starless night.

The bland expression left Tahrek's face, and he pulled Sarenka closer, suffocating her against his knitted shirt.

Convinced that he planned to add her body to the one lying in the streets, she pushed against his chest and tried to free her face.

"Get your illusions back up," he whispered.

Sarenka stiffened but stopped fighting.

His arm around her face was a band of iron as he tucked her head under his chin and shielded her from view.

It took several panting breaths before she managed to push down the panic and raise her illusions.

He released her from the close hold but kept his arm around her shoulder. "Game of dags?" He cocked his head toward the darkened back corner where a target hung.

Sarenka darted a glance about the room. Relieved to find no witnesses, she looked in the direction he indicated. Next to the octagonal bullseye hung a hand-inked picture of her face, covered in slashes and holes from where it had been used for target practice.

She shook her head.

Arm still wrapped around her, Tahrek moved in that direction, taking her with him. He wasn't asking, he was telling. He fake staggered while he walked, making it appear that the two were interested in drunken competition.

She went along with the ruse; a struggle to break free would draw unwanted attention.

In front of the target, he pulled out a set of plain black daggers and handed them to her.

She hesitated before taking them. *Surely if he's going to kill me he wouldn't be handing me a weapon.*

"Relax, I'm not here to kill you. Or turn you in."

She gritted her teeth and gave the dagger a casual flick. It sank into the outside edge of the target. The next hit the wall nearby and the third pierced the top of the target. Glancing about to check for observers, she threw the next two, hitting the bullseye dead center.

Tahrek raised an eyebrow before retrieving the daggers.

"You felt my hair when you brushed against me, didn't you?"

He nodded and flipped the daggers at the target, one after another, in rapid succession. They landed, straight and true, clustered around the center. "Wasn't a braid there, should be more careful with the hairstyles you pick. Why'd you lose control of the illusions?"

She gazed at his ear and decided the truth wouldn't hurt. "I'm Half-H'euman."

"An illegal, like me. I take it that's watered down your abilities."

Her face became hot. "You need to ask? Hasn't it watered down yours?"

He laughed.

"So, it's funny now?"

"No, just not sure how I'd know. Never met my father—" the muscles in his jaw moved as he ground his teeth together— "except once. And I wouldn't want what I saw that night."

"My illusions last about an hourglass turn. My father holds his half a day, easily. It waters down the abilities, being a half-breed. Sometimes I wonder if that's why it's illegal."

"No." Tahrek turned his face away. "It's fear."

"Fear? I don't know about fear being why they kill us. I just know I can't hold the magics if I give in to fear."

"Fear makes everything worse."

She regarded the poster. "Why aren't you turning me in?"

"The posters lie. You aren't a murderer."

She didn't say anything. His faith in her was so stunning that she sobbed.

He cocked his head. "Oh, so you did do it then?"

She turned her face aside, gathering her emotions into tight control before answering, and even then her words came out constricted and strained. "Not on purpose, the Foreveron..."

His face turned pale and his jaw clenched, making the muscles jump. "Knew I was right about you. You aren't a murderer."

Refusing to meet his eyes, Sarenka turned away and struggled for control of her emotions.

"You still addicted?"

"Yes."

He stared at the wanted poster and tapped his d'yroap pouch. "I'm looking for someone. He runs a pleasure-slave business. Wondered if you could help."

"So that's why you helped, you knew I was a pleasure-slave."

"Not hardly. I could've gotten in my questions without killing anyone. That thief deserved to die. So does his pal." He tipped his head towards a man who was lounging against the wall, eyeing the other customers.

"The pleasure houses are simple to find, and one's as good as any other."

Flinching as if struck, he glanced at her and fingered the blade. "This has nothing to do with pleasure."

"Vengeance?"

He didn't answer. Sweat beaded his upper lip, glistening in the low light.

She tilted her head, wondering at the reaction. "I don't know who sold me to the Red Pelican."

Tears glimmered in Tahrek's eyes, but they disappeared so fast that Sarenka dismissed them as part of her overactive imagination.

"They kept me blindfolded after they caught me."

"Doesn't matter. I'll find him." He tossed another round of daggers at the target, but as he returned from collecting them, his eyes narrowed and his face became hard. "Time for me to finish off the rest of the vermin."

Sarenka turned just in time to see the thief trail a customer out the door.

Tahrek set a vial of yellow liquid on the table. "That's all I've got. Sorry for that. Not enough to cure, but it'll help."

She grabbed the vial, hiding it from view.

"You take care of yourself, girl. And get out of Burmtin before it infects you with its rot." Slipping back into his role, he staggered away, a drunk once more.

"I'm trying," she whispered.

She followed him out the door, stepping past the stripped body of the man Tahrek had killed earlier, and searched the street for his broad shoulders, but he was already gone.

I'm such an idiot. I let him get away.

He knows where to get the antidote.

Bet he could get me out of the city too.

A suffocating blanket of depression settled over her as the truth registered. She had missed her opportunity. She worked her way towards the back of an alley and leaned against the wall before sliding to the ground. Her hands shook uncontrollably as she opened the vial and downed the vile liquid. Fire coursed through her veins, and the vial slipped from her hand and rolled across the alley. Dully, she watched it clink to a stop against an uneven cobblestone. Her eyes lost focus.

A man died for stealing tonight, a fate that would've been mine if I had given into the temptation to pinch Tahrek's loops. And what would've happened if it had been Tahrek at the well instead of the spoiled noble?

He wouldn't have hesitated.

I'd have died before I could plant a disarming kiss on his lips, and the onlookers would've stripped my body and turned me in for the price on my head.

For a moment, time became fluid, the paths before her many, and miniscule decisions had infinite results. She lifted free of her body, moving towards the countless lanes of destiny, all connecting, one to another. Her mind expanded and she understood the oneness of the universe, her connection with every person, every thing, every being.

With a snap, like a piece of rubber stretched to the point of breaking, she was alone within herself again. Hand trembling, she rubbed her forehead, desperate to relieve the torturous pounding that plagued her life.

"Mind lost. I'm as mind lost as a..."

But she could not shake off the thought. A man had died and nobody cared. He'd been treated with less respect than a common dog.

Thrice today she had avoided death, but barely.

She put her hands over her face and sobbed.

Kyron, how I hate this city.

CHAPTER 27

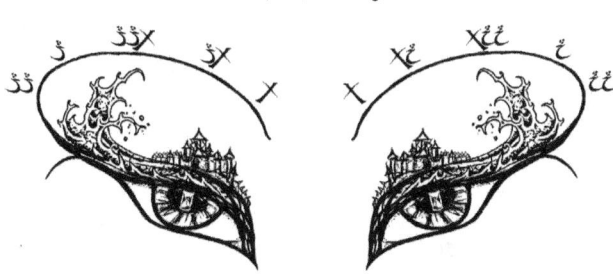

"King Zlakwor,

We present to you the first cat-mount. She has been named Golden Moons, for the night of her birthing, and responds well to that name. She's as large as a horse and able to hunt, as well as serve as a mount. There are twelve in her litter and many more to be birthed this next month.

Now, after 3000 years of study, we, The Allegiance for Superior Animals, beg to be disbanded. Our members would like to pursue other studies and feel there can be no further improvements upon the feline."

Rhain Faughn
M'hakru Geneticist
2018 BB

~*Parian?*~ The word was a bleeding scratch against Parian's brain.

~*Parian! Answer me!*~

~*Please... please... you're hurting me...*~ Parian mind-whispered.

~*What? How am I hurting you?*~

With a moan Parian rolled to the side. His clothing crackled and tore like fragile tissue. He reached into a pocket, tearing it half free, and found only a handful of dust. Bringing his fist upwards, he rested it in front of his face and slowly opened his fingers.

Blackened ash drifted free.

"What's happening?" Still lying on his side he searched the room for clues. "I don't understand."

~Parian?~

Pain shrieked through his mind. ~Airintia, stop screaming.~

~I wasn't. Are you okay?~ Airintia whispered back.

~No... I feel like... like... every part of the inside of my brain has been seared.~

~What! You did it again?~

~Oh Kyron... you're screaming again.~ Parian's thought went forth on a wave of mental anguish. He felt Airintia go pale, and he clenched his hands around his face.

~I'm sorry, let me in to help you mend.~

~No!~ He threw up a mental barrier to block the probe she was sending.

~Come on, Parian, even your barrier is cracked.~ Though she could have gone further, she stopped to mind-whisper, ~You need help, but I won't go on without your permission.~

~Do you remember when we were new and learning to make barricades? The Seven would throw themselves against us, testing our strength.~

~Yes.~

~Do you remember the pain? The raw nerves afterwards?~

He felt her cringe through the connection, and that hurt too, adding to his pain. ~Yes.~

~This is worse, by a million times... it's like... like a cheese grater scraping over the inside of my head. If I can't even handle the breath of your mental voice against my brain right now, can you imagine what touching it would do?~

A tear trickled down Airintia's cheek. ~Don't die. Please.~

Parian laughed, dry and raspy, then clutched his head. ~I won't. Though right now...~

Right now it'd be a relief. He thought, blocking her from hearing that morose thought.

~I had The One.~

~So, he's on the way?~

He struggled, hand-pull by hand-pull, across the room towards a canvas satchel, forcing her to wait for the answer. With each inch forward, his clothing disintegrated, leaving a few crumbling tatters. *~Had. The energy... never seen anything like it... so powerful... knocked me all the way back here.~*

~The One hurt you? And you think this person should be a Seven?~ Airintia's mental voice edged upwards until Parian's gasp of pain reminded her to whisper.

~He... she... didn't do it on purpose... I don't think... just so powerful.~

~You can't go back. Promise me you won't.~

Parian remained silent and dug through his bag, searching for food that hadn't been turned to ash. He fumbled free a piece of scorched venison jerky and stuffed it into his mouth.

~Parian?~ Her voice sent a white hot stab through him, whirling the room towards darkness again.

Parian felt the backlash shatter through Airintia, and her dismay as she was sent sprawling forward onto her knees. The sensation created a loop of emotion and pain. She clutched at her head. A film of fine sweat covered her body, producing a shiver in the chill room. He was caught up; unable to stop the flood of sensations coming from her or from reflecting them back again.

~Oh god! I'm so sorry— ~

~Please, just leave me alone. I need to...~ His voice dropped off.

Airintia sent the tiniest of tendril of thought towards him. It hovered in the room, searching for life, and settled on his slumbering breath before withdrawing.

He's alive, but he can't keep doing this.

The Seven will never come to terms with his search.

It's dangerous.

Unnecessary.

The foretelling never showed this.

It's not supposed to happen this way.

Sarenka's head was seized, shocking her awake, and she surged upwards. Blinded by the fabric pulled tight across her face, she grasped at the hood of her cloak, but her gloved hands fumbled, unable to get a purchase. A blow to the abdomen caught her by surprise, knocking the breath from her and slamming her back to the ground. Pain-wracked and blinded, she clutched her stomach while her heart hammered with terror.

Hands grasped her body, too many, rolling her over and over, making her dizzy. Her cloak tightened, wrapping her as securely as a spider did its prey.

Punches and kicks rained down, knocking her rolling body back and forth across the alley.

Fearful that a rescuer would discover her true face, she refused to cry out for help. Strangled noises seeped out from between her clenched teeth. The beating went on and on, turning every portion of her, even the soles of her feet, into swollen, useless pieces of bleeding flesh.

She curled into a fetal position; sure that death had found her. A final kick landed on her back before a hand pulled at the cloak around her waist. Sarenka curled tighter and the world turned into a dark spinning tunnel.

"Found the loops!"

A pull came at her waist, and there was a sudden release as her d'yroap pouch strings were cut. The search continued as other hands felt along her body.

"Only coppers," a youthful voice sneered.

The coppers showered down on top of her, each ping adding another sharp pain to her misery.

"What the… Pelican… she's Red Pelican!" said a second voice, higher pitched and filled with fear.

"Let's get out of here!" The third voice was older, deeper, a youth bordering on adulthood.

The clatter of metal falling onto cobblestones echoed down the alley, followed by the rapid thud of running footsteps. It was too much, the world faded away.

Caught within darkness, Sarenka climbed the rolling clouds of pain while shrieking banshees scoured every inch of her body. Gasping for air through the suffocating fabric, she reached to pull it free and found her arms bound to her sides by the twisted cloak. Frantic, trussed so tightly that she feared she couldn't free herself without help, she struggled, pushing and pulling against the bloody fabric and making no progress.

She drew in strangled breaths, calming herself before starting over, twisting back and forth on the ground, loosening the cocoon enough to free one arm. Hand shaking, she pulled a tiny opening in the hood and drew in a long ragged breath that ended in a bloodied cough. She whimpered but kept at it for a year's worth of hourglass turns, inch by inch unwinding the sticky fabric from her body.

When at last she could wrench clear of the hood, she drew in great gulps of the cool night air, crying out against the pain which shot through her side with each breath. It became too much, and she turned to quick shallow breaths, unable to get enough air no matter what she did. Sight blurry, she searched the darkness for observers. If there were any, they weren't moving. She tentatively examined the split lip before moving up her face. Her nose was intact, a surprise considering how much it hurt, but where the opening for one eye should be she found only puffed tissue.

A sob broke free, sending pain shooting across her side.

"No time for self-pity… only survival." Her words came out in a slurred mumble.

Surrounding her were gleaming loops of copper, her pouch, and the item that had saved her, the Red Pelican Dagger. She lifted it high, honoring it, before pressing her lips to the gleaming blade. Light caught the eye of the pelican in a ruby flash, a reminder of who it had come from. Shivering, she tucked it back within the folds of her cloak.

After threading a shred of torn fabric through the pouch, she gathered up the coppers, wincing with each move. And all the while she kept telling herself that her eye wasn't ripped out or permanently damaged, that if it were it would hurt far worse. Unable to stand, she set off on hands and knees, but before she could find a hidden recess to hide in the world slid into a mind-lost, sideways angle, going blank.

CHAPTER 28

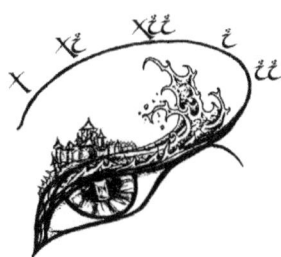

The sun streaked down into Sarenka's eyes when she awoke, making them tear. Glad that she was not blind in one eye, she used her illusions to look H'euman without disguising the abuse. Each cut, each aching bruise, the swollen lip, and blackened eye, she let show through the illusion. She'd need all the pity she could get.

She begged for sustenance that day, and the people who saw her took mercy and threw coppers, some even kind enough to place them in her hand instead of forcing her to scrounge off the ground. She had no strength for work or cunning for stealing. It was all she could do to hold the illusions, beg for meals, and crawl back into hiding. When she slept, it was fitfully and filled with dreams of being taken unawares and beaten to death.

I can't keep doing this.

I need a home, but not people. Never people.

Just a home.

That became her mantra.

After a week the bruises faded and her pride arose, forbidding her to beg. She turned back to the trades she knew. If it couldn't be bought with menial tasks, it could be stolen. She limped through the market, using the awkward movement to distract people while she grabbed the food she needed for breakfast, a roll here, a wedge of cheese there, and decided to end it with what she needed most to finish her healing.

She snagged a small sausage as she passed the butcher and kept walking, pushing it up her sleeve.

A hand clamped around her still bruised and aching wrist in an iron grip. She stared down at the hand in disbelief before it jerked, pulling her around to face three scowling guards.

Sarenka panicked and tried to jerk free but managed to keep her illusions up.

The guard who had caught her yanked the sausage from her sleeve and threw it down on the butchers table. He twisted her arm, forcing her into turning around and pulled it up towards her shoulder blades.

Sarenka gasped at the renewed pain in her ribs, and all the fight went out of her.

The guard loosened his grip, lowering her arm and binding both wrists together behind her back. "Don't fight me girl, or they'll both go back up there, and I can't promise something won't break."

They circled her, rifling through her belongings, searching for other stolen goods. The jostling loosened scabs and fresh blood dripped down her arms and legs.

"Teach you to steal from honest folk. We'll see how you like being cut."

His door at the Refuge Inn rattled and banged, jarring Parian awake. "Who... What..."

The banging resumed and Parian stumbled to the door, settling his illusions in place before pulling it open.

Two men stood at the door, the shorter, stockier man with a fist raised as if to knock. He lowered his hand and tugged the hem of his tailored jacket down.

The taller, thinner man folded a slip of parchment, tucking it into a pocket.

Parian looked them over—linen suits, pinstriped vests, and boots with stone hinges—they didn't belong in this town.

The taller man removed his bowler hat and ran his fingers around the brim. "Parian?"

Parian's heart thumped. "Who?"

"We're sorry to bother you, sir." The other man spoke up, arms crossed in front, tapping his wrist in a kind of tick. "Are you Parian?"

"I'm not sure who you mean."

"We've been informed that there is one Parian Zerelth residing here."

"Oh… You mean that strange recluse with red hair?" Parian pointed to the room next door. "He's in that room."

The men peered at the door then back at Parian. The taller of the two put his hat back on, and his gaze traveled past Parian, taking in the sigils on the floor.

Parian tried to slam the door shut, but it hit a broad shoulder instead. Parian's feet slid across the floor as they pushed the door further open, gaining ground. He turned and ran for the window.

The door crashed into the wall with a bang, and the thrum of running feet came from behind.

He yanked open the window and dived for it.

A cracking, banging sound came from the middle of the room.

Parian glanced over his shoulder as his upper body cleared the window.

Sprawled face first on the ground, the taller man was struggling to stand, feet slipping and sliding on strewn coals and ashes from the toppled brazier.

Jumping over the prostate man, the shorter man barreled towards Parian.

Parian struggled forward.

A fist closed around his ankle, gripping it with vice-like strength.

Desperate to break free, Parian kicked and made contact.

"God, damn it!"

"Bloody seers!"

Parian's other leg was grasped and with a rough yank, he was hauled back towards the room. His face scraped against the window sash, drawing blood, and he landed on the ground with a loud thump. He tried to turn over but a weight landed on his back, pressing him back down. He kicked and flailed but only managed to send the brazier clattering across the room.

They grabbed for his arms.

He avoided their fists and knocked one in the eye.

The man cursed and pressed down on his neck, choking off his air. His wrists were wrenched back and pinned in one meaty paw. Dots formed in his eyesight and the strength went out of his limbs. His neck was released, and he drew a ragged breath.

Parian stared up at the heavier man's sweating face, surprised that the men were strong enough to hold him. Blood ran from the man's nose, dripping onto Parian's cheek. Over his shoulder, the taller man removed a long, thin needle attached to a bulbous ball. Parian renewed his struggles, bucking his body up and down.

"Hold him still."

With a vicious twist, the man with the bleeding nose pushed Parian's arm to the ground and stood on it, pinning it flat.

"Look, you." The heavier man leaned down close to Parian's face. "This can go easy, or it can hurt like hellfire. Which one you want?"

"Okay, okay…" He stopped struggling and forced his muscles to relax. "I'll hold still."

They brought the needle to his wrist.

"You've gotta be kiddin' me!" D'trav stared at the row of Freni-Kyn women with dismay.

Their hair had been bound into tidy braids and fingernails filed down to blunt squares, and each of them wore gauzy bits of fabric that did nothing to hide their voluptuous figures.

"You can't do this! They're like Kyron fuckin' exotic dancers, only with less on."

"They've got to have their needs met, and you aren't up to helping."

"This is torture."

Camille gave D'trav a slow smile, and glanced down at his pants pointedly. "I know."

"I thought the water and the shoes…"

"Made up for everything? Not hardly. I'll be back in a few hours."

He opened the door and poked his head into the next room. A row of cots filled the space, and upon each cot was a spread-eagle tied man with his face covered in a rams-head hood, leaving only nose, mouth, and chin exposed.

"Damned if I don't envy you boys."

Pants tented with arousal, they smiled, obviously game for whatever Camille tossed their way.

He walked down the row, checking to make sure the half-hoods were buckled properly and that they wouldn't be able to see. Satisfied, he returned to the Freni-Kyns. They were clustered together, touching and kissing each other. One of them looked up at him with sultry eyes and he hardened.

She beckoned him closer.

He cleared his throat and stared past her. "Okay, darlins, these are the rules. You've got yourself one turn of the hourglass. Your hair's to stay in its braids. None of *their* hoods are to be taken off, even if they be beggin', and I'm sure as cotton they will do. And you're not to reveal your Freni-Kyn identity. If *any* of you do, you'll *all* be turned over to the city guards."

One of the women ran her hands down over her body. "And what about you, lover-boy?"

"I'm off limits."

She pouted. "You sure?"

"Camille's house, Camille's rules." He nodded towards the closed door. "Go. Enjoy."

Silently, he watched as they sliced the men's clothing away with daggers, and his body throbbed with need.

The woman at the nearest cot gestured for him to join them. Her mouth wandered over the man's skin, licking and kissing.

He groaned and rubbed himself.

This is damnably unbearable.

He took a step forward and stopped.

No.

I can resist.

His cock throbbed angrily.

Maybe.

One by one the women teased the men into heightened arousal, mounting and then unmounting and making them beg before starting again. D'trav was forced to watch each act, lest one of the couples break the rules and put their all their lives in danger.

This is hell. I'm sure of it. I'm where I belong. In hell.

Camille arrived an hour later, just as the first screaming orgasm started.

"They went over the time," D'trav said.

"Told you they would."

She watched for a few moments and fanned herself. "Well now. That's quite the thing."

D'trav groaned.

Pushing Sarenka ahead, the guards marched towards the gallows.

She hung her head and limped forward, shivering with fear. *It's only a matter of time now before they kill me.*

On the edge of the square, Sarenka hung back. A woman was strung up on the platform, every inch of her naked body covered in bruises, bites, and cuts. They tightened their grip and dragged her inescapably closer. Sarenka stared at the ground and focused on holding her illusions as waves of palpable fear struck. Grasping her chin, they forced her to look at the woman.

"That's what happens to thieves," said one of the guards.

"She deserved every cut," the guard holding her arm said. "She thought she could do anything she wanted. Now look at her."

Sarenka sobbed and squeezed her eyes shut.

He slapped her. "I said look!"

Sarenka opened her eyes and stared at the wall behind the woman's body, refusing to focus on the mangled corpse.

"This is how it's going to work. We're going to cut you and let you go. And you're never going to steal again. Understand?"

She sobbed and nodded.

"I *said*, do you understand!"

"Yes… sir."

Satisfied, they yanked her around and pushed her towards the public Shaming Block. It loomed before her, an ominous stone platform. In the center lay a waist-high slab of wood, stained dark with blood. Above that slab a series of fish hooks hung from cord, swinging gently back and forth in the ocean breeze.

Sarenka stepped onto the courtyard square and was jerked backwards by the hood of her cloak. The fabric tightened into a strangle hold as she struggled to keep from falling. Her arms were grasped, and she was hauled upwards and held there while she regained her footing.

A fumbling started on the wrist of her left glove.

She focused her illusions, turning the skin of that hand and arm to brown.

The glove slid free, and the guard twisted her hand, turning it palm down. He gave a surprised grunt.

She froze. Her illusions had failed. Now, instead of a shaming she would get a week of torment at the hands of the Red Pelican; the kind of torture that would make the beating in the alley feel like child's play.

"First offense," one of the other men said.

Sarenka could hardly believe it. They hadn't failed.

"First time caught, more like. She moves like a pro," another guard added.

"You know what that means."

"Well, fuck me. Get that damn hood up and hide the bitch's face."

"Stupid woman, little old to start thieving, aren't you?" He released her wrist with a vicious jerk.

"Learn your lesson. First time offence means mercy and we hide your face." Another added, his voice oddly gruff. "Nobody has to know this is anything but an old accident."

The guard next to him leaned forward and whispered into her ear, "But you listen. If you do it again, not only will it be public, but the matching scars'll announce you to the world as the thief we both know you really are."

He pulled the cloak hood forward to mask her identity and grasped her arm in an iron grip before stepping towards the block. Hidden within the dark folds, Sarenka reluctantly let the illusions covering her face go and focused on strengthening the illusions on her hand. She licked dry lips and sent up a silent prayer. If she could hold that illusion through the cutting, she stood a chance, but it would take all her energy.

They unbound her wrists and shoved her towards the block.

A man with arms the size of her thighs picked up a serrated glass knife. His jaw moved, as if he were chewing something.

Sarenka kept her head bent forward, worried that a spark would manage to float free of the hood, or that they'd change their mind and uncover her face.

A guard grasped her forearm and leaned down over her, using his body to force her forehead to the table and pinning her arm out in front of the Retaliator.

The Retaliator spat, and a wad of warm moisture hit the back of Sarenka's hand. She gagged as the rotted scent of fish chaw filled the air and knew they were making sure she didn't heal fast—or clean. He smeared the chaw over the back of her hand and up over her wrist, luxuriating in it, as if he were coating her with precious ointment. At last, he pinched the skin on the back of her hand into a ridge and pressed a fishhook through the fold.

Sarenka held her breath, enduring the pain as he turned a nearby crank and the line lifted, pulling her skin taut. She closed her eyes as a second and third hook were added and pulled tight enough to tear skin. A whimper escaped her lips.

The serrated blade touched the back of her wrist, cold and sharp, its glass teeth piercing the skin and drawing blood.

Sarenka's body went cold with fear. She stared up through the folds of her hood, fixated, as the beads of blood swelled and slid down onto the wood.

He shifted the blade, getting a better grip and grinding the points in deeper.

Sunlight winked off the honed double edge, blinding her.

Terror filled her. *No! They can't!*

A tear slipped down her cheek, and she bit her tongue, determined not to cry out.

The blade swung sideways in a sudden whir, scraping her wrist and sawing through the taut flesh of her hand.

Sarenka screamed and surged backwards but could not escape the weight on her back, or the lacerating pain. At last, the thin slice of blackened flesh gave way, bouncing upwards on the hooks, and her clenched fist landed on the bloodied slab, spraying the area with red.

"God damn it! Every fuckin' time." The guard flung her wrist aside and stood, wiping blood off his face.

She yanked her hand under her cloak, cradling the cut against her chest. The blood soaked through, wetting her skin and filling the air with the scent of meat.

Her glove landed on the table in front of her face.

Realizing that the guard's weight was no longer holding her down, she snatched up the glove and stood, using the pain as an excuse to stay hunched over.

"You can go. Remember what you learned today, woman," he said from behind, shoving her so unexpectedly that she pitched forward onto her knees.

Something hit her back with a thump.

Another blow smacked the side of her head, and the stench of decaying fish filled the air. High pitched jeers and rotten food rained down around her. Sarenka peered through the folds as a child of barely six launched a rancid piece of meat at her face. She dodged and stumbled away at a run, keeping her head low. The children followed, cursing the day she was born and mocking her thieving abilities.

She endured the yells and the stench of rancid fish for several blocks before the game grew old. Scooping up a piece of meat that squished, jellylike, between her fingers, she whirled about and launched it at the oldest boy. It landed true, striking him in the middle of the chest. Dumfounded, he stared down for a moment, then gave a whistle and the gang melted away, returning to the alleys they had come from.

Sarenka looked back towards the Shaming Square while their voices faded. Only one person still watched, but didn't follow.

She tugged the hood forward, though it could move no further than it already was, and walked a few blocks before slipping into an alley. Upon reaching the back of the alley, she slid down the wall and examined her hand. The cut, while straight and true, was ragged and smeared with chaw. That method had been chosen for the sole purpose of leaving a noticeable scar. She closed her eyes, gathering her strength.

A tear trickled down her cheek.

Now that I can't supplement the odd chores with stealing, how will I survive?

The scent of the chaw, warmed by contact with her chest, filled her nostrils. Sarenka's eyes flew open. Surging to her feet, she took off for the sea at a run. Infection would set in if she didn't get the chaw cleaned off quickly, and then she really would lose her hand.

As the needle pricked Parian's skin, a deafening roar shattered the quiet. The man holding the needle started, and the needle skittered across the surface of Parian's arm, drawing a line of red dots. The grip on his arm loosened.

Parian jerked his arm in towards his body while twisting under the man.

The men's bodies flew across the room, landing against the wall with a crash.

Parian surged to his feet.

Rosalie snarled again and swiped the air in front of the men.

The men backed, crablike, further into the corner she'd trapped them in.

~Go stupid!~

Parian threw the saddle and his bags out the window before launching himself face-first through the opening. Already sore from the struggle, he landed ungracefully.

Rosalie followed, her back claws barely missing Parian's head. She snarled when he grabbed the saddle. *~Are you always so daft? Leave it. We don't have time.~*

Climbing onto her bare back, he gave the saddle one last longing look and held on for dear life as she surged forward.

~That was close.~

~Too close,~ she agreed.

When she could run no further, she curled up and tucked her head under her tail.

Glad for the chance to close his eyes, he leaned against her haunch.

After a while she shifted, pushing out her back legs and him with them.

He mumbled and rolled forward until his head was pillowed by her front paw.

She opened an eye, licked the top of his head, and went back to sleep.

Parian awoke with a stretch and glanced around. Rosalie was nowhere to be found. Shaking out stiff muscles, he pulled a handful of nuts from his bag and tossed them into his mouth, chewing slowly to savor the flavor. A rustle came from a nearby bush and the limbs shook in a shiver of plum foliage. Hardly daring to move, he unsheathed his dagger.

Rosalie stepped forward, squirrel in mouth.

Parian relaxed. ~*Well, at least one of us has fresh food.*~

She dropped the bloodied squirrel at his feet. ~*That's for you. I've already eaten.*~

Parian smiled, grateful. "There's just one thing."

~*Let me guess. You don't eat squirrel.*~

"I don't know how to cook it."

~*It's not turkey.*~

He gave her a you-have-got-to-be-kidding-me look.

~*Just eat it raw, some fresh blood will do you good.*~

"Uhhh no. I like my food cooked, thank you."

~*Suit yourself.*~ She lay down in the middle of the clearing. ~*But time is moving. If you don't hurry, we'll be traveling in the dark again.*~

Parian settled on cutting the meatier pieces of the animal free and left the rest alone. Though stringy, it was better than he expected, and he was glad for the food. It might have been days before he ate next if she hadn't brought something.

For the next few days, their travel was filled with detours and spent mostly off trail. When they reached the outskirts of Darkiorn, Rosalie stood a distance off, nose lifted, scenting the air.

~*I don't like it.*~

"Come on, please Rosalie, we're almost there."

~*Too many people.*~

He scratched at his armpit. "It'll be okay. Think of the steak."

~*Why can't you do these rituals outside?*~

"Too dangerous. I might be discovered, or interrupted… or eaten."

~I wouldn't let that happen.~

"I just can't."

~Too many.~ She returned to her first comment as if it was the most important consideration.

"There'll be lots of male cats."

She took a step towards the city and then stopped. *~If you think that's going to lure me in, you know nothing, Parian Zerelth.~*

"Rosalie, I have to go, with or without you." He stared into her eyes. "I'd rather it be with."

She snorted and started forward, leaving him behind. *~Okay. I'll go, but only because you need protecting.~*

He smiled and hurried to catch up.

Within the turn of an hourglass, she was bedded down in the best of stables with an uncooked steak, and he was sitting in a stone tub filled with hot water. He sighed contentedly, blowing at the suds. He'd cut himself off from the Seven ever since they sent men to collect him. It hadn't been easy to resist. At first, he had just wanted to flaunt the fact that he was still free, but after a while he had simply missed them.

He grabbed the soap mitt and scrubbed himself clean before wrapping a luxuriously thick towel around his waist. They'd never expect him to choose such an extravagant hotel.

He'd be safe for long enough to find The One.

CHAPTER 29

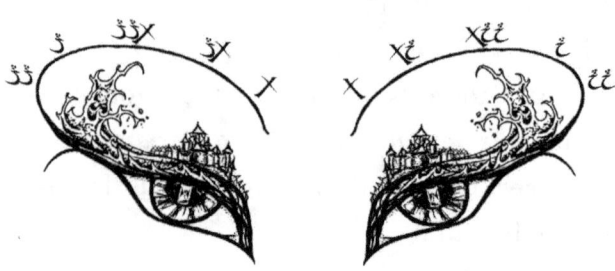

"According to mythology, the Seers are said to have magically guided the Seven Kings of Llayentia in the years before betrayal. There is, however, no solid evidence to support these fairy tales, and all references to them have been struck from official records. Now they are used to frighten silly children into obedience. Sayings like 'you better be good or the The Seven will poison you,' and 'watch out for the Seer, lest your juice turn to poison,' abound in nearly every city."

Valfrids Augstkalnins
Legendmaker
Freni-Kyn Bardic Division

The child wraith bent over Sarenka's body, translucent lips pressed to an ear which twitched, half opening before folding down again. The girl ran feather-light fingers over Sarenka's temples, sliding downwards until they came to a rest against her cheek in a cold caress.

Sarenka's eyes flew open, and her hands balled into fists as she surged to her feet. Eyes wide with fright, she searched the alley. Her energy evaporated and she collapsed in a heap and tugged the hood further over her face.

"Yes, you're alone, don't worry," the wraith whispered, placing her hand on Sarenka's cheek once more.

Sarenka moved her hand in a superstitious ward against evil and touched her cheek through the transparent fingers.

A rustle came from further down the refuse-strewn alley.

The wraith lifted her face, searching for the source.

A pile of rags shifted and moved, separating itself from the crate it was wedged behind, finally forming a man-like shape as it stood.

Can he see me?

Unmoving, the ragman faced her.

She shrugged and bent her head back to Sarenka's ear, whispering.

The rags gasped.

The child wraith smiled. *This should be fun.* She took a step towards the ragman.

He turned and ran, torn bits of clothing flying out from behind.

She gazed down at Sarenka. *It's enough. I've set the trap.*

With a high pitched giggle that echoed off the walls of the narrow alley, she set off after the fleeing man.

Although the frigid touch lifted, the chill remained, sinking down past Sarenka's flesh and settling like a stone of regret in her heart. She moaned at the ever-present pinch of hunger and tapped a fingernail against the stone paving, counting.

Three months! So long... but not enough... how much longer?

Eyes closed, she rubbed away soreness from sleeping on the pebble-encrusted ground. Inns were still out of the question. The wanted posters had been torn from lantern posts and wells, stolen for the tattered parchment they were sketched on. Yet they still hung inside taverns and inns, and they didn't specify that she be taken alive. She peered out from under the cloak edge and settled an illusion of a H'euman crone into place.

Why wasn't I born Sharpra? Life would be so much easier. No magics to dispel. A true body shift. I could sleep anywhere. Do anything.

Removing her glove, she rubbed a begrimed hand over her face. The last of her d'yroaps were gone. She'd spent them the evening before on a snail shell's worth of the meanest drink she could afford. There would be no sweet-drink tonight, nothing to quiet the torment of withdrawal. Pulling the filthy scrap of a threadbare cloak closer, she fingered her pick-tools.

No… Shhh… I can't steal. Stop tempting me.

She stared at the jagged scar across the back of her trembling hand.

It's too risky… especially now. I'm too weak. Too tired…

Pulling the glove back into place, she started forward. The salt laden fog billowed up, obscuring her view and reminding her of the thirst, the Kyron-forsaken-never-ending thirst. Her dangling cup clattered against the links of her coconut shell belt with each step, reminding her of another type of thirst. Sweet-drink, and only sweet-drink, kept the withdrawal at bay.

Her mouth watered. She glanced at the dangling cup and ran a cotton tongue across cracked lips. It was the only thing of value she still owned, and it was all she could do not to rip it free and throw it against a wall.

I can't do this. I can't. Who knows what I'll do? I might kill someone or…

Whispered tales of Freni-Kyn females who had accidentally killed their lovers swept through with a cold shiver. Sarenka's gut twisted and turned at the thought, and she gagged, bending forward to spew forth air in guttural heaves.

A nearby rat squealed and darted away.

Wiping spittle from her chin, she stared at the red tinged liquid, grateful that yesterday's feverish waves of hot and cold had already stolen her food. Though painful, dry-retching was far better than the hours of projectile vomiting she'd experienced the last time she'd gone without sweet-drink.

I'm getting better. Just a few more sweet-drinks, and I'll kick the withdrawal for good.

Glancing upward, Sarenka measured the distance of the two moons from each other and wiped a fine sheen of sweat from her forehead.

Midnight… taverns closing… time running out.

Her heart raced as she rummaged through her pouch, hoping she'd missed a d'yroap. The memory of bones burning like fire and yearning for death came rushing back. She shuddered.

Can't... not again... need sweet-drink... won't survive...

Movement caught her eye. She swung about, reaching for her dagger. Her reflection in a cracked window was all she found. She peered at the broken pane.

Father?

She stepped closer to the window.

What are you doing here? Have you seen what they did to me? Why, father, why make a pleasure drug that needs an antidote? Aren't we cursed enough?

She waited a moment, listening, and cringed.

No, no, no! Don't say that again. It's a curse. The preral cycle is a curse.

Incredulity stole over her face and she shook her head.

I can't be that person. I can't.

Sarenka clapped her hands over her ears.

Stop it! I don't care what you think. I don't care if our ancestors did it to survive the rage wars. I'm not them. I don't care if it's honorable. I can't do it.

She tilted her head, listening.

Yes, I know... I know how I look.

She reached out to touch her face in the glass.

Okay...

You're right of course.

It's the only way to survive.

She shifted into what might appeal to a H'euman male: high cheekbones, honeyed hair, and vacant blue eyes. After tugging the filthy blouse down to expose more cleavage, she blew into her hand and sniffed, then waved it away. The sour stench of vomit couldn't be helped. Then again, the men leaving The Yellow Stain were always drunk.

Surely, one of them...

She stepped from the alley, intercepting a broad shouldered pass-erby whose hooded cloak spoke of ample d'yroap, and reached for his arm.

Breaking stride, the stranger's hand settled on the pommel of his sword.

She hesitated, then tightened her fingers.

He slowed to a stop and spoke with a snarled mixture of question-ing impatience. "Yes?"

"For a price"—voice soft with embarrassment, Sarenka drew a breath before continuing in a rush—"for a price I can give you a good night."

The man bent closer.

Sarenka's hopes soared. She searched the shadowed recesses with-in his hood, trying to find more than the gleam of eyes.

"You don't look like you've got much of a good night in you, girl." The disbelief in his voice was unrestrained. Abruptly he thrust her away, half raising a hand to cover his face. "Kyron! You stink like the back end of a goat!"

"Please. I'll do anything." Sarenka tried to summon up a seductive voice, but the words came out desperate, even to her ears.

The man gave a start. lightning-fast, his hand shot out to grasp the back of her shirt, and he pulled Sarenka towards a guttering torch.

She cringed and held her breath, fearful that her illusions had faltered or that he'd noticed the difference between the illusionary spiraled tresses and the fine fluff of Freni-Kyn hair.

He cleared his throat and spoke with a deeper voice. "Let me see your real face!"

She tried to pull free.

He grasped her arm with his other hand. "I want to know what I'm buyin', girl. Let me see your real face."

Sarenka closed her eyes. Clawing him wouldn't help: she was too weak to break free. *I'm caught. It's over. If only I had found Onglat. I could have cleared my name.*

Maybe he won't remember that they're looking for a Freni-Kyn.

Maybe he won't turn me in for the price on my head.

Maybe I won't be strung up.

Too many maybes…

I can't go on struggling. It's inevitable.

If I'm to meet death, it's going to be head on.

The Foreveron withdrawal had beaten all the fight from her. She let the illusions drop.

Silence hung over them like a bird of prey.

Ayluin Lator, named after his father's father, arrived at the pale blue hut just as the sun set. The handle turned without effort, and he let himself into the dark interior rooms without knocking. He crept through the house, stopping for a creaking floorboard before tiptoeing down the central hallway and peering inside each room, searching for occupants before moving on to the next doorway. At last, he arrived before a tall door, its expensive surface engraved in runes against evil and smeared with green. He leaned forward to smell it.

Sage. Always sage.

Warily, he pushed the door open. A woman sat with her back to him, showing only the tight grey bun above the top of a cushioned chair. A scratching sound came, alerting him to the other occupant. At the desk across the room another woman sat, quill in hand, completely unaware of his presence. He studied the complicated plaits on the back of her head before ignoring the younger woman. Instead he focused in on his target and crept towards the central chair with his arm behind his back.

The older woman's head nodded, keeping beat to music only she could hear.

Stepping in front of her, he pulled the brael flowers out from behind his back with an exuberant flourish and thrust them towards her.

She clapped her hands and smiled and reached for the flowers, but the eyes that met his were blank.

His heart thudded. He placed the flowers in her hands and kissed her forehead.

Staring past him out the window, she brushed the petals back and forth across her cheeks,

"She's lucky to have a son like you," the woman across the room said.

He frowned at the Frevellian herbmistress. "Not lucky enough."

"More than most."

"When was the last time she…"

"Was herself?" the herbmistress asked.

"Yes."

"Three days ago."

"I couldn't get here before now."

"She knew."

He stared at the willow tree through the window. The wind tossed the branches mesmerizingly to and fro, and he supposed that was why she watched them. "Have you found anything to help?"

"Not yet."

He uncoiled his mother's hair and picked up a brush from the nearby dresser. Slowly, gently, he ran it over her thinning tresses.

She closed her eyes and smiled, and he took comfort in that. It was a small thing, but at least he could give her that kindness.

"Has the pain been bad?"

"Some days."

He fell silent, his hand stroking down through her grey locks in a soothing rhythm until he felt they'd both drawn some peace. At last, he put aside the brush and turned away from her vacant stare.

"Find someone else. There must be someone that knows a cure." He set a pile of riseen d'yroap on the desk next to the document the herbmistress been writing. They glinted green in the fading sunlight.

"We will do what we can but…" the herbmistress looked away.

Unable to bear whatever else she might add to that, he left.

The silence drew out as Sarenka waited for him to shout for the city guards.

"How much?" the hooded man asked.

Yanked from the certitude of death, relief washed over her. She licked dry lips. *How much can I get away with?* "Twenty silver loops?"

He barked out a harsh laugh. "For the night."

She hesitated.

"Twenty silver loops, and I get the whole damn night. That's the deal."

Sarenka ground her teeth, causing pain to knife through her temple. Turning her face to the side, she wiped moisture from the corner of her eye. *A whole night! A whole night, but enough silver for a week.*

"Okay, but I get the sweet-drink first, before we start."

"Need somethin' to be with someone ugly as me? Fine." He sounded both satisfied and disgusted. "Put the illusions back on. I'll not be seen with a Freni-Kyn."

The way he said Freni-Kyn. He means slut. Sarenka's cheeks blazed violet but she shifted. *Like most H'eumans, he considers us trash. He can't understand the need, not any more than I can.*

He grasped her wrist in a punishing grip and took off, his longer stride keeping her at a half-run.

"You don't have to hold on so tight."

He didn't respond.

She twisted her arm, trying to free her wrist. "I'm not going to run. I need the d'yroap."

He quickened his pace, refusing to let go.

A tavern loomed into view, and her mouth watered. "Please, can we get the sweet-drink first?"

He passed it without breaking stride or glancing at her. "Later, when we get there."

Their arrival at a windowless shack on the edge of Sad Town sent misgivings shearing through Sarenka. Nobody on this side of town had that kind of d'yroap. When he swung open the weathered door, she yanked her hand loose.

"Show me the loops first!"

He gave a low chuckle and pulled open his d'yroap pouch and tilted it towards her. The multi-colored loops glinted in the moonlight like misshapen rings. She wet her lips. He had far more than twenty silver. With that many d'yroaps, she could bribe her way out of Burmtin and escape the Red Pelican once and for all.

"Satisfied?"

She peered into the recesses of the dark hood, once more trying to find his face. "Yes."

"Well then, in with you." His hand swept towards the hut in mock welcome.

Sarenka stepped through the darkened doorway with trepidation. Night had invaded the tiny shack, sucking from it whatever comforting warmth it should have held and leaving behind the kind of pervasive chill that stripped the bones of heat. Shivering with more than cold, she rubbed her shoulders through the ragged scrap of a fabric she called a cloak.

Her elliptical pupils widened into black pools, adjusting to the dim light as she examined the room. She could define larger objects but couldn't pick out intricate details. Two simple chairs and a small dining table dominated the center of the room. A massive chair sat before the unlit fireplace, and a sideboard leaned against the nearby wall under a cluttered shelf. A single bed, flat and smooth, lay in the far corner next to a large trunk. Though the belongings were sparse, the room smelled only of burned wood. She relaxed; glad not to be adding bedbugs to her list of ails. Apparently not all shacks located in Sad Town were filthy.

With the pale light of the double-moons slanting through the open doorway, he stepped to the fireplace and stacked fresh wood in the hearth, stirring the embers to life before shutting the door. The clunk of the bolt sliding shut was punctuated with a spitting crackle, and the wood caught, filling the room with a flickering dance of shadow and light. And in the moment that those flames burst upwards, he pushed back the hood of his cloak, revealing his face in stark relief.

Gasping, Sarenka reeled backwards and spun around, searching for an escape route.

It was too late.

She was trapped.

Chapter 30

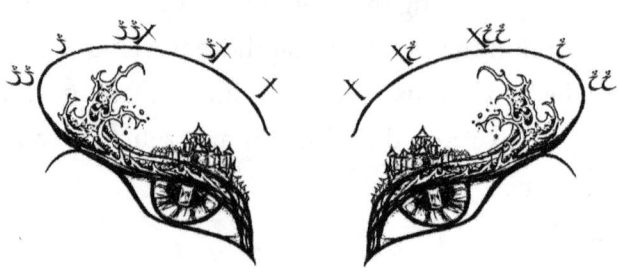

Unmoving, he stared at her with an expression of smug satisfaction.

"D'trav!" It burst from her lips like an expletive.

"What's the matter Sarenka, afraid?" He said, dropping into the drawl she remembered. His jeering laugh echoed eerily as he swung his leather cloak off and tossed it onto a nearby peg. He stalked across the room, eyes narrowing dangerously.

She retreated, step-by-step, until the back of her legs came up against the table. Placing her hands on the edge, she wondered if she had the strength to flip over it before he could attack.

"I wouldn't have castrated you."

"Easy to say that now, isn't it?"

"I left you the key."

"And wanted posters of my ugly mug in every damn tavern."

"I… I'm sorry… I…"

"Well, that's neither here nor there. First things first, *darlin.*" He drew out the endearment, lacing it with sarcasm, and the firelight contorted his slanting smile into a grotesque grimace, shifting with each flickering flame.

Terror crept in a chill warning down her spine.

He drew a dagger from a scuffed leather scabbard with such confidence that she leaned back and flexed her legs, readying for a sideways spin over the tabletop. Firelight winked off the razor sharp edge as the moments drew out. Flipping the well-honed blade in midair, he presented the handle to her.

"A duel?" Sarenka stared at the carved bone hilt with disbelief, eyes traveling from the blade to his mocking leer. The blood rushed from her cheeks. Even when healthy, she couldn't have bested him; he outweighed her easily two to one.

"Take it."

She reached for the hilt.

"I wanna see every nail shortened. Now! Once you've got that done, I reckon I'll give you some antidote."

"You have it—" blood thundered through her veins and her eyesight tunneled, and, for a long moment, her hearing stopped— "the antidote?"

"I do."

"And you'll let me have it?"

"Let's be takin' care of those claws first."

She searched his eyes. *It's too valuable... far more than a night in bed... there's got to be some horrific price...* Sarenka shifted her grip on the hilt and swung it back level with her shoulder in a move designed for only one purpose.

Unafraid, he turned his back to her and laughed.

She hesitated, dagger poised for a downward thrust through his heart.

He swung back around and took a step closer, and there was no mirth in his face, only furrowed brows and piercing eyes.

She flinched.

"You haven't got strength enough to hold that blade steady-like, and you think you're gonna take me out?" His voice lowered into a threatening growl. "Best be givin' that plan a little think over."

Sarenka's hand trembled under the slight weight of the dagger, convincing her that he was right. She didn't stand a chance. Not now. Maybe not ever.

"Do it, girl, or you'll be findin' yourself right back out on the street, without the d'yroap, *or* the antidote."

Her hand wavered before dropping in defeat. *Why lie? He's already bought my service.* Her nails shot out, extending beyond the tips of the gloves. She slammed her hand down on the table and cut flat across them in one quick move. Looking up at D'trav, she flipped the knife into the other hand and raised it to take care of the rest. Her hand shook.

"Careful girl! I want them fingers nice and intact. Last I noticed, antidotes don't be sproutin' legs."

She sighed with disgust for her exhaustion.

"Not like it's gonna walk it's way outta here if you don't be movin' fast enough."

She finished the stroke, slicing through with precision born of many hours at blade practice. Dropping the dagger, she pulled off her gloves and tossed them onto the table, then lifted her hands for inspection. A tiny bead of blood welled up from one shorn claw.

"Told you to have a care!" He grasped her hands, inspecting the fingertips by rubbing his thumb over them. "Welp, it's a start. Edges a bit ragged. We'll deal with what's been left after a bit."

He frowned at the back of her hand and rubbed his thumb across her scar and he shook his head. "Caught thievin' were you? Not sure how you got through the cuttin' without them knowin' who you are. I'm sure it's a tale worth tellin' though."

Sarenka's cheeks grew hot.

Pulling a vial from his pocket, he held it out to her.

Sarenka's focus shifted to the tiny bottle of golden liquid and her illusions dropped away. A waving mass of chestnut brown hair floated about her head, tiny lights flickering among the lengths. Scarlet eyes slanted upwards within a surrounding fringe of inch long lashes. Skin deepened to iris blue.

"Unbelievable." D'trav gave a hungry smile and swept his grey eyes over her body. "So much filth you could plant a garden, but still pretty enough to get most anything you'd be wanting."

Dizzy with anticipation, she stagger forward, eyes fixed on the vial. The hand she stretched forth shook violently in the flickering firelight.

"Damn. You're one sorry mess. I'd best do this, so as you don't go and spill it every which way." D'trav uncorked the vial with a pop.

The unmistakable stench of antidote wafted out, stirring memories of its rancid flavor. Sarenka's stomach churned.

"Open up, darlin. I'm sure you 'member the drill."

Sarenka obeyed out of habit. Her captors had always hand-fed the expensive antidote. He poured the oily fluid into her open mouth and she lost control, gagging on the bile-flavored liquid as it slid over her tongue and hit the back of her throat.

D'trav clasped her jaw and forced her head up. "Keep it down. Keep it down, damn it. I've only got one." He slapped his other hand over her mouth and pinched her nose closed.

A violent shudder worked its way through her body, and she staggered forward.

D'trav released her face and clasped her elbows, supporting her weight until she regained control.

At last she opened her eyes and blinked them several times while the room swam into focus.

Grey eyes narrowed, brows furrowed, he searched her face. "Better?"

"Yes," she said, low and unsure. Acrid oil still coated her tongue, and she felt as if she'd been punched in the gut, but already the ringing in her ears and the burning craving had lessened. "Thank you."

"Good. Strip."

She blinked, surprised at his shift to briskly uncaring.

"I said strip, damn it."

"Why do you have the antidote?" She frowned, suspicious.

His face darkened, and the muscles of his jaw clenched, "Just do, now strip."

Reluctant at what must come next, Sarenka began disrobing.

After rummaging through a basket on the mantle, he threw a handful of red tiles into the fire. Bouncing against each other as they fell, they chinked and turned cherry red before landing on the logs. He grasped the flue handle and pulled sideways. Grating and screeching, the flue shifted, forcing the rising heat into a series of exposed ceramic pipes.

Sarenka traced the pipes to a large bladder of water suspended above a wooden tub. Visible waves of heat radiated from the end of the pipe, surrounding the bladder before rising into a secondary chimney. The flames crackled and popped as her last piece of clothing rustled to the floor.

He turned back, obviously listening. "You're just a slip of a thing now. When's the last time you ate?"

"Yesterday, but I…"

"You lost it. Yeah, withdrawal has that effect. And 'fore that?"

"Three days ago."

"But you kept back just enough copper for sweet-drink, didn't you?"

Sarenka placed a hand on her stomach, empty and flat, and gave a reluctant nod.

"It's not really a drug, you know."

She shook her head, of course it was a drug.

"It's a parasite, grows inside you, eatin' away."

Lying… he's lying… With growing horror she thought of how her stomach had moved the last few weeks, as if something living was inside, trying to get out.

"Sweet-drink only dulls the symptoms. Till you've got the antidote, the cravin'll just claw at your innards like a drownin' cat in a burlap bag."

"I thought… eventually…"

"Don't work that way. Have to have the antidote." He turned to stare at the fire.

Flames flared up, licking at the stones. The tile surface cracked, forming crazed blue fissures before giving one final 'pop' and turning completely blue-white. Sarenka squinted at the blinding white light with alarm.

D'trav's face reddened with heat and he took a calm step back.

Assured that they weren't going to explode, Sarenka wrapped her arms around her body and sank down onto her haunches. She studied his profile in the low light, wondering when the deal she'd made with him would start. This would be the first time she had memories of her liaisons. In her time with the Baron, the only things left after the Foreveron wore off were fragmented images and cuts and bruises. That she sold herself by choice this time only added to the dull throb of apprehension. Tonight would be a mark on her soul.

Doesn't matter.

One night.

Just one.

Then I'll find a way to make d'yroap that doesn't involve... this.

Her eyes swept over D'trav.

I was a fool.

Thinking I could escape Burmtin so fast.

Bigger fool to think I could survive off... what?

A bag of D'yroaps?

Despite the rising warmth in the hut, a sudden blast of cold turned her breath into white steam. She shivered with trepidation.

I'm so upset that I'm imagining... can't be this cold...

Her teeth chattered, loud in the quiet room.

D'trav swung about. "Oh, for the sake of Kyron's pity! You really that stupid? Or just stubborn as a weed?"

She opened her mouth to snap out some tart remark, and then decided silence was safer.

He grasped her arm and hauled her closer to the fire. "Keep yourself warm. Don't need you gettin' sick on me 'fore I get my silver's worth outta you."

Humiliated, she lowered her gazed.

Dear god, this floor...

Knees shaking, she sank into a squat, too afraid of the floor to sit on it. She slid her hand across the wood. It was a dried-out mess. What must have started as tiny splinters had turned into massive splits, some longer than her forearm. She gave D'trav another sidelong glance and, finding his gaze fixed on the fire, experimentally pried at a particularly long splinter. After pulling it half free, she pressed it back down, deciding that it was easily long enough, and thick enough, to be used as an impromptu weapon. Having satisfied her training by finding an emergency weapon, she relaxed. If worse came to worse, she'd have something to defend herself with.

Why... why'd he keep such a tidy hut and leave the floor this way? Or did he leave them as possible weapons?

Sarenka let her gaze roam, searching for other potential weapons. Every item in the hut was precisely placed and every surface clean, but the walls were peeling, the ceiling cracked, and even the support beams buckling. She stared at the thick soles of his boots, considering.

So he's here temporarily...

Probably doesn't care that he's walking on daggers.

D'trav interrupted her thoughts by grasping a carved bone lever and pulling until the muscles of his forearms stood out. With a shriek of protest, the pipes above the wooden tub shifted to the side. He yanked a chain of tiny shells, tipping the bladder until it spilled steaming water into the large wooden tub. The water hit the tub with such force that it spouted back upwards, sloshing over the sides before settling into a gentle rocking motion.

"Get in, you're filtheir than..." he scratched his ear and wrinkled his nose. "Well damn, can't rightly think of one damn thing filthy enough to compare you with."

"I couldn't stay at an inn." She looked from him to the lovely water, and the lure of cleanliness drove her forward. Sinking into its warm and soothing embrace, she closed her eyes.

A sharp clack-thump jolted her back to the moment. On the floor near the tub lay a ceramic pot of cleansing powder that D'trav had dropped. Her gaze traveled from it to his feet, and when he didn't walk away, up to his face.

He tilted his head mockingly sideways, scooped up her belongings in one deft move, and tossed them into the fire.

CHAPTER 34

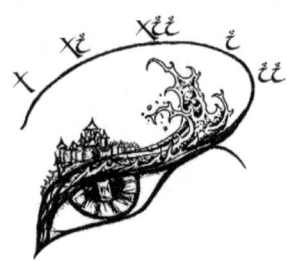

"*The Glidarthian chefs mocked us for our use of Lenan spice. Now they beg to buy it from us. I hear tell they've even made a tooth cleanser from it.*"

Chef Donaldson Randolf
Found scribed in the front of an ancient cookbook.

~Parian? Is that you? What are you doing?~ Lanion's normally sardonic voice was filled with concern.

~Focusing. How'd you find me?~

~I… I don't know. I felt you. You feel… different. We thought you might be… wait—focusing on what?~

Parian kept laying out the chalk marks.

A wave of impatience radiated out from Lanion. *~Focusing on what?~*

~He… she… is calling for help.~

~And you call my one-nighters risky…~ Lanion sent.

~I have to go.~

~No, you don't,~ Shignora chimed in. *~Nobody's ever had to take the time stream to find their replacement.~*

Parian sent the mental impression of a snort of derision. *~Those are Airintia's words. Thanks for giving away my location, Lanion.~*

~Doesn't make them any less true,~ Shignora sent.

~You don't understand.. I can't let The One suffer.. I just can't.~ He lit the brazier and watched to make sure it was burning evenly. The tant wood would burn long and hot, far better than the oak he'd used before, but was tricky to light.

~Then go there. In person,~ Lanion sent.

~I can't.~

~Why?~

~Like I haven't told you a hundred times already.~ The wave of revulsion that rolled out from Parian made Airintia and Lanion shudder.

~It's not that bad,~ Lanion sent.

~It's Burmtin.~

~Then I'll go for you,~ Lanion sent. *~You know all that sexual energy won't bother me.~*

~So that you can go on another drunken tryst, Lanion?~ Airintia's outrage struck both of them, a blind sheet of rage. *~As if the last time wasn't bad enough.~*

Parian rubbed his forehead. *~Airintia, please, not now. Scold him some other time.~*

~You know I'm right.~

~Of course you are, but not now. I'm focusing.~

~I'll go for you, Parian. I'm not Freni-Kyn. It won't affect me,~ Airintia sent.

~No. It's too dangerous. I won't risk you.~ Parian pushed their thoughts away. *~Be quiet. I need to concentrate.~*

Faintly, like a distant whisper, they continued talking without him.

He shook his head, throwing off a shower of green sparks. *They'd never understand. Who could? They'd never had this kind of pull on their minds.*

He paced out the triangle one final time, checking the placement before stepping into the center and closing his eyes. The call for help pressed in and the elements of fire, wind, and water mixed with his earthen body, pulling his spirit-self upwards. He grasped the strand of thought, following its stream until he hovered over a large building in

Burmtin. As the double moons crested the horizon, a stream of people flowed into the building. Skimming surface thoughts, he flinched, his resolve weakening. Lust lashed at his mental barriers, tempting his Freni-Kyn nature and sucking him towards the building.

A sudden blast propelled him backwards through the air, breaking the sensual lure.

Time stretched into an endless stream of flashing days and nights, and he gathered his strength about him like armor before starting towards the building again. He skimmed through rooms filled with iron and bone cages while the distressed call rose to a roar. His spectral hands flew to his temples but couldn't block the scream. It struck, tumbling him head over heels as if he were nothing more than a mote of dust in the wind.

He was expelled from the triangle and slammed into the wall on the other side of the room with enough force to crack plaster. His body slid to the ground in what felt like slow motion and waves of pain wracked his mind. Plaster showered down in chunks on his head.

~Parian!~ a chorus of the Seven cried out.

Parian coughed and spat out debris. ~I... I'm okay.~

The seers shared a wave of relief and worry.

~What happened?~ Lanion asked.

~I told you not to go,~ Airintia sent.

~I think... I think, The One's injured, dying.~ Parian's distress through their link was a heart wrenching sob.

The hum of their thoughts stopped, and Parian knew they'd all thrown up their shields at the same time.

~I'm sorry, Parian,~ Airintia spoke for the group.

He knew they were searching for how to comfort him but didn't care. There was no fix for this.

~It wasn't your fault,~ Rosalie sent.

He didn't answer and kept his next thought to himself. *Of course it was my fault.*

~*You aren't Kyron,*~ she sent.

He blocked their thoughts and leaned against the wall, giving in to the crushing pain of his heart.

Covering his face with his hands, he sobbed, and tears slid down his cheeks.

"You bastard!" Sarenka reared upwards, water streaming down her body in streaks of grayish brown. "What in Kyron's fifth hell do you think you're doing?"

With a sudden whoosh, the garments went up in flames. Horrified, Sarenka's mouth and eyes rounded as she watched her clothing turn into a blackened mass. A puff of thick smoke billowed outwards, bringing tears to her eyes. Blinking rapidly, she swiped them angrily away and choked back a cough. Gooseflesh pimpled her body, and she wrapped her arms around her chest.

Her attention shifted from the blaze to D'trav. She opened her mouth in a threat but snapped it shut again as wisdom sank in. If he was bold enough to burn her clothing, what else might he do? She darted a glance at the splintered floor, glad for the backup plan if things went bad. He seemed not to notice any of this; not the stench of burning leather, or Sarenka's anger, or even the crackling her shell cup made before the heat shattered it.

A flapping sound drew her attention from the shattered cup to the door. She turned her head in time to see D'trav's cloak swing into place, settling over his broad shoulders.

A slow, easy smile slanted its way across his face. "Relax, darlin. You won't be naked long. I'll be back with some clean clothin' and what not. Food too, *if* you behave and make yourself real pretty like. And make sure you clean that hair of yours. I'm lookin' forward to strokin' it."

She cringed. Every legal brothel had a 'no touch' rule. He had to know better than to touch her living hair.

D'trav stepped from the cottage, shutting the door behind him with a decisive thunk.

Sarenka stared at the soaping powder, wondering what hidden menace it contained before sniffing it tentatively. The reassuring scent of lavender and salt wafted up, tickling her nostrils. Relieved, she poured some into her hands and began scrubbing. It might be weeks before another opportunity to bathe came. Every once in a while a noise from outside reminded her that D'trav would soon return.

She sighed.

If she pleased him, maybe he could be persuaded to buy more antidote or at least tell her where to find it. It wouldn't matter how demeaning his demands were if compliance won enough antidote to be free of the withdrawal symptoms. For the first time she understood the desperation that had driven her Freni-Kyn ancestors to prostitution.

Survival was a powerful master.

D'trav returned to a too-quiet home and growled under his breath. Rage arose, momentarily darkening his sight. His eyes skipped past the tub, with its floating coat of greasy dirt, and jumped to his trunk. It sat unmolested, scarf covering its surface, candle still in place. She hadn't plundered it. He took a relieved breath and peered at the lump on the nearby bed.

What's that?

Revenge?

Some dead creature she's done dragged in?

He covered his nose at the thought. A sigh reached his ears as he stepped closer, and finally, he knew. Oblivious to his return, she lay curled up fast asleep in that darkened corner.

Probably first bed she's had since leavin' me standin' with my balls in a sorry state.

He winced at the memory.

After dropping several string-tied packages on the table with a thump, he hung his cloak and bastard sword and went to stand over the sleeping woman. Unlike the last time, there'd be no need to assuage his guilt with excessive alms-giving at the local temple and donations to the poor. This time she'd propositioned him. The covers were a tangled mess, and the teasing glimpses of bare skin brought an aching response from his body.

She's mine.

Least for a while.

His attention shifted to the packages on the table.

Maybe longer now that I've gotten the bribes.

She won't be able to resist.

Nobody addicted to that vile drug can.

Turning back to Sarenka, his gaze roved over her curves before settling on her face. It was surprising how much abuse a Freni-Kyn could take and still remain enticing. He held a hand out to one of the floating strands of hair. It responded, half wrapping its dimly lit length around his finger. The long eyelashes, lying across her cheekbones like dark feathers, gave her such a childlike innocence that he paused, wondering if all Freni-Kyn looked that fragile while sleeping.

Beautiful, of course…

Not the type looks to bed an ugly cuss like me.

His eyes betrayed him, and he saw her covered in the baron's blood, feral with fear. A sudden chill pervaded the room, and his breath puffed out in a stream of white while gooseflesh arose on his arms. Horrified, D'trav took a step back and rubbed his eyes. She lay undisturbed, peaceful and clean.

Now I'm seein' things.

He tossed away the frightening vision with a disparaging shake of his head. The Foreveron drug made people so senseless that anyone could commit murder without meaning to. Still the cold lingered.

Perplexed at the shift from cozy-warm to icy-cold, he glanced across the room. The fire blazed fiercely, firestones white hot. Frowning, he turned his attention to the door. The insulating blanket over it hung slack, with no draft billowing its thick fabric. He looked back at Sarenka, and the image of his sister's face overlay the Freni-Kyn's for just long enough to pierce his heart with grief.

Too damn innocent looking.

He swiped a hand across his face and his cock went limp.

"Son of a vespra-lanir bitch," he muttered with disgust, staring down at his disappearing bulge and wondering why he chose now, of all times, to remember his sister. Purposely staring at Sarenka's full breasts, he willed his body to respond, but every time he felt a flicker of life his sister's face appeared. Turning abruptly away, he strode to the room's only comfortable chair, an indulgence that wasn't shared with anyone. Its broad wooden expanse invited lounging, reading, or in this case, thinking.

"Well, if I can't bed the witch, what in Kyron's hells *am* I gonna do with her?" he grumbled moodily at the fire. The flames grew low while he watched with unseeing eyes, remembering a sister he'd cared for, shielded, fed, protected. Remembering how all his efforts had failed in the end, leaving him alone in this… this…

Thoughts stuttering to a stop, his eyes swept the room.

"This crap hole of a hut." The words, once spoken aloud, lay bare in their truth. His shoulders rounded in defeat. "What am I doin' here, Elsa? Nothin's gonna ever bring you back."

With a grunt of self-loathing, he strode to the table and jerked at the package strings, exposing the contents. Female clothing; each neatly folded article lying like some incongruous pile of frivolity. He flicked at it with a fingertip. The clothing did nothing to relieve the stark reality of a meager existence; one he'd been forced into when he fled the manor, but one which had started in his heart long before that. With longing, he thought of the length of heavy chain in his trunk and how much relief it brought. But no, he had promised Camille.

Bitter with the thoughts of how Sarenka had changed his life, he picked up a dainty sandal and fiddled with the strings. The memory of tying a similar sandal to Elsa's tiny ankle brought tears to his eyes. He dropped it back onto the pile and wiped his face.

These don't belong in my life…

Any more than she does.

He stared at Sarenka for a moment before unwrapping the rest of the packages. A slab of cheese and a loaf of fresh bread, along with eight vials of antidote, joined the clothing on the table. It wasn't enough to cure her, but it was all he could find. Next to these, he counted out twenty silver loops.

I already failed Elsa.

Not gonna repeat that damn mistake.

She's better off elsewhere.

He considered the goods with satisfaction. The past couldn't be changed but he could put aside the guilt for how he'd treated her at the manor.

A drawn out yawn interrupted the memories and regrets. The day had been long, and not as successful as he'd hoped, when he returned with the bribes an hourglass turn ago.

Who am I tryin' to bribe anyway?

Her?

Or my guilty conscious?

His eyes flitted from the woman lying in the bed to the bare space in front of his fire, and he stripped out of his clothes, letting them drop to the ground. Grabbing the extra blanket from where she'd shoved it, he walked over to the fire and stared downward.

"What am I thinking?"

He landed on the edge of the bed with a thud that bounced the straw mattress and shook the frame. Settling into the mattress, he turned his back on her and shut away the knowledge of her naked body lying so close to his.

I'll be struck with lightnin' from the gates of hell 'fore I take to sleepin' on the damn floor.

Not for her.

Not for any woman.

Sarenka awoke to a steady vibrating snore. Momentarily disoriented, she clutched at the nubbed coverlet and pulled it over her head and peered out from under it, just as she had with her cloak for the last few months. Memory of the night before came flooding back, tinting her cheeks violet with shame. Taking in the dimly lit room and the man next to her, the cover slid free, falling in loose folds about her neck and shoulders. She'd sold herself, and the time to pay for that was surely coming, if it hadn't already. But no, there were no tell-tale signs, he hadn't drugged her.

The enticing aroma of lenan spice dragged her from the bed and over to the table. She slapped a hand over her stomach in a useless effort to muffle the gurgling rumble. Mouth watering, hands trembling, she tore a hank of the bread free and crammed it into her mouth, then broke free a chunk of cheese, stuffing it in too. Almost before they could be chewed, she swallowed and snatched up more.

Her gaze darted over each item on the table, all lying in wrinkled oilcloth packaging like discarded peace offerings. Strappy sandals, better than she'd owned in two years. Bodice of brown embossed leather. Chemise, clean and fresh. Skirt of the type that left the legs free for work, short in the front, long in the back. Leggings, warm and strong. Antidote. She ground to a jolting stop.

Antidote? She counted. *Eight vials.*

She stared fixedly at them before stealing a glance back at D'trav. Of its own volition, her hand crept towards the drug.

She pulled her hand back and swore under her breath at the compulsion. "Kyron-be-damned!"

I shouldn't take it.

No, not yet.

They have to be spaced out.

This is…

A bare minimum of two days' worth.

Two days without headaches…

Without the constant ringing in my ears…

Without the burning in my bones that threatens to send me running to the Red Pelican and certain death.

Maybe I'll even be cured…

But how'd he get it?

Only addicts and slave owners used the Foreveron. That he happened to have the antidote gnawed away the trust he'd built by leaving these on the table. Sarenka's gaze settled on the pile of silver loops.

Why'd he set those here?

It's like he's telling me to take the goods and go… but where?

They were still running checks on women at the gates, touching every face before letting them through. Even if her illusions held, which wasn't likely in her weakened state, she wouldn't pass that test. They'd feel the long lashes, floating hair, and elongated eyes.

How am I supposed to get free of this damn city without help?

No, she was stuck here. No way to make a living, no place to live, no one who cared.

Trapped in a city that would swallow her spirit and leave her drained of life if she let it. Sarenka sank into a chair and stared at the man across the room in frank assessment. Not really a good-looking man, but muscular, like any decent guard should be.

Why didn't he wake me when he got back?

She chewed her lip, considering possibilities, and began pulling on the clothing.

D'trav mumbled, rolling over in his sleep.

She froze for long enough to notice the faint light of early morning shining in around the edges of the door-blanket. Concerned that he'd waken, she rushed to finish.

"They fit. I can't believe they fit," she whispered. "Where'd he learn *that* neat little trick?"

She ran her hands down over the leather bodice. It was clean. *She was clean.* The cleanest she'd been since the escape. Lifting a dark blue cloak from the oilcloth wrappings uncovered an empty d'yroap pouch. He'd thought of everything. Except under-garments. The corners of her full lips twitched with amusement before settling into a sideways grin.

Not surprising for a man to forget something like that.

The grin disappeared.

Then again, maybe he didn't forget.

The implications brought a snarl to her lips.

He's just lucky I'm grateful for the goods.

He'd be easy enough to take out right now.

Shock brought with it a sudden whoosh of dizziness, and Sarenka lifted her hand to touch a now cold cheek.

I've come so low.

Nine months ago I wouldn't have considered killing, especially not a sleeping man.

Revulsed, she pushed away the evil thought and wrapped the linen cloak around her shoulders before concentrating on making herself look H'euman. Rushing to the fireplace, she dug through the ashes and pulled free the Red Pelican dagger, ring, and card. Though blackened they had survived. After wiping them clean and rinsing her hands in the cold bath water, she tucked them away within her clothing and placed the loops within the d'yroap pouch, along with the vials of antidote.

With a salute in D'trav's direction, she slipped out the door.

At the sound of the door shutting, D'trav slipped one eyelid open and surveyed the room.

Good, she's gone.

He rolled over, dragging the blanket around him as he went, and shifted about uncomfortably before finally lifting his head to give the pillow a resounding thump.

One problem less in my life.

R'kiax picked up the biscuit he'd just purchased and took a bite before tossing the anxious merchant a few coppers and starting across the market square. A man brushed his shoulder and R'kiax leaned in, refusing to give and knocked the man sideways.

The man turned, hand on sword hilt.

R'kiax smiled, baring pointed teeth.

The man's eyes went wide, and he backed away. "No harm done."

Damn straight there's no harm done.

R'kiax waited for the man to turn away before continuing across the square. Catching an elusive scent, his head went up. He sniffed and swung around, gaze darting from one female figure to another. A woman passed, so loaded down with packages that she had even tucked a bottle of wine under her arm.

R'kiax fell in behind.

His roll landed on the ground behind him with a muffled pluff.

A beggar child darted forward.

A stray mutt snatched up the roll and bared its teeth at the child and growled.

CHAPTER 32

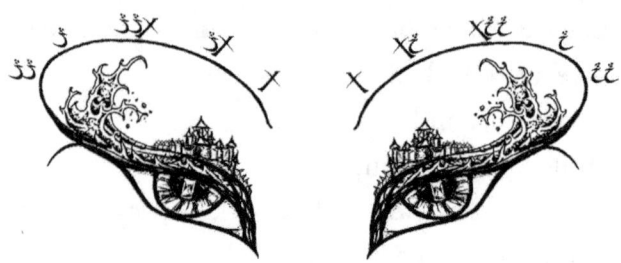

"We can eat them and milk them and use them to make cheese, but we sure as hell can't ride the swamp slugs into battle, I don't care how big and fast they are. And please do not get me started on the slime issue."

Cilleín Ó Lapain
Sharpra War Advisor

D'trav sat up, covered in sweat, heart pounding, and crying out for Elsa in a room so cold that his breath came out in clouds. He stared at the light leaking in around the edges of the door-blanket, and the guilt came flooding back, undoing everything Camille had worked so hard to instill. It was unbearable to go on, to meet each day, without Elsa there to hold his hand and smile her special way. Each day arrived like a crushing weight, unbearable.

If only I could join her in death.

Pushing the candlestick and scarf off the trunk, he threw open its wooden lid and dug through until he found Elsa's old satin robe. Carefully, he lifted it free. It draped between his hands, weighted down with what it contained. He laid it on the bed, and one-by-one, flipped back the folds, revealing an arm length piece of heavy chain.

His fingers slipped tenderly over each link, and he recited his sins against Elsa, all the terrible things he'd done; not hiring a helper to watch her, not bringing her sweets when she asked, staying up late drinking, working too many hours, making her sleep when she wanted to talk, not playing her silly little games enough, running from their parents' home… the list went on.

Leaving the satin enshrined chain laying on his bed, he went to the fire and stirred the embers, bringing them to life. His Banish was made and consumed before he turned back to the bed, as yet undressed. He picked up the chain, wrapping its end around his fist, and swung it back and forth, getting the feel for its weight. It had been so long, almost a year since he'd last held it so. He braced his legs, hip width apart, and brought his forearm abruptly up, flipping the length of chain across his shoulders. It landed on his back harder than he remembered, cutting the skin, and he cried out.

Again.

He slid the chain over his shoulder, letting it clatter to the floor in front of him, and brought it up across the other shoulder, this time taking the pain without a sound.

Again.

He pulled it forward and struck again, and again, until blood flecked the metal. Staggering, sweat covering his body, he let the chain drop to the floor. The pain of losing Elsa was almost bearable now.

A banging came from the door. He hesitated, and struck again.

The door flew open as the chain slid back over his shoulder to the ground. "D'trav! What are you—"

He flexed his arm and stared past her, determined to go on.

Camille grabbed his wrist. "Stop! Stop, dear god! I thought you were past this."

He fell to his knees and wrapped his arms around her waist, and she ran her hand over his bare head, soothing him. Silent sobs convulsed his body, forcing her to brace against the motion or be knocked over.

"Shhh shhhh, it'll be all right."

"It'll never be all right. Never again."

"It will."

"She's gone Camille. Gone…"

"And you'll see her again some day. But you can't do this D'trav. I won't have it."

He laid his cheek against her stomach and cried, and after a time, when he quieted, she helped him to his feet and onto the bed.

"How'd you know I needed you?"

She touched his back with a cloth, gingerly cleaning away blood. "I'm not sure. I had a chill. And for a moment… I… I thought you'd died. I just knew I had to find you."

"How bad is it?"

"Not nearly as bad as the first time I caught you doing this."

"I'll be able to work?"

"Yes, but we're starting the program back up."

He closed his eyes.

"Say it," she said.

"Yes, Mistress."

She leaned over and gently grasped his chin. "You know you need this, right?"

"Yes, Mistress."

"We shouldn't have let up."

"We were busy," he said.

"What triggered it?"

He groaned. "You really don't wanna know."

"I wouldn't have asked if I didn't want to know, luv."

He rolled over and winced as his back touched the covers.

Holding the bloodied cloth, Camille leaned over him with bowler hat tilted at a rakish angle. D'trav's gaze traveled down toward the corseted tailcoat cinching in her waist and pressing her breasts up in an enticing manner. Beneath that, the smallest flap of a skirt brushed the top of her thighs, and snug black leggings stood out in bold relief against the long red skirt that trailed behind.

D'trav ran his fingertip up the inside of her leg, tracing the seam, and felt himself harden. Clasping her hand, he pulled her forward.

She broke the fall, landing with arms braced on either side of him. "Your back, luv—"

"It's been worse."

She swung her leg over his hips and shifted her hips forward and back against him. He gasped, closing his eyes to savor the pleasure. The pain from his lacerations mixed with pleasure, edging him towards satisfaction. He wrapped his hands around her waist and started pulling her closer.

She placed a hand wrapped in fingerless gloves on his chest. "Uh uh. I asked a question."

"The Kyn. She was here… in my hut."

"The Freni-Kyn?"

"The one what got me in trouble."

Camille frowned. "How'd she find your hut?"

He moaned and tried to pull her forward again. "After."

"No. Tell me now."

"She was sellin' herself outside the *Yellow Stain*. My hood was up. She didn't know it was me till we got back here."

Camille's eyes narrowed.

"Shoulda seen the look on her face." He started to smile but changed his mind when Camille frowned. "Cuttin' the bard's tale short, I couldn't fuck the bitch."

"It wouldn't have broken our agreement," Camille said.

"Wasn't that. It's just…" He stared past her at the wall.

She waited.

"Every time I tried… I… I saw Elsa's face…" Afraid to go on, his words faded.

Camille's brows furrowed. "So, she looks like Elsa?"

"Not even close. Elsa was just a child. Pretty and sweet as pie, and blond, and chubby as a puppy, not a…" He swallowed, pressed his fingers to his eyes. "And H'euman, not Kyn."

"So she doesn't look like Elsa, but you saw Elsa's face?"

"Yes."

Pulling off a glove, she leaned forward and placed her fingers against his forehead, shifting her hand slightly from place to place.

"I'm not fever-sick, Camille. It was... well I can't rightly explain. I just kept seein' Elsa's face and I just... well you know..." He shrugged his shoulders. "How's a man supposed to stay all riled up when he's thinkin' bout his sister? So I sent her away... sorta."

"Maybe you couldn't keep it up because she nearly sliced your balls off."

"Bitch!" D'trav growled at the memory, then shook his head with a laugh. "Can't say I blame the girl. Hell, if I was her I'd've struck like a D'yroapbird after a loop, ripped the balls from my body, forced 'em down my throat, and then slit it, without hardly a second thought."

His face turned sad again. "But that wasn't it. It was Elsa's face that did it."

"Well then, consider it a good thing. You may be a pervert, but you aren't the kind of pervert that'd bed a child."

"True enough. But don't change what I did at the manor."

"D'trav, you can't go down that path."

He looked away.

"Stop it."

"Why'd I do it? I should've just left soon as I saw what was goin' down. But no, like the fool I am, I listened to her, and the more I stared at her and that damnable chain, the more riled up I got." He closed his eyes, wanting to turn over but unable to with Camille sitting on top. "And now here she is, makin' it seem like yesterday that Elsa got... I'll never be able to undo it, any of it."

"You can't keep torturing yourself like this."

"What's wrong with me? What kind of hideous creature does somethin' like that?"

Camille swallowed before grabbing his face. "Look at me."

He opened his eyes and stared into her green ones.

"You're a man who takes meat to the beggars, not leftover scraps, but real food. A man who stops to help children with skinned knees. A man who sacrificed a life of ease to rescue his baby sister from worse than death." She pressed her forehead against his. "And a kinky man who happens to enjoy playing with chains. A man who made a mistake, just like any other man."

"But I—"

"Stop beating yourself up over this. It all worked out. You got away. She got away. If you hadn't stopped to listen, she'd be dead."

He threw his arm up, covering his face with his elbow, and his shoulders shook.

Wetting his lips with anticipation, R'kiax followed the scent of Freni-Kyn.

She meandered through the marketplace, stopping twice for more goods before heading down a side street.

R'kiax fell back, concerned she'd see him.

She turned down an alley.

He sped up. He couldn't lose her; this was his opportunity to earn his coral wings. He rushed around the corner and saw her ahead.

She glanced over her shoulder and started walking faster.

R'kiax smiled.

Run away little dove.

CHAPTER 33

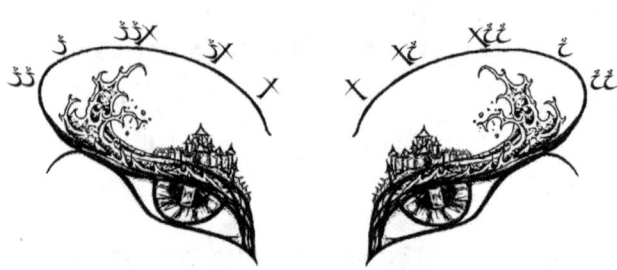

Gaining ground, R'kiax started down the alley after the woman.

She darted another glance over her shoulder, and one of her packages slipped, landing on the ground with a faint rustle. She hesitated but kept going, leaving it behind.

R'kiax kicked it out of the way as he passed, and the tinkle of breaking glass echoed down the alley.

She took off at a run, trying to hold onto her packages. The wine bottle hit the ground with a crash, painting the cobblestones glittery purple.

R'kiax grabbed her shoulder and spun her around, shoving her up against a disfigured wooden wall.

Packages rained down around them as she dropped everything and threw up her arms, pressing palms against his chest with desperation.

He smiled, showing long pointed teeth.

She drew in a deep breath and opened her mouth to scream.

He slapped a hand over her mouth.

She stared at him with vapid blue eyes.

He leaned in close and smelled her neck before running his other hand over her body.

She pressed her hands against his face, trying to push him away.

He threw her down on the ground, scraping her chin against the cobblestones and drawing blood before grinding his heel into the small of her back. "Little more pressure here will break your back. So just keep fighting if you want."

Eyes widening, she stared over her shoulder at him and stopped moving.

Yanking her d'yroap pouch free, he pressed the folds up around his face and drew a deep breath. "just what I thought."

"Take it… take it all."

He grabbed her by the back of her chemise and dragged her to the side of the alley.

She cried out as the cobblestones tore bare skin and tried to crawl.

He flipped her over and set her there, legs outstretched, back against the wall.

"Stay."

He kicked a nearby crate into place and sat on it, then pulled out his dagger and began to clean under his nails. "Now, tell me where you've been today."

She was still sitting there when he left, blood dripping from the hole in her forehead.

A clattering pan and the scent of fish stew startled D'trav awake three days later. He sat straight up in the bed and swung around with his hands already forming fists.

Face flushed with heat, Sarenka threw him a glance before giving a pot one last stir.

"What the hell?"

"Albacore soup'll be ready in a few minutes."

Wrapping the blanket around his hips, D'trav stumbled from the bed and across the room. He tripped on the trailing end, nearly falling face first into the table, before picking it up and slinging it angrily over his shoulder. "Why, in Kyron's third hell, are you back?"

Sarenka sighed. Food always seemed to make her brothers easier to deal with, and she'd hoped it would be the same with D'trav. "I need your help."

"The hell you do. Are you daft woman? I gave you everything you need, now go on, get." His hand waved sideways, ending in a point towards the door.

Sarenka held up a hand, palm down, between them. It shook violently.

D'trav stared at the hand and his jaw muscle jumped.

"I need more."

"What happened to the vials I left you?"

"I drank them."

"*All* of 'em?"

With a nod, Sarenka dropped her hand.

D'trav rubbed the side of his face and turned away.

She stared at his welt covered back and frowned. *What did he do to get those?* The muscles in his shoulders bunched as if he wanted to punch something. "I started craving the Foreveron again. I had to."

"That was enough to last a month, if you'd spread it out."

"I... I thought it would cure me..."

He turned back. "Not enough for that."

"How many do I need then?"

"I don't know, I'm no herbalist... twelve... mayhaps more, seein' as they done been growin' in you a while."

Sarenka collapsed into a chair and covered her face with her hands. "I'm going to die."

"You won't."

Cheeks wet, she blinked up at him and saw the lie. "You know it's true. I'm going to die."

Rubbing the back of his neck, he stared up at the ceiling and seemed to search the twisted beams for answers before looking back down at her. "Kyron-be-damned Sarenka, what do I look like? Some Red Pelican stooge? I can't get stuff like that at a moment's notice."

She sobbed.

"No… don't do that."

She covered her face.

"Elsa come on, don't be cryin'. We'll figure it out. Just… finish cookin' and let me think."

"Elsa?"

He turned away, face wreathed in genuine grief.

She peered up through the fluff of her dark hair. *Maybe he really does have a heart.*

"What is it with you? Why do you keep doing this to me? Are you trying to rip my heart to shreds?"

"I…" Sarenka wasn't sure what to say or even what he meant. Only that she needed help, and that it had taken every bit of nerve she had to ask for it, especially from him. *Cooking, he wants me to cook.* She stumbled to her feet and returned to the pot she'd been tending, catching it moments before it boiled over. With her back to the room, she stirred the pot and listened to the thump of D'trav pacing back and forth.

"We could leave the city together," she said.

"Hell no! I'm goin' nowhere fast with you. You're trouble waitin' to be found."

"We're both wanted. If they catch us we're dead."

"That doesn't solve your problem, and I already stated my case. I'm not leavin' with you."

She stirred the pot long after it finished cooking, hoping that some inspiration would strike and he'd stop pacing. He didn't. He thumped back and forth across the room until the small cooking fire died out.

"Sit down, eat, we'll discuss this afterwards. It's getting cold." She graciously gestured towards the table.

Anger rocked across his face. Jaw set, he obstinately crossed his arms. "No."

"Come on D'trav, it'll waste."

"You think you can just wave a regal hand, and I'll just jump to do your say so."

"No… no… I was trying to be…" She blushed.

"What?"

"Nothing, I'm sorry."

"I'm not eatin' it."

"I said I was sorry."

"No."

"Suit yourself, I'm eating mine while it's warm. So if you want to be an ornery swamp cow—" Sarenka realized she'd gone too far. Even if she was angry, she couldn't show it, not with so much at stake.

D'trav growled.

"I'm sorry… it's habit… my brothers…"

"Shut up. You've said enough."

Sarenka stared down at her dish, appetite gone. *I've got to show my value, make him want me, lure him into eating.* Leaning over a shell filled with steaming stew, she drew a deep breath and tried to regain her dignity. Despite the fact that it reeked of fish, the steam soothed her nerves. She peeked up at D'trav from under lowered lashes.

Eyebrows raised, D'trav stared down at her.

She tore free a piece of brown bread, dunked it in the soup, and lifted it to her lips. And all the while she ate, her eyes traveled the room, refusing to land on the man towering over her.

I can't believe she's back… sittin' there eatin' like… like it's the most natural thing since sharpened blades. D'trav's voice echoed through Sarenka's head, bouncing around like balls in a game of chance, eroding her strength. *I can't do this, not after Elsa. Dear god, what am I gonna do with her? All I wanted was to bed the wench. Unbelievable!*

Sarenka ignored the imaginary whispers and took another bite, positive he wouldn't make it to ten bites.

D'trav's stomach gave a loud gurgle. He grabbed a chair and dragged it across the room.

The scrape of wood against wood brought a satisfied lift to the corner of her lip. *Seven bites. Some things never change. Every man has the food weakness. He'll eat, and then he'll let me stay.*

He flung himself into the other chair and began noisily slopping down the food, rage radiating out with every jerk.

Ever aware of his angry stare, she fell back on childhood lessons and focused on eating with far more daintiness than was needed.

D'trav's thought's struck again, eating away at Sarenka's identity. *Dung! She eats like a high n' mighty noble. Wonder where they caught her. Well, I'm not eatin' like some lord to impress her ladyship.*

Sarenka blanched.

No!

That's twice now.

Not the whispers!

I was cured…

Haven't had them in-in a year…

Can't be true…

Nobody hears what people think…

Just my imagination….

She thought of the day she'd killed the Baron and realized that the whispers had never stopped, would never stop. They'd haunt her past the day she died and straight into eternity.

I'm cursed with the same sickness that led to father's exile.

Her gaze jumped to D'trav's face, concerned.

He can't suspect.

He won't let me stay if he knows I'm mind-lost.

They'll send me to the Isle of the Lost.

He slurped from his shell while glaring over the edge.

Reassured, Sarenka finished her meal. He was angry but didn't suspect anything. She'd know if he suspected. He'd become condescending, like her mother had treated her father. Her overly active imagination could be dealt with after she fought free of Burmtin. She'd find a healer, one who specialized in quieting the mind. There had to be something that worked. For now, she'd ignore the thoughts, and the slurps, as best she could.

She set her spoon down and sat back in the chair. "You could use a window."

Between slurps he grunted out, "Had. A nice little cottage. Wench. With plenty of windows. Before you forced me into hidin' out. Like some puppy what's done its business in the wrong place."

Sarenka pieced together the broken speech with irritation. He was lucky to be alive. She could have taken the key with her.

"Safer in Sad Town with only one access. Less likely to get myself robbed. Or my throat slit." D'trav sucked down another spoonful of soup. His brow lifted and he pulled a splinter bone out of his mouth and examined before using the pointed end to pick his teeth.

Sarenka squeezed the handle of her wooden spoon, determined not to show aggravation, especially since he seemed to be deliberately trying to annoy her.

He looked down at her clenched fist and the corners of his lip twitched. Scooping up the shell bowls and wooden spoons, he dumped them into a bucket without ceremony. "Washin'll have to hold till I've been to the well, haven't enough water to bother heatin' up."

Sarenka's mouth rounded and brows lifted with surprise. "You picked up the dishes?"

"And?"

"I didn't know men… I mean…"

He snorted.

"But, men never help with kitchen care, not unless they're paid."

"Don't abide by the old ways." D'trav scrutinized the room, eyes roaming from surface to surface before settling on her face. "You're not lookin' too good. Get yourself some rest."

Sarenka stood up. "Can we—"

He held up his hand, palm outwards, and gestured downwards. She sat back down.

Lifting his belt from a peg, he swung it around his waist and settled the scabbard to one side before flipping the hinges closed with a snick. "I'll be back later. Stay inside. And don't get too comfy. We're far from done."

Sarenka gave a slight nod.

He threw his cloak over his broad shoulders and, hand on the doorknob, stopped long enough to look at her. One thick brow raised in a questioning arch.

Sarenka nodded her head more firmly.

The door swung shut behind him, and she threw herself across the bed with a relieved smile. What she had dreamed of for months was finally hers, at least until he returned.

A safe place to sleep.

She caught a fluttering of white out of the corner of her eye and jerked her head in that direction. Her eyes darted from surface to surface searching for movement, but she found nothing. Sitting up, Sarenka peered around the entire room and found not a mouse, or moth, or any creature.

A sudden chill crept down her spine.

CHAPTER 34

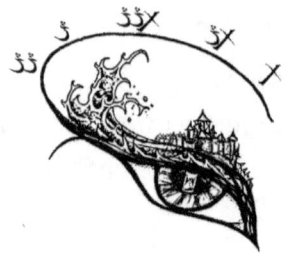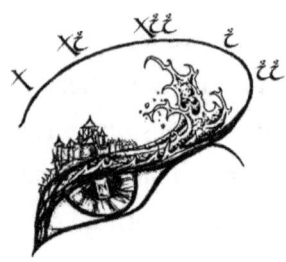

"We are a regimented and frail people, unfit for war. Let us battle with our minds instead. Let us make them pay for our mitigation services, and should they attack, let our defensive devices stop them at the gates."

Kieran Ascal Khidell
Frevell Leader 12 AB

Parian's body lay stretched out on the ground, cold, chest barely moving, as he searched back through time for a solution.

~Parian?~ Rosalie pushed the send, trying to pierce the fog surrounding him.

~*Rosalie stop.*~

~*It's been two days now. You have to come back.*~

~*How do you always find me?*~

~*You smell funny.*~

~*Thanks. I'm not coming back. I haven't found the path yet.*~

~*You'll die. It's been too long.*~

~*I took precautions.*~

Rosalie paced back and forth in her stall. ~*Parian...*~

~*What!*~ Annoyance rolled out with Parian's thought.

~*You smell like death.*~

~*A minute ago I smelled funny.*~

~*The death is stronger than the funny.*~

~*That's enough Rosalie. I can make it one more day.*~

~If you stay too long, you'll get lost.~

~Who told you that?~ Parian asked.

Rosalie's angry snarl roared through Parian's head, and he felt the mix of satisfaction and irritation as she began scratching at the walls of her stall and chewing one of the posts. He watched through her eyes as splinters flew about the stall, and he cringed at the damage.

~Stop destroying your stall! It was Airintia, wasn't it?~

~She cares about you. A cat could do worse in a mate.~

~Oh Kyron. That's funny. She's not my mate.~

~She could be.~

~Not unless we both found our replacements.~

~Then do. Go to Burmtin. Stop being a coward and face this like a cat.~

~I've seen plenty of cats turn tail and run.~

~Not when it matters. You want Airintia as a mate or not? She worth fighting for?~ Rosalie chewed, throwing pieces of wood splinters around her while she waited. Finally she said. ~Well?~

~She'd be the one turning tail and running as soon as she saw my face.~

~It's a good battle wound.··

~Not to H'eumans. Now be quiet, you're breaking my focus.~

~Parian... Don't make me come there.~

Parian waited as the silence stretched out and watched through Rosalie's eyes as she finally threw herself down, pillowing her head on her front paws with a heavy sigh.

He smiled and went back to work.

Now she knows that I can tell when she's bluffing.

Phuh-thump, phuh-thump, phuh-thump.

Muttering curses, D'trav strode towards the west side of town, and each angry step brought an answering, and decidedly annoying, slap of his scabbard against his thigh. The people he passed shifted away from him, sensing the dangerous broil of his emotions. The sun had barely moved across the sky, and he was already regretting his decision to help Sarenka.

Food.

She thinks she can buy me off with food.

How stupid does she really think I am?

And that smart-aleck remark about ornery swamp cows…

He glared at the one man who didn't hurry to get out of his way.

The man glanced up, saw D'trav's face, and took a long step to the side.

I should just kick her out.

What's she to me?

I did my part.

Didn't even make her pay.

He sighed with a mixture of relief and regret upon reaching the Distinguished Dainties. An ocean breeze flapped his cloak, wetting his face with a thin layer of brine. He took a deep breath, savoring the clean salty scent, despite how it had scoured the building's exterior; making it look like it hadn't seen a coat of whitewash within the last ten years.

The back door creaked when he entered. With another sigh of regret, he added oiling hinges to his list. He owed Camille. She'd taken him in twice now, hidden him from the authorities, and helped him create a new life. The least he could do was help her get the place in order before the first hard freeze of winter.

As he passed the open door to Camille's room, he peered into the dim interior. Heavy velvet curtains hung from the window, throwing the room into an early twilight. The bed was unmade, and it would be hours before she touched it, if it even happened at all. Lush costumes littered the room in an explosion of multicolored fabrics, looping over the crystal chandelier, hooked to the top of the curtain, dangling from wall sconces, and draped over chairs. He fought a compulsive urge to straighten the mess with a shake of his head. How she could stand to sleep in there every night, he'd never understand.

Moving on, he worked his way towards a clattering racket, the kitchen. The common-use areas—kitchen, private parlors, washrooms, bedrooms, and latrines—were accessible to all the 'renters.' Camille was the only one he ever found in the kitchen before work hours, though. He supposed she enjoyed the ordinary task of cooking, though he'd never asked. Stopping under the doorframe, he watched her lean over a pot and cautiously raise a wooden spoon to her lips.

Melancholic, hoping to find comfort in familiarity, he took in the details of the expansive room. A long wooden table claimed the center, its scarred surface witness to the many meals it had held over the years. Well-oiled clay pots hung from hooks alongside dried herbs and ropes of garlic. Wooden countertops, scored with knives and stained with a thousand hues of red and purple, ran the length of two walls.

But the star of the kitchen wasn't the table or pots or herbs. It wasn't even Camille. No, it was a monolith of a potbellied stove. It dominated the space, taking a full third of the room over with its gears, pipes, gauges, and perpetually steaming valves; all interwoven with organic elements in an attempt at keeping the use of expensive metals to a minimum. It ran day and night, creating the elixirs that had made Camille her name.

Gears clacking, a carved stone arm shifted a bottle of mint liqueur out and replaced it with an empty one. The scent of fresh clam chowder mingled with mint, incense, stale perfume, and cheap cigars in the close interior rooms, creating such an odd jumble of contrasting smells that he rubbed his nose, trying to repress a tickle. It didn't work. He let out a muffled sneeze.

Camille looked up through a tumbled mass of honey-blond hair. Her heavily-lashed eyes crinkled with delight, and she threw him a welcoming smile.

"Hello darlin, you're early. Come for breakfast?"

He strode across the room and sat heavily in a chair before grunting, "No Camille, just ate."

She flipped the spiraling tresses away from her eyes in a manner that usually had men, and sometimes women, begging for attention. It wasn't meant as a seduction. The move had been used so many times that she did it without being conscious of its effect on other people. Her eyes flicked down over his body, making him aware of how slumped his normally confident shoulders were. But he didn't care. He didn't have to pretend to be anything but what he was in this kitchen.

Picking up a sliced berry, Camille ran it over her lips, staining them a darker red before popping it into her mouth, all the while staring at him. She pursed her lips into a frown and gave the pan a last stir before pulling it from the heat. Her ring bedecked hands wiped down the front of her apron, and she sauntered across the room, landing on his lap with enough force to startle him.

A heavy sigh escaped his lips. He rested his head across her full breasts, and his arms curled in an automatic embrace.

Overbalanced, she wrapped an arm around his shoulder. "What's the matter, D'trav? You look like your dog just died."

"Don't have a dog." He planted small kisses across her bosom, speaking between each kiss. "You know that Kyn I told you I got rid of?"

"Yes."

He sighed again.

"Did they finally capture her?"

"Nope." He froze with his lips pressed against one soft mound, and when he spoke again the words were muffled. "She's in my hut."

~*You haven't come to see me in a week,*~ Rosalie sent.

~*I know.*~

~*Well?*~

~*I will.*~

~When?~

~Soon. Now shut up.~ Parian put a rag over his bloodshot eyes and lay back down.

She sent a blast of anger. *~Listen here you stupid Freni-Kyn. I want out of here. Now!~*

~Soon, Rosalie. Soon.~ He rolled over and put the pillow over his head.

~My legs are cramping. I need to run.~

"Kyron-damn-it!" He threw the useless pillow. *~Fine. I'll come to-night.~*

~I think I have a burr behind my ear. It hurts. I need help.~

~You don't believe me? I said I'll come tonight, and I will.~

Parian splashed cold water on his face, and put on clean clothing before inspecting himself in the mirror. One blue eye stared back, blaming him, the other one wandered the room looking for a different culprit to blame.

"Ugly cuss." He smelled under his arms. "And smell bad too."

Running a hand through greasy hair, he turned back to the tub and stared at it long and hard before shrugging his shoulders.

"Who's going to notice? Rosalie?" Humor tugged at the corner of his lips for the first time in days. Kyron's worlde might have lost The One, but life went on, people still stank, food still had to be eaten, and cats still bitched.

He rooted out his belongings, wiped away the last of the sigil markings, and opened the window to let in fresh air. With a twitch, he settled his illusions in place and left to eat in the common room. He'd be back at the Freni-Kyn landholdings soon enough. It no longer mattered who saw or smelled him.

The innkeep treated him with cautious deference, serving his food with the least of words. For that Parian was glad. Small talk had never suited him, and especially not now. He watched the expensively clad women come and go and felt no twinge of lust, not even for the grey haired woman who passed by so close he could have touched her brocade gown.

~It's been hours. Are you coming?~

Parian laid down his napkin.

~Parian.~

He stood, scraping the chair legs back slowly. *~One moment.~*

The innkeeper hurried forward.

Parian handed over the cost of the meal and then some. It didn't matter, what use did he have for d'yroap now? He picked up his bags and left, determined to put Darkiorn behind. He had to go back through the lines of time, of course. He had to be sure of the death and find a way to undo it, to fix the timeline. But there was no hurry now; his work could be done from home as easily as it could be done here.

He entered the dark stable and made his way towards Rosalie, feeling her growing excitement as he neared. Light slanted in through tall openings, showing the gnawed posts around her pen.

~Rosalie, really...~

~They were pointy.~

He sighed. She was hopeless. *~Now I have to leave extra d'yroap to cover the damage.~*

He swung open the gate and felt a surge of excitement and fear. Parian stopped, sensing a wrongness in the air.

Rosalie shouldn't be afraid.

He started to turn.

Something struck the side of his neck, and the room went black.

Rosalie snarled and leapt forward.

The men backed away, holding up their hands. "He's not dead."

Rosalie nudged Parian's head and listened to his breathing. She sat down with his head between her paws.

The men shared disbelieving looks.

~Rosalie, you have to let them take him,~ Airintia sent.

~You didn't tell me they'd hurt him.~

~He's not hurt. It's just something to make him sleep.~

~He'll be okay?~

~If you let them get him somewhere safe, he will be.~

Rosalie stepped past Parian's emaciated form and went to the door of the stable. Giving Parian one last longing look, she let out a long questioning sound and bounded off into the night.

"What? What's she doing there?" Grasping the sides of his shaved head, Camille pulled his lips away from her breast and stared into his eyes. Her face was filled with dismay.

"I told her to go to sleep, but she's probably playin' at wife and cleanin' or some con'stern other thing. Don't rightly know."

"Well, you're obviously out-of-sorts, or you'd have given me an answer straight up. Never known you to talk in riddles."

"She just showed up."

"She can't stay. Every time she gets near you—"

He held his hand up to stop her, "I know, I do somethin' stupid."

"Wasn't going to say it."

"Don't have ta. Truth is, I owe her." He ground his teeth. "And havin' to admit to bein' grateful for her mercy almost makes me hate her more."

"Oh dear god, D'trav. You owe her nothing."

"She could've left me with no way out. I still wake up in a sweat some nights, thinkin' I'm stuck in that room, with that body and no way out."

"So give her some d'yroap, and send her on her way. She's ruined everything. Look at what you did to yourself, all because she looked like Elsa. What's going to happen if you wake up to her every day?"

D'trav dropped his gaze. He knew what would happen as well as she did. "I told myself she'd done escaped. If they'd found her dead, then the posters would've been torn down long ago. So she had to of got loose, right? Simple logic."

"All right, so get her out of the city."

"You should've seen the sorry state she was in, near starved, clothing ragged, and smellin' of vomit and Kyron knows what else kinda filth."

"That's not your fault, and you know it."

"Easy to hate someone you'll never see again, isn't it? 'Specially after what she stole from me."

"What? What did she steal? A nice hut? Get another one. A fake identity? Those are as common as sand. She's stealing more by being in your hut right now."

"She's dying Camille."

CHAPTER 35

 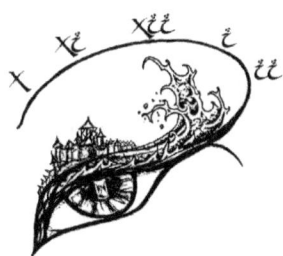

D'trav's words hung between them, chill in the warm room.

Camille shook her head decisively, throwing off the effect. "Again. Not your fault."

"But, I can help her get the antidote."

"You know it's locked down."

"I have to try. It'll make up for... I don't know."

Camille sighed.

"I feel like... like if I help her, I'm somehow helpin' Elsa."

"Fine, but make her pay. That way she won't linger after she's cured."

"Not likely to happen. I'm fair on sure she hates me. But how do I make her pay? You know she can't get a job."

Camille rubbed his head, thinking. "She could work here."

"I couldn't ask that, not after..."

She rolled her eyes. "Well, tell me about her then. She has to have some skills."

He told her everything he could remember, including how she had cooked a marginal pot of soup and forced him into sharing it with her and put on high and mighty airs.

"Wait," Camille interrupted, "she's noble born?"

"Seems like."

"Perfect. She'll do your lettering."

"That *might* work."

"Now, enough about her." Standing, Camille tugged her long skirt up out of the way and straddled his lap. Her legs wrapped about his waist, and she used the leverage to grind against him.

Momentarily distracted by his body's response, D'trav closed his eyes and moaned.

"We've a few hours before opening."

Lowering his head, D'trav resumed the trail of kisses, alternating back and forth between each breast. "I still oughta not done what I did, takin' advantage of her being chained and all. But you know how I am about that stuff. I felt... I don't know... like someone else had control. Ever since then, I've wondered if I'm right in the head."

"You're *my* kind of right." Camille giggled. "And you can chain me up any time you want, luv. *After* we get you back on track."

She swung her leg out from around him and stood, all the mirth gone. "Come on. We've got just enough time for a session."

Watching her curvaceous hips sway back and forth in front of him with longing, D'trav followed her down the hallway. "It was supposed to be your turn."

"My turn will come. This has to be taken care of."

She lifted the chain dangling from her belt, drawing out the moment, and carefully selected a black key. As she inserted it into the lock, she gazed up at him through lashes dyed black. Her lips curved into a slow, sultry smile, filled with promise. The key snicked, unlocking the door to their special room, a room they shared with no one. One they'd put together themselves, each item chosen and carefully placed by the two of them. Their special room.

As the lantern flared, D'trav looked from the carefully placed poles in the center, already outfitted with chains and cuffs, to the rack of whips and slappers, to the smaller toys on the other side of the room: leather dildos stuffed with horsehair, pinching devices of all types, cream colored candles, and bottles of scented oils.

While she walked around the room, letting her fingers trail along the leather whips thoughtfully, he closed and bolted the door. At last her hand landed on the one he'd dubbed the thumper for the way it sounded when it struck. Holding its carved wooden handle, she turned towards him and stroked its length in a tantalizing manner, signaling the start of their game—a game they'd played many times, taking turns at the role of Master.

"Strip."

"Yes, Mistress."

Normally she'd strip him slow, torturing with the tease. But when she said it like that, only one word, she meant to hurry. Fingers trembling over the buckles of his cuirass, he finally pulled it free and tossed it off to the side. The rest of his clothing followed in clunks and shffs, and shzzes of sound, as he tossed them hastily aside. Until, at last, he stood bare in the center of the room.

Camille threw her skirt across a chair outfitted with straps and ropes before walking to him, dressed only in leggings and corset. Grasping his wrist, she lifted it to the top of the pole and buckled the leather cuff around it. D'trav had begged her for the metal ones, craving the cold, the pain, that extra bit of punishment, but she'd insisted on these, and she'd been right. More than once he had collapsed, hanging from them until his knees worked again.

She ran her fingers along his bound arm, across his bare chest, and down to the other wrist. Lifting it, she bound it too, spread-eagling him in the middle of the room. Touching, teasing, she walked around his body and paused when she reached his back.

The cool leather strips slid over his skin, catching on the healing scabs and bringing tiny stings. She wrapped it around his throat and pulled backwards until his ear was pressed to her lips and his air cut off. The tops of her breasts pressed against his back, warm and soft.

"I'm the only one allowed to punish you."

He waited, unable to breathe with the leather clenched so hard.

"Say it." She let go, sliding the whip over his shoulders and backing away.

A rattling of chains came from behind and he felt himself come to full arousal. "You're the only one allowed to punish me, Mistress."

"Spread your legs."

The hours ran passed, too swiftly, until he was spent and collapsed to his knees in front of her.

She pulled his chin up, staring into his eyes. "You come to me for punishment."

He buried his head in her stomach.

Parian awoke to a blistering headache and tried to rub his forehead, but his arm wouldn't reach that far. He turned his head, squinted, tried to bring the room into focus.

~*A manacle?*~ he sent in a scream.

Lanion's pain at the send echoed back. ~*Parian, please. Let me explain.*~

~*I knew someone would be listening,*~ he sent in another yell, letting loose raw anger.

The backlash of pain washing off Lanion struck Parian between the eyes.

He blacked out.

When the room swam back into focus, Parian stared up into the eyes of the bowler hat man from the Refuge Inn.

The man shifted his attention to Parian's arm.

Parian's gaze traveled down to the needle in the man's hand. He stared at the manacles and knew it was hopeless to fight.

The man cocked his head, as if listening to something.

~*Lanion, are you okay?*~ Parian sent.

"He is fine," bowler hat man said.

Realizing that they feared him too much for direct contact, and that they were communicating through the man, shame washed over Parian.

"Tell him, I'm sorry," Parian said.

The man cocked his head, listening again. He moved forward, and Parian realized that instead of just one wrist being manacled, now both were.

"I didn't mean to hurt you. Tell him that," he rushed to say before they could inject him again. The world slid sideways in a whirl of color and went black.

CHAPTER 36

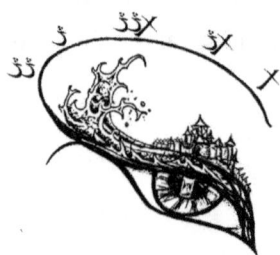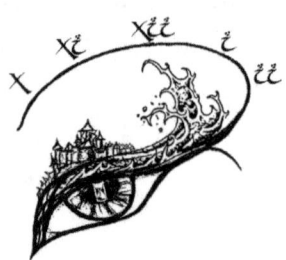

"We sold them Zaernuts, telling them it would make hair grow on their chest, and laughed all the way home at the thought of anyone trying to eat that bitter fruit. Our shock came when next we saw them. They wanted to buy more. Thinking they jested, we gave them the fruit and watched as they peeled away the juicy outer layer and greedily ate the center seed. What started as a jest became the source of our empire."

Willoa A'tnnoris
Sharpra Heiress
3458 BB

"I hate that damn thing," D'trav said.

"The cane," Camille said.

"Stings like fire."

"It brings the most pain for the least amount of damage. You won't even have marks this time. Unlike that chain you used on your back."

"I know, but Kyron's hairy balls…"

"I only use it when you are very, *very*, bad." Camille threw over her shoulder at him with a sultry smile.

He shifted positions, jangling the chain she had locked around his thigh. He looked down at it and groaned as desire began to build again. "Fair enough, but I still hate it."

Camille turned back from the stove and pushed a bowl of clam chowder across the table. "So what are you going to do about her? She can't stay in your hut."

Brought back to the problem of Sarenka, his pleasure shattered, and his cock went limp.

"I'll work out a deal. She'll cook, clean, sew, and take care of some... side business... in exchange for enough d'yroap to pay off the antidote."

Camille's lips pursed at his mention of the 'side' business. She'd tried turning him towards the legitimate earning of loops when he'd first told her of his entanglement with the underside of Burmtin. He'd never given in, with the exception of taking her up on the offer of working as her guard. Despite how much he told her, she didn't know the reasons behind everything he did and never would. That would endanger her life, a risk he wasn't willing to take.

"And after it's paid off?" Camille searched his face.

He clenched his jaw, reading her concerned expression. It hadn't been that long since she'd offered to take him in on a permanent basis and he'd turned her down.

"You can't let her stay. I won't have you hurt by some heartless Freni-Kyn tramp. She puts you in danger, and you know it."

D'trav squinted, shocked by her vehemence. "By birthright the Kyns *are* harlots, but they're hardly what I'd call tramps. In fact, most of 'em are so upper crust they'd make a dead man throw up his last dinner."

"Oh dear god..." She glanced away. "I didn't mean it that way. What right have I to judge? I just meant... Oh never mind. You never answered my question. What happens after she's paid off her debt?"

He examined the worry lines etched into her forehead with sudden understanding. She'd say whatever it took to sway him into ousting Sarenka. For a moment, he wondered if she was jealous but pushed that thought aside as impossible.

"I don't know, Camille. I've got a hankerin' to leave Burmtin. Downright risky stayin' here."

Camille drew in a sharp breath and clasped her chemise with alarm. "No! You won't have to leave, not if you take another hut and turn her in. Nice price on her head right now."

Appalled, he blurted out, "No! No, I can't."

"Why not?"

"You know why the hell not."

"I'll give her a room here, make her earn her keep, and get her out of your hair. With the right lighting and a lot of makeup, we could keep her identity secret."

"I can't be bringin' that risk down on you, Camille. If you got caught hidin' her, they'd kill you."

"Well luv, I've got a cellar full of Freni-Kyns already, but I can't keep discussing this all day. I'm willing to help if you change your mind."

"Speaking of those Kyn women you've got stashed." D'trav deliberately moved the discussion away from Sarenka. "It's damn near broke me, but I've got 'em set up with passes through the gates."

"That's lovely." Standing, Camille smoothed her hair and threw him a stiff smile.

D'trav watched with trepidation. This discussion wasn't over, and he knew it. Camille passive was a storm brewing.

"Would you take a look at the stove? I think one of the valves is broken."

He considered the contraption and rubbed his hand across his chin, scratching at the line of beard edging his jaw. He had no idea where she'd found the device and had decided the first time he saw it to steer clear.

Fixin' it might... he glanced at Camille again.

Who am I kidding?

Fixin' it won't make her accept Sarenka.

"That thing scares me so bad it makes my danglies downright... well... dangly," he said with a shake of his head. "Anything with that many gauges has gotta be dangerous. I'd blow the place to the northern reaches, most like."

"Well, okay. Couldn't hurt to ask. I'll get Randy to take a look. He's handy with these sorts of things."

D'trav went to stand guard at the front door, adjusting the loosened vambrace straps as he walked. Working as the brothel's official bouncer didn't pay much, but it kept food on the table and served as another go-between for his more lucrative business.

One of the gigolos left his room as D'trav walked down the hall. The man coughed and looked awkwardly away.

D'trav shrugged his shoulders. What did it matter what the renters overheard or thought? They loved Camille and wanted to protect her, but she'd established the *no interruption* rules for them long before he'd come along.

He gave the scantily clad man a nod. "G'day, Randy."

Camille sent both women and men to tease the chain locked around his thigh that night, knowing it would bring frustrated pleasure.

Burk watched Lance saunter down the long white hallway in low waisted pants and a bolero jacket, drawing the eye of man and woman alike.

Several feet away, Lance stopped to rake long fingers over his scalp, ruffling dark hair. He held the pose, leaving his arm up far longer than was necessary.

Burk smiled. "Won't work on me, ya dandy. I'm immune to your charms."

Lowering his arm, Lance cocked his head to the side, and his gaze roved over Burk's body. "You sure? I'd give you such pleasure. I'd even play Randy-the-gigolo, just for you."

"Sounds more like a torture session to me. You have a report?"

At Lance's nod, Burk tapped on the door behind him.

"What!" The rage filled shout made both men blanch.

Burk hesitated. "Lance here, sir."

"Send him in." The reply was controlled, all trace of rage suppressed.

Burk gave Lance a worried frown and mumbled, "Glad it's you and not me."

Lance entered the sequestered room and glanced about, at once comfortable in the familiar velvet and leather room. He sauntered over to the plush leather seat and sat, stretching his legs out in front and sliding down into a lounge position before speaking. "New quill?"

Nonplused, Captain Lator just stared at him.

Lance cleared his throat and sat a little straighter in the chair. "So, I've been in place for three months, and there's no sign of Sarenka. No Freni-Kyns at all. Camille doesn't hire them."

The captain tapped his chin, then gave his head a dismissive shake. "She has to surface eventually. Stay there."

"But—"

The captain cut off Lance with a dangerous look from under lowered brows.

Lance's breath quickened and a rush of longing raced through his body.

"Anything else of interest? Captain Lator asked.

Lance licked his lips, pushing away the longing ache the captain always stirred. "She services a regular. Kinky bastard doubles as a guard. I figure he's working off the fees."

"Interesting. Keep an eye on Camille and the guard. I want to know everything about them. Information like that is useful." Lator didn't smile but his face relaxed. "Anything else?"

"That's it. For a bordello it's pretty clean. She even ousts you for taking illicit drugs. Boring, really. I'm sure you could use my talents elsewhere. Surely there's some wealthy slut somewhere that needs wooing."

Captain Lator stared at him for so long and so dispassionately that Lance became uncomfortable.

Lance cleared his throat and pulled a valve from his pocket. "Almost forgot, I need this replaced." Leaning forward he set it on the desktop.

Lator raised one brow.

"Had to break it as an excuse to come here. Being the only one who can repair that stove of hers is paying off. Smart of you to sell them to the whore houses for so cheap."

The captain gingerly picked up the greasy valve between two fingertips and placed it on a clean piece of parchment. He folded the parchment around the valve before carrying it over to a chest whose surface was covered in tiny drawers. After setting the parchment wrapped valve in a wicker basket on top of the chest, and fastidiously wiping his hand on a kerchief, he pulled open one of the drawers and produced its replacement. He returned to his chair and placed the valve at the edge of the desk.

"This concludes our business," he stated, pushing the valve towards Lance with a fingertip.

Lance leaned forward to snag the valve. "I'll report back in a month or so, unless I get wind of something."

"Very good."

Lance sauntered over to the door and turned to gaze at Lator. The man was already engrossed in a document. Lance's mouth opened to say something but he changed his mind and left. Once the door closed behind him, he breathed a wistful sigh. "So strong... So alone..."

Burk turned an incredulous look on him. "You're going soft man, or mad. He'd skin you for breakfast if you gave him a chance."

Lance pinched his lips in a bitter frown and turned to leave, glad for those few moments alone with the captain.

"Maybe," he threw over his shoulder.

The captain pulled out a ledger and flipped through the pages before running his finger down a list of names, stopping on Distinguished Dainties. Next to Camille's name he wrote:

11th of Dust ---- Unknown Lover ---- More Information Needed ---- Possible Bribe?

He snapped the book shut and turned to reading reports. The Freni-Kyn had been spotted in several locations. Unfortunately, those sightings had turned out to be yet more false trails. However, they were closing in on Onglat. Soon they would know, decisively, whether or not he had murdered the Freni-kyn.

The captain's thoughts drifted to R'kiax, the ace in the hole that had turned out to be a vast disappointment. He had thought that sending a Sharpra to chase a Freni-Kyn would guarantee success, given the racial hate. Now the man was missing and presumed dead.

He picked up the ledger that tracked active agents and flipped through to the Sharpra section. Perhaps R'kiax had decided to return to his clan. One never knew when a Sharpra's duty to clan would interfere with business.

Sarenka watched beggar children squabble over a scrap of cloth through the open doorway and fidgeted with boredom. After so long on the streets, the hut felt small and confining. She had solved the problem by tying off the heavy blanket to one side and propping open the door, letting in sunlight and fresh air. But she'd been awake for hours now. The day was growing old and temperatures dropping, and still no sign of D'trav.

Shutting the door, she paced back and forth, then picked up the stone candlestick and waved it around, testing its balance. For the first time in months, her mind was abuzz with energy. She turned to searching the sideboard and found nothing of interest but the tiny fire-squares and a knife. Her eyes settled on the trunk, and she looked from it, to the door, and back. She rushed over and flipped up the scarf that covered it. Beneath, embedded into the trunk, was an ivory lock. Staring at the intricate mechanism with consternation, she sat back on her heels.

"Stupid damn D'trav, melting my pick-tools like that."

She started to search the room for a key, but a sudden thought changed her mind. Tentatively, she pulled up on the lid and was both pleased and disappointed when it opened.

Can't be much in here if he didn't bother locking it.

She flipped it back and was surprised to find it full. Wetting her lips, she peered at the door again.

Could be really bad if I get caught digging through his stuff.

She shrugged and began unloading the trunk, laying the items out in rows so that they could be replaced in the exact same order. Near the middle, she flipped open a small shell box and sat back on her heels with shock. Within were a plethora of wax seals representing all the major houses around the city, as well as some she didn't recognize. Setting them to the side, she continued until she came to beautiful, but worn, piece of satin. She caressed the fabric and unfolded an arm before realizing it was a child's kimono.

She stopped with her hand still pressed to the slick surface and peered at it.

Strange…

Tentatively, she turned back another side and uncovered a length of heavy chain.

Sarenka recoiled in horror.

My god!

He's a monster!

CHAPTER 37

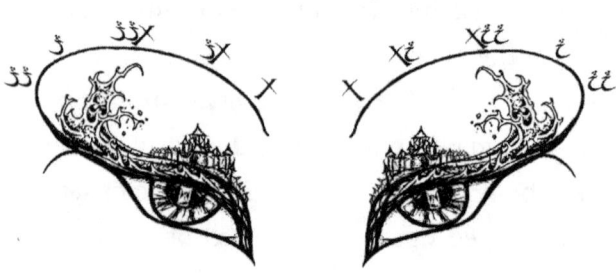

She smoothed her fingers over an embroidered name—Elsa—and it was almost more than she could bear to cover the chain and keep unloading items until she reached the bottom. It was odd, higher than it should be. Running deft fingers along the seams, she discovered a tiny lever which popped open a panel of wood in the bottom. She flipped it back and rifled through a pile of parchments.

Phoneys. All of them.

Gaze settling on the box of seals, she tapped her lip and considered the implications before refilling the trunk and settling the scarf back in place.

Well, that explains having d'yroap and living in Sad Town.

The antidote… maybe.

The kimono and chain…

I can't even think of that…

Surely not what it seems.

Bam! The door slammed open.

Sarenka jumped.

D'trav marched in carrying a small bundled packet. Dropping it on the table without acknowledging her presence, he unwrapped the string bindings and folded back the sides of the packet, revealing a pile of papers. These he sorted into new piles, studying them as he worked.

She joined him at the table and waited for him to speak.

After a while, he slid two sheets of parchment over to her. "Can you duplicate that"— his finger jabbed down on a scrolling signature— "onto this here piece of parchment?" He jabbed at a second document which had only a blank space where a name should be.

She considered the implications. "I've not copied someone's mark before."

"I didn't ask if you'd done it before. Can you do it?"

"I'll need to practice."

D'trav pushed another piece of parchment towards her, followed by the inking shell and quill. With an abrupt scraping of chair legs against wood, he stood. "Start practicing. I need it by morning."

Walking to the fire, he lifted the pot lid. *Strange comin' home to the smell of food. Been a long time since—*

"It's not done yet," Sarenka mumbled without looking up from her hunched position over the paper. "Been a long time since what?"

"What'd you say?" D'trav started, turning towards Sarenka with a frown.

"The food's not done." She glanced up, momentarily confused, before returning her attention to the parchment. "Don't get upset, it'll be cooked soon enough."

With a frown, he scratched along the edge of his beard. "Must've said it out loud."

"What?" She asked in a vague tone, too focused to really hear him.

"Try loosenin' up your shoulders. It'll show in your marks if you don't relax."

Sarenka rolled her shoulders before continuing.

A loud splashing sound came from behind. "Kyron-be-damned!"

Startled by the yell, Sarenka streaked a line across the page.

"I told you not to go out!" His angry shout was trailed by a string of curses, in which Freni-Kyns in general, bulls, and Kyron all did improbable things together and in every position possible. The odd clanking sound that accompanied his expletives provoked Sarenka into twisting around in her chair. Barely contained rage darkened his face nearly as much as the front of his clothing was darkened by a wet stain. He jerked the pail back and forth while a puddle spread below his feet.

Sarenka pressed down the threatening quirk of a smile and hastened back to the writing, hiding her face from view. "I needed water."

"From now on, you just keep your-con-stern-little-self right here." He thumped down the pail for emphasis. "And let me do the fetchin."

"Then you'll have to get up earlier. I need it in the morning, not when the double moons have already crossed," she murmured, focus centering on the page.

Hours later, D'trav broke her concentration by laying a large clam shell of food next to her. "Take a break and eat."

Sarenka realized she was holding her breath and let it out in a rush. She rubbed her eyes, leaving them cold and wet. Peering at her ink-stained fingers with alarm, she knew she had just smeared the ink across her face. "Harder than I'd have thought."

He looked up in the midst of shoveling in an overlarge bite and watched her stretch and crack her knuckles from under furrowed brows. "But you can do it, right?"

"I think so. Might keep me up all night though." She grimaced, trying not to look at his mouth. *His table manners…*

With distant eyes, he gave a barely perceptible nod and took another bite. *If she can make the signs, we won't be needin' to pay outsiders. That alone reduces the risk of information leakin' out.*

Hands shaking, Sarenka rubbed her temples, trying to massage away the echoing voice along with a building headache. *I'm mind-lost as a… have to be, who else hears voices?*

After washing the dishes, D'trav flipped the chair around and straddled it backwards. "Now we talk particularities."

She glanced up from the parchment and bit her lip, knowing what he had to mean. "I'll fulfill my original deal of course."

Pupils widening, he shifted uneasily, and his gaze settled on her breasts.

Sarenka cheeks grew uncomfortably hot.

His gaze traveled back to her face, and the hunger dropped away as abruptly as it had arrived. *Fuckin' vespra-lanir bitch! When in Kyron's hells did Kyns start blushin' over sex?*

Sarenka blocked the whispered voice by digging her nails into the palm of her hand.

D'trav's eyes narrowed into distrustful straight lines. His hand hit the table with such a thud that made it her jump. "I don't want your body."

He thumped the table again. "I'm not sure I want your cooking."

The last time he hit the table it groaned with the force. "I *know* I don't want to share my hut with someone who'd slice a man's dandies like you did."

"I promise I won't use my nails, unless you want me to."

His rough laugh was so disparaging that she stiffened with anger.

"Your nails don't scare me, darlin. It'd be less than nothin' to make sure they stayed short. I just don't want you."

Shocked, she could do nothing but blink.

He laughed again. "Haven't heard that much, have you?"

"You know I can take on any face, right?" Ace-in-the-hole evaporating, her voice edged upwards with desperation. "Not for long, but long enough."

"Course I know. What's the chance I take you back to wherever you hail from, and they give me a nice bit of d'yroap for my considerable effort?"

"None." A flood of memories washed over Sarenka. Wide wooden halls and riseen-black fixtures gleaming under elegant chandeliers, her brothers' cruel pranks, the grasping men her mother entertained, her mother's disapproval over everything she did—everything she was. And lastly, the day she was promised to Sir S'dansc, a nobleman of renowned brutality who had already seen two wives to their graves.

All that malevolence masked behind stiff smiles and knowing looks. Her life was to have ended at fifteen—no, before that—since she was to have been chained to her studies, awaiting the marriage day like a goose readied for the mid-snow fest, deprived of the freedom that had kept her existence livable. No, where she came from wasn't his business, nor was she going to discuss it.

There's that look again. What is that? Fear? She looks just like... D'trav glanced away with a frown. *Why the hell does Elsa's face appear every time I look at her?*

Sarenka's entire body tensed as the whispers resumed. A wave of dizziness hit. Her fingers dug into her legs, wrinkling the skirt. She hummed a silent tune, trying to drown out the fragmented whispers scratching at her brain.

"Well then. Here's the deal, Darlin. You'll cook and clean and sew and do just about anything I don't have a hankerin' to do. And you'll make the signatures for me."

She shook her head, remembering the seals. "It'll get us hung."

"That's the deal. Take it or leave it." He began unstrapping his armor, not looking up until she went too long without answering. "Well? What's it to be, darlin?"

She stared at the parchment on the table. "What do I get?"

"A roof over your head's not enough?"

"You know what I need."

"One silver a day, but you pay for your own damn antidote."

"You can get it?"

"I'll do what I can."

She picked up the quill and started writing.

"An' don't be gettin' too settled in, this is just till we see if you're up to the job."

She sighed. It was something.

He stripped down and threw himself across the bed. "Can't risk you gettin' yourself seen either. From now on, I do the shoppin', hear?"

She rolled her shoulders and thought back over his words. She wouldn't have to use her body to keep from being kicked out. He was letting her stay because she could use a quill. A surprising turn of events. Neither of them had mentioned that she'd have to labor for a year to repay the antidote money.

D'trav awoke to a scratching noise. *Rodents. Again.* He lay still, pinpointing the direction before slowly rolling over, dagger prepped to throw. Sarenka sat hunched over the table, scribbling away. After sliding the dagger back under his pillow, he studied her ink smudged face, taking in the dark circles under her eyes.

Her stiff posture was a grave contrast to the flowing movements of his usual counterfeiter; a man who's skills had left D'trav more than ready to fork out the extra d'yroap, despite the irk of hiring for parchment work. It wouldn't be too long before she was as good, her progress the night before proved an aptitude for the trade.

His stomach rumbled. He stretched, yawning noisily, glad for the small flames flickering off the crumbling remains of a log. If not for that, the room would be cold enough to see breath. He made no effort to squelch the squeak of his cot when he arose, yet she remained tense with concentration, bottom lip caught between her teeth. Peering over her shoulder, he watched her finish the signature with a sweeping loop.

She let out the breath she'd been holding and placed the quill to the side before looking up. "Good enough?"

He compared the two documents side by side. More than good enough. The original owner would be hard pressed to tell the difference. "It'll do. Go get yourself a bit of sleep."

Standing, she took a stumbling step towards the fire. "I'm supposed to cook—"

D'trav arrested her movement with a hand on her shoulder, guiding her towards the bed instead. "I've fended for myself for years. You've done enough. Get some rest."

Irritation crossed her face, but she crawled onto the bed. On hands and knees she leaned forward, stretching the crick from her back before dropping flat with a groan.

D'trav watched with understanding as she reached behind to rub her rear. He knew, only too well, the exacting toll a wooden chair took on a person's rear end after an entire night of sitting. He examined the documents. She'd never know his satisfaction or how many lives might be saved.

No. That'd endanger everything.

Sarenka groaned.

He peered into the darkened corner, trying to figure out what she was doing. Her bodice landed on the floor next to the bed. He looked away. "Take the antidote I brought home last night?"

"Yes," she yawned, stretching the word into something that sounded like a barred owl call. "Not too long ago."

As her breathing deepened with sleep, he seated himself before the trunk. Grasping a tiny latch on the edge of the weathered bone lock, he pushed in its matching key and started turning it. A frown creased his forehead when it didn't budge.

Thought I locked this.

He ran his fingers over it, searching for damage. Outwardly it was a simple mechanism that any peasant might own. But in reality, the deceptively complex trunk and lock would cost the average Sad Town dweller several years pay. He twisted the key, locking and then unlocking it to a satisfying series of clicks, then stared at Sarenka's slumbering form with another frown.

She better not have.

Flipping open the weathered trunk, he peered at its organized piles of supplies and clothing with relief. She hadn't picked the lock and rummaged through. Like his hut, the belongings were neat and tidy. Sadness flowed over him.

Easy to be organized with no wee ones around to get into things.

He brushed his hand over Elsa's satin robe and the chain it hid, sighed heavily, and pulled free a seal along with its matching orange candle. After sealing the document, he leaned over to inspect the *House of Anor* seal, a flying horse, and the resin laced wax tickled his nostrils. Satisfied, he rubbed away the sneeze and smiled. With this letter came freedom for at least one person. He tossed the granite seal into the air and caught it behind his back before stowing it away.

Good investment—

Sarenka turned over, drawing his gaze.

—and so is she. A silver a day's nothin' compared to what I'll make off her signs. Now, to send this letter and get my pay. Finally, luck swingin' my way. Placing the document within his tunic, he peered at the sleeping girl again. *Have to get faster, though. Can't be sittin' up every night.*

"Shut the hell up," Sarenka moaned, turning over restlessly.

Great. She talks in her sleep.

With a repressed shudder he took in the curvaceous form, barely disguised by the thin blanket.

Needs a sleep gown and a separate bed…

Just plain disturbin'…

Sleepin' with someone that reminds me of Elsa…

Or watchin' her undress…

Or bathe.

Damn it. Larger hut's startin' to sound downright peachy.

Sarenka grabbed his pillow and put it over her face.

D'trav shrugged. *Apparently she's a light sleeper.*

Chapter 38

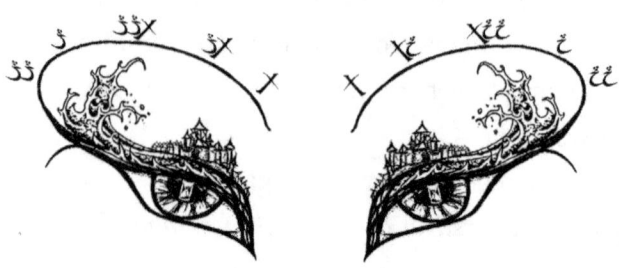

As requested, we've worked on slogans that downplay the use of manark dung in your herbal-bean mixture. We still feel there must be some disclosure as this could lead to a credibility issue in the future. We've included some recommendations and, as soon as you've made your choice, artisans will begin lettering your signs.

~sincerely,
Venali Cluhurach
Spinmaster Extraordinaire

- *Mornings weren't meant for sleep. Get roaring with Banish.*
- *Discover life, discover Banish.*
- *Banish. When tea just isn't enough.*
- *Cut the z out of morningz with Banish.*
- *From the heart of the swamp to your table, a drink meant to bring you to life: Banish.*
- *Let the rich, woody, lemony zing of Banish brighten your morning.*

The next evening D'trav returned with a heavier d'yroap pouch, a package of food under his arm, and two buckets of water. His cheerful whistle of an old bar tune petered out when Sarenka turned from the fire, scowling face beaded with sweat. Her hair hung semi-limp in the humid room, strands waving dispiritedly, tips reddened by their own inner light.

"You bring water now?"

D'trav's celebratory mood evaporated. He scowled back. "My hut. I do what I like."

"I told you, I need it earlier in the day."

"Look, this is the deal. You stay here, do my papers, clean my shit, feed me, and I pay you a silver a day, get your damn antidote, and, if you're really nice, maybe a way out of Burmtin. That's it. You don't get some fancy man that caters to every want under the double moons."

"But—"

"No buts. It's a simple, mutually rewarding arrangement. We aren't supposed to be friends, just business partners. And I'll tell you this straight up. I don't pay people to yell at me when I walk in the door."

She snapped her mouth shut, biting off whatever she'd planned to say.

"Look. I know you're exhausted from bein' up all night, and the Foreveron critters are eatin' at your innards, but this is the way it has to be. I'll not come home to this every damn night."

She turned back to the stove. "I'm sorry."

Still angry, he thumped the water buckets down near the sideboard and the package on the table before dropping the empty pails by the door. "Woke late. Bought two more buckets so I can get water mornin' and night now. Food in the package on the table."

She stirred the pot.

"When's dinner done?"

"An hourglass turn ago." Wrestling a slab of meat onto an oversized scallop shell, she carried it to the table. "It's overcooked. And try to eat it all. It'll be bad by tomorrow night."

He sat with a frown. "You went to the market again?"

"I was fine, kept my disguise with no problem."

He grabbed her arm as she walked past, giving it a rough shake. "I'm tellin' you, don't do that again!"

"What was I supposed to cook? You have no cold cellar. The food was spoiled already."

"If you can't do what you're told, you'll be findin' yourself back out on the streets. I'm not lookin' to get myself strung up and tortured next to you." Face blazing red with rage, the muscle along his jawline clenched and unclenched.

Sarenka eyes widened with fright. "Okay, I won't. I promise."

Reassured that she was taking him seriously, he let go of her arm and his anger, and gave a curt nod. "Good, make sure you keep it."

She sat across from him and began eating her meal with studied concentration.

From under furrowed brows, he glanced at her between bites, expecting her to start talking at any moment. The silence between them drew out to an unbearable gap. "You plannin' on ditchin' our deal?"

"What? No. I'm not stupid."

"Good. Far as I know I'm the only one that'll sell you the antidote."

She glanced up sharply and spoke as if her throat were being squeezed. "Did you get more?"

"In the cloak," he mumbled around his bite.

"Was the signature good enough?"

"Yes." He relaxed a little. Maybe she wasn't planning on leaving. He did hold all the winning cards.

With a distant look in her eyes, she chewed a bite of meat far longer than necessary before asking, "Bring anything for me to do tonight?"

"No."

Sarenka sighed, leaving him wondering if she was disappointed at not having work to do. He started to ask but changed his mind. Now that she'd ruined his night, he wasn't in the mood to entertain. Having her in the hut was weird enough already.

"What do you do for work?"

He half-smiled at her.

Now he got it. She was fishing for information. "I'm a bouncer at a brothel. They've got an openin' too. I'm thinkin' you might take a shine to fillin' the position. Help pay your way round here."

Sarenka choked on her bite so badly that D'trav gave her back several hearty wallops. She gulped down some water and sat silent, all questions driven out.

D'trav chewed his meal, more than a little alarmed that she'd almost choked to death over his joke. But it had ended her inquiries. He didn't need anyone delving too deep into what he did for a living.

R'kiax set his M'hakru whiskey down on the countertop and pushed back a hank of greasy blond hair, exposing the slight point of a Half-Frevell ear. It had been weeks since he'd last seen the woman. He glanced down the room at the dag-board. Next to it, riddled with slashes, the Freni-Kyn's wanted poster hung. He ground his teeth together. He'd caught her scent more than once. And now, like an unranked fledgling, he was forced to skulk about town rather than tell the Red Pelican that she'd escaped the city.

A cloud of perfume enveloped him, making his eyes water.

"Tahrek?" A woman leaned over his shoulder and stared him in the eyes.

R'kiax stiffened as invisible fluffs of hair brushed against his face. He stared at her tightly woven braids. Freni-Kyn. Masking her scent with a revolting amount of perfumes. He rubbed his nose, trying to keep from sneezing.

"I knew it was you." She flashed pearl white teeth in a broad smile and pushed her way up beside him, turning around and leaning against the bar.

R'kiax hesitated, then smiled back. "How'd you know?"

"The ear, silly. What other Half-Frevell goes around Burmtin showin' it off like that?"

R'kiax threw back the rest of his drink and slapped the empty shell down on the stone countertop. "Gives me away every time."

"So, did you find him?"

"No. Not yet."

"I asked around. He ain't been seen by nobody. Least not anybody that be talking. Likely done went to ground after the warehouse burned down."

There had been only one warehouse fire in recent history. A building owned by one of the illicit pleasure houses. R'kiax nodded. "Most like."

"Shame about all those people bein' killed." She leaned back and ran a fingertip up and down the tattoo on her left breast.

R'kiax smiled, suddenly hungry for more than whiskey, and wondered if they were real or illusions. "How about we take this discussion elsewhere."

Her face closed up, becoming doubtful. "Thought you didn't do that."

Damn. I've blown it. "I'll make an exception. This once."

"Well, I don't know…"

"Ten silvers."

She smiled broadly, but it wasn't the friendly smile she'd given him when she approached, now it was the smile of a professional. "Well, why didn't you say so sweetheart?"

He grabbed the crook of her elbow and guided her from the building. As they walked, he worked hard to be charming, and their arrival at a seedy inn occurred without any more awkward mistakes.

Opening the door, he ushered her in.

She threw him a smile and held out her hand.

He dug through his embossed pouch and dropped the silvers into her palm, counting them as if it really mattered.

Sashaying into the room, she pocketed them.

R'kiax pushed the door shut with his foot and followed. Locking his hands together, he brought the double fist down on her back as she neared the bed.

Silent, knees buckling, she fell across the bed and gasped for air.

He climbed onto her back and held her throat, squeezing just enough to be painful. "Lose the illusions, bitch."

The illusions fell away, revealing skin the color of a pale rose.

"Kyron-be-damned." He started to let go, then changed his mind. "Tell me about your friends."

Sarenka lay in bed, eyes closed, listening to the now familiar sounds of D'trav dressing. His morning routine never varied. After a month and a half of listening and watching, she could tell what he was going to do before he did it. When the door of the hut thumped closed, she sprang free of the blankets, rushed to the door, and cracked it open enough to watch him disappear down the street. She hurried through pulling on her sandals and cursed when her fingers fumbled over the ties, using one of D'trav's many colorful expressions. Rolling her eyes at that atrocity, she promised herself that she'd never use those phrases again.

Not only hasn't he given me enough antidote, but he hasn't gotten me out of the city.

And I'm even starting to sound like him.

Time to take things into my own hands.

She stepped out the door, face flushed red beneath the careful illusion of a middle aged woman with an overlarge wart near her bottom lip. Rushing through the streets to gather supplies, and stopping only long enough to renew her illusions, she arrived back home with a basket loaded down with twelve jars of assorted jams, preserves, honeys, a handful of kor nuts, and a selection of packaged ground nuts. She tucked the goods under the head of the bed, worried that their combined weight would shatter the vessels, especially if D'trav threw himself down on the mattress too hard.

She walked around the room, checking to be sure the basket couldn't be seen. Satisfied that it was hidden from all angles, she sat at the table with quill and paper and worked through a signature for D'trav. It was to be finished by this eve and hadn't seemed difficult, but with the sun already approaching midday, she was worried.

The sun set just as she was finishing, and still D'trav hadn't returned. Standing, she bent backwards, forcing a satisfying pop from her back before turning to the day-old stew. She stirred the contents and frowned at the formless mush it had become.

"I should have gotten us some rolls, or something."

"Oh no, you shouldn't have," came a growl from behind her shoulder.

CHAPTER 39

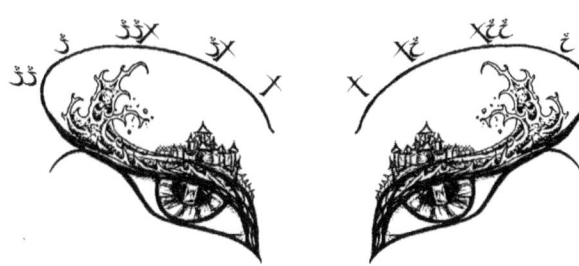

Sarenka hunched into a defensive position and swung around. Hot liquid splattered across D'trav as she swung the ladle at him and scrabbled to pick up a butcher knife. A shower of red sparks flew from the tips of her hair, dispersing into nothingness before they could land on the ground. At the sight of D'trav's wide eyes and raised brows, she came out of the fighting stance and giggled. The color on the tips of her hair faded to pale pink.

"You surprised me."

He wiped the mess off his face and dropped two loaves of bread onto the tabletop. "Where'd you learn that move?"

"On the street last year. Girls got to survive, you know."

A fleeting look of pain crossed his face. He turned away.

Sarenka stared at his back, wondering what she'd said wrong.

That evening he hardly spoke, except to thank her for the signature and pay her the last week's earnings.

Long after he'd gone to bed, Sarenka sat by the fire. After a while, she began murmuring out the lines of a haunting lullaby. When at last the fire grew low, she pushed away the nostalgia with surprise. It had been many years since she'd thought of that song, so many that it was a wonder she still remembered the words. She stumbled wearily to her feet, and, as she turned from the fire's warmth, a white fluttering caught her eye.

Pale form shimmering in the shadowed room, the whiteness lowered until nearly touching D'trav's lips and paused.

Frozen in terror, Sarenka could do nothing, neither run, nor cry out, nor defend.

As if sensing her vulnerability, it lifted free of D'trav, shifting its spectral body before soaring across the room towards her.

With a shriek, Sarenka raised her hands to shield her face.

R'kiax stared at the whimpering woman with satisfaction. She'd squealed like a swamp cow being cut in half. He now had the name of a whorehouse with a roomful of Freni-Kyn. That should buy him something.

He drew his blade.

She crawled backwards across the bed.

He grabbed her leg and pulled her back towards him.

She kicked at his hand with the other leg.

Dropping the knife next to them, he grabbed her legs and yanked until he was pressed up hard between her legs. He shifted into his Sharpra form, shoulders broadening and gaining a ruff of hair, ears moving upwards, hair turning long and banded with dark brown stripes.

Horror replaced the fear on her face, and she struggled against his hold.

His members throbbed and thrummed against her flesh, and he laughed.

"Please don't kill me. Please."

Letting go of one leg, he sprang, throwing himself across her body and pinning her to the bed. He grabbed her hair, wrapping its floating mass in a clenched fist.

She screamed and bit down on his shoulder.

He jerked away, but she refused to let go. Grabbing the knife near him, he held it to her throat.

She released his shoulder and lay panting under his body.

"As you can see, I'll not be taking pleasure in your body whore, but..." No. He wouldn't take her. Not when it meant a permanent attachment to her that could result in his death. No slut Freni-Kyn was worth that risk.

Closing her eyes she breathed out a prayer so faint he couldn't make out the words beyond 'Kyron'.

"I know... I know you're Sharpra, and you won't take me because of the bonding, but please... please don't kill me. I've never harmed one of your kind, and I never will."

"I've other uses for you." He rolled off and pulled her to her feet by her hair.

She screamed, turning white.

He looked at her clothing, still rucked up in the back, and let go.

She fell to her hands and knees on the ground, as if he'd stabbed her, and panted while sweat ran down her face.

R'kiax furrowed his brows and glanced at his blade, wondering if he'd somehow cut her. He nudged her with is foot. "Get up."

Her hair floated around her head, throwing off embers.

He reached for it, and she began struggling to rise.

"I am. I am. Please." Tears streamed down her face as she stood.

"Get your clothing in order."

She tugged down the back of her burgundy skirt and pulled the corset up over her nipples, covering the blackening areas.

R'kiax grabbed her chin and touched the bruise under her eye. "That won't do. Hide it."

She closed her eyes. Her illusions flickered before settling into a blond haired, blue eyed H'euman with unmarred skin.

"We're making a trip." He held up the blade. "If you run, you're dead."

"What!" D'trav's roar from across the room startled Sarenka into shrieking again.

"What? What's a matter?" D'trav hauled her up from where she huddled on the ground and shook her lightly.

"I saw something. It-it came at me." A white flutter out of the corner of her eye caused her to swing around and point. "There! There it is."

The white blur soared down and landed gently on the table.

D'trav snorted and walked towards it. "Well, it is the biggest moth I ever did see, but not somethin' to get riled up about."

Sarenka's cheeks blazed violet-red with embarrassment.

Picking it up by its wings, he held it out to her but she shook her head no, she didn't need a closer look. He took it to the door and tossed it outside where it sailed off into the dark.

"I'm sorry... I..."

Instead of the mockery she expected, he only shrugged. "It's not a thing, now get yourself to sleep. The night's fadin' fast."

She nodded, glad for his closeness. Despite seeing it land on the table, she couldn't shake the memory of something far bigger than a moth flying towards her.

R'kiax's trip to the Red Pelican headquarters went without incident. A terrified woman can be a very compliant thing. Of course, his beating beforehand had softened her up. She had sobbed and wailed while he dragged her down the halls, and it was all he could do to resist a fist to her throat. At last, he threw her into one of the bone cages and fought off an urge to bathe before delivering his report.

Filthy Freni-Kyn whores.

Their stench should be wiped off the face of Llayentia.

Revealing to Lator the location of a Freni-Kyn nest left him smugly satisfied. Although Lator never cracked a smile or offered him a bonus, R'kiax left with an additional mission, find the whore house and watch it.

As he sauntered away, a slap and the cry of a woman echoed down the hall. He fingered his dagger, wishing he could be part of that interrogation.

Airintia rubbed her forehead. How much longer would the debates continue? ~*We can't keep arguing about this.*~

~*You're right. So what do we do? Lock the asshole up? Kill him?*~ Lanion asked.

~*You're more Freni-Kyn than he is, Mr. Drama. You know I don't want that. And he's as good as locked up already, chained to a bed with an enchanted manacle. He can't even use his illusions.*~

~*Agree, the manacle was a bit of an overkill, but I'm not so sure he doesn't need to be locked up for good,*~ Lanion sent.

~*That's quite enough.*~ The reprimand in the elder's voice was sharp as a whip. For a moment, none dared speak. ~*But they are right. The longer we stay in debate, the less time we have to fulfil our duties.*~

~*But his life's at stake,*~ Airintia sent.

She felt the agreement in the others' psychic scent.

~*How much time have you spent in the last few months searching for your replacement?*~ the elder asked.

Airintia was silent, ashamed.

~*Any of you?*~ the elder asked.

None answered.

~*I thought as much. We've all held our breaths and hoped Parian was right. We let him risk his life on the chance of finding the One. What does that make us? Cowards? Voyeurs?*~

Airintia gazed through her window at the wildflower strewn field. She was guilty, and the silence must mean that the others also felt the sting of guilt.

~*So, we make a decision based on facts,*~ the M'hakru contingent sent. ~*Agreed?*~

~*Agreed,*~ Airintia reluctantly sent.

The others joined in with consent.

~*So what has he actually done?*~

~*He spent months jumping time streams at the risk of his own life and health. Did you see what he looked like when we caught him? Skin and bones. Pure skin and bones.*~ Lanion flashed them with an image of Parian's legs.

~*He hid from us,*~ Airintia added, still feeling the sting of that hurt.

~*He claimed to have found the One several times, and then not,*~ the Frevellian contingent sent.

~*He blasted us all with rage through the connection and nearly killed Lanion.*~ The elder sent, bringing Parian's primary crime to light.

Silence hung between them.

Airintia sobbed, knowing the truth but not wanting to face it.

~*We all know what this means. Parian has lost his way. He is unfit as a Seven and must be replaced,*~ Sadness infused the elder's send.

~*I wasn't hurt that bad.*~ Lanion tried to mask the panic, but Airintia felt it through the connection.

~*She's right, Lanion,*~ the M'hakru sent.

~*I demand a vote,*~ Lanion sent.

~*Very well. All in favor of declaring Parian insane? You have my vote already,*~ the elder sent.

~*I abstain. I'm too close to this to make a fair decision,*~ Lanion sent.

~*Aiy,*~ the Frevell and M'hakru mind-spoke at the same time.

A well of horror rose in Airintia's gut. ~*Please, we can't do this. He's a good man. Against. I'm against.*~

~*Aiy,*~ the Watrelk's send was faint, reluctant.

Airintia leaned forward, squeezing back a wail.

The majority had voted.

He was lost.

A gust of regret blew through, touching all their hearts, and the silence drew out.

~Very well. We have our decision, heartbreaking though it may be. I'm sorry, Airintia. I know you were close. This is one of the more difficult decisions we face as a Seven and why we were chosen. We must have the strength of will to do what is right, even when it tears our hearts out.~

~So, what do we do then? We have no replacement for him. He never took an apprentice,~ the Frevell sent.

~We find someone. His teacher is still alive, he will have to return to service.~ The sadness that accompanied that thought was almost too heavy a weight for the rest of them to bear.

Airintia stared at the field, watching the wind flatten the flowers. Grey clouds bundled on the horizon. A storm was coming. *~And Parian?~*

~You know the rules,~ the elder sent.

~Will he remember us... afterwards?"~

~It will be kinder if he doesn't.~

~How long?~

~Before I get there?~

~No, how long before he's stripped of his powers?~ Airintia asked.

CHAPTER 40

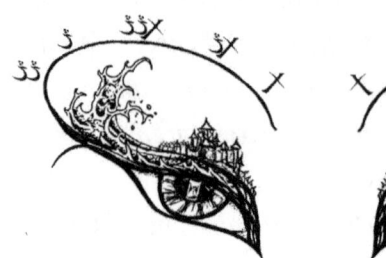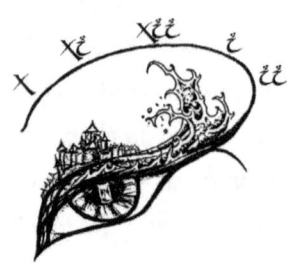

"They've left sir, the whole damn lot of them. Took to flight an hour ago. We've got reports coming in from all over of V formation Glidarthian regiments, all heading north. It seems tearing their wings off has done the job after all. Teach them for hiring out to drop flame buckets on our troops' heads."

Desmond Borges
H'euman Regiment Captain
War Minutes

D'trav snuck up on Camille as she bent over the stove. He grabbed her waist and pulled her hips backwards.

She squealed and whirled around with a knife in her fist.

He threw up his hands.

The fear left her face. With a laugh, she tossed the blade away and threw herself at him.

"Damn, girl. Nearly skewered me," he said around the kisses.

"Your own damn fault, too."

After several long kisses, the stove began to hiss. She gasped and rushed to pull the pot to safety.

D'trav settled himself at the table. "Second time in a day I've been threatened by a cook."

"How so?"

"Sarenka. She turned around 'bout the same way you did."

"Teach you not to grab women from behind."

He reddened. "I didn't. I just said something and startled her. And damned if she don't seem jumpy. Woke me in the night screaming about a moth, of all things."

Camille gave the pot another stir and leaned against the counter, facing him. "Truth tell, I've not slept well for the last few months myself."

"Why? What's wrong?"

"I keep having nightmares about someone breaking in and killing us. Sometimes it's Red Pelican, other times I'm not sure what it is. Then sometimes I just wake up, and I swear there's someone in the room. So I have to light a lantern and walk the grounds before I can sleep again. I mean, what— we're haunted now?"

D'trav gave an uneasy laugh, knowing it was his fault she was afraid of the Red Pelican. "I just keep havin' these disturbin' dreams about women wrapped in chains."

She held out her wrists, "Any time, luv."

His cock gave an answering throb, and his gaze traveled from her wrists, to her face, then dropped back down to her breasts. The musky scent of her Jasmine perfume wafted upwards, luring him in. D'trav pulled her close and growled playfully and the kisses turned into nips along her neckline. "You're sooo bad. I might be forced to go to the considerable trouble of spankin' you."

"I know. I am." Camille purred out and wriggled against his growing bulge before pulling away.

D'trav went into a role he'd played many times, one that came with rules. He dragged her across the room and sat, yanking her down onto his lap with a rough jerk. Grasping her hair, he pulled backwards until her back arced, and her breasts thrust upwards. With his other hand he tugged down the ruffled edge of her blouse, uncovering rosy nipples, already half hardened.

He stopped to savor the sight. She was a thing of beauty, all voluptuous mounds and sensuous valleys. Cupping a creamy breast, he pressed upwards, drawing the hardened nipple towards his lips. He brushed barely parted lips over skin soft as velvet, bypassing the nipple, making her wait.

D'trav released her breast and stood, swinging her over his shoulder and drawing a gasp of surprise. The chair rocked backwards, landing on the floor with a clatter, and he strode from the kitchen.

Camille kicked her legs against his back in mock fight, barely suppressing a giggle.

D'trav rewarded the effort with a sharp slap to her ass, but her voluminous skirt caught at his hand, muffling the sound.

Habitual caution stopped D'trav outside Camille's room. His eyes flitted from surface to surface, searching for hidden dangers, before coming to a rest on a tall mirror. He savored the view of a marauder claiming his prize before striding in with one thing on his mind. With a quick flip forward, and her accompanying squeal, he deposited her on her feet in front of the silken bed. Moving his hands to her waist-string with familiar ease, he waited, drawing out the moment before yanking the string free so fast that she jumped. The fabric fell about her feet in a jade puddle.

He took a step backwards.

Under his inspecting stare, Camille rolled her hips suggestively and stepped towards him, lifting her arms to encircle his neck.

D'trav gave a tiny negating shake of his head and grasped her wrists before she could touch him. He smiled, slow and sure, and abruptly spun her around, pushing her across the bed.

Sand drifted downwards through the hourglass, and the building came to life around them as time passed. At last, the two landed in a limp heap over the side of the bed. For a moment they lay—half on, half off—catching their breaths.

D'trav moaned as the sparks of light cleared from his vision, enjoying the lingering laps of pleasure that rocked gently through him.

He ran his hand over Camille's reddened ass before bending to kiss it lovingly.

With a low laugh, she wiggled under his lips, playfully asking for more. "I might be a wee bit sore today."

"Teach you for temptin' me in the morning."

Reminded, Camille shook her ankles, rattling the chains, "Oh no! We need to hurry."

D'trav groaned and released her ankles from the shackles.

Camille sprang to her feet and began rushing around the room.

After half-heartedly pulling at his breeches, D'trav decided his knees were too weak to stand. He fell forward, landing backwards on the bed with enough force to make the tantwood frame bounce.

Camille looked down at him, eyebrows rising. "I had this bed specifically designed not to do that. I think we broke it."

D'trav smiled lazily up. "Take it out of my pay, darlin. It was well worth it."

She shrugged and turned away. "It's no matter, just won't hire that carpenter again."

His eyes drifted closed while she rushed to get dressed. The sound of splashing water was followed by rustling fabric and latches snapping shut. At the soft sound of leather cord being pulled through corset eyelets, he gave a relaxed sigh, unwilling to give up the last few minutes of aftershock pleasure. Surges of ecstasy shot through his body, revealing itself in the occasional betraying jump.

The unexpected weight of Camille landing on top of him brought a woof from his lungs.

His eyes flew open.

She straddled his hips and took his face between her hands with a smile, before softly kissing his lips. "It's good to see you relaxed, now get up you big, mean, bad-guy." She punctuated the words with kisses. "We've got to get moving."

With that she jumped to her feet and began applying the face colors of her trade.

D'trav frowned, preferring her natural skin tone to the dramatic teal swirls she was swiping onto her cheeks. She was long past the day when she serviced customers, but she still wore the costume and he supposed it was comfortable, a uniform of sorts.

A blaze of warm gratitude washed through him. How fortunate he'd been to meet her somewhere other than here. Their friendship had become so much more than the tryst it had started with. He was sure their relationship would never have blossomed into what they had now if he'd been just another customer.

Stepping to the washstand, he swished freezing water over his semi-hard member and watched it shrivel into a tiny wrinkled mass with disgust.

So much for feelin' like a sex god.

He looked over at her as she painted a bird under one eye. "Thanks Camille."

"For what, luv?"

"For bein' here for me. For... everything... just every damn thing." His hands spread wide in an all-encompassing gesture.

She walked towards the door, hips swaying, "Not another word, luv. What're good friends for if not to comfort each other?"

With a wink over her shoulder, she stepped from the room.

CHAPTER 44

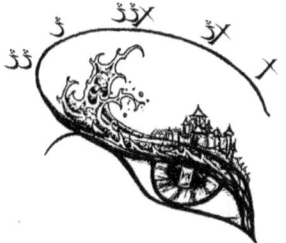

The next day dawned early, and like the one before, Sarenka lay waiting until D'trav left before darting out the door. This time, instead of masking her voluptuous figure behind an unappealing form, she shaded her skin to honey brown, masked her folding ears behind H'euman ones, turned her hair satin blond, and her eyes pale green. It was time to woo a man, or so she hoped.

Basket over her arm, she sauntered down the streets and frowned when each bust-jiggling step drew attention. She paused long enough to wrap her linen cloak closely about her body, shielding it from hungry stares. As she approached her goal, a unattended cart outside of a local brewery, she slowed in pretended exhaustion. Sarenka stopped to lean against the brewery wall and wiped imaginary sweat from her brow while checking the street for watchers.

Boldly grasping the handle of the empty vendor's cart, she dropped her basket in and pushed it away. After turning the corner, she went into a near run and by the time she reached the baker's house, she really was sweating. She paused on his doorstep to catch her breath. The curtain moved and the door swung open.

"Good morn' sweet one." The baker said, leaning over her, each word carried between rotted teeth on a puff of sour breath.

Sarenka resisted the urge to cover her nose and took a seemingly shy step backwards. "I'm here to pick up some sweet rolls that were ordered yesterday by mistress Delange."

"Aiy, I've got 'em all ready for you. At fifteen coppers each that will be..." His eyes rolled upwards, staring at the sky overhead, as he tried to count out the sum.

She waited impatiently, knowing from past experience that he'd never believe the sum if she did the math for him.

"Ummm... three hundred coppers and that's... three... three silvers, 'tis." He beamed, and she wasn't sure if he was happy because he was making three silvers, or because he'd figured out how much she owed.

Gritting her teeth at the overcharge, Sarenka handed it to him without a word.

"Anything else I can do you for?"

"I think not, though I dare say I could have gotten these at a better price elsewhere."

"They wouldn't be as good, would they now? I'm the best in these here parts." He leaned even closer, making her skin crawl.

She gave the cart a shove, moving away with a lurch, and spoke over her shoulder. "Good day to you."

"Any time, m'dear."

Sarenka waited for the soft snap of his door shutting before stopping to arrange the rolls, jars of trimmings, and shell spoons. If her plan worked, she was well on her way to escaping Burmtin.

She arrived in front of the Glidarthian Jump Tower just as the sun crested the city, throwing rays of soft pink over the sleek stone walls. Rolling past with measured, slow steps, she reached the corner and turned back, this time stopping at the building next to the tower. She pretended to rearrange her wares while watching for the Glidarthian who always left at this time for breakfasting.

After waiting for what seemed like forever, her shoulders slumped. He wasn't coming today, and she'd wasted over a month's worth of earnings. A shadow moved across the sun, throwing her into darkness for an exaggerated moment. She peered up at the top of the tower just in time to see a Glidarthian glide to a running stop.

Disappointed, she sighed and started to turn away just as the door at the bottom of the tower opened. A man with wings painted in garish orange and green stripes walked out. Turning his back to her, he left, long strides taking him rapidly away. She grasped the handles of the cart with renewed hope and started forward.

"Sweet honeyed rolls, fresh made," she shouted,

His step faltered.

"Strawberry, nuts, and blue honey toppings, no extra charge for first time buys."

He stopped in his tracks and turned abruptly around, hurrying towards her.

She threw him a sunny smile as he approached, stomach jiggling with each step, and was amazed that those thin wings could lift him into the sky. "What can I do you for?"

"Two rolls—" He caught sight of the plump, sticky bits of pastry. "No. Make that five. And you say no extra charge for the toppings?"

"First topping free for first time buys. If you want more than one I'll have to charge you."

"Very good." His chubby cheeks creased in a huge smile and his eyes lit up.

"That'll be…" She copied the baker, pretending at having to add up the sum by hesitating over the price. "Five silver, unless you want more toppings."

"And I do." He grinned. "Three toppings each. It would be a waste not to try each one, right?"

"A terrible waste." She nodded. "That would normally be another twenty five copper for each topping, but seeing as the first topping is free, it only comes to… seven silver and fifty coppers."

She leaned against the cart and watched him smear jams across the buns. "You live up there?" She jerked her head towards the tower.

"Not hardly. They don't have proper kitchens in those things."

"Then where?"

He waved the spoon towards a wooden building across the street. "We rent that. They wouldn't let us build a proper stone house."

"You don't sound very happy to be here."

He loaded down another roll with a pile of preserves but paused to look up at her, one brow raised. "I'm not. This is the worst post. They use it to train us because of that. Longest flight to get here, so our wings are always aching. We aren't allowed to bring our families. And worst of all is the food. It's abysmal."

Unable to wait any longer, he lifted a bun to his mouth and took a massive bite. His eyes slipped closed and he moaned. "Ooooh my... this is... heaven... it's just heaven."

Sarenka grinned with amusement. "I was hoping you'd enjoy my cooking, but you had me worried when you said the food was abysmal."

"Oh dear no, I'm sorry. No, this is most excellent. Forgive me." He blushed and gave a short bow. "If these fair hands created this temptatious feast, then your hands are fairer than your face."

"You flatter me." Sarenka focused on raising her cheek color to a faint flush.

He spoke around the rest of the roll he'd stuffed into his mouth. "No, my dear, I speak the truth always. You ravish me with your cooking."

Sarenka's cheeks burned hot in truth now. She'd heard the Glidarth had food fetishes but this was the first time she believed it.

Head bent over the cart, preparing another bun, he didn't seem to notice her uncomfortable silence.

"Do try the zaernuts, not only are they delicious, but they're said to make you healthy. Perhaps they'll help with the sore muscles." She gestured towards the nuts she'd cracked open the day before and spent an hour chopping.

"Is that what these are? A new culinary treat. I shall be the envy of the tower today."

"You know, if those don't help with your muscles, I could try rubbing them for you."

He glanced sharply up, and his wings fluttered nervously, before he dropped his gaze and fumbled in loading down the bun with preserves. "I-I… err… um… I-I don't know what to say."

"Say yes. You complimented my cooking already, what could be better to follow that than two bodies touching? And I have the most luscious fruit flavored oils, too."

His cheeks blazed red and he spoke hesitantly. "You… have known my people before?"

She shook her head in pretended innocence. "No, why?"

Looking down, he studiously drizzled honey over the top of the bun, then began to meticulously sprinkle nuts over them. "Nothing… n-never mind." He peeked at her before turning his attention back to the food.

She changed the topic, worried that she'd moved too fast. "So you deliver messages then?"

The relief that washed over his face was almost comical. "Yes, most days."

"How long can you fly?"

"The entire day if I have to."

"Wow! That's amazing, you must be ever so strong. Ever deliver people?"

CHAPTER 42

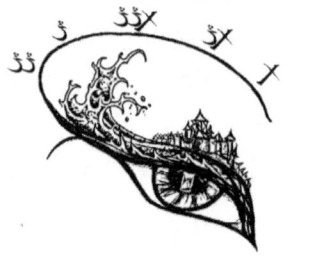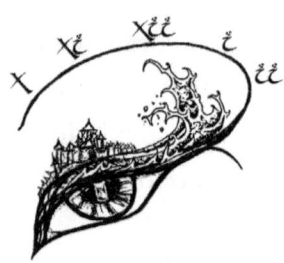

"This spring the Alumoon trees blossomed and the wind blew, strewing the ground with pink confetti, promising a bright new year. It was a lie. Instead, we reaped bitterness and death when our king was slain in front of us."

From a Glidarthian songsmith's diary
Year of Betrayal

"Every once in a while."

"Aren't they heavy?"

"Yes, but we have a system that makes it easier. We take turns trading off flyers until we get them to the next tower."

She nodded, though she wasn't sure what he meant.

"We don't do it often, not from Burmtin in any case"

"Why?"

"Well first, it's expensive."

"Really? How much?"

"Fifty gold is the least I've ever heard of them charging."

Sarenka's heart sank a little.

"Then they have to have papers. And right now there's a ban on both M'hakru and Freni-Kyn females, so the guards have to be here to check all passengers."

Her heart plummeted to the bottom of her stomach. There was only one thing she hadn't tried.

"I'd give anything to fly. Why, I'd cook for a month if someone took me for a ride. It'd be so"—she gave an exaggerated shiver—"delicious... all those pastries... the wind in my hair..."

His wings fluttered half open, and though he had nothing in his mouth, he swallowed, and his face flamed red. "I-I... well I have to get to work now. Here's the coin." He counted out the eight silver loops. "Do keep the extra, these were worth every copper, and please do sell them here again. I'll tell the others too, I'm sure you'll sell out."

She grasped his hand before he could rush away. This was a one-time shot. It would be more than a month before she earned enough to buy the ingredients again, and all the carts would be locked down once the missing cart was reported to the guards. "Are you sure you wouldn't want to fly with me today."

"I'm-I'm..." Face purpling with embarrassment, he rushed off.

Sarenka lingered, hoping he'd send out one of the other Glidarths. She left an hourglass turn later when the strain of holding the illusions became a pickaxe against her brain. After rounding the corner, she loaded the rolls and spreads into her basket, abandoned the cart, and headed towards home, stopping only long enough to visit a place she hadn't been to since moving in with D'trav. Under the back awning of the butchers shop a man lay, curled on his side with the ragged vestiges of a cloak pulled around his hunched form.

She leaned over to give his shoulder a shake.

He opened his eyes, showing only white spheres. "Who's there?" He sniffed the air several times, and licked his lips. "Shore do smell sweet."

Sarenka set the basket down in front of him. "Brought you a treat, father."

"Ah, it's that little beggar girl what liked to take my best sleep spots."

He patted around on the ground in front of him.

Sarenka picked his hand up and placed it on the rolls, showing him by feel the treasure trove of food she had brought. "Got you enough rolls for a few days, and some other treats too." She grabbed his other hand and put an open jar in it.

"Strawberry preserves. I can smell them from here. Guess you're making up for all those times you made me take the cold spot."

Sarenka smiled. She'd always given him the choice locations. He just to teased her because the first time they'd met she'd been sleeping in one of his favorite spots.

"Thank you, little one." He patted her cheek, finding it with un-canny ease. "You're smelling a lot better now. Not like the meat market. Like a Kyn ought to."

Sarenka stiffened, glancing up and down the street to make sure nobody heard. "I told you not to talk about that. How'd you know anyway? I never did anything to give it away."

"My secret, lil' one. Now you get yourself off before your illusions drop."

Arriving home, she stood in the doorway and accepted the dark gown of depression that settled over her shoulders. Her illusions evap-orated as she shed her cloak. Shivering with cold, she shuffled over to tuck away what remained of her coin. Knowing she should add wood, she turned towards the fire but changed her mind and crawled into bed, pulling the blanket over her head. Under the cocooning warmth, wrapped in dark thoughts, she sniffed back tears until the sun set.

The door creaked open. A man's heavy boots took two cautious steps into the darkened hut.

Sarenka stiffened with fear.

"Hello?" D'trav called out.

"I'm here." She relaxed and pushed the blanket off her head.

"What's the matter? Why's the fire out? And why do you sound funny?"

"I fell asleep. Don't feel too good."

An 'oof' as he bumped into a chair leg was followed by several choice words and the sound of logs being added to the fireplace. Sarenka pulled the cover back over her head, determined to shut out the world. Before long, yellow and red flickered through the weave of the blanket, intruding on her black gloom. Preferring the darkness, she rolled towards the wall and listened to the thump of D'trav's feet against the wooden floor, drawing ever closer.

Dread filled her. She couldn't talk about how she felt.

"Get you something? Stew's cold, but there's bread and wine."

"Not hungry."

He sat on the edge of the bed. "Stomach hurt?"

"Yeah."

"Okay, well, get some sleep. If you need anything let me know."

Sarenka drifted off to the sound of him moving about, and awoke to his hand on her forehead. She pushed it away.

"Got no fever brewin', in any case."

"I'll be fine, please, just leave me alone."

He grunted and went to sit by the fire.

Sarenka lay in the dark and thought of all the things she missed. The dappled shade of oaks, alumoon trees blanketing the ground with pale pink petals, sun shining through cosmos flowers like colored glass, and cool grass tickling her ankles. The sweet-tart taste of freshly plucked carlt grapes. Fine food and a feather bed. The scent of pine trees whispering outside her bedroom window while the double moons lulled her to sleep. But mostly, freedom to be herself.

A sob slipped out.

D'trav stirred again.

She gulped, but it was too late, she could hold them back no more. One after another, more sobs broke free, and before she knew it he was thumping his way back to the bed.

"What's the matter, Sarenka?"

"I hate this city. I hate not being able to go out and do things. I hate not being me and having a price on my head. I hate my life."

"Keep saving your coin girl, you'll have enough to buy your way out of here eventually." His face was long and grave in the flickering firelight.

"You don't believe that."

"It's a fact. Enough d'yroap buys most anything."

Oddly reassured, she rolled away and stared at a crack that ran down the wall of the hut.

Instead of walking away, he lay down behind her.

She slept, though for how long she didn't know. A hand on her cheek awakened her. Icy cold, it sank through her flesh and made her teeth ache.

CHAPTER 43

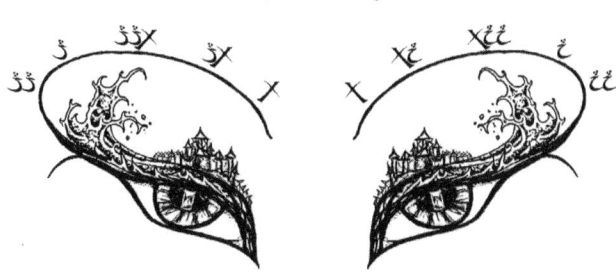

Startled out of a dead sleep, Sarenka sat straight up in the bed and stared about at the predawn room. Light filtered in through badly daubed cracks and around the edges of the door. The unnatural touch which had awakened her still lingered on one cheek. She pressed her fingers to the still-cool flesh with a shudder.

Not a dream… real… but how… what… Her stomach gave a grumbling protest, and she rubbed it, pushing away the fright. *No. It has to be a dream. I'm just mind-lost.*

Rising from the bed, she stirred the fire to life and threw a handful of ground Banish into a pot. Sarenka gave the congealed pot of stew D'trav had made a disapproving frown before scooping up the cold mass and planting it atop two slabs of brown bread. The stew jiggled, catching the dim light as if it were an expensive dessert, before sinking into the bread. Relieved, she rubbed her hands down her skirt.

D'trav let out an especially loud snort and rolled over on the bed.

She jumped and gave a nervous laugh before rushing to pull the spluttering water from the heat and turning her attention to D'trav. He lay sleeping, fully clothed, without even a corner of the blanket covering him.

"Hey!" Fearing D'trav would regret his gentleness of the night before, she shook his shoulder with their former gruffness. "Food's ready. Get up."

"Gah! Stop yelling in my ear." He stomped across the room and stumbled out the back door to relieve his bladder.

Used to his early morning irritation, she turned back to the table and poured the Banish into the shell cups and gave a relieved nod, glad for the normalcy.

He arrived back at the table looking more awake. "Feelin' better, I take it."

"Yes."

"Signatures." He nodded towards the papers on top of his trunk.

"I'll finish them while you're gone."

"You sure you don't need me to stay home?" His voice softened a little.

"I'm fine."

He finished wolfing down the cold breakfast and scalding beverage. "I've got some things what need attention. See you tonight. Get those signatures done, they were supposed to go out this morning."

"I'm sorry."

"It's okay. Long as they get done today."

Over the course of the next few weeks, Sarenka began visiting bars whenever she had no signatures to do and returned to her original goal, finding Onglat. That, and only that, would clear her name and return her freedom. If she happened to pick up some extra d'yroap or a bottle or two of antidote along the way, well, that was a nice bonus. And with enough bonus finds, she might be able to leave the promise of death behind once and for all, even if she never found Onglat.

H'euman face half-concealed behind a mop of dishwater brown hair, Sarenka opened the door and stumped into *The Shipyard*. She limped past a crowd of people circling one of the tables and made her way to the bar. Sitting cautiously, she gripped her gimp leg and swung its stiffened length around to face the pubkeep, then scowled up at the beverage and food sign above his head.

"Ale." She tossed down a few copper d'yroaps.

Attention centered on the milling crowd, he barely looked at her as he clipped them to his belt and poured a pale, foamless liquid into a shell tankard.

Sarenka took a cautious sip and was surprised to find it tasty. She nodded towards the crowd surrounding a table and lisped around a missing tooth. "What they playing?"

"Not a game. Captain's doing a fast draw. I'd be watching too, if I didn't have to be back here."

"Fast draw?"

"You know, fancy-art-like."

She slugged down her ale before swinging around, dragging the bad leg behind. With concerted effort, she lifted herself from the seat and moved into the crowd, shoving herself between onlookers until she could peer under a man's arm at what the people were arguing about.

"Seven coppers," the man in front of her said.

"One silver."

"Four silvers."

The bids escalated rapidly.

She understood why. It was the finest drawn boat she'd ever seen. Rough waves slapped against the side of a ship shaped like a massive wave. Tilted, on the verge of capsizing, wind shredding the billowing sails, sailors worked to keep the ship afloat. Its mast was broken, the windmill top hanging precariously above the sailors' heads, ready to crash down on them at any moment. Even with her childhood of finer life, she'd never seen a picture so alive.

Someone used the crowd cover to grasp her ass.

Sarenka took a step back, setting her heel firmly down on the offender's foot and heard a satisfying yelp. She turned, grinding her heel in as she did.

He let out a shriek.

Shifting nervously, hands moving to weapons, the crowd grew tense, and the sea captain paused to stare at her from under unkempt brows.

She finished swinging around until she was face to face with the offender. Sarenka shifted her heel off the man's foot and gave him a gap toothed smile. "I'm sorry, did I step on you? Can't feel a darn thing with that foot."

His cheeks blazed red while he jumped up and down with the injured foot cradled in his hand.

She limped past, took a wrong step, staggered, and bumped into him, nearly knocking him over.

He grabbed her arm to steady himself.

Sarenka swayed back and forth, nearly toppling both of them several times, before pulling free and stumping out the door with his d'yroap pouch pressed tight against her thigh. Outside, she combined his meager loops with her own and tossed his pouch behind the building.

Two streets away she stepped into an alley and pulled her hood forward, obscuring her face in shadows. She settled down onto her haunches and picked idly at the loose threads of her work gloves. Her eyes slipped closed, but she forced them back open.

She flinched when voices drew near. Sailors and merchants strolled the busy streets, hailing—and sometimes accosting—strangers. Getting rounded up for dock work would reveal her face. Though exhausted, she had to go back, this was too big of an opportunity to miss.

When she could handle the magics again, Sarenka tinted her skin the shade of a midnight shadow and shifted her hair to ruddy brown. Staying close to her true coloration made the illusions easier to hold. She staggered to her feet with a grimace. There was no time for tiredness when she needed the agility of a cat.

She slipped from the alley and started back towards the pub, boldly strolling down the middle of the street. After walking past and doubling back, she melted into the shadows of a dilapidated warehouse across the street, invisible, unless someone looked directly at her.

Moneybag in one hand and drawing stick in the other, the Captain walked out of the pub with a satisfied grin on his face, moneybag in one hand and drawing stick in the other.

Sarenka smiled.

He's alone.

Fortune's shining my way.

Motionless, she waited.

He strolled away, stopping for occasional two-step dances and was almost out of sight before he rouded a corner, heading towards the nicer part of town.

She rushed forward at a half run and found herself staring at an empty street. A cold knot of despair landed in her stomach.

He's gone. I missed my chance.

She started to turn away but movement drew her eye to a secluded pathway. Peering closer, she discovered the captain fumbling at the door of a merchant class home. When it swung open he turned to look up and down the street with a smug smile on his face and then slammed the door shut.

Sarenka stalked past his house and walked around the block before hurrying home. Rushing in the door, she tossed her cloak on the hook, gave the stew a quick stir, and threw herself across the bed, exhausted. Her eyes were closed before she hit the mattress.

Awakening hours later, she squinted at the rays of light slanting in around undaubed beams and jumped to her feet. She needed the writing tools in place, the signatures well in hand, and her hands and face smudged with ink before the sun finished setting. Lest D'trav start wondering what she did all day.

The door swung open, throwing moonlight over her page.

She peered up at D'trav, a black outline against the night sky.

"Hey there, darlin," he spoke with no trace of the old cutting mockery.

Setting aside the quill, she relieved him of the packages tucked under his arms. "You ought to let me get some of the food stuff."

"Too dangerous." He spat on his thumb and started to rub it over the bridge of her nose.

She dodged the hand. "Stop that. I'm not a child."

Eyes saddening, he turned away. "Sorry, old habit."

She put the basket of fresh eggs on the table along with a flat brown package. Grabbing a damp rag from a nearby bucket, she wiped her face, cleaning off most of the ink. "I kept my identity hidden for months with no problem."

"No, Sarenka. You can't. Your life isn't the only one in the balance. There are dozens of people who'd die if you got caught."

"Surely you jest. Dozens?"

"Dozens, and it's no jest. It's not a blink of trouble to stop at the vendors, just let me handle it."

With a shrug, she started readying their meal. *Good thing he doesn't know what I do every day.*

After he'd eaten hearty bowls of stew and discussed the effect of the early morning fogs on shipments to and from Burmtin, along with an assortment of other minor topics, D'trav threw himself across the bed and was soon snoring. Sarenka looked up from where she was finishing her signatures and smiled. She'd grown so used to his snoring that she doubted she could fall asleep easily without it in the background.

I'm going to miss that.

Tiptoeing over to her cloak and pulling it on, she deposited her newly purchased pick-tools into an inner pocket, along with a hunk of bread, a paring knife, and the Red Pelican dagger. D'trav rolled over. She froze, waiting until his snores resumed before slipping out the door. What she needed to do was worth the risk that he'd wake and find her gone.

Face and hair darkened, she strolled across town without bothering to slip into the shadows until she reached the Captain's street.

From that corner she worked her way to his house, sneaking through one yard at a time to the yap of barking dogs.

She crept around the perimeter searching for signs of life and decided he was either asleep or out creating more art. At his back door she studied the metal lock. It was pricey for a mere captain, but she supposed some did better than others and this one better than most. Fumbling with the lock, bending her tools time and again, she finally let it fall back to the door with disgust. The lock thumped against the door and lay there, an ugly piece of rusted metal, mocking her abilities and her mediocre tools.

Sarenka sighed. *It's no use.*

She pocketed her tools and started turning towards the street.

The unmistakable sharp snap of a lock opening made her stop.

She whirled back around, pulling her dagger as she turned.

Behind was only the door and the lock, hanging lopsidedly open.

Blinking her eyes at the impossibility, she stared at the lock and her mouth rounded with amazement. If she had unwittingly sprung the lock, dropping it would have opened the mechanism, but it had snapped open after she turned to walk away. Locks didn't do that, or at least none of the ones she'd ever picked. Perplexed, she bit her bottom lip, and her eyes darted from shadow to shadow, searching for close hiding places.

Only a M'hakru could have moved fast enough to have opened it, and if there's a M'hakru involved, I'm dead. Reluctant to touch the metal again, she gritted her teeth and grabbed the lock and tossed it off to the side.

Unlike the rusty lock, the door moved freely, gliding slowly ajar on oiled hinges. Pupils widened, she entered the unlit room and picked out a simple kitchen, the details crisp in black and gray tones. She tiptoed towards a doorway across the room. A chill ran up her spine, and the hair on the back of her arms rose.

Sarenka froze.

A long scratching sound was followed by a high-pitched squeal.

She glanced behind her at the open door and freedom. *Run!*

A 'tick, tick, tick' sound drew closer.

No—I can't run. I have to do this.

A great wooly dog with a graying head that reached nearly to her chin padded from the open doorway. Old bones too tired to do more than pace, it walked forward, head level, and gave no sound of greeting.

She slipped a hand into her pocket and clutched the knife, waiting for it to draw closer.

Two paces away it sat, cocked its head sideways, and its great tongue came rolling out. It panted, loud and heavy in the silent house.

She smiled, positive this was no guard dog.

Its head turned, following something she couldn't see.

Alarm ran a shivering path down her back. Sarenka searched for the thing that wasn't there, and the hairs on her arms rose once more. *Kyron, everywhere I go I see things...*

Can't do this...

Can't fall apart...

Not now...

When its head could turn no further, the dog stood to follow its invisible quarry from the room.

Shivering, Sarenka followed from a few paces off. She'd come here with a purpose and was determined to complete it.

Halfway down the hall, the dog threw itself to the ground and rolled onto its back. It gazed at her upside-down, tail thumping expectantly and tongue rolling out.

Sarenka drew near and raised a hushing finger to her lips.

It panted happily, tail moving in a slightly faster wag.

After checking the hall once more to be sure they were indeed alone, she leaned over to scratch its chest and belly. Finally, she examined the door it was laying in front of.

She turned the handle and shuddered at the scratching sound, loud in the quiet house. Pushing the door open ever so gently, she peered through the crack, and her gaze flitted from surface to surface, scanning a room lined with books and appointed with stools, quills, desks, and the great shadowy depths of comfortable chairs. Everywhere she looked books were strewn across surfaces, haphazardly stacked, and lying open as if the owner had wandered off moments before. But mostly they were shelved; tidy lines of labels, begging to be read. This was the type of room her parents used for school lessons, a study, or library, as some preferred to call them.

Large rolls of creamy parchment beckoned her towards a far corner. She crept across the room, tripped on the thick carpet, and pitched forward, landing with a 'whoof' over the back of a chair. She struggled to stand in the dark, trying not to tip the chair over.

A loud snort came from within the room.

Still draped across the chair, as though ready for a childhood paddling, she jerked her head up and searched the darkness.

A loud snore followed that snort, drawing Sarenka's gaze to the source. The captain lay within the darkened recess of a great overstuffed chair, head flopped to one side, legs extended, feet resting on a wooden chest, one hand folded over an open book in his lap, and the other draped over the chair arm. Below that dangling arm a pipe lay, unlit ashes falling from its bowl.

Sarenka shook her head at the foolishness of falling asleep while smoking and slowly pushed herself free of the chair. She worked her way step-by-step past the litter of stacked books and papers, until she arrived in the corner with the thigh-high pieces of rolled parchment and canvas. Just as her hand was about to touch a roll a soft sound came from behind. Turning, she saw the Captain scratching at his chin, eyes still closed. She watched, transfixed, as his hand drifted downwards and settled onto his chest. He scratched idly at the chest hair peeking through the loosened laces of his poet's shirt before gradually stilling.

Sarenka waited, measuring the time in counted heartbeats before deciding he wasn't going to awaken, and grasped a roll, tucking it under her arm. One after another, she gathered the rolls, filling both arms so full that she worried the book littered room couldn't be traversed without dropping one of them. She considered putting some back, but the act of bending forward threatened to landslide into an avalanche of paper and canvas.

Softly turning, she made her way back towards the door. It swung silently open as she approached. Sarenka tensed to run, thinking that she'd roused an occupant, a wife, or child, or servant. The dog padded into the room, sniffed the wooden floor, and began turning in slow circles, nails clicking with each turn.

Letting out a pent up breath, she relaxed.

"Stop fidgeting and set your sorry ass down," came the captain's gruff voice.

Chapter 44

"Once upon a time, long long ago, all the races worked together. And in that time, they wanted to trade for goods, rather than take them by sword, so the kings of the seven lands had rings made to trade with. These are the loops they created:

> *Copper.........star...........(Freni-Kyn)*
>
> *Silver...........wave.........(Watrelk)*
>
> *Gold...........arrow........(Sharpra)*
>
> *Riseen.........tree............(M'hakru)*
>
> *Breyt...........gavel..........(Frevell)*
>
> *Airnelk.......wing...........(Glidarth)*
>
> *Nighshk......map............(H'euman)*

And if peer at the inside of a loop today, you will find those symbols still there. But even with the most costly of metal, nighshk, those loops alone were not enough. Men must always have more. So gems were inset into the nighshk, creating even higher currencies.

The wars came, and the races were not happy with the symbols and created plans to mint new ones. But after the Glidarths withdrew to their Megatropolis, they refused to cooperate, saying the loops were meant to remain the same, for eternity.

And today, so many years later, there are some who still look upon their loops, staring through the ovals at the double moons, and wish for unity.

And when they do, it is said that Kyron grants them luck in all their endeavors."

Kyron's Wish
A simple H'euman fairytale

Parian struggled to break free of the shifting fog. How long? How long have I been here? He pushed at the mist and found Rosalie.

She rubbed her muscular body along his side, nearly bowling him over, and a great rumbling sound vibrated through her chest.

Weak kneed, he wrapped his arms around her neck and buried his face in her soft fur. ~You betrayed me.~

~*I had to.*~

~*I did nothing bad to you, and you betrayed me... why?*~

~*You turned dark*~

~*So you let them chain me?*~

She stopped purring. ~*I feared...*~

~*What? What could be so great that you'd let them chain me.*~

~*I feared you'd take the long dark walk, the way of death.*~

He was silent, arms still wrapped around her neck.

~*I might have.*~

~*It'd be a waste of good Freni-Kyn meat.*~

He laughed, unsure what she'd meant to say, but certain that was not it.

~*You're happier now?*~

~*I'm chained to a bed. No. I'm not happier. Just angrier.*~

~*Angry is good. Angry brings the lust of the hunt. Angry keeps you alive.*~

He sighed. ~*I suppose so.*~

She ran a rough tongue over his face. ~*I must go, Parian-Time-Walker.*~

He let his arms drop to his side, feeling the chains once more.

~*Run with the wind, Rosalie.*~

She bounded into the fog, leaving him alone, and it swirled up, trying to claim his mind.

"Parian? Are you ready to come back to us?"

"Lanion?" Parian peered at the figure over him and found only the shorter of the bowler-hat men. The man held a needle with orange liquid dripping from its tip. Parian blinked his eyes and shook his head. "Hallucinating, I'm hallucinating."

The man frowned. "I don't think he heard you."

"No. I heard. Yes, Lanion. I'm ready to come back." He tried to smile but his face remained still and numb.

After a moment the man lowered his arm and turned away. After placing the needle on a nearby table, he turned back to Parian, tipped his hat forward, and tugged down his cream colored under-vest. "Good evening, sir. My name is Naertho of the house Indros. How might I be of assistance?"

Parian looked at his arms. "Getting these off would be a good start."

"I'm sorry, sir, that is not within my ability at this moment. Is there anything else I might get you?"

Parian shook his arms and tried to sit but gave up after moments. "Food, and a drink, water, wine, I don't care."

"Very good, sir." Naertho gave a curt nod and left the room.

Parian leaned forward, testing the limit and strength of the chains. Sweat broke out over his body, and he wondered how long he'd lain there.

~*Hello?*~ he sent.

No answer came.

"So that's to be the way of it." Not that he blamed them.

The steaming food arrived and Naertho sat down to feed him.

"If you just free one hand, I can feed myself."

"I'm sorry, sir, that is not within my ability at this moment."

"Of course it's not."

Naertho tucked a napkin under Parian's chin and brought forward the first bite.

Parian dutifully opened his mouth and grimaced when it dripped down his neck.

Naertho put the bite into Parian's mouth and patted at the drip on his neck, ever so patient.

After several more bites Parian could stand it no longer. "Enough. Go away. I will eat again when you allow me to feed myself."

"Very good sir."

"I don't suppose you could ask one of the seers to talk with me."

"I'm sorry, sir, that—"

"Don't say it."

"—is not within my ability at the moment." Naertho left, closing the door behind him. A cane that was propped behind the door fell with such a clatter that sent it pain shooting through Parian's head.

Parian groaned.

The next several days were a ritual of disappoints for both of them. Naertho would appear for meals, Parian would refuse to eat and ask to speak to the seers, Naertho would tell him he couldn't and leave.

On the third day Airintia finally spoke, ~Why aren't you eating?~

~Because I don't want to be fed like a baby.~

~We can't let you go, Parian.~

~Just one arm. That's all I'm asking for. Just one.~

~When you deliberately blast with raw emotion and the backlash is enough to knock yourself out, you've gone too far. And you injured Lanion.~

He groaned. ~I know. I'm sorry.~

~He is still tender from that thrust of rage.~

~I wasn't in my right mind. That drug they gave me.~

~Stop it Parian. The drug had nothing to do with it.~

~I didn't mean to hurt him.~

~Another lie.~

Parian shook his chains, frustrated. ~What do you want me to say? That I did it on purpose? I already told you I wasn't in my right mind. That part is true.~

Dust floated, twisting and turning in the golden rays spilling through a window across the room. How long would it be before they trusted him again? The curtain lifted and fluttered in a slight breeze and he realized the window was open.

~Just one arm, Airintia. What can I do with that?~

~Just one,~ she echoed back.

That night he sat on the edge of the bed and ate a meal with one hand and stared at the open window.

The captain's gruff words almost made Sarenka drop the scrolls.

She wondered what excuse she could give for her actions as she turned back.

The captain lay as she'd seen him last, head lolling to the side, arm dangling over the edge, and open book across his chest.

With a groan the dog finally lay down.

Sarenka realized the Captain's words were for the dog and slipped out the door. She padded down the hall, gaining speed as she went. Relieved to have made it to the kitchen, she sped up even faster and tripped over the rug. Her arms flew out as she fell, sending the scrolls flying. She landed against the table, flipping it forward onto the chair and sending a metal tankard bouncing across the room. Clanging like a bell, it rolled to a rest against the far wall.

"What in—" The captain's alarmed shout from the library cut off abruptly.

Sarenka scrambled to her feet and snatched at the scattered scrolls, clasping as many of them to her chest as she could. From the hallway, the heavy slap of shoes against the wooden floor turned into the thrum of a run. She jumped out the back door and took off at breakneck speed, both arms full of rolled canvas and parchment.

A bellowed shout for the guards rang out, startling her into jumping behind an overgrown bush. She lay under its sheltering branches, catching her breath and listening. The sound of running feet and raised voices gradually petered out as the guards took off in the wrong direction.

Using her knees and hands and a nearby rock to hold down the corners, she spread the scrolls out flat, one atop another, until she created an awkward pile of uneven parchment. She tugged at the edges, aligning them as best she could, and rolled them into one long scroll before tucking the bundle under her belt and sliding it behind her back.

She didn't bother to change her disguise before stepping from behind the bush and making her way towards home, keeping to the deeper shadows. The night was dark, the double moons not yet risen, and even with Freni-Kyn eyes, she'd struggled for sight in the darkened home. At the sound of running feet, she stopped to watch two soldiers troop past and couldn't help but smile. They hadn't seen her. She'd make it home with her treasure.

The sound of more running feet, this time on a route that would bring them too close, caused her to dart into a pub. A dull throb began behind her temples, and she paused to rub her forehead before making her way to the bar.

"Frevellian wine, if you've got it."

The pub's man pulled a cork from a previously opened bottled, filled a spiral shaped shell.

"One silver," he announced, gently placing it in front of her.

She fished the silver loop from her pouch and handed it to him, along with some copper for a tip, before sitting at a table in a darkened corner. Setting down the delicate spiral cup, her gaze flitted about, looking at each patron and worker, taking in their clothing, their demeanor, and their full coin pouches, before moving onto the next.

A man leaning against the far wall lifted his head, as if sniffing the air.

She squinted. Not only was he completely out of place, but there was something familiar about his slovenly clothing and mop of greasy blond hair.

Catching her eye, he lifted his tankard in a toast with one hand, pushed his hair behind a slightly pointed ear with the other, and gave her a knowing wink.

Tahrek!

She half rose, anxious to go to him, to ask for help in fleeing the city, but stopped herself and swept another glance across the room. Now was not the time. Or place. This tavern, with its patrons waving lace kerchiefs and wearing satin skirts, was so different from where she normally drank. Her roughly woven skirt and leather bodice set her apart. If she were to cross the room to talk with Tahrek, she'd be remembered; every detail, from the color of her skirt to the rips in her blue linen cloak, recounted later for their amusement or the ears of the searching guards.

Tahrek, likewise, seemed uninterested in approaching and leaned back against the wall with his eyes half closed. Though he looked drunk enough to doze off, Sarenka thought it a sham.

She noted the door three paces away and hoped it didn't lead to a dead end. Sipping the wine, grateful for that tiny surge of energy, she considered her options. If she went out the front way, she'd be spotted on the street and stopped. If she left by the back, she could hide in an alley until morning before moving. Her gaze settled on the man who had served her wine, doubting he'd let her exit that way.

Before she could decide what to do, two men entered wearing guard uniforms. She scooted her chair back further into the shadows and sighed with relief when they turned to the barkeep. The animated discussion that followed soon drew an audience from the rest of the patrons. Hands flew about in broad gestures and the excited tones could be heard even from where she sat.

Turning to point in her direction, the barkeep fell silent.

CHAPTER 45

The guards stared, eyes wandering up and down her body. They looked to each other and nodded before starting across the room. Sarenka sprang to her feet and ran through the nearby door. The crashing sound of falling tables and chairs came from behind.

Sarenka startled the red faced cook rolling out dough and threw herself through the next door, turning to slam it behind her. Finding herself in a private office, she grasped a walking stick and rammed it under the handle. Her breath came in frightened pants as she ran to the window and tried to turn the crank.

It moved an inch and stuttered to a stop.

The door rattled and shook.

Sarenka looked back with horror. Each thrust of the guards sent the stick incrementally inwards. Grasping the crank with both hands, she threw her weight behind it, alternatively pushing and pulling, and each turn, though as fast as she could make it, seemed to take hours. A hand reached around the edge of the door to grasp the walking stick, and Sarenka pushed herself through the barely opened window headfirst.

She landed in a roll and darted down the alley, choosing to run towards an end that led to an unlit avenue, rather than the one that led back to the main street. Fear hammered in her ears as she dashed down the cobbled road without pausing to search its inky depths. It ended, buildings on both sides butting right up to the towering city wall. Cornered, desperate, Sarenka turned towards the advancing soldiers. Though she was still hidden within the shadows, she knew she was caught. A hand clapped over her mouth. Her eyes went wide with surprise. The ground gave a sudden heave, falling away under her feet.

She let out a screech, but the hand around her mouth tightened, letting no sound escape as they landed in a sprawl. She stared upwards, and flailed her fist at the attacker in the pitch-black room. Dirt landed in her eyes, and painful tears streamed down her cheeks, as she gasped for breath.

"Be quiet, you fool," a voice whispered into her ear. "They'll hear you."

Sarenka stopped struggling.

The hand across her face lifted.

From above came the thud of moving feet and muffled voices. Finally, when all she could hear was the soft sound of their breath, she felt a hand on her shoulder. It moved downwards, sliding over her skin, groping in the darkness.

Angered, Sarenka strove to push it away.

The hand grappled with her for long moments before grasping her arm and pulling her to her feet. It let go, leaving her stranded, alone in the darkness.

Sarenka's breath quickened with fear. She raised her hands, feeling about for a wall, and found only air.

The sound of flint being struck came. A tiny torch sprang to life, barely bright enough to see the shape of the person next to her. Sarenka squinted, though the face remained shadowed, the body was female.

"Who are you?" Sarenka's voice sounded desperate, even to her own ears.

"Never you worry about that. Let's just get you out of here." The woman turned on her heel.

Sarenka caught sight of the woman's forward bent ear and her focus immediately centered on the six-fingered hand holding the torch.

M'hakru. She shivered, but pushed back the fear that had immediately struck. If the woman had intended to kill her, she'd already be dead.

The M'hakru trooped off, giving no signs of noticing Sarenka's hesitancy.

Her rapid march forced Sarenka into half running to keep up, but no matter how hard she tried, she fell further behind. After a time Sarenka bent forward, gasping for breath and holding her ribs.

The light around her dwindled as the M'hakru moved steadily forward.

"Please… I can't go that fast."

The light stopped and the woman looked back. "I forget sometimes about your disabilities. Sorry."

Sarenka chewed over these words as they started off at a much slower pace. So the M'hakru considered the other races disabled, and perhaps they were. Perhaps they all were. Maybe people were supposed to have all of the abilities; the Watrel8k water-breathing, the Sharpra shape-shifting, Freni-Kyn illusions, M'hakru speed, super intelligence of the Frevell, and wings of the Glidarth to see the world with.

Wouldn't that be a wonder?

She tried to visualize it but tossed the thought away.

Mind-lost.

Not the sane thoughts I need for survival.

Almost as mind-lost as hearing voices and seeing things.

After walking for miles, the woman drew a jagged sword and turned towards Sarenka.

Halting, Sarenka grasped the hilt of the Red Pelican dagger hidden within the folds of her cloak.

Instead of attacking, the woman tapped the ceiling with her sword.

Sarenka watched with relief, thinking that the M'hakru was trying to trigger some hidden mechanism.

Nothing happened.

The woman tapped again.

After a long moment, an uneven patch of ceiling lifted upwards, letting in moonlight. Silhouetted against the night sky, two women reached down to lift them up, depositing Sarenka on an unfamiliar street.

The M'hakru pointed south. "Two blocks down is the southern-most well. Can you find your way from there?"

"Yes, but… who are you?"

"Someone that doesn't exist. Someone that doesn't like the guards any more than you do. You take care now."

"But why help me?"

"A friend sent us, one of our type." The M'hakru winked, gave a curt nod, and melted into the shadows.

One of our type? "What do you mean?"

Sarenka stared at where the M'hakru had faded from view, hoping for a clue to her identity or perhaps to form an ally. No answer came. The woman and her companions were no longer anywhere nearby. She shook her head with both admiration and alarm.

M'hakru… too damn fast.

She thought back over the tavern scene and settled on Tahrek, leaning against the wall in pretended sleep. *They have to be with him. It's the only explanation. But why? Twice now he's rescued me.*

"Nobody does that in Burmtin," she whispered and turned reso-lutely towards the well.

Upon finding the southern town square, she set off for Sad Town, arriving home within scant moments of daybreak. The rumbling of D'trav's snoring as she crept into the hut filled her with relief. She smoothed the rumpled scrolls, sorry for the damage that had been done, and slid them cautiously under the bed.

Resisting the temptation to climb in, she rubbed her aching legs before turning to the preparation of their break fasting meal, knowing that feeding D'trav was the fastest way to get him out the door. Within the turn of an hour glass he left, taking the signatures she'd completed the day before.

Sarenka sank into the bed, sleeping several hours before getting up and unrolling the scrolls on the table. She tossed most of the pictures to the floor behind her, while interesting and artful enough, they were not what she needed.

Unrolling one of the smaller scrolls, she finally found it; not a piece of art so much as a ship diagram; each detail precisely drawn, as though the artist had used a knife blade to make the lines straight and true. She leaned down over the drawing, tracing the lines with her finger, soaking in all the ship parts; port windows and doors, rails and sails and hatches, even where the ropes were attached to the sides, every detail sketched out in perfect accuracy.

After pulling a blank sheet from the pile of parchment D'trav gave her to practice signatures with, she redrew the boat. All her practice with the quill of the last month made her lines fast and straight, if not precise. She turned the parchment over, rolled up the drawing, and tried again, rapidly drawing a crude ship on the parchment. Satisfied, she unrolled the Captain's drawing and compared the original with her rough sketch. With a frown for the inaccuracies, she tried again, testing her memory.

When D'trav arrived that evening Sarenka was still at it, though the stolen pictures had been hidden under a loose floorboard. He stared over her shoulder and scratched his hand back and forth over the stubble lining his jaw.

"Oughta stick to signatures. Don't think you'll earn a livin' that way."

She jumped and let out a squeal, streaking a line across the page.

"Sorry Lass. Thought you knew I was here."

"Didn't hear you… focusing too much." Turning back to the drawing, she cocked her head, for the first time appraising it for artistic value. "It is pretty bad isn't it? I'm afraid I've wasted some parchment."

"Don't mind the drawin.' Just don't neglect the signatures."

"So it's okay if I use the ink and parchment to draw?"

"Don't see why not, though I can't imagine why you'd take a hankerin' for that."

"Makes me feel good. And I get bored. The signatures are all finished."

"Well, I'm glad you finally found somethin' to keep you happy. And don't you worry, before you know it you'll have enough saved to get out of this city for good." With a nod, he went to the trunk and opened it in front of her, having weeks ago stopped hiding what he did with the signatures. Pulling the box of seals out from under several layers of clothing, he finished the documents before placing them in his cloak.

"What's to eat?"

"We only have cheese and bread and eggs. I already cooked the eggs, but you may want to save them for the morrow."

"It'll do."

Sarenka put away her drawings, served their dinner, and fell into bed, sore but satisfied.

Soon, she'd be free from the trap that was Burmtin.

D'yroap pouch in hand, Sarenka jumped, landing on the edge of a box. As it flipped over she jumped again, this time landing on the barrel above it. Balanced on the teetering lid, she glanced over her shoulder.

Three angry men were pushing past vendors, scattering merchandise in their rush to catch her.

Three more jumps propelled her over the pile, sending boxes, crates, and barrels tumbling down behind her with each leap. Alighting on the patchy cobblestone street, to the cacophony of scattering goods and angry shouts, she broke into a run, sliding around the closest corner before dashing forward again.

Strangers gaped at the sight as she dashed past, skirt gathered into a roll around her waist, thin legs adorned only in plain brown leggings, and soft leather boots making hardly a sound. Her black hair streamed out behind, and she was sure they'd have taken her for a messenger boy had she not been wearing the corset.

Almost immediately an alleyway opened to her right. She grabbed the corner of the building next to it and used her forward momentum to catapult into the darkened recess. As she flung herself into the alley, she glanced back down the street, checking to make sure they hadn't rounded the street corner and seen her duck out of sight. She stopped only long enough for her eyes to adjust before darting towards the wooden gate at the far end of the alley.

Sprinting at the towering barrier with breakneck speed, she waited until the last possible moment before dropping as low to the ground as possible, skidding the last few feet into a crash against the wood. Her feet slammed into the bottom plank, throwing it out of sight, and she slid to a stop on the other side of the fence. Scrabbling to grasp the plank, she pushed it up against the fence, hooking it over convenient wooden pegs, and stood to dust herself off.

She searched the length of the alley and let out a relieved sigh. She was alone.

The sound of running feet came, pounding past the alley on the other side of the wooden fence.

Sarenka pulled a leather strap from under the roll of fabric encircling her waist and hooked the coin pouch to it. Unlatching the remaining leather straps from around that fabric roll, she let the roughly woven skirt drop to the ground, covering both her legs and the pouch. As a final touch, she pulled free a wine skin and doused the bottom of her skirt with water.

Sighing, she drew a deep breath, closed her eyes, and focused long enough to turn her hair straight instead of curly, and her features that of a freckle covered youth, still pale, but not the angular strong face she'd been wearing. Now she looked like Tamika's sister instead of Tamika herself.

Opening a nearby wooden crate, she pulled free a wet bundle of fabric and threw it over her shoulder, settling the weight against her back before striding to the end of the alley and merging with a group of washer-women. The women, bundles of newly washed clothing strapped to their backs and faces ruddy from ocean spray, laughed and joked as they strolled towards their homes and soon Sarenka was caught up in the camaraderie.

The three men who had been chasing Sarenka rounded the corner just as the washer-women neared the crossroads. The men stopped to glare at them with legs spread and arms crossed.

The washer-women faltered for only a moment before moving forward.

Eyes blazing with intensity, a man with a nose like a hawk stepped towards the lead woman.

With a calm demeanor Tamika stopped and outstretched her arms to halt the rest of the women. They lined up next to her, hands on their hips, and glared at the men.

The man's companions stepped forward to grasp Tamika's arms.

An alarmed expression spread across her face and she jerked back, trying to pull her arms free.

The hawk nosed man hiked Tamika's skirt upwards, revealing striped stockings, garters, and bare skin. The men gaped.

Tamika gasped and broke free of their grip. Her hand shot out, catching the man off guard in a resounding slap that could easily be heard a block away.

The other men backed away as the hawk nosed man rubbed his reddening cheek. He looked the women over once more and his gaze settled on Sarenka. "Get her."

Hesitant now, they stepped forward and reached for her arms.

Sarenka glared at them. "Touch me like you just touched her, and I'll…"

CHAPTER 46

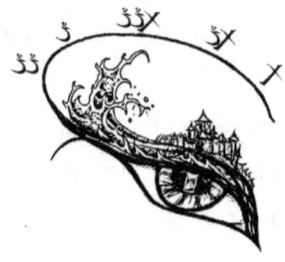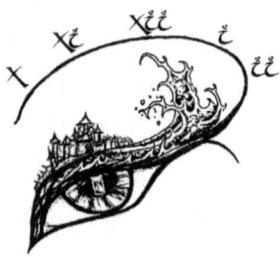

~Parian?!~

~Rosalie.~

~This one you seek, across time. It is in trouble.~

~What?~

~Something bad… bad people… circling.~

~Circling what?~

~This one, they are circling,~ Rosalie sent.

~How do you know?~

~You leave a wide trail.~

~I don't…~

~You do. I followed… saw… felt. I went alone this time.~

~Dead. The One is dead.~

~Not dead. Live.~ Rosalie bumped him from behind.

~I wish this weren't a dream and they were.~

She nipped his ear.

~Owww.~ He rubbed the ear and felt wetness. *~You made me bleed.~*

~Not a dream. They live. You must help.~

~I can do nothing. I'm trapped here. They've chained me.~

~Stupid Freni-Kyn. Must I rescue you every time? Can you not use simple leverage to break the chains?~

Parian sat up in bed, suddenly wide awake.

Why didn't I think of that before?

He searched the room for something he could use to pry the chain loose. Why his mind had supplied the answer in a dream, he didn't know, but he was grateful.

Nothing. There's nothing.

He lay back on the bed and abruptly jerked his arm upward, testing the strength of the chain. Rolling off the side of the bed, he tiptoed towards the window, bringing the chain taut before grasping it with both hands and dragging the bed. It moved, not silently but quiet enough, rucking up the thick carpet as it went. Beyond the window, only predawn darkness waited. Satisfied that it could be done, Parian pulled the bed back to where it had been and smoothed the carpet.

Sleep came quickly and he awoke to a clatter as the cane fell over. Startled, Parian's eyes flew open.

Naertho crossed the room towards him, food tray in hand.

Parian struggled to sit up, twisting about awkwardly with one arm still chained.

Naertho waited to make sure he was stable before setting the tray down and leaving.

Uncomfortable eating without illusions to cover his face, Parian had established that he preferred eating alone. When the door shut, he pried at the chains with the handle of the spoon but only succeeded in bending it.

Parian sighed. *There has to be something.*

He scanned the room as he ate. Desk on far side, quill, inking well, parchment, the bed he was laying in, and the chair Naertho had sat in to feed him. He stared at the window.

No loose bars to prop the window up and too small for Rosalie to leap through.

Not that she would come anyway.

He chewed as he considered and then gave up.

There's nothing.

It was just a dream after all.

Naertho swung the door into the cane as he entered, scraping the metal across the ground with a screech.

Parian covered one sensitive ear with his unchained hand and turned the one he couldn't reach away.

Naertho picked up the cane and propped it behind the door.

"I don't know why you bother. It's just going to fall over again," Parian said.

"Sometimes we have… guests… that need it."

Parian stopped chewing and stared at the cane. *Maybe, just maybe…* He jerked his gaze back to his food. "Almost done, couple more bites."

"Very good sir."

"Can I ask you something?"

"I am at your service, sir."

"Why engrave runes into the shackles? I can't harm anyone with illusions, or use them to escape."

"There have been occasions, in the distant past, when we had Sharpra and M'hakru guests."

"Well, not letting a Sharpra shift into something thinner makes sense, but why slow a M'hakru?"

"They tend to be most violent, sir."

"Well that makes sense, but this seems a waste of magic, do you have no other shackles?"

"After the wars started, it was decided that all manacles be outfitted with runes."

Parian nodded and after taking a few more bites, lay back with pretended exhaustion. "I'm so tired."

"You could engage a surgeon to repair your face, sir. I would be most happy to inquire into that for you."

Parian shook his head. "Doesn't matter… most of the time."

"I'll leave you to your rest then."

That night Parian dragged the bed around the room until he was covered in sweat and his legs and arms burned. The next day he paid for it with muscles that didn't want to move.

Naertho, noticing the pain, called in the taller man to check him. He rested his hands against Parian's head and poked and prodded and asked questions.

Parian dutifully answered, waited two days, and repeated the bed pulling exercises. He wasn't as tired this time, or as sore.

His nightly ritual of dragging the bed across the room continued for the next two weeks. Finally he could shift the bed without being sore the next day. Satisfied that he had regained his strength, he put his plan into action the very next night by pulling the bed over near the door. He grabbed the cane in a rush, anxious for freedom, and applied it to the chain. Nothing happened. Neither metal bent or budged.

Parian stared at the chain with disbelief.

There has to be a weak link.

Searching for one that was partially open, he ran his hands over the links until he reached where it was joined with the bed.

No... not after all this work... there has to be a way.

He rolled over the edge and lay on the ground to examine the fastener. Pushing the cane between it and the wood, he began rocking it back and forth and was still doing that when the sun began to shine in the window. He propped the cane behind the door, dragged the bed to its spot, and collapsed.

Later, when they brought him food, he waved his hand, far more interested in sleep. Again the herbalist poked and prodded searching for what ailed. Parian pretended to a wheezing cough, and they brought him a syrupy sweet-drink. He tossed it back and waited for them to leave the room before spitting it into his chamber pot.

That night he began again, prying at the anchor pin, rocking it back and forth until, with a crack, the wood splintered and the pin fell to the ground. For a moment Parian was so surprised that he just lay there. Then he sprang into action, wrapping the chain about his wrist, ripping the blanket from the bed and tying it around his neck like a cape.

Parian opened the window and froze as a dark shadow fell across him, blocking out the double moons. A barn owl hooted. He relaxed and jumped out the window, landing on a cushion of wet leaves before starting forward at a half run, angling between trees and searching for a landmark. A rustling sound kept pace, stopping when he stopped, moving when he moved, and an unmistakable warbling howl made the hair on the back of his neck stand at alert.

Killian Wolves!

Kyron no... we can't still be in the Darkiorn area!

Another howl went up, filling the night with dread. A second and third howl joined the first one.

The sound was undeniable, killian wolves. Natives of the Darkiorn area, they were said to be the offspring of a misbegotten genetic manipulation gone wrong. If he didn't find shelter soon, he'd be ripped limb from limb. Stopping to lean against the bare trunk of a pine tree, he searched the sky for chimney smoke.

If worse comes to worse, there are always trees.

He turned to look back the way he'd come and came face to face with two blue eyes. His ears filled with the sound of great rushing waves and his heart pounded with fright. Vision swimming, he reached for his blade with a sweat slickened hand.

A cold nose gently touched his.

The fear drained in a whosh, and he staggered. "Rosalie?"

She turned her head sideways and rubbed it across his face.

He stepped backwards and came up against a tree.

She stepped forward.

"I'm not going back."

~I'm not here to take you back, stupid Freni-Kyn. I'm here to help.~

He let out his breath in a relieved sigh. "How'd you find me?"

~I've been with you the whole time.~

"So the dreams..."

~*Were real,*~ she answered.

"And The One is…"

~*Alive.*~

"I need somewhere safe, somewhere they can't find me."

She crouched, offering her back, ~*I know.*~

He climbed on, and she gathered herself for a leap, shifting rapidly from foot-to-foot and forcing him to grab the sides of her neck or slide off. Her muscles bunched under him, coiling hard and tight, and she lunged forward, bounding from the clearing before settling into an easy lope. Head back, pine scented air streaming past in cold gusts, he stared at the double moons. She might not be a real person, but she was the best companion he'd had since joining the seers. It was all he could do not to let out a whoop of delight as they raced across a land of dappled grey.

For three days they followed her schedule, running for an hour-glass turn, sleeping for a while and then taking off again. Deliberately she'd dash through the brush, flushing quail and other creatures, and forcing him to cling for dear life as she leapt into rough bloody landings, gathering and eating them raw.

When he asked her where they were going, she simply sent, ~*The opening.*~

She began to climb the side of a mountain, terrifying him with leaps and scrambling jumps over loose debris, and he asked again and got the same reply.

~*The opening.*~

At last she slowed, padding reverently onto a grassy plateau.

Parian stared past the open area at a giant black hole. He should have known. "So, a cave."

She nudged him forward. ~*Go. Look.*~

Stretching stiff muscles, he strolled to the edge of the opening and placed a hand on the wall before leaning into the great open maw. Within lay the black of night, cool and dark.

No, not night. It's blacker than night. It's the black of water so deep that the bottom can't be seen, the black of octopus ink, the black of—

His fingers brushed across an engraved design, interrupting his thoughts. Pulling free of the darkness, Parian stared at what lay closer, the edge of the arch. He traced the lines with his fingertips, trying to discover its pattern. The pathway behind his tracing began to glow, taking life from his mere touch.

Shocked, he pulled his hand back.

The glow remained, pale and green.

Experimentally, he touched again, bringing forth more green lines, but stopped when he realized he must be crushing some creature, releasing its life essence in order to create light. His gaze traveled past that design to the side of the wall, stopping to rest on an irregular shape which didn't belong. Striding over, he discovered a torch, its rag bound surface so old that it was shredding away.

As he walked back towards the engraved arch, his foot kicked a small item, launching if forward, where it bounced against the stone pavement, twisting and turning before coming to a rest.

Rosalie pounced, picked it up, and shook it before looking up at him. Her ears wilted and she dropped it, as if embarrassed. With a look of sheer disgust, her mouth dropped partially open.

"You look like you ate a giant moth made of vulture vomit."

~Gaw… that smells of man… tastes even fouler.~

Parian scooped up the bit of metal and snapped apart the two sides. "It's a flint and tinder."

~Which is?~

"I'll show you." He set to work, placing the torch on the ground between his feet and hunching over to strike the two pieces together. Sparks flew, and the rag surface went up with a whoosh, catching fire immediately.

Rosalie backed away, blinking. *~So, a fire maker.~*

"Probably left by the same person that left the torch. It seems a welcome of a sorts, don't you think?"

She sent a wave of distrust.

Parian lifted the torch high and nodded agreement before turning to the arch.

CHAPTER 47

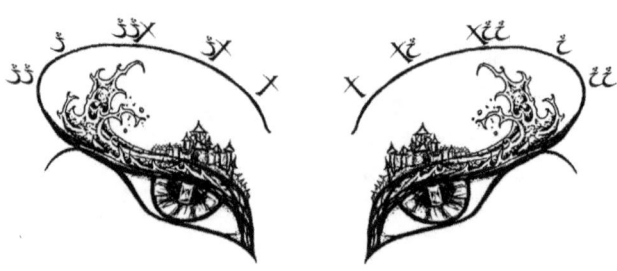

"You'll what?" the hawk nosed man asked.

"I'll call the guards," Sarenka said, placing a hand on her hip.

Tamika, long black hair swaying, moved to stand beside Sarenka. "And I'll second the report."

Heartened by the bravery of their leader, the rest of the washer-women stepped forward. "And we'll stand as witnesses." One of them announced.

The man's face turned redder with rage, but he backed away, hands in the air. "All right now. Don't want no trouble."

Tamika gave a tight smile. "I bet you don't."

He nodded at the two men before turning to leave. "Backtrack, we must have missed her." The men trudged off down the street, checking each alley as they went.

After they turned the corner, the group of women broke out in giggles.

"How much did you get this time?" asked Tamika.

"No idea, but enough to feed us all for the week, I'll wager." Sarenka hauled her skirt up and unlatched the bag. Reaching into its recesses, she produced handfuls of the winnings for each of the women. They took no time to count out the loops, glad for whatever came to them as the luck of the draw.

"Don't know how you do it. You must be M'hakru-fast to get the bag and run away before they see your face."

"Just clever enough to keep my face turned away is all," Sarenka said.

"Till next week." She gave them a nod, tucked the almost empty bag away and walked off, heading back towards the other side of town.

Once out of sight, she ducked into an alley and opened her fist. A vial of liquid, pale gold in the shadows, rolled back and forth. She lifted it to her nose, making sure it was antidote before tucking it away within her linen cloak.

That's seven… just five more and I can leave.

She shifted her face to chubby and pink while shortening her hair into a blond bob. The pain behind her eyes rose to frightening levels, and she rubbed her temples. If she didn't get back soon, she'd be forced to find shelter for an hourglass turn.

Shoulders brushing, Parian and Rosalie stepped into the great black maw.

Parian gasped.

Within were rough and natural walls, with great gaping arches made by men, edges lined in patterns that set his heart to dancing. He hurried forward, moving from chamber to chamber, each rough and empty, lacking furnishings or comforts, until he reached a room with a large brazier in the center.

He touched the torch to the pile of wood and watched as it flamed upwards.

And then he sat, the wind suddenly sucked out of him. "I can't believe I found it."

~You found it?~

"We've looked so long"

~You found it?~ Rosalie asked again, petulant.

"No, of course. You found it. But still. It's here. I'm here."

~It's a cave with a firepit.~

"Yes." He smiled at her, rubbed under her chin. "Yes, it is, and so much more."

He wanted to reach out to the Seers, tell them he'd found the Unity Hall, but he couldn't. For now, it must remain a secret.

Rosalie paced the perimeters of the room before settling down near the fire. *~It's just a cave.~*

"A very special cave. How did you find it?"

She rested her chin on her paws, and closed her eyes.

"Rosalie?"

She flicked her ear and opened one eye.

"How did you find it?"

~I was making it very obvious that I didn't want to talk about it.~

"Please Rosalie, this is history, I need to know"

~After I... let them rescue you——~

"You mean betrayed me."

She closed her eyes.

He waited for her to start again but grew impatient after a while. "Rosalie?"

She didn't reply.

"Okay, okay, you rescued me."

~After I rescued you, my chest hurt so I ran. There are wild cats here, did you know that?~

He shook his head.

~Cats as big as me that live free to do whatever they please, and for a while it was good. You were in the fog land, and I couldn't go there often so I just ran. But then the storm came...~ She stopped to lick a paw.

"And?"

~Long jagged light, streaking from the sky and making fire. I was out hunting, alone and desperate for shelter, so when I found this place I entered.~

"So you got no... mental nudge to come here?"

~Perhaps a little… in where to hunt. Not in where to shelter. It smelled of man, but old and distant. And while the storm raged, I had nothing to do. So I found The One you seek.~

"So, Kyron guided you here."

She let out as disparaging a snort as a cat could have. *~Why must men always search for the supernatural? I hunted. It stormed. I sheltered. I found. That is all.~*

Unwilling to discuss theology with a cat, Parian held the torch aloft and peered at the walls, looking for answers.

The day was cold and bleary when next Sarenka saw the washerwomen. Trudging down to the water's edge, she hiked up her skirt and waded into the waves with dirty clothing in hand. She'd learned the techniques from them and had even bought the special leather straps they used to secure their skirts.

Tamika glanced up with a grin. "No angry crowd following you this time."

"No, just the washin'. Easier to do in the ocean than in the hut. Rinsing there takes forever." Aware of Tamika's thoughtful gaze, Sarenka began beating the stains out of her chemise.

"You ever want to hire out, let me know. I'm sure I can get you into the guild."

"Someday maybe."

Fog drifted across the water, obscuring the wave-shaped boats anchored along the coast.

"Ever wonder where they're going?"

Tamika looked up from the shirt she was scrubbing and squinted at the boats. "Not ever."

The sun caught the regal angles of her face, reminding Sarenka of the spell that had washed over her during their first meeting. Tamika was a woman born to lead. It seemed almost fitting that the hard life age her, adding wrinkles where there should be smooth skin, lest she seem too young to be taken seriously.

"I wonder how far they travel. Maybe they go somewhere pretty, with lots of flowers and gold laying on the ground for the taking."

The women around her giggled at the notion.

"All I know is, they leave for about twenty-one days at a stretch, most times," Tamika said.

"How far do you think they can travel in that time?"

"Travel and come back, you mean."

Tossing the shirt she was beating into a basket, Tamika drew forth the next item and swished it delicately in the water. "Old man Stergon's been having the runs lately. Think he may not be long for the world."

Sarenka stared at the oily bits of floating green and yellow that washed off the undergarments and took a step back. She swallowed several times and looked at the shore with longing while she waited the long moments for the current to wash the debris away.

Unaware of her discomfort, the women around her tutted and shared knowing sad looks.

"He's such a kind man. Always tips well and gives us fruit on the holidays."

"Cause he wants in your knickers."

Sarenka half-listened to the gossip. Her real focus was on the long boats gliding past. "Anyone know when the next ship sets sail?"

"Always with the tide, girl. Every day. But with the tide."

"When it comes in or... Oh. I get it now. They use the tide to help them leave."

Uninterested in something they'd seen daily for most of their lives, the women returned to their gossip.

"I'll see if I can't rustle us up a bit more coin soon," she said, bundling her clothing into a knot and throwing it over her shoulder. "I've got to go make the morning meal for his majesty."

"T-t-teach... teach you for t-t-takin the... the vow," the youngest of the group stuttered out. "N-n-not... n-not... not the life for me.

I'm g-g-going… I'm g-going… going to stay free as the wind till the… the… till the d-day I die."

Surprised that she'd spoken at all, Sarenka smiled at the girl and waved goodbye. She'd have liked to have given them hugs, knowing she'd never see them again, but didn't dare, lest they feel her Freni-Kyn hair.

Upon arrival back at the hut, she threw the clothing in with the dirty laundry to be washed and woke D'trav for the breakfast she'd set out before leaving.

He wrinkled his nose.

"What's wrong?" Sarenka asked.

"Must be a storm coming in. Smell the salt in the air?"

Sarenka darted a glance at the soaked clothing and moved to stand between the pile and D'trav. "Definitely smells like a storm. Fair amount of fog today too, can't hardly see out the door."

Three evenings later, while D'trav was away on business, Sarenka set a goodbye not on the table and slipped out of the hut. Bundled into a small tight bag on her back were extra clothing, three apples, a round of cheese, and a turkey leg wrapped in greased paper; enough to survive a fortnight, she hoped. As she closed the door there was a white flutter above the note. She shivered.

"I won't be missing that."

For the first time in many months, she pulled the dark blue cloak down over her face and started forward without her illusions. The fog billowed about in heavy drifts, helping to hide her movement. Cobblestone turned to sand and muffled calls drifted past, sentries working their way down the coast.

At the shoreline she rolled her cloak into a ball and tied it to her belt with the extra straps she'd sewn on. Bundling up her skirt at the waist, she secured it far tighter than the washerwomen did and hoped that looking like them would work in her favor if anything went wrong. Her slippers joined the jumble of things hanging from her waist.

The double moons pierced the fog, liming the waves in silvery-pink light. A sign. She was favored. She took her first hesitant steps. The water washed upwards, icy against her legs. But she continued on, one determined step after another, until she was deep enough to raise her legs and let the undercurrents drag her towards the boats. The last few days had been spent throwing daisy petals into the waves one by one, wailing for a sailor lost at sea while actually calculating the direction of the undercurrents. At first she drifted as the petals had, but gradually the currents took her further out to sea, leaving her positive that she'd miss the boat which was to set sail today.

Fearful of the creature that lay beyond those boats, Sarenka turned towards the cresting front of the nearest wave-shaped ship and swam. For once her father had been right; she *did* need swimming lessons to survive. Slightly winded, she grabbed hold of the barnacles clinging to the side of the boat like overgrown fungus, and began moving around the boat, searching for the way in. Finally, a line streamed past, silver in the light of the double moons, leading from railing to water.

Gritting her teeth against chattering, she grasped the rope, placed her bare feet on barnacles, and hauled on the line. The Istoarm resisted, pulling downwards and forcing her to strain against its watery embrace before releasing its hold. She surged upwards so fast that her foot slipped, and she scratched her forehead against the exposed barnacles. Blood trickled down her face as she drew a deep breath and continued, handhold over handhold, working her way upwards.

Reaching the rail, she stopped to listen and hoped the drunk she'd pumped for information was accurate. Right now the Burmtin Tavern should be hosting a rowdy crew, intent on their last drunken binge before setting sail.

Please let them be gone...

Sarenka clambered over the railing and scuttled into the shadows, pausing only to dredge up memorized details of the wave-vessels before starting forward, dodging from one covering to another, until she arrived at the main deck. She paused, leaning against the cabin to catch her breath, and stared across that wide-open space towards the hatch to the hold. This was the riskiest part of her endeavor. To cross that space risked being seen.

A long creak sounded.

She stopped and held her breath.

Soft footsteps came from the upper deck, barely audible against the gentle lap of waves. Instead of moving on, they stopped above her head. A sharp click-zsht sound came as flint was struck, and sparks flew downwards in a shower.

Squinting against the light, she pressed herself flat against the cabin wall.

The sound came again, followed by the dim glow of a newly lit lantern.

Sarenka grasped her dagger and drew it forth.

The light grew brighter and the pirate moved on, throwing long, angular shadows across the wooden planks. The soft scuff of his steps faded into the night.

She took off at a crouching run, sliding into the shadows behind a stack of barrels with relief. She waited for another round of the guard's circuit before darting forward and yanking up on the hatch. It creaked as it opened. She froze, listening for the sound of approaching footsteps. When none came, she threw herself into the darkness below and pulled the hatch shut.

As her eyes adjusted to the almost solid darkness, Sarenka started forward, using details she'd memorized from the drawings to guide her. She reached the end of the hall and was about to open the furthest compartment, the one that held her prize, when a muffled "mmmpfh mmmpfh" caught her ear. She cocked her head, listening to the noise, and realized the sound was coming from the door she'd just passed.

Mind-lost. I'm mind-lost to even be thinking this.

Taking a step back, she pressed her ear against the door.

The muffled 'mmmpfh' came from within, more distinct now.

Sarenka shook her head no—told herself no—even as she cracked open the door wide enough to peer in.

I just need the antidote and a way out of Burmtin.

What, in Kyron's name, am I thinking?

The room beyond, little more than a wooden cave, was lit with a lantern, its wick trimmed almost to the point of extinguishing. It hung from a beam, rocking slowly back and forth, throwing shifting and distorted shadows across the space.

With growing alarm, Sarenka stared at the source of the noise. Eyes burrowing into hers with silent pleas for help, a woman sat, mouth gagged, wrists and ankles bound together with strips of white muslin.

Sarenka slipped into the room and started to pull the gag free.

"Don't do that. She'll scream."

CHAPTER 48

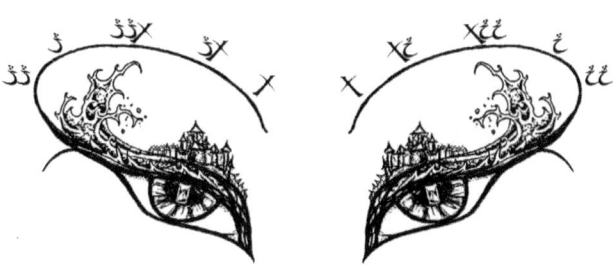

"The price of a slave in this war torn land? My axe across the throat of any that stand in the way. Why bother with those time slaves, who you only own until their debt is repaid, when you can own someone forever?"

M'hakru Soldier
Found on the Barren battlefield

Thought to refer obliquely to the M'hakru blood collection ritual, whereby they tie slave's souls to them in the afterlife.

Sarenka spun around.

Within the shadowy recesses of the shelved wall behind her was a row of men and women, all in various forms of confinement. Sarenka groaned. "Oh my god. Of all the ships, in all of Burmtin, I pick a slaver's ship to stow away on."

"Bad choice, that," the woman who had spoken before said.

Sarenka settled down on her haunches and held her head in her hands. "What to do... what to do..."

"Cut these ropes and we all escape. Easier to get out as a group than as one person."

Time was running out and the sailors would be returning soon. A large group of burly pirates was too much for her to deal with alone, even if they were drunk. She moved to the woman's side and sliced free the bindings around her wrists. "How do you figure?"

"If you have to fight, and you will, you'll stand a better chance of survival."

"Kyron-be-damned!" Sarenka swore, but handed the woman her extra knife and went to work freeing the other prisoners. When she came to the one whom she'd seen first, the older woman stayed her hand.

"We can't take her. They gagged her for a reason. She won't stop screaming. Can't help it, mind-lost."

"What's your name?"

"Escrach."

"Tell me, Escrach, would you want to be left here? Even if your mind was gone? We can't leave her." Sarenka clasped the bound woman's neck in a firm grip, and used two fingers to pinch a specific spot. The woman slumped to the ground with a let out breath.

"You killed her!" Escrach hissed, drawing back with horror.

"Death would be better than slavery, but she's just unconscious. We all go, or none of us goes." Leaving the gag in place, she cut the unconscious woman free of the bonds and motioned to the two strongest prisoners. "Grab her. If she wakes up, let me know."

Sarenka scrutinized the twelve men and women. "Any of you have fighting skills?"

With a nod, Escrach shifted her blade into a defensive position that Sarenka recognized from her training.

A burly man stepped forward.

Sarenka pulled down the lantern and handed it to him.

"Use it as a weapon if you have to. I don't have another knife."

Nearly plunging the room into darkness, the man swung the lantern around, testing its weight. "It'll do."

"Are there any other prisoners in the holds?"

Escrach shrugged. "We had enough to do taking care of ourselves without trying to find more of us."

"You're in charge of defense, Escrach, if this all goes bad I expect you to get as many out as possible."

They filed from the room, a ragged group of half-starved people and Sarenka nodded at them as they passed, taking in the mixture of disbelief and hope mirrored in their eyes. She quickly opened the other doors lining the hallway. The first held another hapless collection of prisoners, none as hysterical as the one they were carrying. After equipping them with assorted found objects, they moved onwards. The rest of the rooms proved to carry provisions. Sarenka stared at the goods wistfully, wanting to plunder them, knowing her precious antidote lay within. A last wave of regret washed over her as she closed the doors and headed for the hatch.

"Get that light out," she hissed.

Behind her came a clinking sound.

The hall plunged into heavy darkness.

Lifting the hatch, Sarenka peered out, searching for the location of their guards. After several long heartbeats, she closed it. "Guard passes every quarter turn of the glass. After he passes we leave. Be quiet and be fast."

A few mumbled, "Okays," drifted out of the darkness.

She pushed the hatch up a crack, straining her ears, and soon the steady thump of feet passed them on one side, then again on the other as he moved to the far side of the boat. After they faded, Sarenka pushed the hatch all the way open, clambered out, and guided them to the darkest shadows before nodding towards the side of the boat. She made eye contact with the nearest and knew they understood before she ran for the side.

The first woman dropped her skirt and dived over the side, creating a loud splash

Sarenka cringed. While one splash might be ignored, twenty wouldn't. "Everybody over and swim for shore, fighters last."

Seven prisoners spread out into a half circle perimeter around the jumpers.

After a few splashes the sound of running feet came from the forecastle deck.

Sarenka shared an understanding look with Escrach. It was possible the rest of them would die. Sarenka stepped towards the sound and melted into the shadows.

Shedding encumbering skirts and cloaks, the men and women leapt over the side three, four, and five at a time. As the last few non-combatants jumped, a guard rounded the corner. He paused before bounding towards Escrach, loose shirt billowing in the moonlight.

Sarenka let him pass then threw herself on his back, bearing him to the ground. "Hold him down."

The man half raised himself from the ground.

She clung, refusing to let go.

His elbow flew backwards, catching her in the eye.

Escrach's body joined hers on top of the man, and he went down with the extra weight.

Sarenka caught the flash of a blade in the man's hand.

"Hell with that, I'm killing the bastard," Escrach snarled while grinding her foot into the man's wrist, forcing him to drop the dagger.

"No! They'll hunt us forever if you do," Sarenka panted out between dodging his elbows and fists.

He flipped over and reared upwards, nearly throwing them off.

Two more women and a man joined the fray, bearing him back to the ground. Escrach grabbed the man's hands and pulled them upwards, stretching him out so that he could no longer fight.

He twisted and kicked until one of the women rolled over onto his legs.

Sarenka slammed her hand into the man, and while she was close gave a hidden pinch to the man's neck.

With a sigh of let out breath, he went limp.

"D'rather 'ave killed him." Escrach let go of his wrists, rubbing the palms of her hands down her skirt as if the touch had made her feel dirty.

"Why didn't he call for help?"

"Pride makes people stupid, girl."

Escrach and the other two women climbed onto the ledge and balanced, ready to jump.

"What are you going to do about her?" Escrach pointed to the slumbering woman. "Don't know about you, but I'm not strong enough to swim with her."

"I'll have to use the ramp."

"Your death, not mine." With those words, Escrach dove over the side. The last two women joined her, leaving Sarenka alone to rescue the unconscious woman.

She donned the pirate's clothing before pushing the man into the hold and securing the hatch. After wrestling the dead weight of the woman onto a rolling crate, she added her belongings and threw her cloak over the top, hiding them from view. She surveyed her awkwardly balanced parcel and licked dry lips, hoping the captive didn't awaken too soon.

Taking a deep breath and creating the most scar-covered, gnarly, female figure she'd ever tried, Sarenka started towards the ramp, running when in the shadows. At the last darkened area, she paused to stare at the final obstacle: a twenty strides long ramp that seemed to go on forever.

Beyond that, the bulk of the bow rose from the water in a curving half circle: a cresting wave with painted froth sparkling white in the moonlight. She took courage from the symbol of perseverance and rolled the crate towards the ramp. It bounced and jumped over the uneven wooden boards, each jostle threatening to capsize, while the shore-side pirates ignored her approach. They had to have heard her and were only intent on keeping people off the boat, not the other way around.

With raised brows, the pirates looked up from slapping palms together in a game of chance.

"Hey! How'd you draw the lucky straw?"

At first Sarenka didn't realize they were being sarcastic. Then she gave her shoulders an exaggerated shrug, stopped, and wiped the sweat from her brow in pretended nonchalance.

"Just lucky like that," she finally grunted out. "Got one more load then I'm off."

"Gonna get yourself a maaaan?" said the slimmer of the two.

She drummed up a loud bold laugh. "Most like, most like. If I can find one drunk 'nough to stand lookin' at me."

They laughed and she pushed the crate forward again. As she passed, one of the men cocked his head sideways, and a confused expression crossed his face.

"What's the matter?" the other man asked.

"I didn't recognize her, did you?"

"Hold up just a moment!"

R'kiax watched the steady influx and exodus of patrons from the bordello, knowing that he needed to go in. His skin crawled and he scratched his arms, adding to the long red marks already there. Venomous thoughts dripped into his blood as he considered Lator, sitting behind his desk, doling out orders, comfortable as a king in his cushy office.

To give an assignment like this to a Sharpra had been a reprimand of the most subtle type. Lator had to have known he couldn't hire one of the women. That risked the bonding, and death. Instead, he'd been forced to watch the building day and night while the filth of all the races came and went, willing to spread their legs for what? A moment's pleasure?

He tapped his top-hat forward, shading his eyes as a passer-by glanced in his direction. When the stranger didn't look away, he fingered the hilt of his Red Pelican dagger.

I'll make him pay for this, one way or another. And then I'll leave. I've had enough of Burmtin. Wolf Clan village sounds less dull by the minute.

A woman, breasts bare, walked past an open upper window and his double cocks throbbed.

And less torturous.

A man left, wavering on his feet as if drunk, and R'kiax fell in behind. When the drunk entered a tavern less than half a block away, R'kiax cursed. He stared back at the brothel and then at the tavern, considering which was more likely to pay off.

Six and a half to a dozen... one way or another...

He tapped his cane against his heel and walked in. Within a heartbeat, he knew he was overdressed and needed a reason why. Sitting next to the man he'd followed, he removed the top hat and carefully placed it on the counter before rubbing an imaginary spot from its brim.

The man looked over at him, pupils widening and narrowing as if he were having a difficult time focusing. His lip lifted in a sneer. "Half-breed."

R'kiax dropped his gaze with pretended shame. *Well at least we agree on that, they should all be wiped out.*

Producing a triangular deck of cards, he rapidly shuffled them and held out the deck to the man. "I might be, but I bet I can read your mind. Pick a card. Any card."

A flicker of interest lit in the man's eyes and he drew one, peeking to see what it was. His face went pale and he gulped.

R'kiax waited.

The man set the card face down on the counter and slid it back over with a fingertip.

"What? Don't want me to guess what it is? Not very sporting of you."

"I'm sorry for the insult."

"Did I say I was insulted?" R'kiax slid the death card back into the deck before pocketing it. "On the contrary, all half-breeds should be wiped from the face of Llayentia."

The man gulped again, keeping his eyes on the countertop. He started to stand. "I think I need to—"

R'kiax grasped the man's wrist and slammed it down hard enough on the countertop to bring a wince. "I think not. You will stay. And you will buy me the best damn vintage they have. And after I've gotten rid of the foul taste in my mouth your company gives me, then we will talk."

The man sat clumsily, with his hand still clamped to the countertop.

R'kiax gestured for the barkeep and ordered the curtained booth in the far corner, as well as a bottle of Frevellian Crenach wine. It arrived, surface beaded with sweat in the hot room, along with two fragile shell glasses. R'kiax waved the serving wench away and poured it himself, holding up the cork for the man to smell.

Taking a sip, he let out a loud sigh and twitched the curtain closed. "Is there something wrong with the wine? Drink up."

Hands shaking, the man lifted his cup and took a scant sip.

R'kiax tossed back the drink and refilled his glass. "Now then. Tell me all about the brothel you just came from."

CHAPTER 49

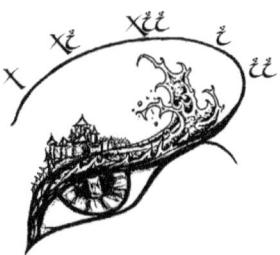

"*Dearest Glendora,*

I'm afraid I'm not long for the worlde. I took a M'hakru push dagger in the abdomen today, all three ~~pierc~~ blades piercing to the T shaped hilt. I'd never seen such a wicked weapon, four inches long, with pieces chopped free so it did the most damage. They are either demons or genius. I saved it for you. The blade.

They've drugged me good though so I'm not hurting too bad, and given me quill and parchment to write with. I suppose that's well enough. ~~I don't understand this war. Three months ago these were our friends. Now we slay each other like wolves with the froth mouth....~~

~~I fear~~...I'm sorry for the scribbles. It's so hard to focus. I feel faded grey. Please take my house and care for Chandra. I don't think~————~~~~"

H'euman Inheritance Records
First War
Year of Betrayal

As the streak shows, this letter was never finished. The soldier died before signing. This case went before the frevellian courts for settlement.

    Sarenka took off at a run, crate thumping awkwardly along in front.

    The sound of their running footsteps grew.

    A figure flew towards her from the side.

    She flinched and swerved, thinking one of the drunks had come back to the ship early and was moving to intercept.

The figure sailed past, and the sound of fighting broke out from behind.

Sarenka swung around, pulling her blade free.

A woman thumped one of the men from behind with the handle of her knife.

He crumpled to the ground and the other sailor turned towards the woman.

She threw her shoulder into his gut with enough force to toss him backwards into the water and shouted, "Run!"

Sarenka took off at breakneck speed for the better part of town. Common Sailors wouldn't be tolerated there, especially sailors chasing women.

Escrach caught up with her and grabbed a side of the crate, helping to propel it forward.

From behind came splashing, followed by the rapid thrum of running feet.

They made it two streets before the wheel hit an upheaved cobblestone. The crate pitched forward and shattered against the ground, sending the unconscious woman flying. She landed on a piece of crate and slid a few more feet while Sarenka's belongings rained down around her. Afraid that she'd been killed, Sarenka ran forward. She pressed her fingers to the woman's throat and was relieved to find a pulse and no sign of damage.

Drawing the stolen pirate sword and her Red Pelican's blade, Sarenka turned to face their pursuer.

Escrach had already started advancing, blade glinting white in the moonlight.

The man skidded to a stop.

Sarenka dropped into a defensive position and bared her teeth.

His gaze shifted back and forth between them before settling on Sarenka's ugly, scar covered face.

She snarled, frightening him into backing away.

Escrach stopped advancing.

Without looking behind or taking his gaze from theirs, he stepped back another ten paces.

The women waited, sweat slickened hands clenching sword hilts and muscles wound tight.

He spun around and ran back towards the docks.

"Probably going to get help," Escrach said, dropping out of her fighting stance.

"We'd best get out of here then. I'm just not sure what to do with her." She nodded at the unconscious woman before gathering her belongings and tying them all into a bundle.

Escrach glanced at the woman, then squinted to peer up and down the street. "No witnesses. That's good. You've done enough, I'll take her to a healer. Maybe they can fix her."

Sarenka held out the sword. "Here, use this to pay for it. I can't keep it."

"You're all right, for a Freni-Kyn."

Sarenka blanched, for the first time realizing that she'd revealed herself to the woman. "Please. Don't tell anyone."

"Are you kidding? We all saw you. They already know. Just get back to wherever you've been hiding, and you should be fine. Not like any of them know where you live."

"Thanks for sticking around and helping."

"Couldn't let a murderess show me up, could I?"

Sarenka smiled.

Escrach scooped up the unconscious woman and began walking towards the wealthy side of town.

Sarenka darted into the shadows and worked her way towards Sad Town, taking many double-backs to make sure none of the prisoners followed. She arrived just as the double moons crossed in the sky and slipped in the door, staggering with exhaustion. Picking up her goodbye letter from the table, she tossed it into the fire, then she stripped off the entire pirate ensemble and threw that in too. The clothing flared up, much as hers had months ago when D'trav had burned the filthy rags she'd seduced him in.

Without bothering to unknot her wet belongings, she tossed them behind the bed and slid under the covers naked. She'd sleep in today and hope D'trav didn't notice that her clothing wasn't hung on its usual peg, or piled near her on the floor.

She stared at the moons through the curtain and sighed with a bittersweet mix of satisfaction and disappointment. She was still captive to Burmtin, but she'd saved some people from a terrible existence, one that would've robbed them of their dignity before taking their lives.

The next day D'trav walked in, tossed packages of food onto the table, grabbed buckets and headed back out the door. Sarenka looked up as he grunted over his shoulder. "Back in the turn of a hourglass."

She nodded and went back to working on the signatures, ignoring the packages.

When he tramped in carrying four full buckets, she bundled up all the writing supplies and loaded down the table with dinner. He placed his elbows on the table and covered his face.

"D'trav?"

Keeping one hand over his eyes, he waved the other at her in a don't-bother-me way.

She put a hand on his shoulder and found he was trembling. "D'trav, what's wrong."

He shook his head, unable to answer.

She pulled up a chair across from him and tried to pull his hand away from his face.

"They killed a bunch of washerwomen today—" he broke off with a sob.

Sarenka felt the breath sucked from her lungs.

"Was a child in the group. Wee bit of a thing, strung up in the square with the rest of 'em."

The room whirled around her.

"I knew 'em, not real close, mind you, just worked with 'em sometimes." D'trav paused and took several deep breaths. "The leader was as fine a woman as I ever did meet, hair black as coal and... they... they done shaved her and cut off her woman parts. Oh dear god..."

The world went black.

A soft wet patting on her cheek brought her back to the room. "Sarenka? Come on girl. Wake up."

Flat on her back, she pushed away the rag and stared up at the ceiling, wondering why she was laying on the ground.

"I shouldn't 'a told you. I'm sorry."

She gripped his arm and stared up into his tear streaked face, remembering. "No. It can't be true."

"I'm sorry, girl."

Rolling onto her side on the floor, she curled up. "This is my fault. This is all my fault."

"Sarenka stop." He carried her across the room and laid her on the bed. "It's not."

"They were my friends."

"You knew them?"

"Tamika, the leader's name was Tamika."

"You knew them."

Tears streamed down her cheeks, and she covered her face with her hands. Time moved on, meaningless. At last, wooden, she walked to their cold meal and sat.

"Signatures nearly finished," she said in a voice devoid of emotion.

He stared at her a moment, as if unsure what to say, before finally pulling a chair up and dipping a hunk of bread into the jellied soup. "That's good, I suppose."

"Any more?"

He paused before continuing to chew and mumbled around the bite. "Nothing for the rest of the week."

She sighed and stirred her soup without looking up.

"I know you're itchin' to earn some extra gold so you can buy more antidote."

Sarenka bit back the wave of sorrow. "I just need out of Burmtin, don't really care about the d'yroap."

They gathered the dishes without more talk, each consumed with their own thoughts, and D'trav set a bottle of Vengeance on the table.

"I-I… have to go aid the families…"

Sarenka half stood.

He pressed her shoulder downwards. "You can't. You know that."

Sarenka looked away and he left.

She stared at the door for a few turns of the hourglass before opening the bottle and tipping it up. The liquid burned its way down her throat and into her stomach. Stumbling into the chair next to the fire, she threw back swig after swig. Tears ran down her cheeks, soaking into her bodice and making her think of the blood-soaked garments she had witnessed at the torture block.

"It had to be the antidote. If I hadn't taken so much… so often… wouldn't have mattered. Nobody would've come looking."

She staggered to the bed and fell asleep cradling the bottle against her chest.

The morning sun slanted in the window, sending spears of blinding light into Sarenka's eyes. With a groan, she rolled off the bed, landing on her hands and knees on the ground. She stared at the ragged floor for a few moments before pushing herself up onto her feet and going to the water pails. After splashing the cool water against her face, she gulped it down, feeling as if she could never drink enough.

"That's one hell of a wicked drink you downed last night."

She rubbed her eyes and squinted at D'trav.

He lay in bed, hands folded under his chin, staring across the room at her with a neutral expression.

"You as much as gave it to me."

"I did."

"Could've warned me."

"You needed it."

She sobbed. "Doesn't make it go away."

"No. Just makes it bearable for a night or so."

"How do I go on?" *Knowing it's my fault.*

"You just do. It gets easier with time, but it never goes away."

She picked up a pan and set it back down with a groan for the throbbing headache. Rolls and water for breaking the fast, she decided. Then she had some things to get rid of. She wouldn't risk anyone else's life.

D'trav's return that evening was quiet. He was expecting to find Sarenka a mess, instead he found the meal cooked and the room cleaned. While they ate, he broached the topic he'd started the night before.

"Place where I work's lookin' for girls. It's not easy but it'll shore 'nough get you out of the city faster."

Sarenka's cheeks darkened to a reddish purple, and she lowered her eyes, hiding them behind inch long lashes. Her normally deft fingers slipped on the knife she was using to cut meat, sending up a spray of broth. She licked her lips nervously, and peeked at him before dropping her gaze again.

There it is again... turnin' purple... and that's not anger... she's blushing! And Kyn damn well don't blush about sex. Ever. He pushed a large piece of meat into his mouth and chewed, staring at her thoughtfully.

Because of the baron?

He shook his head.

No, not with the Foreveron. With that drug she'd have next to no memory left of the night. Nope. Gotta be somethin' else.

Sarenka's shoulders lifted in a cringe. Placing her fork on the table, she closed her eyes and rubbed her forehead. After a few minutes she returned to eating, humming under her breath between bites.

He watched through narrowed eyes, and his chewing slowed to a halt. The battle-scarred hands holding the utensils drifted to the table, forgotten.

She can't be... no trace... but then... illusions could hide that. I've done seen her unconscious while she was a slave though, and here. Just never did think to look for somethin'... unusual... He studied what he could see of her exposed skin, searching for the tale-tell signs of a half breed: tiny scars, irregular bumps, anything that would show past surgeries.

"When's the last time you were with a man?" D'trav asked, as another pressing concern struck. He didn't need her endangering them when the Preral sickness drove her mind-lost with lust, and there was only one way to prevent that.

Glancing up sharply, she gave a quick reply. "Two weeks ago. I'll be okay for two more weeks, minimum."

"Two weeks?" He glared at her. "You took a man while staying with me?"

Sarenka tried to smile but couldn't force her face to do that. Instead, she stared at her food. "Had to."

"You won't be doin' that again. I'll get somethin' set up at the brothel before the time runs round again."

"No! I-I..." she stuttered, "I pick my own men."

"Too risky. I'll set it up."

"You're here. Long as we have sex every four weeks, I shouldn't need another man."

"No."

"No?"

"Done told you. I don't want you like that. Oughta be clear as ale by now."

Sarenka slammed her hand down on the table. "I'm not going to get the Preral sickness.

"Awful picky like for a Kyn." Pulling a chair over to the fire, D'trav poked at the logs, building a higher than normal blaze.

"Yes. I'm picky and I'm not a fool. I take care of my needs before that could ever happen, and I'll pick my own man, Kyron-damn-it!"

"Fine, I'll make sure there's a *reasonable* selection, but you'll pick one of 'em."

"I have to stay hidden." A shower of red sparks fell from her hair.

"We'll work out a disguise for you afore hand."

Without finishing the meal, she abruptly gathered up the dishes, slamming them about with enough force to make him jump a few times.

Helluva temper… I can almost hear the hiss from across the room.

She stripped down, yanking at her clothing angrily before climbing into bed naked.

He watched, glad that he'd forgotten to purchase a sleep gown.

"Too damn hot in here," Sarenka said.

Stifling hot. He added another log to the fire, pretending not to hear.

She gave a disgusted grunt and shifted about on the lumpy mattress, thumping the pillow a few times.

Out of the corner of his eye, the covers sailed to the ground.

Finally she became quiet.

He waited, stoking the fire with impatient jabs until positive she'd fallen asleep.

Holding his breath, he crept close.

Her naked form was a vast disappointment. It answered none of his questions, and he found no obvious signs of other heritage. Unenhanced with illusions, her figure remained a perfect hourglass, her eyelashes still feathery long, her ears still ruffling downward in sleep, occasionally perking up as though dreaming of hearing things. More importantly, there were no signs of the surgical alterations that some parents performed at birth, thinking to save their half-breed children from slaughter. If she was a half-breed, it was completely hidden.

Thinking, he rubbed his hand back and forth across his jawline, creating a rhythmic scratch, scratch, scratch noise in the quiet hut. If the rumors were true, the scars were invisible when the operations were performed on the newly born. He shook his head. No, she was too perfect for that; her petite sizing, combined with hourglass figure, would've taken years of surgical operations to create. It was one thing to reshape an ear or remove an extra finger, another to reform an entire body.

He continued rubbing his hand back and forth along his jawline. *And then there's the illusions... half-breed Kyns can't harness the magics, can they?*

Beads of sweat formed above her lip.

Gonna be a damn uncomfortable night for the both of us, darlin.

Discouraged, and more than a little confused at not discovering the reason for such un-Freni-Kyn-like behavior, he dropped onto the bed next to her.

At the sudden movement she mumbled and rolled over.

His eyes raked one final time over her body. No. She had no surgical scars. Not one. He was positive. And with a body like that, she should be covered in them. She had to be a pure breed. D'trav rubbed his chin thoughtfully, then pulled off his boots and undressed, bouncing the mattress with each move.

"Kyron-be-damned," she mumbled.

Tomorrow. I'll figure it out tomorrow.

Awakened by the rumble of D'trav's incessant snoring, Sarenka lay staring at him. A few tears slipped free. She pushed away thoughts of her friends' deaths. Now was not the time to focus on what she'd caused. Not with the threat of being forced into a night of sex with a stranger. Fear drove through her mind like a dagger.

How am I going to get out of this? He's not stupid. He'll know I'm a half-breed if I tell him I don't get the sickness. And if he finds that out, he'll turn me in or kill me outright.

Not like it was my fault being born.

Not like I chose my parents.

Her fuming turned as sizzling hot as the room temperature.

She shifted position, searching for a cooler spot.

I have to find a way out... something... her thoughts jumped from one solution to another like a cornered rabbit *...anything.*

A trickle of sweat rolled down her back. Irritated, she shoved the covers he'd piled between them further away.

I wish that oaf would stop throwing logs on the fire before bed. It's hot enough in here most of the time anyway. And last night was the worst ever. He just kept going and going, one damnable log after another.

She considered D'trav, not the least bit attracted, but the idea of visiting the brothel was beyond horrifying.

I could end up with someone far worse, someone cruel and disgusting like...

No, D'trav wasn't her type. In fact, no man she'd met was her type, but if it kept her from bedding a stranger, then so be it. She grabbed the wad of blankets from between their bodies and threw them over her shoulder. A rustling flooffe came from behind as they landed on the wooden floor. Scooting over, she ran her hand down over his chest and across his abdomen.

D'trav pulled her close, his body responding with hot need. His lips wandered over her neckline.

Sarenka fought not to stiffen in his arms.

"Camille," he murmured, breath hot against her neck. "You always in the mood, darlin?"

Surprised, she waited a heartbeat before running her hands around his back and rocking her hips forward against his erection. Like a gulp of muddy water, revulsion filled her middle with nausea, but she continued. Despite the sweltering heat, an icy chill settled over her, bringing up goosebumps.

His lips covered hers.

Sarenka opened her mouth to his plunging tongue.

He pulled away and his eyes slipped open, widening as shock spread across his face. "Elsa?"

"D'trav, I—"

The shock turned to disgust, and his arms shot out, propelling him backwards off the bed. He landed on the rough wooden floor with a loud thunk. "What in the name of Kyron's third hell? You Kyron-be-damned, vespra-lanir, swamp-gas-filled, loaded dung hole of a—"

Sarenka leaned over the side of the bed. "Are you o—"

"Keep back!" Hand raised in a panicked warning, he propelled himself further away, sliding across the floor. With a howl, his face turned into a mask of surprised agony, and the same hand he'd been holding up shot to his backside.

CHAPTER 50

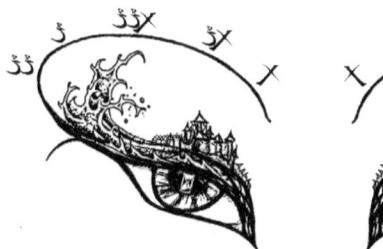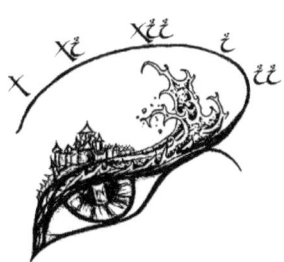

"This exquisite Jeridite specimen was taken from the beast that capsized the Frothy Oyster in 3000 BB. After devouring most of the seamen, it was slain. This small portion of its 100 man span shell weighs almost as much as a full man and yet the magical creature stays afloat. The Glidarthian Crafting Guild, who use Jeridite shell for both armor and adornment, was most generous in its donation to the museum."

Irvetta Charybdis
Glidarthian Museum of Craftsmen

"D'trav, you're hurt!" Sarenka leapt from the bed and grabbed his hip.

He pushed her away, leaving a bloody print on her arm. "Wrap somethin' round yourself!"

"Stop being ridiculous! We're both adults. Turn over." She gave such an unexpected heave that it rolled him over, provoking another cry of pain.

With growing alarm, Sarenka stared at the splinter protruding from his backside like the end of a maple syrup spike. Blood seeped around the edges of wood and for a moment, the sight of a M'hakru Push Dagger—buried to its T-shaped handle in living flesh—flashed before her eyes. She swiped a hand across her face, burying the memory.

Let's just hope it's not as deep as a M'hakru dagger too. Three inches of blade can do a lot of damage.

"D'trav, don't move. Just lie there." She rushed to his trunk and realized it was locked. "The key! Give me the key!"

He fumbled through his discarded clothing from the night before and groaned with pain before pulling free the bit of bone that served as a key.

Racing across the room to grab it, her hand struck his and the key flew into the air. She snatched at the key, and it tumbled across her fingertips before disappearing in a bouncing skitter under the bed.

"Kyron! This can't be happening!"

She dove for the key, outstretched fingers barely grazing the intricately carved bone. Beneath her breast, pricking the skin, a wedge of wood stood out. With horror, she stared from the splinter to the key and strained forward, stretching her arms and fingers into painful numbness. The splinter dug at her chest as her fingers caught the side of the key, wriggling it closer.

A drop of blood slid down her breast.

"What're you doin' under there?"

Startled, she lost her grip on the key.

She glanced over her shoulder at D'trav then back to the splinter digging into her chest before turning back to the key, now caught against the raised lip of a loose board. Wincing, she worked at the board, rocking the bone back and forth, fearful that it wouldn't budge.

A scuffing sound came and D'trav let out a loud groan.

"Stop trying to move," she said.

"You're taking too long."

She gave a quick tap on its edge, flipping the key into the air and past the board. It landed in her palm. She shut her eyes and breathed a thankful sigh as her fingers closed around it.

"Got it."

She pulled free of the shadowy recess and dashed to open the trunk. The first shirt her hand landed on flew across the room, landing next to D'trav. Filling a shell stein with hard liquor, she banged it down before him and sloshed half the liquid over the side.

"Drink this."

"No. Gotta work today." Using the bed for leverage, he propelled himself upwards but fell back to the floor with a jarring thump. Gasping, he gripped the edge of the bed, digging into the mattress.

"D'trav, this is serious. You have to let me help you." Sarenka placed her hand over his and was startled to find it cold and clammy. Alarmed, she examined his face.

His normally bronzed face had gone pale and a fine sheen covered his skin. He gulped, as if fighting the urge to throw up.

Her voice shifted to soft persuasion. "It's going to hurt like the blazes when I pull it out. You need the drink."

His jaw clenched in an audible grinding sound.

"Take the drink."

"Gotta special order comin'. Gotta go in."

"Stay home."

"Just pull the damn thing out already, Sarenka! I felt it. I know what we're dealin' with."

"I don't think so D'trav. The end sticking out is easily an inch across, and who knows how long."

"Dammit all to tarnation, just do it already!" He slammed his hand down, pounding the rickety floor with enough force to rattle the dishes across the room.

Sarenka drew a deep breath, steeling herself against the worst: a gush of blood she couldn't stop, D'trav passing out, his screams attracting a visit from the city guards. A plethora of gruesome scenarios ran a quick gamut through her mind as she worked her fingers under the edge of the wood.

The sound of his heavy breathing and grinding teeth unnerved her, nearly making her insist on calling for an herbalist. The scent of blood hung in the air like freshly slaughtered meat, reminding her of the man she'd murdered, and further shattering her nerves. She flexed her nails, sharp now that he trusted her enough to let them grow, and sank them deep into the wood, pausing when he gasped.

"This is going to hur—" With a hard backwards yank, she pulled the splinter free before he could tense up more than he already had.

D'trav's anguished scream was followed by a fluid string of curses. Having grown used to his tirades, she focused on stopping the blood before it became a stream. He started to roll over, but she put her knee on the small of his back, a pin that normally wouldn't have worked.

"Stop moving, you idiot," she snarled. "You'll make it worse." Dropping the bloodied sliver, Sarenka grabbed the bottle of lenan rum and poured it on the wound.

D'trav yowled and reared upwards, half throwing her off his back. He proceeded to curse her, her mother's mother, her father's ancestors, and any animal they'd ever owned, back through eight generations.

The curses became ridiculous enough that Sarenka had to press her lips together to stop a giggle. She lowered her head, letting her hair fall over her face, and held the old shirt to the wound, staunching the thin flow of blood.

D'trav pounded the floor, punctuating his cursing with thumps and the clatter of rattling dishes.

Sarenka waited, afraid to move, surprised at how little it bled. The wood had been easily four inches long. Though sleeker in shape than a M'hakru push-dagger, she'd expected something the size of an animal tooth and ended up with something the length of a tusk.

His cursing trailed off into panting breaths. "Can you bandage it?"

Sarenka chewed her lip, concerned.

"Well?"

"Not easily, I think it needs a surgeon."

"I'm not some limp wristed Kyn dandy boy. Wrap the damn thing up."

Sarenka's lips thinned at the insult. "Give me your hand. No, the other one." Grasping the proffered hand, now warm instead of cold and clammy, she pressed it against the wound.

"Aiiiy." He winced. "I didn't mean it that way."

"Now who's being a limp wristed Freni-Kyn dandy boy?"

Blood seeped around the cloth, and she pressed her fingers down on his hand again.

He groaned. "I'm sorry already."

"You think I'd do this if it wasn't needed? Press hard, damn it. Don't let it go, you hear me? Not even for a moment."

"Okay, okay! Just you hurry it up." His lips moved in what she supposed were silent curses.

Taking this self-control as a good sign, Sarenka rummaged through his trunk and pulled free the most worn of his cotton shirts. She raked her claws downwards, ripping the fabric into strips before returning to his side. Folding a large piece into a pad, she said, "You're going to have to stand up."

"Son of a…" he snarled through gritted teeth and struggled to his feet, slapping away her helping hand with enough force to sting.

Ember colored eyes narrowing with anger, she examined the wound, surprised once more with how little blood was seeping out. Placing the pad against the wound, she pulled the first piece of cloth around his hips with more force than necessary and began wrapping the wound. She was still silently seething over the slap when she stepped back and tossed D'trav his pants.

With a gasp of pain, he grabbed for the flying pants and gingerly pulled them on, each tug accompanied by a sucked in breath through clenched teeth. "Gotta go. Get any later and hair's gonna start growin' on my eyeballs."

"Here!" She tossed him another shirt. It fell short, landing on the ground. "You may need to make another bandage. I'm sure one of the ladies will be happy to help."

He stared down at the shirt, grunted, and turned towards the door, leaving it on the ground.

"D'trav, we need to talk," Sarenka snarled, thrusting the shirt into his hand.

"You ain't tellin' me somethin' new girl," he muttered, stepping through the doorway.

Parian sprang to his feet and ran to the central chamber where he hurried through piling ingredients on the fueling vessels. Stepping to the center, he threw himself into the time stream towards Burmtin. Pain, confusion, anger, joy, the emotions had ricocheted through his sleep, drawing him into a frenzied rush to connect. If he could grab those strong emotions, he'd find The One, but time was running out. Of that he was sure.

He soared over the city, following a clear stream of light towards the far side.

It flickered out.

Parian's forward rush came to a halt.

Only death stopped a 'calling stream' so abruptly. Paniced, he searched about for another cable of emotion. Before him, where the cable had been, a figure of a H'euman child formed. He floated closer, thinking perhaps that he'd been wrong. This youth couldn't become a seer any time soon. She had years of childhood before she'd be ready to join them.

~Uh uh uh~ she sent, raising a hand and wagging a single finger at him. She blew across the palm of her hand, raising a force so strong it threw Parian back into his body.

He struggled for breath before gasping out, "My god, such strength!"

~Did you feel that?~ he sent.

A chorus of yeses answered him.

~What was it?~ Lanion asked.

~I'm not sure… thought maybe she was The One but… it just doesn't feel right.~

~She?~

~Yes, she.~ He sent them a vision of what had happened.

~If that's The One, then she's stronger than was foretold,~ Airintia sent.

~And younger,~ Parian agreed.

They felt Lanion's mental shrug. *~Well, if she's The One, she's too young. And if not, she clearly told you no. I'd say you need to cool your heels, brother.~*

~Perhaps,~ Parian sent, closing the connection before they could figure out where he was hiding.

"Damn that woman, have to get her out of my bed." D'trav limped through town, unaware of the way people were weaving a wide berth around him. Had he noticed the attention he was getting, he might have stopped glaring at them. His arrival at Camille's place only aggravated him more when she insisted on checking the bandage, fussing over it enough that he wished he'd stayed home.

"Camille, can you send some feelers out for a two-room hut?"

"Anything for you, luv."

"Keep it in Sad Town and as close to the center square as possible. Need a well she can go to without my help." He nuzzled into her neck. "Wish we had more time. Could use a bit of lovin' this morn."

She laughed. "Not sure you're up to it, luv. Mayhaps tomorrow."

His hearty chuckle joined hers. "I'm up, trust me, but it'd be real painful like. And not in the way I'm hankerin' for."

As D'trav wrapped a cloak around his shoulders that evening, Camille pressed a slip of parchment and a key into his hand. "There's the address for your new hut, luv, right next to the well so she can get her own cursed water. I already secured it. Consider the first month on—"

"Didn't have to do that, Camille, I—"

"Stop!" Resting her hands on her hips, she finished, "As I was saying… the first month's on me. I need my guards fit. Coming in wounded from fighting a Freni-Kyn off isn't working for me. It's the best solution."

He nodded and pulled her to his chest. She thought just like him at times. "Tomorrow? Early?"

She answered with her lips.

By the time D'trav arrived at his destination the pain had settled into a horrid, throbbing ache, and he was cursing the day he'd met Sarenka.

"That cursed sweet-drink she tried to push on me sounds like a damn right fine idea now. Stupid bitch. What in tarnation was she thinkin' gettin' all cozy like and all."

He surveyed the weathered hut with a critical eye. Wind-driven salt water had scoured most of its whitewash away, leaving the exterior a mottled brown, but true to Camille's word, it lay directly across from the common well.

One headache out of the way.

His gaze slipped over the surrounding area, taking in alleys, access points, what little lighting there was. A pock-infested man, who was rubbing his crotch through threadbare breeches and leering at every female that walked past made D'trav frown with disgust. Once again Sad Town was living up to its reputation for attracting the most unsavory sorts. It would take a few bribes to make the man disappear.

Finally, he gave a nod of satisfaction.

Not as secure a location as I'd like, but good enough.

As he pushed the unlocked door open, the mingled odors of unclean bodies, rancid fish, and other unidentifiable things struck.

What in Kyron's name is makin' that disgustin' stench?

Clamping a hand over his nose, he surveyed the pillaged room. Every piece of furniture had been deliberately ransacked and destroyed, leaving behind only smashed remnants.

Let's just be hopin' they didn't take out their rage on a person too.

Last thing I need to be dealin' with is another dead body.

He scuffed the floor with his foot, kicking aside a littering of shattered pots and piles of rotted vegetables. Satisfied when no flecks of rotted wood broke free, he gave it one final test, stomping down with enough force to send stabbing pain running down his leg.

Good and solid.

A smashed chair lay in front of a doorway, forcing him to step over it before peering into the second room. Taking one look at the only intact piece of furniture, D'trav decided he'd found the primary source of the stench. A mattress covered in dark stains and green with mold.

He shuddered.

Who knows what lives in that mess.

It'll have to be burned.

Stepping back into the main room, he experimentally touched the walls.

"Damn it!" He drew his hand sharply back, and wiped it down his breeches, grimacing at the long greasy streaks his fingertips left behind. "It'll take a solid two days' work to get this place livable."

He frowned, remembering the signatures he needed Sarenka to work on. "Guess that leaves the cleanin' to me. Still, better than havin' the witch in my bed."

He shuddered again with revulsion.

And better than seein' Elsa's face every time I think about beddin' her. If it weren't so hard to find a forger, I'd just ditch the temptin' little bitch. Make life a lot easier.

The idea of secretly moving here without her was an entertaining thought. He tried telling himself that he wouldn't have a hole in his ass the size of a small knife if not for her, but knew he couldn't choose the simple way out. Besides, their working relationship, while uneasy, offered some protection from authorities and eased his conscience. For now, he'd keep her around. His gaze drifted to the side wall, taking in the tattered remains of a cloth hanging over the top of a window.

Sarenka'd be glad for that bit of sky, though it's crisscrossed with protective jeridite-shell plates.

He sighed.

Elsa would've been glad too.

The safety plates, like everything else in the hut, were covered in filth. Experimentally, he drew his dagger across the greenish black straps, creating a high-pitched screech. Flecks of brownish red fell to the ground, revealing solid shell. He grimaced. Though the creatures were brutally captured, there would be no remnant of death.

Someone had been murdered here.

Not surprising. This was, after all, Sad Town.

He looked back to the window, pushing away grim thoughts.

Needs coverin's. Can't risk some scumbag peeper seein' Sarenka without her illusions.

Turning to the back of the room, he opened the rear door and checked to see how thick it was before slamming it a few times to make sure it was solid.

Be nice havin' a back way in, but gonna need a better lock.

He surveyed the room one last time and gave a nod of approval.

It'll do.

Lot of work. Not sure whether I should thank Camille or curse her, but it'll do.

With trepidation, Sarenka looked up when D'trav arrived. He could very well blame her for his injury. "Hello."

He grunted and moved to the pot, ladling his own stew into a bowl before leaning cautiously against the table and slurping down his meal.

Not that the rough wooden floors were her fault, though she might have recommended that he fix them. Instead, too afraid of removing part of her back up plans, she'd lived with them, keeping them as they were, rough and splintered, just in case things ever went really bad.

By the time she realized that he didn't plan to chain her up and abuse her, she'd grown used to the security of knowing there were weapons in the house that most people would never notice. And in Sad Town, where criminals and thieves stalked the streets only slightly less than hunger did, that was a definite advantage.

"How's your wound?"

"You mean the splinter in my ass," he said.

"Is it bad?"

"You mean the wound I wouldn't have if you hadn't woke me like you did."

"I was just trying to—"

"Hurts like Kyron's ninth hell." He began looking around the hut, all the while rubbing his hand back and forth across his jaw, and counting under his breath.

Sarenka decided to leave him alone. If mentioning the wound made him feel the need to count, then he hadn't cooled off yet.

After dinner he dropped a packet of papers onto the table without sparing her a glance. "Need these people's signs copied. You've got yourself two days."

Sarenka blew her breath out, creating a hiss as the air swished between her pursed lips. "That's the only thing you're going to say to me tonight?"

"I hate it when you do that."

"Do what?"

"Breathe out like that. So annoyin' it makes me want to…"

All thoughts of avoiding a confrontation evaporated. She rolled her eyes. "Well at least I can hold a normal conversation. Should have let you bleed to death you… troll."

He surprised her by not even blinking at the insult. "We're movin' in two days."

"Moving? Where?"

"Cave under a bridge," he said.

Sarenka blinked, surprised that he'd cracked a joke without batting an eye. And she might have found it amusing, if not for the serious look on his face. She opened her mouth to respond sarcastically.

"Two room hut next to the well," he said.

She shut her mouth, considered the news. *Good… maybe… but he's still so…*

"Has a window."

"Who's Camille?"

He focused all his attention on Sarenka for the first time that evening. Narrowed eyes and a suspicious frown replaced his casual mannerism as he whipped out, "How'd you get that name?"

Sarenka jumped at the sharp snap in his voice. "You thought I was her... this morning... you..."

He snorted, returning to his former nonchalance. "Figures. A friend. Runs the brothel."

Sarenka's cheeks colored and she turned away. She'd always assumed his job had side benefits but hadn't ever wanted details. His payments probably included time spent with an expert at sexual pleasure.

"And who's Elsa?" she asked at last, afraid of learning yet more sordid details.

Surprised, D'trav sucked in his breath. *So I really did call her that. Kyron-damn-it all!*

She rubbed at her temple. *Stop talking to me!*

"My sister."

Sarenka turned back, slanted brows lifted in surprise. "Your sister? You thought I was your sister?"

"Don't wanna talk about it." He picked up the papers on the table and tapped them down, evening up their edges before setting them down and shifting them about pointlessly.

"No wonder you don't want to be with me. Do I look like her?"

"No... and yes." An expression that landed somewhere between wistfulness and loneliness flitted across his face. His grey eyes lifted to stare at her before he exclaimed, "Not gonna talk about it. Change the subject."

Sarenka chewed her lip a moment before saying, "Drop your trousers."

CHAPTER 51

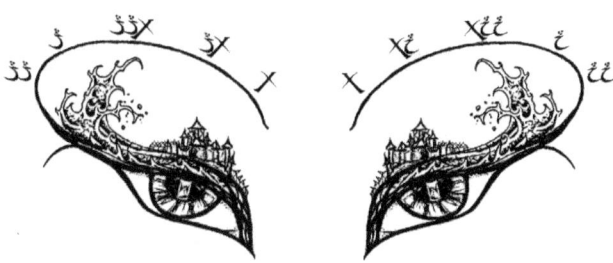

D'trav's mouth dropped open instead.

"Oh, stop looking so appalled. I need to check your bandages and clean your wound."

"Son of a swamp cow, Sarenka!" He found his voice in a sudden angry shout. "Watch how you speak! Man could get a wrong impression."

"Stop being such a prude." Sarenka snickered. "You work at a brothel and deal in stolen documents, for Kyron's sake. It's just body parts."

She grabbed his shoulders, turning him towards the table. "Now. Either undo the pants, or I will."

Two mornings later, D'trav's first thoughts were for the hut he'd obtained. It was perfect on many levels, most of which had nothing to do with Sarenka and the well. The informants would be able to move freely around the central square, instead of having to come up with reasons to be on an isolated avenue. Unlike the more secluded streets, where strangers were treated with suspicion and watched like a hawk, people on the square hardly gave passers-by a second glance.

There would be no more incidents of having to tell a nosey neighbor why 'cousin Tremont' was visiting yet again. No more fake birthdays, or organized games-of-chance. With the ability to come and go with ease, there' would be better income and less danger, always the most important thing he considered in any place he set up business.

Ultimately, that's what matters, the business.

He was determined to continue no matter how many obstacles Sarenka threw in his path. She'd spoiled his plans by killing the Baron of Leanon Manor too early, forcing him into establishing a whole new operation and moving agents into new locations. Then she'd weaseled her way into his life, and he'd managed to turn that into extra d'yroap. Now she'd caused an injury that would leave him limping for weeks, maybe longer, but even that was manageable, as long as he didn't get into a fight.

Yes, I'll succeed. One way or another, I'll get my revenge for Elsa's death and rid Llayentia of at least one corruption.

Rolling out of bed with satisfaction, D'trav winced. His hand went behind, automatically clutching at the embarrassing wound. But even that stabbing pain couldn't drive away the pleasurable thoughts of Sarenka's finished forgeries and their upcoming move. The renewed throbbing just reminded him to move carefully.

He groaned.

Sarenka's insistence on stitching the wound closed had been followed by hours of driving pain. His inflamed skin had swelled, puffing up around the thread like rising bread with string tied around it. The stitches pulled every time he moved; a constant reminder of her caution about the dangers of tearing the healing tissue.

Despite the discomfort, he smiled. Today would be a good day. He'd make a huge profit on the signatures and finally get the Freni-Kyn out of his bed. To top that off, Camille had informed him that she had men lined up for Sarenka's Preral cycle. Five days from now Sarenka's needs would be taken care of at the brothel. Then he'd relax, at least until next month.

Yes, a good day.

No. Not a good day… an excellent day.

The kinda day that makes a person wanna break open their finest whiskey and hand it out to every sad son of a dog that wanders by.

By early afternoon Sarenka had already gathered their meager belongings, stacking them in the center of the room. D'trav acknowledged the effort with a nod when he arrived. After creating the illusion she always wore when going out with him, that of a middle-aged woman with an overly large nose, the two walked to the new hut, carrying what they could.

Sarenka stared at the hut, eyes traveling from it to the nearby well before she turned to D'trav with a smile. "Thank you."

"Weren't me, thank Camille."

Her smile faded at the thought of the brothel.

As they entered, Sarenka stifled a grimace at the lingering odor of uncleanliness that her sensitive Freni-Kyn nose detected. Though he'd worked hard to clean it for the last two days, leaving early and returning late, filthy and exhausted, something would have to be done about that stench. Herbs for the ground, she decided. Walking across hyssop, or maybe meadowsweet, would make it smell better. She started to set her things next to the single narrow cot that occupied the main room.

"Uh-uh." D'trav's chin lifted towards the only interior door. "You sleep in there. This one'll be mine."

He's giving me a whole room?

Sarenka blinked with surprise but walked to the other room. The putrid smell was stifling in the enclosed space, but the tiny area appeared freshly cleaned. She examined the coarse bedding and decided they were crisp enough to be brand new. That was so startling that she couldn't help but turn to stare at D'trav.

With a thump, he dropped his battered trunk into place next to the small bed he had claimed. Scooting the trunk over a couple of inches, he squared it up precisely with the head of his bed, and left to collect the rest of his things.

Sarenka sank onto the edge of the bed.

My bed.

She smoothed a hand over the bedding and stared at the bare wall.

"His sister. I look like his sister. Is this room because of her?" Her soft words felt loud in the silent hut. "Well, he wouldn't be reminded of her if he really knew me."

She chewed her lip, considering the odd turn her life had taken. Living with a stranger who was beginning to treat her like a sister felt wrong somehow, especially after such a short time.

He's changed. He's not the cold hearted bastard that tried to take advantage of me... how many weeks ago... She tapped her finger against her skirt, counting off the weeks since she'd moved in, and decided that maybe, just maybe, it had been enough time to form feelings of friendship.

Even if he still has that weird chain wrapped up in Elsa's kimono.

It means something, but what?

She'd watched him with the beggar children, even followed him a few times, and he'd never shown any type of perverse interest in them. It had taken her a while to figure out that he wasn't throwing their left overs away but was dropping them off with one of the orphan gangs, exchanging a full bucket for an empty one.

I'll never be able to live up to his dead sister's memories.

I should leave. If I don't, he'll be sure to get hurt.

But not yet.

Have to save up some more d'yroap.

Or end up back here, begging for help.

Sarenka ground her teeth as D'trav escorted her to the brothel the following week. His eyes darted, as though expecting an attack at any moment, and even with a limp his rapid stride forced her into an occasional double-step. She glanced at him nervously, knowing she couldn't let another person die because of her. Her plans to separate from him had been put into place that week, but it would be three more months before she had enough d'yroap.

A pebble shifted under his foot. He stopped to grasp his thigh with a sharp intake of breath.

She glanced from his clenched hand, to the pain reflected in his face, and knew she'd stay until he was healed. Even with plenty of d'yroap, she couldn't abandon him. He would never have been injured by that floor if she hadn't been trying to seduce him. They resumed walking at a normal pace, which had the unfortunate effect of giving her more time to dread what was coming. Her thoughts swarmed like a pack of hungry mosquitos after fresh meat, and she squared her shoulders, sticking her chin out stubbornly. This night would just have to be dealt with.

It's either that or tell him the truth.

Not an option.

Despite her resolve, she balked when it became obvious that their destination was the Distinguished Dainties, a dilapidated old building that looked like it might blow over in a stiff wind, she balked.

D'trav took one look at her face, locked his fingers around her elbow, and pulled her forward. "It's not as bad as it looks on the outside."

She shook her head, though doing anything but complying rished creating a scene.

He swung open the door and propelled her into what seemed like obscene luxury after two years on the streets.

Sarenka let out a relieved breath. *Perhaps I won't catch a disease after all.*

A middle aged woman with honey blond tresses hurried towards them. She winked at D'trav and Sarenka a once over. "Just a bit of a thing, isn't she?"

D'trav glanced at Sarenka, seeing her through a different filter. "Suppose so. You gotta room ready?"

"Of course." She turned business woman and gave Sarenka a curt nod. "If you will be so kind as to follow me."

With that she spun on her heel, leading them quickly towards a dressing room where pots of creams and powders littered a small table. She nodded towards the chair. "If you will take a seat, I'll be right with you."

Sarenka started towards the chair.

From behind came a schzt-snap.

The hairs on the back of her neck rose as she grasped the blade hidden within the folds of her skirt and turned back.

"You'll need to drop the illusions, child."

Hand on blade, Sarenka sat, allowing the illusions to fall away.

"Oh my, quite lovely. But then again we'd expect that from a Freni-Kyn, wouldn't we? Tis a shame you can't work here. You'd make yourself a pretty d'yroap."

Sarenka repressed a shudder. "Can you hide my heritage?"

"Not completely. But once I'm done, it won't be a total catastrophe if your illusions falter. The makeup'll give you a bit of time to turn away and get them back up again." Camille walked forward, rubbing her hands together.

Seems like she'll enjoy covering my face.

While Camille applied an assortment of concoctions, D'trav watched with arms crossed. "You look tired, still havin' the dreams?"

Camille glanced at D'trav. "Ever since she killed the baron, luv."

Sarenka froze, heart hammering.

"Yes, I know who you are girl."

"I shouldn't of come here like I did," D'trav said.

"Had to go somewhere, didn't you now? What with them plastering Burmtin with your face."

Sarenka felt an odd mix of shame and irritation. "If he hadn't—"

"I know what he did," Camille interrupted.

"Camille, it's not her fault."

Camille pursed her lips.

"If you're gonna blame someone for the nightmares, then blame me. It's me what could've brought 'em here on my heels."

"She's the one that killed the man."

"The Foreveron."

"Well, she shouldn't have gotten herself caught by the slavers to begin with."

Sarenka watched her cheeks redden to violet in the mirror.

"Camille!"

"Okay, okay." Camille picked up another pot of color.

In the uneasy silence, Sarenka stared in the mirror as the slant of her eyes were downplayed, lips artfully thinned, skin tone masked with dark, earthy colors, and cheekbones made less pronounced. It was almost magic what the woman could do with face paints.

When Camille began adding heavy ornamental wires to the filaments of her hair, weighting them down and keeping them from floating, Sarenka couldn't help but flinch with pain and grip the chair arms. But she kept silent.

D'trav watched from over her shoulder and lifted one eyebrow in obvious surprise.

Sarenka chewed her lip at the expression on his face, concerned that she was tolerating this far better than he expected. After fighting for the last four days over the planned brothel trip, he had probably thought he'd have to tie her up to get her here. Yesterday, with all her plans in place, she'd stopped fighting, creating the first peaceful evening all week. He'd actually sighed with relief when they made it through their meal without harsh words. Hoping that he knew enough about the Preral sickness to know she should be shaking, but not enough to know she would have been shaking all week, she'd pretended to shaking hands too.

He shrugged his shoulders, looking reassured.

Relief washed over her. He was buying the deception.

As they left the room, Camille handed her a brightly colored mask but stopped Sarenka when she started to put it on. "Not for you, luv, it's for him." She poked at the black eyeholes, showing that they were covered. "Less likely to see you in a slip-up."

When presented with a row of men, all in various stages of undress, Sarenka was glad for the greasy face paints Camille had insisted upon, positive that her face had gone bright violet with embarrassment.

Her gaze traveled down the group, and she rejected the youngest two automatically. Though beautiful, they wouldn't do for her purposes, not with an adolescent desire to prove themselves that guaranteed boasting. No, she needed a man who could keep his mouth shut. She also rejected the man who seemed more intent on admiring D'trav than watching at her; he was a wild card that she didn't want dealt. Another man, rubbing his crotch suggestively, provoked such a strong temptation to lash out with a kick to the balls that she clasped her hands tightly behind her back. The rest of the men she caught, and kept, eye contact with as she passed. D'trav thought she was choosing someone attractive, but it didn't matter one bit what they looked like. What mattered was who they were under the skin, the real person.

One of the gigolos glanced furtively away instead of staring boldly back.

Sarenka stopped.

Perfect.

He was a little embarrassed, which meant he was new to this life, but old enough—judging by a few wrinkles at the corners of his eyes—to stay silent.

She hoped.

Sarenka indicated her choice with a wave of her hand.

The man peered at the man next to him then back to her before pointing at his own chest and mouthing, "me?"

Sarenka nodded.

He stood in a rush and led her to a private room.

Sarenka scoured the chamber for details and was disappointed to find no exit beyond the one she'd entered by. It was filled with the type of opulence she expected: a shiny coverlet edged in beaded fringe, a chandelier draped in translucent red stones—cut so that they caught and diffused the light, basking the room in a pink glow—walls covered in luxurious maroon taffeta, and heavy stone candelabras, already lit. She memorized the candelabras scattered placement. They, at least, offered a possible weapon.

With a casual toss, the mask landed on a nearby table, sliding until it nestled against the base of one of the candelabras.

She gave a satisfied nod and sat on the bed before looking at her companion and patting a spot opposite her.

The man's brows rose slightly, but he sat without question.

CHAPTER 52

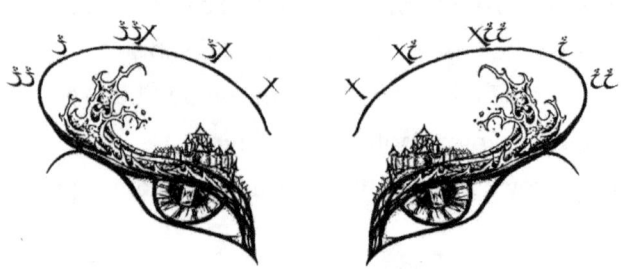

As the door shut, Camille winked at D'trav and grabbed his elbow, guiding him towards her room.

"I promised I'd work tonight, darlin."

"Well, I guess your duties will start now then." She opened the door and gestured him in. Candles flickered from surfaces, warming the room.

D'trav considered the line of toys on her bed, ending with a piece of chain, and felt himself harden. "You sure know how to make a man an offer he can't resist."

"You know what to do."

He walked to the bed, listening as the door latched behind him, placed his legs shoulder width apart and undid his belt.

She reached around from behind, tracing a finger along the line of his bulge.

"You want the armor off?"

"No. Tonight you will be the warrior who gives everything... *everything*."

"And what do I call you?"

"M'lady will do nicely."

"Yes, M'lady."

She pulled the tie of his breeches, relieving just enough pressure to tantalize him more.

Closing his eyes, he waited for her to stroke him.

Instead, she tugged the pants down over his hips, carefully avoiding his stitches. Her fingernails traced over his ass, circling the injury. "Healing nicely. Swellings completely gone."

"Yes, M'lady," he moaned, wanting more than that teasing touch.

"Kneel," she said.

D'trav stared at the oiled chain she had used to keep him aroused for the last few hours and shuddered and fell to his knees, spent. "Oh god, Camille."

The chain landed on the floor beside him with a jangling crash, sending up a puff of jasmine and sandlewood scent.

Camille sat on the bed in front of him and stroked the lines of his face.

Wrapping his arms around her, he shuddered as waves of electric aftermath went through him.

"What's your name?" Sarenka asked.

"Dick," he paused, and his face flushed faintly. "Dick Charmer."

Sarenka coughed but couldn't hold back a giggle.

His flush deepened.

"Nice name. You can call me... Myrddyn." Opening her waist pouch, she poured out a new set of dice and a pile of copper flats. "We're playing Sharpra s'tideu."

"For clothing items?"

"No. Just to win."

Though his eyebrows rose again in surprise, he asked no more questions.

She nodded with understanding; after all, he was paid to do, not to question. The two were soon caught up in a challenging game of skill and chance.

A light tap at the door interrupted Sarenka's concentration. She looked up, hand poised in the air with three triangular shaped cards ready to be laid down. Dropping the thin metal plates, she climbed onto the bed and grasped his hands, pulling him up to join her. Making exaggerated moaning sounds, she began jumping. When he didn't immediately do the same, she moved her hands up and down, and raised her brows at him in a manner that said come-on-do-it.

The look of realization that struck his face was almost comical, but he began to jump, making the types of sounds a man in the midst of sex might make.

Sarenka fought a giggle, and her illusions faltered, but she had them back in place almost immediately. Dick gave no sign of seeing the slip, and under their energetic sounds came the faint scuff of leather shoes walking away. The two slowed to a stop, listening for a few minutes before sitting.

Sarenka started gathering the cards that were strewn across the bed. "We'll just replay that last hand since I already revealed mine."

"You're right, that would've given me an unfair edge." Dick pulled his cards from his waistband and dropped them on the bed face up.

"Humph! I won that hand, or would have."

"Yep, you would have." Dick grinned and helped pick up the rest of the triangular cards. With an apologetic look on his face, he held out a card that had been bent during their jumps.

She snatched it from his fingers and peered closely, examining the edge. "Well dung! Those cost me a week's labor. Now I'll have to pay to have it rolled flat and trimmed."

Though popular among some circles, the game was not usually played by the poor, mostly due to the expense of the cards in their metal-poor world. Her attempts at finding cards made from other materials failed, leaving her with the necessity of several risky trips and a few picked pockets, before she finally commissioned a set of thin metal cards from Danielson.

Dick watched at her with so much concern that she leaned forward and patted his knee. "Don't worry, wasn't your fault. I'll just get my blacksmith friend to fix them."

Several hours rolled by before Sarenka decided enough time had passed. She dropped her engraved playing cards onto the embroidered bedspread and strode to the corner where a tall mirror stood. She stared at her reflection in the heavily gilded surface for several long moments before giving in to the urge and sticking out her tongue. With a quick swipe, she smeared the thick red goop that covered her lips and savagely twisted a pinch of neck skin, sucking in her breath at the pain. As a bruised welt developed under the makeup, she simulated the same with her illusions. Turning back to Dick, she pulled ten silver d'yroaps from her waist-pouch.

"This is to keep silent about tonight. We had sex. That's all they need to know."

Dick looked confused but took the coin. "You do know this was prepaid, right?"

"Yes. That's for the silence."

"Very well, Myrddyn. Will we have *sex* again next month?"

Laughing at his daring, Sarenka rumpled the bed covers more convincingly.

Sure, why not?

It'd be simpler if she didn't have to find the right man every month. It wasn't a surprise that he knew she was Freni-Kyn and would need monthly servicing. Despite her best efforts, her illusions had weakened several times in the hours they'd been sequestered. She'd picked the right man, of that she was now sure. If he had enough control to hide his surprise when her illusions winked out, then he'd be able to keep the fake sex a secret from the prying of someone like Camille.

"Yes. But I'm bringing new dice. You cheated."

"Who me?" He spread his arms and widened his eyes innocently.

"I like you."

He smiled. "I'm glad."

A sudden thought came to her, one that would assuage her guilt. "You want to earn some points with Camille?"

"Always."

"Meet me in the third south alley off the southeast square tomorrow at sunrise."

He scratched his earlobe, looking leery.

"Trust me in this. It's going to buy you big points."

They left the room and walked down the velvet-draped hallways towards the main chamber, with its gilded furniture, plush carpets, and beaded sconces. Men and women lounged about the room in various states of repose, chatting with each other. Sarenka's gaze swept over the crowd—unsure which were clients and which prostitutes—before finally landing on D'trav. He stood at attention against a wall, staring straight ahead like a common guard.

Dick sauntered away, joining a group of men near the oversized fireplace

She walked towards D'trav. "Let's go."

D'trav nodded in answer, and she supposed that he was trying to stay professional.

Doorknob in hand, she half-turned back towards the room.

A man she'd rejected slid his hand around Dick's waist and pulled him in for an intimate kiss.

She cocked her head sideways as their bodies pressed against each other's, and her eyebrow rose.

D'trav glanced back and gave her a nudge. "Some of 'em prefer other men."

Sarenka blinked at D'trav vacantly.

"Come on, stop gawking. It's natural enough."

She left the building, still stunned.

How'd I miss that?

CHAPTER 53

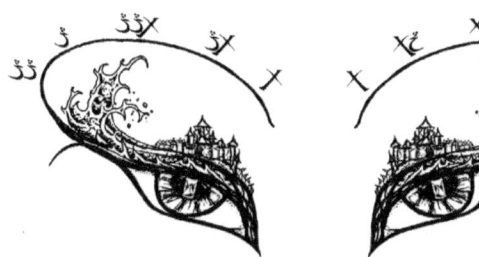

Wearing course trousers and a simple bloused shirt, Dick stepped hesitantly into the filthy alley the next day.

A growl came from the dark.

"Hush, now. Shhh." Sarenka stepped forward, leading a group of Shepherds.

Dick backed up and held out his hands in front of him.

"Here, take the leads."

"No… I…"

"Hurry! The owners will be out to feed them soon. You have to get these to Camille before then."

He took another step backwards.

"Are you going to force me into taking these to her myself?"

"I don't like dogs."

She glanced from him to the dogs with sudden understanding. "You're afraid?"

A door opened behind them and Sarenka took off at a run. Six alleys and three streets away she leaned over, panting for breath, and pushed away the happy licks of the dogs. They jumped around her, overjoyed with the freedom to run.

Dick leaned against a nearby wall, breath coming in wheezing pants.

She grabbed his hand and put the leads in it.

"Take them to her. Tell her they are from both of us and not to ask where we got them. They'll guard the place, and she can get some sleep. And tell her I said to pet them. A lot. Or I'll take them back."

He peered at his hand and then at the dogs. They wagged their tails happily. "You better be right about this."

The next four months were spent in learning the counterfeiting trade and saving her silvers while D'trav came and went with his work at the Brothel. The nights he returned long past the crossing of the double moons left her curious, but she had learned, after the first few explosive conversations, not to ask where he'd been.

She'd made it through two more visits to the Distinguished Dainties without a problem, always choosing Dick for a partner. Camille had been more than civil and walked with Beast, renamed Dante, at her side at all times. Sarenka took great satisfaction in seeing the unloved dogs doted on by both patrons and workers.

Her next visit was looming over her head, but she refused to focus on it. If Dick wasn't available, she was positive she could bribe another of the men into silence. She even thought Dick's lover, Randy, might be a good choice, especially since he preferred men.

Her relationship with D'trav had moved from reluctant partners, to mutual respect, and then on to something she was unwilling to put a name to, lest it evaporate and leave her back where she started, with nobody. Her contentment had grown so much that she'd created one excuse after another to stay instead of leaving when her silvers accumulated.

Now, she didn't even bother with the excuses. She'd stay for as long as D'trav would let her. He'd turned out to be a completely different person than she expected. There were days when she wanted to ask why he'd demanded she serve him at the manor instead of setting her free, but she didn't. Asking might ruin what they had, a friendship that went beyond being paid to make counterfeits.

It would forever remain a question in her mind, one that needed no answer.

Sarenka's hand jerked at the coded tap on their back door. With a frustrated sigh, she started the signature over. Since the move, their night visitors had increased in frequency, always coming at the most inopportune times.

Like when I'm bathing, or sleeping, or eating, or... well just about any time.

Loosening his blade, D'trav rose from his position in front of the fire. He paused at the door, listening cautiously before swinging it open. The dip in outside temperatures brought a chill breeze whipping through the room, and Sarenka pulled the blanket closer. She'd taken to wrapping herself in it during the evenings, preferring to save her cloak for outdoor travel.

With a sigh, she returned to the steady practice she'd been engaged in. This signature, more difficult than the others she'd worked on, was taking too long and D'trav was becoming impatient. She bit her lip in concentration, barely noticing the soft murmur of voices in the background, but a name sliced its way through her awareness, causing her scribing to abruptly cease.

Ink spread across the document in a growing blot as she listened with heightened senses, every detail stretched out in cold relief: the scent of stale fish and salt riding in on the rustling breeze, the warm flicker of red and yellow as the fire jumped, the unnerving wail of a cat screaming with heat.

The wind lifted the corner of her parchment, coldness seeped through her blanket, the candle flickered and threatened to go out, but still she stared at the growing blot, ears lifted so high that the pleats along the outside edge were nearly gone. Their business drew closer to farewells and Sarenka fidgeted. She must have imagined the name, or perhaps they were done discussing him.

The crackling noise of exchanged papers signaled the end of the transaction.

Finally the stranger said, "We'll have some more for you next week, Onglat. The information looks good, and seems to be a solid run. We'll all be rich soon, long as everything goes as planned."

The conversation murmured on, but Sarenka's ears were so filled with a rush of blood she couldn't hear.

D'trav is Onglat?

No! No, it's not possible.

All this time he's been right under my nose.

What a fool I've been.

Suddenly aware of the drawn knife in her hand, she hastily pushed it back into the hidden pocket she'd sewn into her skirt.

I can't believe I did that after all this time. Guild training never really disappears, no matter how long you're away from them.

She pushed thoughts of the training away, it didn't matter and it might even save her life.

Now's not the time to deal with Onglat, not with witnesses, and certainly not with a kitchen knife.

Grabbing the quill, she returned to scribing. The sound of the door swinging shut, followed by his nearing footsteps, provoked her into slamming the quill onto the table. She snatched up the parchment, with its tellingly large ink blot, and created a suitable distraction by standing fast enough to rock the chair backwards, nearly toppling it over. Stepping to the fire, she tossed in the now-wadded practice sheet with all the vengeance that was seething through her veins.

Onglat is D'trav...

D'trav is Onglat...

It chanted through her mind, and the deception pushed her into anger that didn't have to be faked.

How could he deceive me like that?

How could I be so dense?

The seals, the meetings, all the signs were there.

"I don't know if I can do this one!"

He gaped at her for a moment but quickly said, "Course you can, darlin. You've got loads of talent. Just need to break for a bit."

And now he's forcing me to a decision I don't want to make.

He looked away, eyes roaming the room before settling on the kettle. "Here, I'll fetch you some tea. Then you can get back to it."

Letting out a disgusted breath, Sarenka pulled the blanket closer and her blackened fingertips, which seemed as much a part of her life now as breathing, reminded her of what she'd been doing to earn her keep.

Helping Onglat... Dear Kyron... I've been helping Onglat. The most wanted man in Llayentia.

Probably helping him foil the Red Pelican.

If they ever find out... Kyron...

I'm as good as dead.

Desperate for something, anything, to keep him from suspecting that she'd overheard his conversation, she grasped at normalcy. "I need some warmer clothes soon. I'm cold all the time."

"I'll rustle up somethin' tomorrow. Winter cloak, too. Anything else?"

"No, I don't think so," she murmured, voice trembling, and slumped tiredly in the chair, hoping the feigned exhaustion covered the barely suppressed emotions surging through her.

I could slit his throat right now, while his back's turned.

He trusts me, and that death's far kinder than what awaits him.

CHAPTER 54

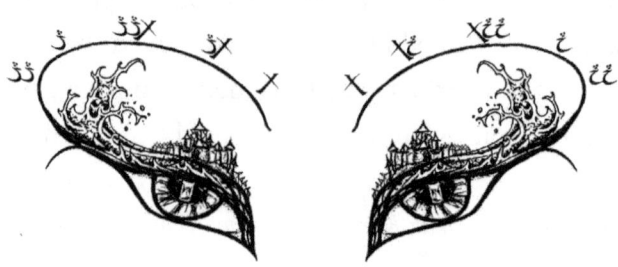

D'trav carried the shell of mint tea to the table and gave her an encouraging pat, along with a jar of honeyed seaweed. "Just take a break."

She frowned. *He's not making this easier.*

Misunderstanding, he smiled sympathetically and pushed the tea closer, encouraging her to drink it. "Don't you worry yourself, Sarenka. I'm sure you can do it. I've seen you make some pretty fine signs over the last few months."

Sarenka moved to the only soft chair, the same battered, wooden chair he'd owned when she moved in, now equipped with cushions bought just for her. Slumping deeper into it, she stared morosely at the flickering flames. Since the move he'd relaxed, even slipping into a brotherly attitude—one she enjoyed.

What must be like, to have an older brother to care for me as he had for his sister? Things would've been different, very different. For one thing, I wouldn't be on assignment to find Onglat the Slippery.

Not find…

Now I've got him!

I should be rejoicing, instead I'm wondering about giving him a mercy killing.

She ticked off her choices on her fingertips, trying to think of something she'd missed.

She could turn him in, which would bring her back into good graces with the Red Pelican, probably a monetary reward, and most definitely ensure his slow, torturous death. The easiest, safest, choice.

She could run, take the silver she'd earned and escape. Nobody hurt that way, but that took time to set up, time she didn't have. The price on Onglat's head was far higher than the price on her own had ever been. And if she'd found him it was only a matter of time before someone else did.

She could kill him, a coward's way out in many ways, but far kinder than the torture awaiting him if she went with the first choice. Of course, killing him carried its own dangers. If they discovered who he was afterwards, she'd be in more trouble with the guild. Another breach of orders on her account would definitely result in her own death, unless she found a reason to do the killing.

In the end, her training won out.

He has to die.

He betrayed the Red Pelican. No one gets away with that.

An ice cold hand gripped her shoulder.

Nerves on edge, she swung around, breaking the grip.

Across the room D'trav rummagws through his trunk, no doubt prepping for something else that would get her in deeper trouble. Finding no one behind her, she returned to working on the signature.

Bad enough I'm hearing voices. Now I'm jumping at shadows and imagining touches.

I'll contact them while he delivers this letter tomorrow… if… if I don't take him out tonight.

She angrily pushed away the tear slipping down her cheek.

Damn him! Now I'm crying like a wee one.

Drawing in a breath, she balanced herself using techniques the guild taught. So focused was her attention that she didn't notice D'trav climbing onto his creaking cot or his droning snore. When she scribed out her final work and lay down the quill, it was well past the crossing of the moons. She stood, stretching to release stiff muscles. The blanket slid to the ground, forgotten. D'trav's peaceful snoring filled the room with a familiar drone.

Now's the time to do it.

He won't know the hurt of betrayal…

Painless.

In every way.

On noiseless feet she crept across the darkened room, pausing after each step until she reached his cot. She leaned over his recumbent form, firelight reflecting blood red off her drawn blade.

Sensing her presence, his eyelids slipped open. "Elsa? Go back to sleep, 'lil one… gotten us well enough hidden… bad men won't find us here, baby," he mumbled, patting her blade arm, eyes closing.

Startled, Sarenka drew back and stared at him with horror. Slipping the paring knife into her skirt, she wrapped suddenly cold arms about her midriff and turned to bed.

I can't do this.

Oh dear Kyron…

But I have to…. I have to.

Parian drifted in close to a small hut in Sad Town. The mood radiating from the building was a bitter mix of sadness, anger, and fear. Whatever was happening, it wasn't good. Knowing that another burn-out might kill him, he paused to check the energy levels before sinking through the roof.

Raw energy sizzled through the rooms, abrading his nerves and reminding him of the energy he'd faced in the pub. It pulsed, buzzing against his mind like the voice of a thousand people all speaking at once.

He swept through the tiny hut and found only a man and a woman, no girl-child. That brought both a wave of relief and regret. Though she could annihilate him with a thought, the child held more power than he'd ever encountered, and he longed to see her again.

Instead of attempting contact with the people in the hut, he tasted the crackling energy and found it foreign, unlike any he'd ever shared before. His eyes leapt from the woman to the man, confused. He had no idea which it emanated from but felt certain he should recognize the flavor of their thoughts.

Time accelerated. The moons crept across the sky, and still the Freni-Kyn female lay staring at the ceiling. He plucked her name free from the whirlwind that was her mind—Sarenka. Conflicting thoughts pulled at him, drawing him in, confusing him.

Gritting her teeth with resolve, she slipped from the bed and padded from that room to the main one, where a single man lay—D'trav.

Parian lurched forward with alarm. If she killed this man, this D'trav, then either The One would be dead, or The One would be too corrupt to ever become a Seven. At the doorway his astral form bounced against an invisible net and caught. Energy radiated along the net, and the girl-child appeared in the corner of the room.

Tears trickling down her cheek, she stared past him, drawing his gaze back to the bed.

Pulling free a dagger, the Freni-Kyn drew several deep breaths before reaching towards the Ileuman's forehead with her free hand.

Just as she was about to touch him, the man coughed and rolled onto his back.

She jerked her hand away, freezing in place for endless moments.

Chapter 55

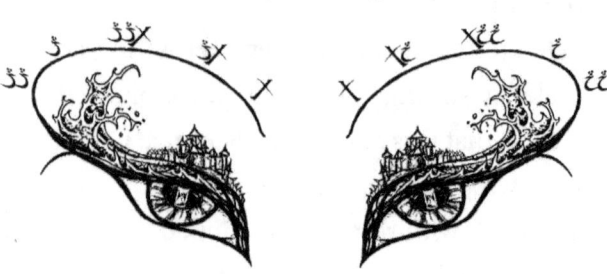

Parian dared to hope, to believe in the basic kindness of the universe.

Sarenka yanked the man's head to the side and sliced across his jugular vein.

D'trav's horror filled eyes flew open.

She drew the knife away and shifted position, staring into his face.

His hands grappled at the gaping wound, trying to stop the spewing blood.

Sarenka watched, her gaze never leaving his.

Red sprayed between his fingers for an eternity before turning into a trickle, and as his life force seeped from his body, the man's gaze drifted past Sarenka, focusing on the far corner of the room. His face fell slack.

"I'm sorry..." Covered in blood and a stifling cloak of regret, the Freni-Kyn woman sobbed. "I'm so sorry."

She fell to the ground and rocked back and forth on her knees, moaning out her regret. Tears ran down her cheeks, mingling with blood and washing the neck of her nightgown in watercolor shades of pinkish-red.

Unable to pull himself free from the energy web or use his powers to heal D'trav, Parian watched the girl-child lay her cheek, oh-so-

softly, against the man's chest. To the dull accompaniment of sobbed remorse, the moment stretched towards eternity.

At last the child stepped back and held out her hand expectantly towards the dead man.

The whisper that was D'trav lifted free of his body, and a great sadness filled his face as he stared at Sarenka. He mouthed a single word, *"why?"*

Turning to stare at the girl-child, his face transformed like a vessel being filled with the wine of joy.

She giggled and jumped, landing in his outstretched arms with the agility of a fawn.

He caught the child's body against his chest and cradled her for a moment before turning towards the door, sparing not a glance for the Freni-Kyn whose whimpering cries of grief still echoed behind him.

As he stepped through the wooden door the time stream faded, and Parian fell to his knees within the symbolic triangle. He looked to the fuel and was surprised to find it had barely been touched.

"I've failed. Oh Kyron, forgive me. I've failed you." He clutched his chest as grief cut a jagged path through it.

~Parian! Wake up! You're sending! And we don't need to share your nightmare,~ Lanion sent, interrupting Parian's laments.

Drawing in an audible breath that was part scream, part strained air, Parian jerked upright. Unsure of where he was, he stared about wildly before clutching the cloak to his chest and falling back onto the blanket-covered pile of sweetgrass. A remnant of tears cooled on his cheeks. He rubbed at them, pushing away both the wet sensation and the sadness. He felt Lanion's questing probe and raised his guards, shutting the Seven off from finding him.

It hasn't happened yet. Or perhaps it has, on another time stream.

But it could still happen, if he didn't get there to stop this chain of events. The next time he'd travel with the names D'trav and Sarenka. That, at least, was something.

The child though. He shook his head sadly. *It's too late for her.*

Sarenka awakened with a start at the sound of a door shutting. After a night plagued by dreams of pale ghosts and assassins carrying Red Pelican daggers, she was glad for daylight, though her head was such a jumble of thoughts and emotions that it felt like a mix of dried leaves and cotton. The previous night's events came rushing back, accompanied by a thud of dread.

With a groan she rolled over.

She either had to kill him or turn him in, and that decision needed to be made today.

The biggest problem was that she knew, beyond a shadow of a doubt, what was in store for D'trav. The guild would make an example of him by torturing him for as long as they could keep his body alive. Then, at the last moment of life, after he'd earned his death a million times over, after he'd begged to die and been denied that pleasure more times than could be counted, after his body was a shattered mass of quivering raw flesh, they'd deliver the killing blow with a Red Pelican dagger. His mutilated corpse would be strung up for the world to see, another ghastly reminder of the power, and the ruthless scope, of the Red Pelican Assassins' Guild.

But why? What horrific act had he committed? What had any of their 'examples' done? She'd heard rumors, of course. One guy skimmed off the top. The other hadn't killed the target he'd given him; a child barely six winters old. Some had tried to leave the business. There were countless reasons, some valid, some less so, but they never told you ahead of time what the targets had done. All she knew was that he'd flagrantly slipped through the snares they'd set for him time and again, giving the Red Pelican yet more reason to despise him, to want to make an example of him.

The thought of D'trav being tortured to death roiled through her vivid imagination, turning her ill enough to forfeit her break fasting meal, but there was no way to avoid turning him in and still save herself from that same, torturous death. She was destined to become the traitor her mother accused her of being when she'd refused to wed for the good of the family. But this time, she was selling out the man who had found her the antidote countless times and had fulfilled his end of the bargain when it would have been easier to oust her.

In fact, he's saved me twice now.

Self-hatred seared her heart, pushing her into action. Yanking on her clothing with force to abrade her skin, she strode into the main room. On the table lay an opened package containing the winter clothing she'd mentioned the evening before, along with a small pile of silver d'yroap. D'trav—*no, not D'trav*—Onglat had to have gotten up earlier than normal to get the clothing. Sarenka closed her eyes, and her stomach churned about in unrelenting turmoil.

Why'd he have to do that, today of all days?

This would be so much easier if he'd remained the disgusting bastard I used to think he was.

This last month he had been especially... A parade of bitterly pleasant memories ran through her mind.

She gritted her teeth, already regretting what she was about to do, and closed off the part of her that cared. Tugging the cloak from the pile, she threw it over her shoulders and left the hut without eating, heading towards an old, burned-out house. She sifted her way through the charred landscape towards a skeletal back door where wooden posts rose from the ground like the grizzly remains of tilting rib cages, picked clean by scavengers. She couldn't help but think how much the building was like her own heart.

Burned out.

Empty.

Without hope.

From the doorway, she walked a measured pace to a spot she'd prayed never to return to. One she'd last seen the week after the washerwomen were killed. Kneeling to dig at the dirt with her knife brought forth an unexpected sob of heartache.

Oh Kyron… why… why… so much death… and always my fault.

She clutched the fabric of her bodice leaned forward, desperate to ease the stabbing pain. Long moments passed before she could draw breath.

"This won't do. Follow orders—live. Disobey orders—die. It's simple."

Resolute, she scrubbed a hand across her cheek, leaving behind a dirty smear.

Unearthing a simple wooden coffer, she opened it and withdrew a heavily greased dagger, followed by a thin triangle of flat metal. She stared for a moment at the emblems of her job, emblems of her life, emblems she'd walk away from if she could. Twisting several wide leaves from a nearby plant, she wiped away the grease before withdrawing a rag from her skirt and polishing the blade. The eyes of the pelican, carved into the coral inlaid hilt, stared accusingly at her. She shudder.

No one escapes the eye of the Red Pelican.

Not me.

Not D'trav.

Turning her attention to the triangular death card, she wiped it clean before slipping it into her deck of metal playing cards, a necessary precaution. She could claim to having found the dagger, since they were left behind as warnings or sometimes lost in fights. The death card, however, was never *accidentally* left behind, and none but Red Pelican members would dare carry one. If it was left behind, it was for a reason, one that involved a dead body. A simple spy, she'd fooled herself into thinking she'd never have to use the card. Or so the lie went, the same lie she'd used to convince herself to join the guild in the first place.

As she made her way to a plain warehouse in the merchant division, Sarenka silently rehearsed her words. She slid sideways past the wagon that sat—half-in half-out—of a massive doorway, and scanned the workers for a familiar face. Finding no one she recognized, she made her way towards the underground entrance and was intercepted by a middle-aged man, whose leather vest and stitched armband identified him as the clerk.

"An' what might I help the misses with this fine day? Would you be needing to hire a bit of space here? Or perhaps rent wagon services? We have good strong brutes for helping with loading." Peering at her through round eyeglasses, he patted, then pinched the pockets of his knee-breeches.

Sarenka shifted the palm of her hand in a manner that might have been missed by a less observant person. Filtered daylight flashed across the surface of the embossed death card and caught on the eye of the pelican in a small wink of red.

Giving a curt nod, the clerk waved her past the brawny helper who stood nearby, idly sweeping dirt in a seemingly random pattern across the floor.

She took in the sweeper's stout form, six fingered hands, and the hood that hid his ears, knowing that though the M'hakru's eyes never rose from the ground, he was watching and would kill her on the spot if she did anything suspicious, probably faster than she could see his hand move.

Upon reaching a massive crate that appeared to have been there forever, she grasped an edge and slid it easily aside, grateful for the hidden wheels. She stared into the gaping maw that had been revealed, a staircase leading into the inner offices of the Red Pelican Assassins' Guild, and warily began her descent. From behind came a rumble as the crate slid back into place, followed by the scratching *whisk* of a broom as dirt was pushed around its base.

With false confidence she marched forward, keenly aware of the loud click of her shoes against the polished surface beneath her feet. Sarenka concentrated on a bored expression, and her eyes darted past faces of both strangers and acquaintances. Not daring to let herself be distracted, she focused on reaching her objective: the leader who'd be expecting her report.

She stopped in front of her first obstacle—a blond haired, blue eyed man sitting on a stool.

Burk glanced up from flipping through a document, and a sudden dazzling smile replaced the former boredom. "Well heeello, lovely one, long time you've been gone."

"Shut it Burk, I need to give my report." Sarenka tipped her head towards the dark tant-wood door behind him. "He in?"

The charismatic smile Burk put on when trying to win favors vanished. "My, my, aren't we in a mood? Yeah. He's in. But he's busy so give me the report. I'll pass it on."

Sarenka sighed. She should have known Burk would want to appear important. "No, I need to pass it to him this time. When will he be free? I only have a couple of hours before I'll be missed."

Burk let his eyes traverse to her feet before coming back up to her eyes.

Inwardly Sarenka cringed. He had to be noticing that she looked healthy, not like someone on the run.

"You didn't show up after the murder, thought the drugs might have killed you."

"Well, they didn't. I found a source for the antidote. Obviously, you didn't search very hard for me. Were you hoping I'd be strung up?"

"Did you hear? We caught one of Onglat's compatriots." He changed the subject in a transparent effort to deflect attention.

She supposed he was hiding either his own inept search or that he'd been told to let her hang. Whatever he was hiding didn't matter now.

"Soon as he cracks we'll have the Weasel's location."

"Really?" Sarenka covered her surprise by pushing a strand of waving hair out of her eyes and pitched her voice for restrained excitement. "It's about time. Hope they kill the bastard slow, especially since he's going to cost me a promotion."

She knew Burk mentioned the capture to rub her nose in her own incompetence. Acknowledging that failure was the easiest way to circumvent yet more awkward reminders of her ineptitude, and the look of surprise on his face confirmed her beliefs.

"I'm sure it will be as bad as his friend. I heard they scalped him, then covered the bleeding flesh with acid. They're going to tear his nails off next, one by one, then they have this special creature, a vespra-lanir, they're going to let it have a go at his genitals, devour them while he's still alive, then…" he trailed off, distracted by a fistfight down the hall.

"Hey! You two! Break it up. Now, I say!" His booming voice echoed, bouncing off the walls of the unadorned hallway, and he took a step towards the culprits with hands fisted, drawing both the opponents' and their onlookers' attention.

Sarenka gulped back the nausea that had risen to her throat. Positive that she'd gone pale, she pinched color into her cheeks while his back was turned. Resolve shaken, she wondered which was worse, knowing she was about to condemn D'trav to death, or having to live with herself after they tortured him.

As the combatants moved away from each other, Burk turned back to her, changing the subject. "Your… *needs*… been taken care of?"

With effort, Sarenka fell into a familiar role. She rolled her eyes before saying, "Really Burk, this is getting old. Do you see my hands shaking? If my needs hadn't been taken care of, you know they'd be shaking. You aren't my watcher, Burk. Stop trying to chat me up and get me in."

He grinned, this time putting on his innocent-little-boy face. "Can't blame a man for trying Sarenka. You know my offer of sharing your cycle is always open."

"How could I forget? You tell me every time you get a chance."

He shrugged and, without turning around, tapped twice at the door behind him.

At the muffled 'enter' that followed, he swung the door open.

"Sarenka's back, sir. Says she needs to give a report."

After a long, anxious silence, came the simple words that were the first part of her key to safety. "Send her in."

Sarenka entered the elegant office with reluctance. No matter how plush the appearance, the room's stifling closeness weighed heavily, reminding her of a coffin. Her gaze flitted from surface to surface, nothing had changed. Captain Lator sat, a permanent fixture behind a wide length of tant wood desk, with a document and quill. The beauty of his long golden hair, pulled back in a tidy braid, and his elegant, pointed ears, adorned in simple nighsk studs, was negated by the strict tailoring of the traditional Frevell suit he always wore. In another setting, in other clothing, his Frevellian heritage might have made him a handsome man. But here, in this office, he was jury and executioner.

He didn't bother looking up, but instead left her standing by the door for longer than he ever had in the past, a sure sign of displeasure.

With growing unease, she waited until the captain waved towards an overstuffed leather seat before perching on the front edge. As his emotionless eyes scanned a document, her mind betrayed her, replaying D'trav's acts of kindness over the last three months. D'trav had taken better care of her than her own family ever had.

"Well?" the Captain asked, still not looking at her.

Sarenka's resolve crumbled. She couldn't do this to D'trav, but if she didn't give them proof of her loyalty, her own life was forfeit. She'd come expecting to win favor and remove herself from danger. Instead she would become a traitor to the Guild, and she had mere moments to find a solution.

"I failed, Captain. No sign of him at the manor."

No, she wouldn't turn him in, she'd do the unthinkable and kill him herself. Like the shuffle of playing cards, killing strategies flipped through her mind in rapid succession, landing on poison. The night before had proven she couldn't slit his throat. After standing over him with a drawn blade for what seemed like forever, she'd gone to a bed of troubling dreams.

Poison was the answer. He'd fall asleep, never knowing she'd slipped it to him or the pain of betrayal. To avoid guild repercussions she needed a plausible reason for owning the poison and slipping it to him. It could be done, with the right herbalist.

"Yes, botched it, I would say." His eyes remained glued to the document. "You know you won't get paid for that, of course."

"Yes sir."

His eyes finally rose in a bird of prey sweep over her body before leveling on her crimson eyes. "Why did you kill an ally?"

She cleared her throat, nervous that the focus had turned to the death of the baron, instead of her failed objective.

"He drugged me with Foreveron and didn't trim my nails." She held up her hand, flexing the fingers so that the blades of her nails slid clear of the nail-beds. "I have no memory of the kill."

What she thought at first was a grin spread across his face, forcing her to suppress a shudder when she realized it was a silent snarl.

CHAPTER 56

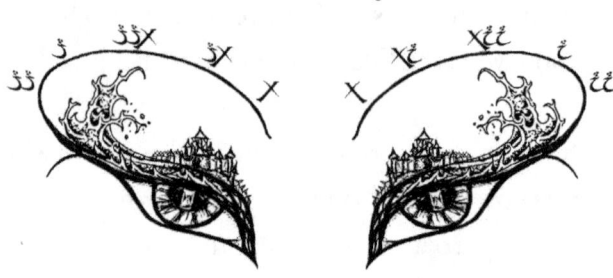

Lator moved a hand down his countenance, replacing the monstrous mockery of a smile with the detached look he usually wore. Now that she knew what it hid, that face, the one she'd always thought meant careful neutrality, took on a new macabre meaning.

"Why now, Sarenka? Why show up now? Why not months ago?"

Sarenka licked dry lips as her plan slid into place. "I was addicted to the Foreveron, had all the withdrawal symptoms. I thought maybe, when he'd heard what I'd done, that he'd attempt contact. So I visited the bars for weeks, just like any normal person."

"In disguise."

"Yes." She didn't drop her eyes, though the urge was there.

His own went back to the document. "And?"

"Never showed up and never made contact, even though I let my identity be known to the people I thought might be sympathetic to him."

"Yet you are clean, decently clothed, and in obvious good health. How is that?" Picking up the quill, he dipped it carefully in an inking shell before scratching it across the parchment.

That Captain Lator only half-listened, writing while he talked, boded ill.

"I... my cycle... I took a man. I've been with him ever since. We had an... arrangement. He got the antidote. I provided for his needs."

Despite her determination to give no outward sign of the cloaking half-truths, Sarenka stiffened.

He didn't respond. His pen scratched across the parchment, and the silence drew out, leaving her wondering if he'd heard. Forcing herself to draw steady breaths, she waited while he finished writing. Yet when he spoke, she was so startled that she jumped.

"Sign in. Go see your watcher. We should have another job for you soon."

She cleared her throat, hoping the sudden tremble in her hands wasn't visible. It had been far easier than she expected to feed him the lies. The next one was the most dangerous. "I've got a lead on Onglat, sir. A connection I made at the Yellow Stain started talking. I'd like the time to explore that lead. Shouldn't take more than a week and... after that I-I need some time off. A year, probably."

Lator's pale blue eyes lifted, staring into hers without taking away from the inscrutable expression on his face. He was the most enigmatic person she'd ever met. A perfect example of what a Red Pelican Assassin was supposed to be.

"I've been ill in the mornings. I'm..."

His gaze drifted towards her stomach.

"You should have come in for the matings. That would never have happened here." For the first time a trace of anger edged his voice, though his face remained a deafening mask of calm.

"I was afraid I was being watched, caught a follower a couple of times. Needed to look like a simple addict, just in case it was Onglat." Her lies were stacking up. If they got uncovered she was dead, and that death would be every bit as painful as the one she knew they planned for Onglat.

"This will mean a twin demotion."

One for failing the mission. One for the baby. From the moment she decided to feign being with child she'd expected this. Pregnancy, or lack of control as it was considered to be, was not acceptable.

"One year, Sarenka, that is all. The brat belongs to us. Make sure to bring it with you when you come back. Send Burk in on your way out." The captain dismissed her by scratching out a quick succession of words across his parchment.

She waited several turns of a minute glass before opening the door and stepping into the hallway. Feeling as if she'd been held underwater to her lungs' limit, she drew a deep breath. After the stifling office, the hallway air was refreshing, clean, wholesome even. She took no time to savor the victory and barely noticed the strange expression on Burk's face, instead her mind raced ahead.

He'd captured one of Onglat's men, which meant that her game could end at any moment. She had to lay down the winning pieces before time ran out.

Tonight.

I'll do it tonight.

As Sarenka traversed the labyrinth of underground halls and offices which comprised the Burmtin headquarter division of the Red Pelican, Burk stepped into the captain's office.

"Yes, Sir?"

"You heard?" Lator's steely blue eyes burrowed into Burk's, demanding truth.

Burk's face colored and he cleared his throat nervously. "Yessir."

"Follow her. She's holding something back. Find out what it is. Take her out if necessary." The death sentence was given without emotion or gesture. Her life was insignificant, a troublesome insect.

"Yessir!"

Outside the room he rubbed the inside of his elbow across his brow, mopping at the profuse nervous sweat and took off down the hall in a rush. He rounded a corner at a near run but, upon catching sight of Sarenka, turned aside to chat with one of the new trainees, disguising his pursuit behind seemingly casual conversation.

Burk stood in the shadows across from the squalid hut Sarenka had entered and frowned.

Damn the girl, putting me on the spot like this.

A H'euman male with a limp entered, in all appearances a commoner, nothing suspicious, but Burk knew better than to leave off this quickly. Giving the accomplice a knowing nod, he faded back into the shadows, and within the hour he had personally placed a series of spies to watch the couple day and night.

We'll have it worked out soon enough. If she's even up to something and not just stupid as a rock.

Shame to kill her.

Little more sweet talk and her next cycle…

He pictured Sarenka draped across his bed, gesturing him closer, then shrugged.

Oh well.

Win some, lose some.

Not like I've got problems with the ladies. Just curious…

If even half the rumors are true…

He grinned, imagining the wild night he'd have.

An hourglass turn later, D'trav stepped out the door and started across town towards Camille's brothel. He caught a slight movement within a nearby shadow, but his stride went on uninterrupted. Mind at instant alert, unwilling to let the watcher know he'd been spotted, D'trav shot glances from shadow to shadow, hiding the scans behind casual movements. He continued across town, watching for followers and assuring himself that every stranger he passed was just that; a random passerby.

He's watching the house but didn't bother following me.

Sarenka's in danger!

Looping back around, he stalked towards the hut by a different path, securing a vantage point for observing the stranger.

The man shifted from foot to foot continually, looking bored and foot sore.

Lured in by the watcher's lax attitude, D'trav crept forward, determined to take him out.

The stranger's shoulders stiffened, and he leaned forward intently.

D'trav's eyes narrowed, and his gaze shot past the man, catching sight of Sarenka exiting the hut. *Damn me, if she don't look like she's goin' shoppin' with that basket over her arm. If I told her once...*

He gritted his teeth as the sudden urge to catch up with Sarenka grated through his body.

She's risking everything.

Again.

Drawing a calming breath, he forced himself to stand his ground instead of chasing her down and shaking some sense into her.

Like that would do any good anyway.

He almost snorted. Sarenka had long ago figured out that he was all bark and no bite when it came to her. If this person was intent on robbing them, now was the time.

The man leaned against the wall and released a huge yawn.

D'trav slipped further back into the shadows and ran his hand back and forth across the line of his beard, considering the implications.

So... a spy...

Only one group interested in me...

He worked his way across town until he reached the Distinguished Dainties and circled it twice. When he was positive no one was watching the place, he rushed through the back door.

"Camille!" he shouted, hurrying down the hall and peering through open doorways.

"Camille!"

A door slammed behind him.

He spun, drawing his sword, and found only an empty hallway. A noise from the other direction made him spin again, sword out, snarl lifting one side of his lip.

Camille froze with his sword under her chin.

He pulled it away and stood there panting.

Her face went white and she raised a hand to her forehead. "D'trav, what in the name of darkness has gotten into you?"

"There anyone here?"

"You mean clients? No."

"Nobody else?"

"Just the renters. You look ill. What's going on?"

"Not here. Somewhere private."

"Dante!" she called.

The Shepherd came bounding around a corner, tail wagging, ribbon bedecked, and licked D'trav's hand.

"Put that away and come with me." She gestured towards his sword before leading him to her office.

With reluctance, he sheathed the weapon, but his hand never left its hilt, even after she had closed the door behind them.

"These walls are double thick, but keep your voice down. You'll frighten the renters. Bad for business." She sat in the chair and stared at him from across the whitewashed desk.

D'trav glanced around the room. He'd always thought the pink padding on the walls was just another of Camille's extravagances, but he should have known better. She did everything for a reason. "The Red Pelican's found me. I've gotta get out of Burmtin today. Can you help me?"

Camille stood, hand to her throat. "What? No! Are you sure?"

Dante whined, looking back and forth between them.

"I've got men on my house, and the shame of it is they aren't lookin' to rob us." He blinked, and then half grinned at the irony. "Now that'll be words I never thought would cross my lips."

She sat so fast and hard that D'trav feared she was fainting, but when he started to go to her, she waved him away.

Dante nudged her hand and whined again.

"Okay, okay, let me think. You need guards paid off at the gates. I'll have that done within an hourglass turn. I've got clothing and travel things you can take. How much coin do you need?"

"Don't worry about the guard or the coin. I've got somethin' set up for emergencies already. We have a worse problem."

"Which is?" She seemed borderline exasperated.

"I've gotta go back by the hut. That's what I need help with."

"No! You can't. Leave your stuff. Nothing's worth the risk."

"Sarenka's there. I won't leave her to be tortured by those—" he abruptly shut up, half afraid that if he started saying what he thought of the Red Pelican, the rage would take him, and he'd do something stupid.

"Knew that bitch would be the death of you. But do you listen? No. Of course not." She began pacing. "Fine. I've got a few tricks up my sleeve. Expect a wagon crash outside your hut. I'll make sure enough people show up to create a bit of a mess. You should be able to sneak out then."

"Thank you, darlin. I'll repay you. I promise."

"Stop talking. I'm not done. That won't be enough to get you to the gates. There'll be a fire on the east side of town. I've got a side business there that I'm tired of dealing with. It's isolated enough that nothing else should catch, but they'll still ring the alarms. That should pull most able-bodied people away from the streets. This is going to take me"—she tapped her bottom lip, thinking—"three hourglass turns. Maybe a little longer. Be ready to go."

Reaching into a drawer, she pulled out a pocket-watch and held it by its chain. "You know how to use one of these?"

"Yes. But keep it. Draw too much attention for some lowlife like me to have one of those contraptions. I'm a good judge of time. I'll be ready. I've just gotta let a few people know what's goin' down, and pack a couple of bags."

"Too dangerous, give me the names and I'll see it done."

D'trav blanched and shook his head. "No. Can't put you in that kinda danger. We've got us a plan for situations like this here. Just gotta talk with one man. He'll carry the tale to the rest."

"Be careful, D'trav. Please." Camille's eyes turned sad. "I'm going to miss you."

D'trav pulled Camille close and cradled her face in his hands. "I'll come back. I promise." He watched her fight back tears and felt helpless to console her. They were pragmatic enough to know that his vendetta was more likely to end in death than with a happily ever after.

"You better come back, or I'll come hunting you. If you think the Red Pelican is persistent…" She let the words hang unfinished, and though she smiled, he could see the pain behind her eyes.

He stared at her, unsure how to say goodbye.

"Kiss me, you lump." She drew him close in a passionate kiss.

As the moment turned bitter-sweet he pulled away, ending it with small, poignant farewell kisses. Stepping into the hallway, he was surprised to see one of the gigolos lounging against the wall. He glanced worriedly at Camille.

Her lips tightened, she'd be careful of the man. "Next time I'll need more than a quickie, luv," she said loudly and threw D'trav a playful wink.

"Any time, darlin."

"A little chain play maybe?" She gave his ass a swatting pinch.

Spinning on his heel, D'trav shoved her up against the wall. He grasped her hands and held them above her head before plunging his tongue into her mouth.

She responded by pushing her hips forward and exaggeratedly grinding her pelvis against his.

He released her as quickly as he'd grabbed her, and turned to walk down the hallway, throwing over his shoulder with a grin, "Course, darlin."

"Don't forget I need you here early on the morrow," she called after him.

"I'll be here."

Nearing Randy, he gave the gigolo a curt nod.

Randy's face was flushed, and the look he turned on D'trav was filled with promises. When he spoke it was sultry and low, meant for D'trav's ears only. "You can play with me like that any time you want, lover boy."

D'trav forced a slanting, good-humored smile and gave him another nod, but his eyes narrowed after passing Randy. The man might not be a turn-coat, but his presence in the hallway was suspicious enough for them to have flung themselves into roleplay, despite the precious time it took. He was positive that their little act would throw off all suspicion, and that Camille would come through for him. Though she hated Sarenka, she was a practical sort that would put his safety above romance.

The thought of Camille, and romance, brought a frown to his face. He'd been increasingly aware of how much she cared for him, and that, in turn, brought an uncomfortable and confusing warmth to his body. She was the only person in Burmtin he'd miss. If he hadn't known how much it endangered her safety, he might have considered settling down with her.

Maybe one day I'll come back for her.

Maybe.

If I manage to survive.

Sarenka worked her way towards the local herbalist who had set up shop in the warehouse district. If anyone knew how to poison someone painlessly, he did. Stepping into a crowded room filled with hanging herbs, Sarenka stifled a large sneeze, letting out a little 'peep' instead. Eyes watering, she took shallower breaths.

Kyron! I hate these places; they always make me feel like I'm drowning.

"Hello," she said.

A rustling noise drew her around a ceiling-high stack of seasoned kegs. Nothing but a huge bin lay on the other side.

"Hello?" She said, raising her voice, and wondered if she'd imagined the noise.

The rustle came from behind the bin, drawing her forward once more. Heart pounding, muscles tensing, she prepared to flee or fight. A cat jumped from the bin and landed in front of her, startling Sarenka into a backwards scramble.

It cocked its head sideways before walking towards her.

She shifted backwards uneasily.

Cats too? Kyron's thirteen hells, I need to get out of here.

"Hello!" she shouted.

"No need to yell, young miss, I kin hear just fine." An elderly man, with a heavy commoner's drawl, worked his way out from behind a pile of neatly stacked boxes. What was left of his hair had been combed to one side, and his leathery skin seemed to exude grime from its pores. He patted his hand against the side of his stained apron, sending a billow of dirt into the air, and convincing her that he was, indeed, nothing but a great H'euman dust-making machine.

The thought brought a brief grin before another sneeze broke free, this one coming on so suddenly, so unexpectedly, that it escaped in an abrupt explosive burst.

"Excuse me. I'm sorry." She pinched her nose, trying to ward off the incessant tickle that seemed to have moved in like an unwelcome relative in the middle of winter.

"So, I'll be takin' it, you've done found yourself in a heap of need."

"Excuse me?"

"When a person done been caught up with somethin' they ought not to be, it kin take a mighty special somethin' else to fix things. If'n you know what I mean." He winked at her conspiratorially and rubbed his hands together.

Sarenka's skin went cold under the illusions.

He knows!

He's one of them.

Somehow they knew I'd come here, and he's here to remind me to do the right thing.

A warning.

In a pretense at smoothing down her skirt, she slipped her hand into the folds and grasped the dagger hilt. "And what special something would you recommend?"

"Now don't you be worrin' yourself none, we'll get you right fixed up in no time. I've got just the potion what'll kill off that sneezing sickness once and fer all." He patted her arm with such a freezing cold hand, that Sarenka realized he wasn't rubbing his hands together because he wanted her to offer a bribe, he was trying to warm them.

She let out a relieved breath. He wasn't Red Pelican after all.

"No. No, I'll be fine. I just need something to kill rats. Only I don't want them to suffer," Sarenka blurted out, impatient to get what she'd come for and go.

The cat wandered closer.

Sarenka shifted position, putting the man between her and it.

Pursing his lips, the elderly man looked her up and down. "Why would you be carin' if the varmints be a suffering?"

"Well..." She blinked, momentarily at a loss for words.

"You one of those crazies what be feedin' the rats? That'll get you fined, and fer good reason."

"No! Never! But just because I want a creature dead, doesn't mean I want it to suffer. I was thinking, something that made them fall asleep, and not wake up." Rubbing at her watering eyes, she added with a pleading note of desperation, "Please, do you have something?"

The silence hung between them.

She tried to appear nonchalant and gazed about the herbalist shop. One day she'd discover what always triggered the spring sneezing in these types of places.

"So, you're just wantin' them to drift off to sleep, real cozy like, and never know what hit 'em, right?" A trace of sarcasm edged the herbalist's voice.

Sarenka nodded, shifting attention from the room to his face. *Is he starting to suspect?*

He returned her questioning stare with a frank one of his own.

"I do be thinkin' I have just the right thing fer you. Be careful with it though, t'would kill a grown size man, if'n it were to, accidentally like, make its way into food." He peered at Sarenka from under bristled eyebrows with such a piercing stare that she was convinced he'd figured her out. But without another word, or waiting for an answer, he shuffled off. Plucking a bottle from a back shelf, he paused long enough to blow away a heavy coating of dust, eliciting another sneeze from Sarenka. "Ten silver loops fer the bottle."

Sarenka's mouth dropped open. "What? That's just ridiculous. It's for killing rats, for Kyron's sake!"

He licked his leathery lips, but instead of wetting them, they looked even drier. "I do be havin' a cheaper one, but it don't never make 'em sleep, be right painful, tis."

Sarenka shook her head.

"Their mouths start up frothin' an—" He began slowly setting the bottle back down.

"No."

His hand stopped, hovering over the shelf.

"I'll take it, and one more. Two bottles."

A look of smug satisfaction settled over the old man's face.

Counting out the loops, she snatched the bottles from his hand and headed out the door.

With dinner.

That's when I'll do it.

CHAPTER 57

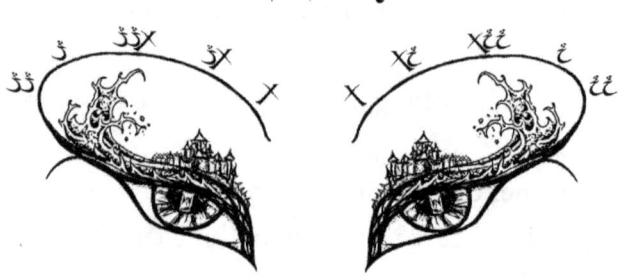

Burk approached the captain's office with trepidation. It was bad enough that he'd been caught eavesdropping, but now he had to carry in bad news. That alone was enough to make any agent break into a cold sweat. With no time to waste on a bath, he hoped that his body odor didn't throw him into further disfavor.

Lance slipped out the door, closing it softly behind him as Burk drew closer. He leaned against it and fanned himself with the document he was holding. "That man…"

Mistaking the gesture, Burk grimaced. "He angry already?"

"What? No. Well, not at me anyway. I dare say I've earned a promotion with my bit of news. But the heat he stirs in me… it's just—" he brushed his hand back through his hair, striking a pose— "unbearable. I could use some release, and you could use a bath. I've got two hourglass turns before I'll be on duty, care to join me down at the coast?"

Burk snorted. "Not hardly. I'll be lucky if I live through the next few minutes."

"Well, if you change your mind…" Lance pushed himself off the wall and sauntered away.

Burk gave the door a brisk tap and straightened his clothing.

"Ow! Son of a—" a man exclaimed from down the hall.

Burk turned in time to see one of the new recruits rubbing his ass and glaring at Lance's retreating back. Despite his trepidation at going into the office, Burk snickered. Any man who had been here a while knew not to bend over when Lance was around.

"Enter!"

The demand jarred him back to the moment. Turning the knob, he edged the door open and was surprised to find the Captain staring at him instead of looking at documents.

"What did you find out?" Lator demanded, without waiting for Burk to speak.

"She's living with a H'euman, bald man with inks on his left cheekbone, tribal, probably Sharpra origin. Slight limp, think he may be lame. They get visitors at strange hours, always come to the back door, drop off packages, take packages." Burk spoke in rapid succession, not bothering to cover his nervousness. It was pointless—Lator would see through it in a heartbeat—and concealing it might be construed as a sign of deception.

"How are packages in broad daylight considered odd?"

"Sorry sir. I was trying to be brief. Street kids, they'll tell us anything for a sweetstick, said they can't sleep in that alley anymore, too many people coming and going at night with packages."

"And it was confirmed with the neighbors?"

"Yessir. Insomniac lives in the hut behind them. Says they have visitors coming and going all hours."

Captain Lator tapped a random pattern on the desktop and stared off into space.

Burk shifted his feet, wondering how much longer he should stand there waiting, or whether he should just leave.

"Any pattern to the drop-offs?" The captain unstoppered a scent vial and dribbled some into his candle, filling the closed space with the aroma of lenan spice.

"No sir. Not that we can tell from what the neighbors say. Some nights nothing, some nights several visitors. I'll keep someone on it till we find the pattern, of course." Corner of his eye twitching, Burk stared fixedly at the scent vial before remembering to return his gaze to his leader's face. That he smelled bad enough for his leader to so pointedly use the expensive oils surely meant a demotion.

"Follow them. The visitors too. Track them all."

After Burk left, Lator sat in the silent room, fingers steepled before his face, putting together all the bits of information he'd received that day. The candle on his desk guttered, nearly going out before springing back to life, painting his face with flickering shadows. Coming to a decision, he reached for his quill, along with a fresh sheet of parchment, and scratched out:

I think we've found him. Prepare an interrogation room for two.

He folded the letter with precise care and poured wax into the center before twisting off his ring, breathing on the surface, and pressing it into the red puddle. Counting out the seconds before rocking the ring free, he examined the imprint, satisfied with the crisp impression of a pelican in flight. He scribbled a false name beneath the seal and scratched a salutation on the other side, where his signature should have gone, finishing the illusion that he didn't know how to properly address a message.

Annoyance with the lack of proper etiquette, which went against all his formal Frevell training, caused him to shake his head. Even he, with all his rank, was required to follow the rules.

After exchanging his outer garments for a weathered merchant's jacket, he touched a hidden button on the edge of one of his many mirrors and listened to the clicks as the mechanism sprang into action, unveiling a secret passage.

When he reached the Scarlet Scroll—a discreet postal shop with access to the Glidarthian flight service—the merchant at the desk greeted him with his usual banter. Soon, the letter had been bundled, double sealed, and was on its way. Though it had to travel half the continent, it would arrive by nightfall.

After leaving, Captain Lator stopped by his favorite bordello and ordered three bedmates sent over. Indulging in the rare wine of satisfaction, a flit of a smile touched his lips.

I'll be promoted for this capture... a sweet, sweet revenge.

Glancing at the hourglass, Sarenka gave the spit one last turn, searing the venison. She sat back to wait and anxiously smoothed the wrinkles from her skirt. Through the course fabric the cold glass reached, death pressing at the veil of life, stopping the downward sweep of her hand.

Her fingers lingered over the concealed vials and she bit her lip as the nagging worry returned.

What if even two bottles wasn't enough?

He deserves this...

A last good meal...

A peaceful death.

Just let it be enough.

Her training as a spy required combat and subterfuge, not poison dosage.

D'trav walked in the door carrying rolled up burlap sacks and surveyed the room, eyes shifting from surface to surface before settling on the roasting venison. His stomach rumbled, loud in the quiet space. "Get your things packed. We're moving."

"What? Why?"

"Just get packed. Only one bag's worth." Tossing a burlap sack towards her, he moved to the foot of his bed and snapped open the lock on the trunk. Clothing landed around him in rumpled piles as he dug through the trunk.

It was pointless to keep asking questions. Whenever D'trav gave orders like this, he wouldn't talk again until they were obeyed. Sarenka picked up the bag and walked towards her room, pointedly ignoring the white flutter out of the corner of her eye. The last few months of seeing and hearing things that weren't there had almost inured her to that distraction.

She opened her drawer and stared in without seeing. The truly important items, like the cache of antidote vials, had been carefully wrapped in fabric and secured within her cloak earlier that day. The rest would only be a dull reminder of what she'd lost. Halfheartedly grabbing a few meager belongings, she returned to the main room and gave a dispirited shrug before dropping them next to his.

Staring at his belongings, she decided that it wasn't a complete waste of time. She wouldn't have to sort out the valuables, he'd already done that for her. She need only throw them over her shoulder and leave town. In a year she'd tell the Red Pelican that the babe had died at two months. Perhaps by then her heart would lose its ache over killing someone who was more family than her brothers had ever been.

"I'm packed. Why are we moving?"

"Cause they've found us."

Despite guild training, Sarenka's heart thudded to the bottom of her stomach. There was only one 'they' in her life, but surely he didn't mean *them*. "Who, D'trav? Who found us?"

"The Red Pelican. Now grab yourself some victuals. We'll be hidin' out for a few days, and I'll not have you puckish... least not till—" Grunting, he heaved his storage trunk over and opened a compartment Sarenka had missed. He pulled free a leather satchel, straining with its obvious weight, and heaved it across the room. With the unmistakable sound of jingling loops, the satchel landed next to the burlap bags.

Sarenka's heart raced and her cheeks went cold.

They've found Onglat...

But don't know I'm here with him?

D'trav took one look at her face and murmured, "It's gonna be okay, Sarenka, I've got us a way out."

She tried to breathe but couldn't.

The hourglass continued its slow trickle as the moments stretched out, surreal. D'trav stepped towards her. White fluttered from the distant corner, impossible. The meat sizzled, dropping bits of fat into the leaping flames.

I should turn it. It'll burn.

Her breath returned, ragged in the quiet room.

Grasping her arm, his warmth a fire against her clamminess, D'trav guided her to a chair.

He thinks I'll panic…

Panic's not a friend…

It causes mistakes…

And mistakes get your throat slit as surely as pigs get run through the slaughter gauntlet.

"How'd they find us?" she asked.

"Don't know, must've made a mistake," D'trav answered.

Sarenka realized that she'd spoken aloud.

They must have followed me.

I've brought death to our very doorstep.

"Camille's arranged for a wagon accident and a bit of a stink. Soon as that starts up, we slip out. This time of day, common well's as crowded as a dock whorehouse, so there oughta be enough millin' about to hide our movement."

"That won't be enough."

"It will. Camille's sendin' more, plus stagin' some other ruckus to keep the watch busy."

"How—" her voice cracked on the word, "how will we escape? They're everywhere, every city."

"One thing at a time, Sarenka. First we escape Burmtin. Next we find somewhere safe to hide from the Red Pelican."

D'trav scrutinized the room before pulling the charred meat from the fire and setting it on the table. Steam rose from its surface in billowing waves as he sliced through it. Without bothering with the niceties of dishes or utensils, he held out a chunk for her. Blackened around the edges, blood dripped from the raw center, pooling on the tabletop, a reminder of the death that had started her down this path months ago.

One moment of fate, a mistake that wasn't mine...

And now we're destined to die.

Staring at the blood, her hand went to her throat as a scream fought to break free.

A quick death by poison...

Or a horrible, gruesome type of death...

Doesn't matter...

Still death.

He shook the knife, bringing her back from the edge. "Take it Sarenka. We need to eat while we can."

She flinched, shifting away from the dangling chunk of meat. "No. I-I can't."

"If you want my help escapin' you will! I'll not be luggin' someone about who doesn't have the sense to eat when they've got the chance."

Kyron! If they catch me with him... the torture. She grasped her skirt, clutching the empty bottles through the fabric, and wondered if it was enough poison to kill them both. *Far better that quick death than what the Red Pelican will do to us.*

"Damnation Sarenka. Take it!"

Grabbing the meat from the knife tip, she crammed it into her mouth, then spit it out into her hand.

His brows went up.

She tossed the meat back and forth between her hands, cooling it.

Slicing free another piece, he took a cautious bite.

He was right, of course. If they were going into hiding, it could be days before they ate again, especially if they ended up having to ditch their bags. Of course, that wouldn't matter if they died of poisoning first.

The two chewed in silence until Sarenka noticed a funny expression on D'trav's face. "What's wrong?"

He wrinkled his nose. "Tastes kinda odd like. You sure it was fresh?"

"I tried some different herbs. And it's still half raw."

He dug in with earnest, tossing back bites and blowing out mouths of steam around the meat before grinning at her with satisfaction.

"And now you look like you've won a bet," she said, faintly annoyed.

"I did. With myself." His grin turned into a wide smile. "Guess you do know how to eat like a normal person after all, *m'lady*."

Her annoyance flared higher, and she set down her knife, leaving the last bite for him. "We could die at any time, and you choose now to mock my eating habits?"

He snickered. "Looks like I'm creatin' one undignified monster."

They were brought back to the gravity of the moment by the sound of a loud crash outside their door, followed by angry voices. At that signal, the two stood. Camille had done what she'd promised, creating the first distraction. Tossing the last bite into his mouth and picking up his bags, D'trav peered out the front door then waved her forward.

Sarenka grabbed her pack and gave a quick shrug of dismissal.

Mistaking her shrug for a ready signal, D'trav slipped out the door.

She followed, noting a spiral of smoke rising from a fire on the other side of town. *Fire in the mercantile section. Good idea. The Watch'll take care of that before even thinking about dealing with a rumble in Sad Town.*

In front of the hut, two wagons lay smashed together in a tangle of splintered wood and canvas, one laying precariously on its side. The owners shook angry fists and screamed obscenities at each other. Goods from the wagons lay scattered across the cobblestones, creating a free-for-all in the frenzied crowd. Street children slipped through onlookers' legs, filching vegetables, tools, and other finds before darting away like beads of quicksilver.

More people rounded the corners of buildings, hurrying to join the fray. A pack of dogs arrived, bounding through the crowds and snatching up prize pieces of meat. Sarenka recognized Beast\Dante and started to call him to her side but changed her mind. She couldn't endanger the Shepherd that way. Packages in hand and confused expressions on their faces, three Glidarths glided into awkward landings, buffeting onlookers with their painted wings.

Behind the tumultuous crowd, abandoned but for one man, the well stood out in surreal relief, a reminder to Sarenka of how far she'd traveled in the last year. The pendulum of her journey had swung from desperation, to hope, to despair, and now all she wanted was an end to it all. No more running, no more fear, just peace. Through it all, the well had been both a source of sustenance and an unavoidable risk. Now, just as the common folk had abandoned it in a wild scrabble for random goods, she too would abandon the past, the well, the city, in a reckless run towards an unsure future. Probably death.

Leaning against the well, feet crossed in front of him and an amused expression on his face, was Tahrek. He caught her eye and gave a quick salute, as if to tell her she was doing the right thing. Next to him the transparent figure of a child flickered into view, her face tilted up to stare at Tahrek. Sarenka rubbed her eyes and looked again, seeing only Tahrek.

D'trav wove through the crowd, pulling Sarenka out of her thoughts, as he worked his way towards a side street. Her gaze darted about; searching for what she knew must be present. At last she found them.

One...

Two...

Three...

Three assassins.

But had they not been searching the crowd instead of participating in the free-for-all, she'd never have noticed them. They wore the dusty breeches, sweat stained shirts, and peace tied weapons of common laborers, though, as she watched, one light haired man tugged at the strings, loosening his blade for use.

Ducking her head, she shifted appearance to a Frevell face. The new, slimmer visage—with skin the color of fresh cream, and stick straight brows slanting up into blue-black hair—was a bold move. One they might not expect. And it could backfire, making her more noticeable in the primarily H'euman city, yet the sheer audacity of choosing that face might throw the Red Pelican off.

She glanced down at her clothing with a grimace, it was all wrong, of course. A Frevell would be wearing a restrictive jacket and tailored skirt, instead of shapeless peasant's clothing that had never been pressed. But this was Burmtin, where people often lost their way and the races took on each other's habits.

Sarenka looked the other way and locked gazes with a woman who had obviously witnessed the shift, Escrach. The woman winked and threw herself into the fray. Behind her, following like a shadow, the mind-lost woman they'd rescued let out an ear piercing scream that had no end.

D'trav jerked Sarenka sideways, taking her out of the crowd and into the shadows of a nearby building. Still feeling as if she was watching life from a distance, she gazed over her shoulder at the well, hoping for one last glimpse of the enigma that was Tahrek. Instead, she caught sight of a child wearing overlarge slippers with turned up toes.

The Red Pelican behind the youth noticed D'trav and surged forward.

The child knelt to pick up a cabbage and his outstretched leg tripped the assassin.

The man flipped forward, landing on his face just in time to be trampled by a string of scurrying children.

Sarenka smiled, but not at the sight of the man falling, her smile was for the youngster.

Clinging to a cabbage with blackened hands, he struggled to stand and tripped over his blacksmith apron. The little beggar had taken her advice after all, though she'd never know why he kept the silly slippers she'd traded for his pick-tools.

The assassin sought to pull himself up, using the boy as an anchor.

The boy's hand balled into a fist and thudded home, striking the man's cheek with enough force to throw the assassin back to the ground.

Though Sarenka knew half the reason it had worked was because of surprise, she was glad to see the child's limbs were no longer skeletal, and that his hair was as clean as any blacksmith's apprentice would be.

D'trav glanced back and gave a start, almost dropping her hand. She watched with amusement as his eyes flitted over her, taking in clothing he knew well. She threw him a knowing wink, and his shoulders relaxed. He turned to working his way down a side street, dodging animal refuse and discarded trash while drawing them ever farther from the shouting curses.

Pulling her into a doorway, he whispered. "I've paid off guards at the west gate. If we get separated, work your way towards it. They're expectin' a H'euman so take a different face before gettin' close. Tell 'em I sent you."

At Sarenka's understanding nod, D'trav moved off at a semi-run, hand clasping hers as he picked up speed.

Fire bells began to clang, calling for all able-bodied to aid in carrying water.

Soon as... corner... stab the... quick. Fragments of words and garbled phrases pierced her mind. Sarenka grabbed her forehead and bent forward with a groan.

Alarmed, D'trav stopped. "What's wrong? You sick?"

"No." She stared at the corner of the building he'd almost stepped around. "Headache. Let's go a different way."

D'trav's eyebrow rose in question. "This is the fastest route."

"It's just... I have a bad feeling about this, let's find a different street."

"That's a helluva mind-lost thing to say, and I don't do anything based on what a person be feelin' at the moment. I set this up earlier. It's the best route, and we're stickin' to it."

Sarenka nodded. He was right. She was mind-lost, just like her brothers always said she was, and his decision was completely logical.

Despite this, she tensed with expectation as they stepped around the blind corner. Crates and barrels lined the abandoned warehouse street. Camille's fire was working like a charm, emptying what would normally be a crowded avenue. She hurried forward, impatient to get to the gate that stood a few hundred feet away.

Movement out of the corner of her eye, and the jingling thump of a d'yroap bag hitting the ground, brought her up short.

She dropped the illusions and the bags, pulling twin daggers from the folds of her skirt.

CHAPTER 58

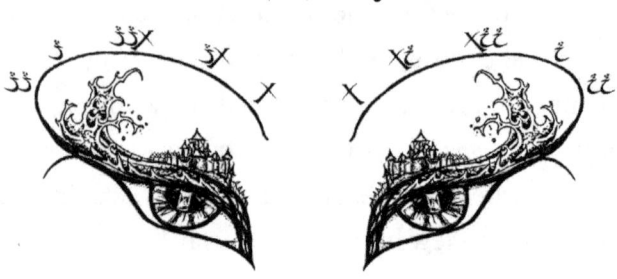

She spun, assessing the situation at a glance, and guild training kicked into gear.

Two men… even odds if I'd kept up my training.

I'm rusty as…

Her undercover position had meant going almost a year pretending to be an ordinary Freni-Kyn. And though she could have run through some practice exercises while D'trav was at work, she'd spent that time learning the art of forgery, searching for a way out of Burmtin, and enjoying what little freedom she could. She'd pay for that lax of caution, but not before she made them work for her death.

With the skill of a well-trained warrior, D'trav swung his bastard sword at the assailant in front of him. Cloak flying out behind, muscles flexing, he whirled through a two-handed stroke designed to remove a limb.

Surprised by D'trav's fast reactions, his attacker jumped backwards, losing the advantage of an inside hit to D'trav's exposed abdomen.

At the sight of her drawn blades, the man who had been rushing to attack Sarenka slowed, feinting to her right. A flash of dull red on the cross guard of his sword drew her attention to the inlaid pelican emblem. If not for the well-honed Red Pelican blade, she'd have thought the assassin a common beggar.

Ragged cloth hung from his gaunt frame in disheveled streaks of brown and gray. His skin was begrimed, and in that strange way that time telescoped when in danger, she noted that his nails looked as if he'd been grubbing in the dirt. Long greasy chunks of hair fell half way down his back. He was either too lazy to cut it himself or favored the tangled mess. But there was nothing lazy about his eyes. Their piercing green depths were calculating her every move.

"Best back off, little man, or you'll be begging through extra holes in your face." She circled, waiting for him to make the first move.

"Give it up, Freni-Kyn, you don't have to die today."

"Right. Let you take me in so they can torture me first? I'd rather die fighting."

"It's your death—" The rag man darted forward, testing her skills.

She dodged to the side, narrowly missing the longer reach of his sword.

A taunting grin lifted the man's lips, and he took several more swings, making her look inept with his finesse.

She dodged the blows, though not gracefully.

Changing tactics, he lunged forward, aiming for her chest with a killing blow.

She twisted sideways, barely escaping the blow.

Unable to stop the momentum, he plummeted past.

The reek of his unclean body lent disgust to her resolve as she undercut, slicing through his rags and striking flesh.

His cocky smile disappeared under a determined sneer.

Ringing clanks and exclamations came from behind, reassuring her that D'trav still battled for his life.

Dust blew through the area, eliciting a sneeze, and in that moment she felt her legs swept out from under her. Mid-fall she flipped over, landing on her back with enough force to knock the breath from her lungs. She braced her daggers defensively, sure that the killing blow was on the way.

Savoring the moment, the ragged man paused, sword poised for the final blow, and a mocking sneer twisted one corner of his mouth.

Panicked, Sarenka fought the freezing grip around her chest, struggling to draw even a thimble of air. She couldn't move fast enough, couldn't defend herself, not lying on her back with the energy draining from her arms.

As the moments slipped away, he gripped the hilt in both hands and slowly lifted his arms higher, raising the sword above his head.

Light caught on the edge of the blade in a flash, momentarily blinding her. A tear trickled down the side of her face. Struggling for breath, arms turning to lead, Sarenka's hands lowered, exposing her chest to the killing blow.

He stabbed towards her heart with lightning speed.

Moments before it would pierce her chest, a sword intercepted the blow, knocking it enough askew that it thudded into the ground next to her, barely missing her throat. With a quick flip of his wrist, D'trav twisted the weapon from the surprised man's hand and sent it flying across the alley. He finished with a return swing towards the man's abdomen, forcing the assailant to throw himself into a rolling jump for his weapon.

Sarenka pulled her knees to her chest and drew a desperate breath.

D'trav stood guard, sword in one hand, dagger in the other, and a soundless snarl on his face. He met her eyes for a fraction of a moment. A shadow fell across her face.

Sarenka stared past D'trav with a growing horror as a figure loomed up, blocking the sun, blade poised for a killing blow.

Alerted, D'trav slung about just in time to stop the sword the larger assailant was aiming at his unprotected back.

The sound of the beggar scrabbling to reach his sword pushed Sarenka into action. She jumped to her feet, searching for any edge that would give her the upper hand.

"Almost had you girl. Next time there won't be someone to rescue you."

Her hair threw off a shower of red sparks. "Don't think so, novice. A year ago I'd have taken you out in minutes."

He jabbed, forcing her to take a step backwards. "Yet now you struggle to keep up. You've grown fat and lazy."

"Well, at least I don't smell like I've been licking ass."

He snarled and gave a savage thrust.

Dodging the blow, she pulled on the knowledge of the street fighting she'd witnessed as a kid, searching for a usable strategy.

The beggar settled into a series of slashing swings, backing her up, step by step, towards a nearby wall.

The longer reach of his sword had her at a disadvantage. She needed to get in under one of his swings, and she was running out of time. Discarded refuse lined the edge of the street, forcing her to keep an eye on the ground and her opponent at the same time. She ducked into a mock fall, grasped a handful of fireplace soot, and threw it at his face.

He staggered backwards, coughing, and raised his arm to rub across blinded eyes.

She gripped his shirt collar with one hand, and yanked him forward, slamming her shoulder into his chest.

He gave an 'umph' as air was forced from his lungs. The force of the maneuver threw his head forward, towards the dagger she'd raised, but the ragged shirt gave way, and, instead of impaling the man's skull from under his jaw, he was left with just a scratch under the chin.

Staggering backwards, his eyes flew open in alarm, and he swung his sword blindly towards her.

Knowing that speed was more important than finesse, she dropped to the ground and kicked the man in the knee.

Though he didn't give the satisfying screech that meant it was broken, he did fall forward onto one knee.

She flipped, shoving him over and pinning his sword arm to the ground with her shin. Her Red Pelican blade sliced through his neck, spraying blood over her clothes and face.

The beggar's free hand went to the gash in his throat.

Dropping her other dagger, she leaned in close and covered his mouth to keep him from crying out.

With a last convulsion, his bloodied hand slid across her face, streaking it red.

As the pounding in her ears slowed, Sarenka became aware of an almost unnatural silence. Fear quickened her into a scrabbling search of the last place she'd seen D'trav. With an accusing look on his face, he stood to the side, leaning on his sword hilt as though it were a cane. His bloodied dagger lay on the ground, forgotten. Next to it, hand severed at the wrist and shirt covered in blood, the other assailant lay. Such a dizzying flood of relief cascaded through her mind that she swayed.

"You're Red Pelican."

Sarenka glanced at the pelican emblem on her dagger and stood. She searched his face, unsure of his reaction, and found the hurt of betrayal. "Spy, not assassin. Yes—and no. Not anymore."

He lifted his sword, holding it ready.

She tensed.

"And you know who I am?"

"Onglat the Slippery." Her hands tightened on her daggers by reflex alone. She was too tired for another fight and wouldn't beat him anyway. What little she'd seen of his fighting abilities, combined with his muscle mass, made him an opponent who would beat her every time. Her only chance against him was surprise, and the time for that had come and gone.

"You turned me in, didn't you?" Anger infused the accusation.

"I considered it. It would have bought a promotion, and a lot of d'yroap too. But no."

D'trav's head dipped until he stared at her from under furrowed brows. "Why?" He growled the word, drawing it out.

Surprised that he seemed angrier at not being turned in, Sarenka flushed, too embarrassed to admit that she valued his friendship.

Instead, she shrugged out a lie. "I owed you one. Come on, we need to go."

Suddenly aware of the taste of blood in her mouth, Sarenka swiped the back of her arm across her lips and spat with disgust. She stared at the assassin's bloody throat, and a wave of dizziness struck.

"Dear Kyron, I've just killed a man. Now I really *am* a murderer."

D'trav grabbed her arm, keeping her from running towards the gate. "Do what you been trained to do girl. Muddy the damn trail. Those men matched us far too closely in skill to have been a chance encounter."

"Then the Red Pelican miscalculated either our training or our strength." She pushed aside the raw emotions and forced herself to wipe blood from her blade across the dead man's rags and rummage through his pockets, searching for Red Pelican emblems. To do anything else would make D'trav suspicious of her motives. Without checking the value of her finds, she added any and everything to her bags.

"Just sayin, there's probably more on their way." D'trav followed her example and collected the short-swords the two men had carried as well.

"Just tell me this D'trav, what did you do to betray the Red Pelican? I'd like to know what I put my life on the line for."

"Killed one of the dogs who murdered my sister. Was gonna take out another one, but you sure as hell threw a smoker into that fire."

Sarenka blinked. She'd thought, with all the forgeries, that his betrayal of the Red Pelican would be something far more selfish. He'd surprised her once more.

"Now, my turn for a question. Why'd you blush just now? What're you hiding?"

His question slowly sank in. *Why did I blush? Why did I find the fact that I like him so embarrassing? Surely now, with death so near, I can be honest. Is it because he's the first man to treat me like a person instead of a possession?* She shook her head. *This is foolish. We'll be dead soon, regardless of what we do. Best not to fog it up with sentimentality.*

"Let's get going. We just have to make it a little longer without getting caught." Sarenka started towards the gates, but D'trav grabbed her arm, smearing the blood that covered it.

"You're bloodied. Can you get your illusions up?" He leaned over to wipe the blood from his hand on the pants of an assailant, then surveyed his clothing for more traces of blood. Other than a few flecks that could have been gotten shaving, and a large splattering across his left arm, he was clean.

She grimaced with distaste at the reminder. "I can try." Closing her eyes, she drew in a few deep, calming breaths before grasping the inborn magics that would change her appearance to H'euman.

He watched the attempt with a frown.

She peered down at her arm. The blue of her skin shown faint through the illusion, making her appear ill.

He pulled her cloak close about her body, hiding her arms and face. "Still showin' through. You've gotta keep this on till we're out the gates, and for Kyron's sake, don't look up. Those red eyes'll have 'em on us like vultures on a carcass." He pulled his own cloak forward over the left side of his body, hiding his bloodied arm.

As they started forward again, she staggered. The use of illusion, after everything she'd been through that day, was so exhausting that she wasn't sure how long she could hold them. It had been months since he'd taken her in, and she'd forgotten how tiring the illusions could become, especially after a fight.

D'trav wrapped his arm around her, half supporting her weight, and moved forward with a limp, taking her down a side path instead of towards the gate.

"You get any more of those *feelins'* of youruns, you make sure and give me a heads up."

A cloaked man rounded the corner and stopped to take in the dismemberment and brutal deaths. He shot a furtive glance down the street for witnesses before checking to see if they were alive. After a careful scrutiny of their bodies, he skirted the area, scouring the ground. At last he stooped to examine a set of footprints leading away from the fight.

His eyes narrowed. They trailed no blood. If they were injured it was minor.

"They'll pay for this…"

"But first, a little blood for my collection." Reaching for his pouch with a six fingered hand, he withdrew a vial and knelt next to the men. He squeezed their wounds, dribbling blood into his vial and gave the corpses a scornful smile.

"I'll see you two on the other side of death. Hope you enjoy being slaves."

He paused to concentrate, shifting into a Half-Frevell with dirty blond hair, and took off for the west gate.

CHAPTER 59

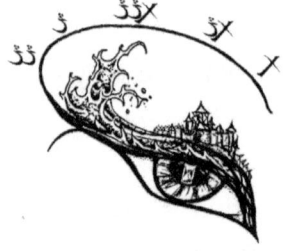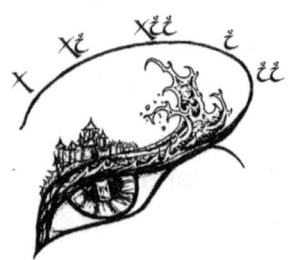

"You should see an herbalist about your leg."

D'trav grunted. "Should've gone when you first told me to."

"I'm sorry."

"For what?"

"For the splinter, for ruining all your plans, for everything."

"Oh, just... put a cork in it," he said impatiently. "What's happened, happened. Can't be tryin' to undo the past."

"How bad is it?" She'd seen him drown out the pain many nights with M'hakru whiskey and knew it had to be bad if he was limping.

"Let's just hope I don't need to fight again."

Fear coursed through Sarenka, and her skin went cold and clammy. If neither of them were able to fight well, their next encounter would be their last.

"Don't let them take me alive." She grabbed his arm, locking eyes with him. "Promise me that."

"I'll take care of both of us, if needs be."

She started forward again. "Till then, we keep going. We only have to make it a little longer."

Parian hovered above the Half-Frevell assassin and watched him select the perfect spot to strike from—an area shadowed by so many different levels of buildings and structural angles that he'd never be sighted. After inserting the five-blade bolt into his crossbow and cranking it tight, the assassin laid it on the stone barricade and leaned forward, sighting along the weapon, making sure he had a clear shot.

Parian threw himself into the air and zoomed through the city. Moments later he was hovering above Sarenka and D'trav. They were bloodied and exhausted, dodging the bolts would be impossible.

He touched D'trav's mind and sent, *~Go another way! Take Rustle Avenue.~*

D'trav plodded steadily on, passing Rustle Avenue.

Too tired…

He's too tired.

Parian turned to Sarenka. If anything she looked more exhausted than D'trav, but he had to try.

~Danger!~ he shouted into her mind. *~Don't take Outer Wall Road!~*

She stumbled and sighed.

~That's right! Outer Wall Road! Danger! Assassins!~

She trudged onwards, leaning against D'trav for strength, giving no sign of having heard.

No!

This can't be happening.

After all this…

They can't be brought down by a simple bolt.

He tried once more to leave an impression, but his energy drained when he touched their minds, and he was forced to withdraw.

He couldn't do this alone. He needed the rest of the Seven, but they weren't with him. Even if he called for help now, they wouldn't hear him from within the time stream. He launched himself into the air again and landed next to the Half-Frevell.

They're almost here!

He'll slay them!

Parian touched his mind and grimaced with understanding.

No, he's not going to kill them.

His positioning in this exact place was more significant than Parian had believed. He planned to slice through enough important areas in their legs that they would be unable to walk. Then he'd take them in to be tortured. All for the reward of a pat on the head from his superior.

After guiding them through what seemed like a week's worth of exhausting loops, false starts, and double backs, D'trav led them straight towards the gate. The walls towered over them as they drew near, throwing the area into chill shadow.

Sarenka shivered at the omen, drawing her cloak closer.

A pale flickering, like the reflection of light against a mirror, drew her gaze towards the shadows. Immediately tense, she searched for more assailants but found none. With relief, she put the sighting down to yet another flight of her imagination and wondered if D'trav would have brought her along if he knew she was mind-lost.

Parian watched Sarenka and D'trav approach the assassin unaware, and sighed. He had no choice, he had to break the code of Seven. There was nothing else he could do.

The Half-Frevell tensed, adjusted his crossbow, lifting it just enough to aim.

Parian touched his mind and discovered it to be Sharpra instead of Half-Frevell, and hoped he wasn't too late. He'd never studied an assassin's mind, had rarely even encountered them. He shivered with unexpected waves of cold and hot.

The assassin shifted again, placed his finger on the trigger.

Parian panicked, searching for just the right spot.

The assassin's finger began to slowly press the trigger.

Parian darted a glance at D'trav and Sarenka as they neared the ambush. He pressed deeper, sifting through the assassin's skull, and memories of the man's past kills flashed past, sickening him.

Face going lax, the assassin stiffened and fell to the ground, weapon landing on the stone he'd been bracing it on.

Parian gagged and threw up. Instead of the fluid evaporating as soon as it left his ethereal form, it landed around the assassin's body in a gelatinous splat. He stared at the fluid in disbelief and wondered how much this would cost his real body.

He'd done it. But the victory was bitter; the carnage he'd witnessed would scar his mind for years. He'd never known that people could be killed and tortured in so many ways. He pushed at the alien memories, trying to shut them away, and stared at the assassin with disgust.

Yes, a bitter victory, and a forbidden one.

But necessary, and harmless… mostly.

Triggering that area of the man's brain would leave him unconscious for hours and vulnerable to the many thieves of Burmtin. He just hoped it was enough time for Sarenka and D'trav to escape.

He shifted, jumping the time stream in search of them.

When they finally neared the small side gate, Sarenka leaned against D'trav and watched his suspicious gaze travel up and down the route leading towards the opening. "Why didn't you escape Burmtin after the baron?"

"I hadn't killed all the bastards yet." He leaned over, rubbing his thigh.

Sarenka stared at him in horror.

His face was such a mask of hate that it sapped what little warmth was left from her body.

She shuddered.

That was the type of hate that didn't die. The kind of hate that buried itself, hilt deep, in someone's chest. She vowed to never do…

whatever it was… that would bring that wrath down on her head. He might be treating her like family, but he was not a man to betray. That thought brought a faint smile to her lips. An alliance with a man who took revenge so seriously was strangely comforting. He was as strong a guard for her back as she was for his.

"We just have to make it a little longer," she said.

He gave her an odd look and started forward, dragging Sarenka along for the first couple of steps, until her feet caught up with her brain and started moving again. She bumped against a wall and heard the faint tinkle of breaking glass.

So now I've broken the empty vials. How fitting.

"You carryin' somethin' that'll leak out an' betray us?" D'trav asked.

She shook her head.

The scent of green wafted through the gate and hung in the air, promising freedom, before mingling with the wisps of smoke from the fire behind them.

Sarenka stared at the guards and took a step back into the shadows. "No. It can't be."

"Come on, girl, we're almost out."

She dug her fingers into his arm, keeping him from stepping forward. "You don't understand. That's Brandon. You can't bribe him."

"Damn sight right, that's Brandon. Easiest guard in the city to bribe. Let's go."

"No. D'trav. He hates Freni-Kyns. He wants us dead. All of us. Whatever he's promised, it's a lie."

D'trav stared at Brandon and his eyes narrowed. "Well then, this may be a sight harder than I thought."

"Remember your promise."

"I'd sooner kill him than you, darlin. Let's go. Keep those illusions up, if'n you can."

Outwardly, he merely nodded at the approaching guards, but his hand flickered through a quick succession of signals.

Sarenka held her breath and took the last few steps, too exhausted and afraid to do more than keep shuffling one foot in front of the other.

Brandon lowered his hand towards his sword, and she tensed for a fight, but it bypassed the handle, scratching at his crotch instead. She didn't dare peek at his face but kept her gaze leveled below the waist. Her cheeks flushed.

He knows. He has to know. He's got a raging hard-on.

D'trav sent another signal and the other man signaled back as they stepped between the guards. The last step loomed before her, and she took it, stepping beyond the grays and browns of a broken city, a city filled with sorrow, and into the open field beyond. The small, single lane track leading from this little-used gate, welcomed her, calling her away. Her gaze traced the road as it roped its way over rolling hills, losing itself in the distance.

"I would have done this months ago, had I known it was that easy. How much did you pay them?"

He stared straight ahead, face clothed in concern. "Too easy, but enough to keep 'em silent for a while longer. We aren't outta the woods yet. How far can you walk?"

The light drained from her eyes, and her shoulders slumped. "As far as I need to."

"Determination isn't always enough to keep a person alive."

"We just need to go a little bit longer," she woodenly said.

"Why do you keep saying that?"

She didn't answer but started walking, cutting across land towards the nearest grove of ginger maples.

Stepping into an invisible hollow, she tripped and would have fallen if D'trav hadn't grasped her arm.

"Slow down, urchin."

She blinked at him, confused, but before she could respond he looked away.

"Sorry. I know you aren't… It just sorta… slipped out."

Sarenka walked on in silence, pausing often to get her breath or shake out a cramping muscle.

"You called her that, didn't you?" she finally asked. "Your sister, I mean."

"Yes, but not in a mockin' way." They crested a hill and stepped down into a valley that would hide them from the city.

Sarenka started to sit but he grasped her elbow.

"No restin' yet."

"How much longer?"

"Now you *sound* like her too." He gave a gruff laugh and nodded towards the grove. "One more hill, we'll rest once we hit those trees."

She clutched her stomach, and leaned forward as a cramp struck.

"You okay?"

"I will be." She started forward again.

He grabbed her arm, stopping her. "How many days since you had antidote."

She avoided his eyes. "I... a week."

"Get it out and take it now."

"D'trav no. Let's just keep going. It can wait."

"Do it now Sarenka."

She sighed and pulled free one of her carefully swaddled vials, held her nose and drank it down. "Satisfied? Let's go." She struck out, broken glass clinking in her skirt with each step.

As they crested the last hill, Sarenka turned to look at Burmtin. Its dirty brown folds were a discarded garment, lying in rumpled disarray on the green and blue carpet of the land. She stepped into the welcoming coolness of the tree line and sighed. "We're free."

"Well, not quite," a suave voice spoke from the shadows.

CHAPTER 60

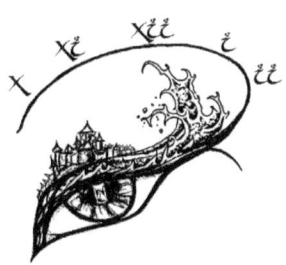

"I saw it today for the first time. A metal black as a moonless night and strong as a diamond. We fought to break it free from the stone and our picks bounced back, nearly impaling us each time we accidentally struck the metal. With the most valuable metal in our hands, I can buy the most magnificent of aerie."

Unknown Author
Upland University Museum
Thought to be pre-betrayal Glidarthian

D'trav's sword rang as he pulled it free of the scabbard.

Sarenka yanked out her daggers but knew it was useless; she was too exhausted to put up a decent fight. Her keen Freni-Kyn eyes searched the shadows, picking out two men, both leaning nonchalantly against tree trunks.

"Show yourself," D'trav growled, stepping forward.

"Stop, D'trav. Two men, and they don't have weapons drawn." Sarenka kept her voice low, hoping only D'trav would hear.

One of the men sniffed disdainfully and propelled himself off the tree. He sauntered into a beam of golden light and stood there, waiting for their recognition.

"Randy?" Sarenka asked.

With a cock of his head and a raised brow, he pulled free a dagger. "Lance."

He held the blade casually, wrist half limp, before peering down at it with a expression of surprise on his face, as though curious to have found it in his hand. Lifting a fingertip to support the point, he turned the blade in the filtered sunlight. The Red Pelican emblem stood out in stark relief against the black blade, and the light reflecting off the nighshk metal momentarily blinded them. A drop of blood rose from his finger, and he lifted it to his mouth, looking at them through a fringe of bangs.

"You look tired, Sarenka. What say we get you back where you belong?" He jerked his head at D'trav. "We'll just take in this traitor together. No repercussions."

"No," she spoke through clenched teeth.

D'trav's grip on his hilt tightened and his muscles tensed.

Sensing his readiness, Sarenka prepared herself for the onslaught.

Lance gave another short cock of his head. "Somehow I knew that would be your answer. Told Burk that too. He'll be so disappointed when he arrives and finds you dead."

"Fuck Burk!"

"I do believe that's what he had in mind. This is hardly a sporting fight. Neither of you will be a challenge. Ready, lover?"

The man behind Lance drew a sword and stepped into the light.

Sarenka gasped.

Dick appeared shaken, and his grip on the sword was unsure. "Sorry, Sarenka."

"So that's how you knew I'd head towards the trees," she said to Lance.

He half smiled at her.

"And you! You betrayed me!" She glared at Dick. "I thought you were my…"

Red crept into Dick's cheeks, but Sarenka wasn't sure if it was shame or anger.

Lance's smile grew. "Yes, all those late night discussions about how much you love trees, and how the first thing you were going to do, when you left Burmtin, was find some trees to sit under. You made it too easy, really. Are you sure you won't come with us?"

D'trav's urgent voice startled her into looking at him. "You should go, Sarenka." His eyes were intense, pleading.

"I'm not running off with these two—" Her gaze settled on Dick's pale face with disgust. He probably couldn't fight well, and, though it would leave a seeping wound in her heart, she'd take him out or die trying. "—lying, good-for-nothing, lizards."

Lance's eyes narrowed. "Very well then, let's get this over with."

He paced towards them with Dick following closely behind.

Sarenka braced herself, willing to let the assassins make the first moves. Out of the corner of her eye, she noticed D'trav do the same.

As the distance closed between them, Lance's face went slack, and he fell to the ground.

Determined to pierce Dick's chest, Sarenka leapt forward, dagger held out for a killing blow.

Dick dropped his sword as he threw himself to the ground.

Sarenka's blade sliced through the air where Dick had been standing. She landed just beyond him and swung around in a crouch.

D'trav stood above the two men, sword lifted, ready for the killing strike.

Dick ignored them, pressing his ear against Lance's chest.

D'trav shared a disbelieving look with Sarenka before springing into action and collecting the fallen blades.

Sarenka pressed her blade to Dick's throat.

Dick held out empty hands, showing no other weapons. Next to Lance's body lay a round thing with a quill sticking out of it. "I couldn't let him do it. Not to you Sarenka."

"Dead?" Sarenka nodded towards Lance's body.

"No, he'll come around in a few hours. Probably have a hell of a bruise where I injected him."

"You're not Red Pelican," D'trav said.

"Hardly. I've been desperate, but not stupid. No offense Sarenka."

She sighed. He was right, joining them had turned out to be the stupidest move ever. "What do we do with him?"

"Leave him here and he'll track us. We should just kill him," D'trav said.

Dick stepped in front of Lance's body. "No! You'll have to kill me first."

As if that was the best option, D'trav stepped forward, raising his sword.

Sarenka grabbed his arm.

D'trav spoke out of the side of his mouth. "Let me handle this."

"He's my friend."

He gave her an I-can't-believe-you're-doing-this look. "I won't kill him, just the assassin."

"Please, D'trav, no."

Braced for an assault, Dick watched the exchange with wide eyes and his lips pulled into a fearful frown.

"I'd say tie him up and leave him, but that's not a death I want hangin' over my head." D'trav grimaced at the thought and sheathed his weapon. "Lettin' someone slowly starve to death's a low down cowardly way to kill."

Sarenka's stomach cramped again. She leaned forward, grasping it. A fine sheen of sweat broke out over her body.

Dick grabbed her arm. "Sarenka?"

"She's okay. Just waited too long to take the antidote."

They guided her to a tree, and she sat beneath it, gazing up through the leaves at the purpled sky. Her vision blurred in and out of focus as her eyes watered.

"Troops are supposed to collect you in the morning. I'll wait here with him and make sure nothing attacks," Dick said.

"Nothin' much gonna attack him round hereabouts. Too close to the city. All the big animals wiped out by hunters ages ago." D'trav waved his hands around. "Long as he's awake before nightfall he'll be okay, and you can't stay. They'll set you out as a bloody example for the rest of Burmtin to see."

Dick blanched. "I know, was trying to figure out a way around that. Could just run back to the city before they arrive, but he'll know I tricked him. He's smart enough to figure it out."

"I 'spect so," D'trav said.

"So there really is nowhere safe for me in Burmtin now. Let's get him tied up then, he'll wake soon enough."

"D'trav," Sarenka said as another cramp started. "I don't think this is from the Foreveron."

He looked down at her with a puzzled expression. "What then?"

"The meat."

"It did taste odd." He rubbed his hand across the edge of his jaw. "But I'm not sick, girl.

She closed her eyes, too tired to talk.

They wrestled Lance onto a wide tree branch and tore his silk shirt into strips, using them like rope.

Dick picked up Sarenka's pack and helped her to her feet. "So… where we heading?"

She felt her cheek with her hand, it felt cold in the noon day sun.

D'trav snorted. "And then there were three."

Dick's eyes darted back and forth between their faces. "It *is* okay if I come with you, right? I can pay for supplies with favors if you want."

D'trav's eyes jerked in Sarenka's direction and he shuddered. "Okay, you're in. Long as you take care of her needs."

Sarenka frowned and looked at Dick with concern as a wave of dizziness hit and the knots in her stomach grew. His face mirrored her own anxious thoughts. He was as worried about their secret being revealed as she was.

"D'trav's in charge, we go wherever he leads." She tried to give his arm a reassuring pat but threw up instead, splattering the ground with a blackened congealed mass.

D'trav grasped her arm, keeping her from falling forward.

She tried to straighten and retched until it turned into empty heaves.

"Dear god, Sarenka. We've gotta get you out of here." D'trav handed his bags to Dick and scooped Sarenka up into his arms.

"Have to put a lot of distance between us and that grove of trees," D'trav said.

D'trav tossed another log into the freshly lit fire. He glanced over with concern as Sarenka huddled further down into her cloak for warmth. *She looks so different now, so young.* It had been hours before she'd been able to walk again, and both of them had suffered from stomach cramps and loose bowels.

"You gonna be okay?"

She glanced away from the fire , eyes vacant.

"Sarenka?"

"Huh?" Coming to herself with a shake of her head, she answered, "Oh, yes. Just a bit chilled."

"Had me sweatin' thorns there for a while."

She moaned and leaned to the side, throwing up into the small hole he'd dug for her.

"D'trav, I have to tell you something."

"It can wait."

"Not if I'm dying it can't."

"Come on girl. Isn't the cramp grass you ate making you feel better yet?"

She fumbled in her skirt, turning out the pocket with the broken glass. It landed on the ground, green tinge visible even in firelight.

D'trav peered at it with a frown. "What was that?"

"Poison."

He stood, dumping the bowl in his lap onto the ground. "Why would you—"

She held up a hand. "Wait. It's okay. I didn't do it."

D'trav sat, a look of betrayal on his face as the implications sunk in. He shook his head.

"They sent you to kill me."

"They were going to torture you." Tears seeped down her cheeks. "I couldn't let that happen. The herbalist said the poison would be painless."

"So you poisoned us both?"

She shook her head. "No. I couldn't do it. Better to die fighting like men, not poisoned like rats."

"So the meat…"

"Was bad," she whispered as her eyes slid shut.

When she awoke again the hole had been filled and the cramp grass had started working. She rolled to her side, prepared to hurt, and was surprised when it didn't. Gingerly she sat up.

The men, who had been discussing cards, stopped talking.

At the sound of a hooting hiss, she ducked. "What was that?"

"Yeah, what was that?" Dick picked up a stick to defend himself with, ignoring the sword lying next to him.

D'trav grunted. "Bird, sort of, doesn't have a beak though. Harmless. Probably huntin' mice. I'm takin' it neither of you've spent much time outside the cities."

"Just the trip to Burmtin, and I stayed on the road for that," Sarenka said, grateful that he was treating her the same.

"Burmtin, born and raised," Dick said.

"Well then, you've got yourselves a heap of learnin' to do."

"How long do you think it is to the next city?"

"Few days, give or take. Give us time to figure out a way to create new identities. Can you dye that Freni-Kyn hair of yours?"

She grasped a hank of the floating mass and pulled it under her chin. "I-I don't think so. I'll just use my illusions."

"Be better if you didn't have to rely on 'em too much."

Catching on, Dick rubbed his hands together and grinned. "Oooh… disguises! I'm good at costumes!"

D'trav looked at him and raised a brow.

Dick's smile faded. "I just thought, well it *is* something I can do."

"What do we eat out here?" Sarenka interrupted. After her long talks with Dick, she knew he was more Freni-Kyn than she'd ever be. D'trav would just have to get used to it.

"That'll be the first thing I give you, huntin' lessons."

Dick paled. "No! I can't kill animals."

"Then eatin'll be mighty slim pickin's. Hope you like roots and bugs and the like."

"I'm not eating bugs. I'll learn to hunt," Sarenka said.

Dick sighed, and Sarenka knew he was resigning himself to the fact that he'd need to learn to hunt. "How are we going to hide from the Red Pelican?"

"Now don't you be worry'n 'bout that. I've got me some pretty good connections. We'll be someone else soon enough."

The fire burned higher, warming the area and she lay back.

"That simple?" Eyes blinking closed, she considered a new life, as a new person. It had never occurred to her to take another identity when she ran away from home years ago. "Can we become treasure hunters, raid the ruins of..."

"Nothin's ever as simple as it sounds," D'trav murmured as her voice trailed off, tucking the edge of her cloak under her chin.

Sarenka tried to respond but her eyes wouldn't open. She sighed, rolled over, and drifted off to sleep.

The next day dawned clear and warm. After camouflaging their campsite, they left, moving towards the highest peak between Burmtin and the grasslands. They trudged forward, panting and pushing themselves to the limit, and cleared the wooded area within the hourglass turn. Stepping onto the crest of the next hill, the land rose before them, unmarred by the hands of man.

Sarenka drew in a deep draft of clover scented air. At last. Freedom from Burmtin. She savored the rolling fields, scattered groves of trees, and sprinkling of blue daisies, enjoying the first flutter of lighthearted joy she'd felt in years. Laughter bubbled up, and without thinking, she hugged D'trav. Setting her bag down, she stripped away the corset she'd been wearing. The breeze picked at her blood splatted chemise, whipping its sweat soaked fabric about.

D'trav stared back the way they had come. "I'll never get my revenge for what they did now."

Sarenka glanced at the storm in his face and her brows drew together. "Revenge isn't worth dying for."

"Sometimes I reakon it is."

"If you die doing it then they win."

D'trav glanced at her sideways then squinted at the city and spat. "True 'nuff."

"You can always go back later, get them when their guard is down."

"Look who's gotten all wise on me all of a sudden like."

Sarenka laughed and started pulling the chemise over her head.

D'trav turned to studiously studying the path before them.

Drawing out a sky blue corset—one she'd always refused to wear because it seemed too free, too lovely, for Burmtin—she admired the shine of the brocade threads in the sunlight, a luxurious garment D'trav had bought her after catching her flipping the latches of his boots. Though it would have brought a lot of silver, she'd kept it as a symbol of freedom. She glanced at D'trav's back and smiled. Laced with kindness. Her gaze dropped to the metal latches. And strength.

She stared at D'trav with new eyes, taking in his brawny frame and assessing both his strengths and weaknesses. He was quick tempered and kind hearted, a double-edged sword. She couldn't have killed him; no matter how much the Red Pelican wanted her to be, she wasn't a murderer. It would take cunning to soften his temper and keep them out of trouble.

Her gaze shifted to Dick, a man with more inner strength than she'd ever suspected. Their friendship had saved her from the mortification of relations with a man she didn't want, but she'd always thought it shallow; a companion for a price. He'd proved her wrong and lost his lover in the process, earning his place at their side.

She smiled at the thought of the three of them, traveling the world, seeking fortune wherever it might call. They were companions now, fellow traitors, and they would die to protect each other.

"You can turn around now."

D'trav turned back as she wrapped the corset around her torso and gave the latches quick flips of her fingertips, snapping them closed. At each 'snick' her body lost some of the artificial age with which the city had weighted her down, leaving her looking like the youthful six- teen year old she truly was. He watched the transformation of Sarenka with dumbstruck amazement. He'd never have expected the sight of fields and trees to cause someone to change so dramatically. She was far younger than he'd thought. When she wrapped her arms around him in another genuine hug, he responded with uncertain pats on her back.

She clung for a moment, then passed her bag to Dick and grasped their hands. "Come on, let's run."

"Ummm… Sarenka. How old are you?" Dick asked.

"Sixteen winters."

D'trav shared a concerned look with Dick.

"Freni-Kyn winters, you dolts," she added. "That means I've been an adult for over a year."

"Like that makes a hill of beans worth of difference," D'trav mut- tered under his breath.

"Actually, it does," Dick said. "Frevell kids don't mature until they're older, forty or sixty or something like that. And really I met one once. He was supposed to be twenty five but he acted like he was twelve. If the Freni-Kyn people say their kids are adults at fifteen, then I believe them."

D'trav grunted. He'd seen Sarenka do some rather immature things over the last few months. Not a lot, but enough to put the Freni-Kyn's-are-adults-at-fifteen-rule into question. He scratched along the edge of his jawline. Then again, he'd seen H'euman thirty year olds do some childish things, so maybe Dick was right.

With the burden of the city behind, Sarenka's fatigue seemed to melt and giddy happiness covered her face. She yanked them forward, and the slope did the rest of the work, sending them into an awkward lope. They came to a breathless stop under a lenan tree, and D'trav pulled a leaf free, crushing the foliage and filling the air with its spicy scent. Taking in Sarenka's violet flushed cheeks, he let loose a laugh of his own. It was good to be here, now, with her.

His eyes blurred for a moment, and he was sure his sister stood next to Sarenka laughing. Elsa's hand clasped Sarenka's free one before reaching for his. Shivering, he held out his hand as she faded from view.

Sarenka grasped the hand he held out, hiccupped, and covered her mouth with her hand. "Excuse me. Don't know what got into me."

That night, Sarenka tossed and turned while D'trav stood guard. He frowned and leaned over her, checking her head for a fever.

Eyes wide open, she sat up with a look of terror on her face and grasped his arm. ""We have to go back!"

"It's okay Sarenka, just a dream."

Her eyes focused on his face. "The poison, it's still in the vegetables."

D'trav shook his head, confused.

"The beggar children D'trav. They'll notice we aren't there and eat it. We have to go back. Tonight!"

Parian drifted above, watching their exit from the city with relief. *Now...*

Just to follow them…

I should be able to intercept them somewhere safe.

He watched Sarenka shed the burdens she'd been carrying and D'trav relax. The further they were from the city, the freer they seemed. They had gained a new companion but his thoughts seemed harmless. Parian's mind drifted upwards, ready to return home, when a fourth figure appeared between them.

What the…

Between D'trav and Sarenka a child now stood, hands stretched out to hold theirs. Parian shook his head.

The girl child?

Where'd she come from?

This is wrong.

Something's gravely wrong.

Sarenka reached to grasp D'trav's outstretched hand, and the child flickered out, appearing again behind Sarenka. She moved forward, turning to light as she stepped into Sarenka's body. Parian's hand shot forward, closing on empty air, and Sarenka hiccupped.

The area became a whirlpool of swirling colors as Parian was sucked away.

Below him a Freni-Kyn woman lay chained to the floor. Nearby a H'euman lay dead, his broken body laced in slashing cuts. Blood covered the two, covered the area, cloaking the stone room in the scent of slaughtered meat. He reeled upwards with shock but couldn't escape. Though his tether was invisible he was anchored to the room as much as the woman was.

He understood the ramifications. He'd shifted to another time stream, another possibility. Yet once more, Sarenka had killed the baron. That event alone was the constant in a shifting realm of probabilities, the one event that always happened, no matter what occurred the day before. No matter whether the Baron argued with her before drugging her, or whether she went into the stupor relatively conflict free, this event always occurred.

It was simply meant to be.

As her eyes began to twitch, she tossed her head back and forth and moaned, "No... please no... I can't..."

Parian breathed a sigh of relief. Sarenka lived still in this time stream.

There was time.

Her eyes flew open and filled with horror. She scrambled away from the dead man and the door swung wide open.

A long haired man stood frozen in uncertainty before backing out of the room in a rush.

"Guards!" D'trav roared. "Sound the alarm!"

Chapter 64

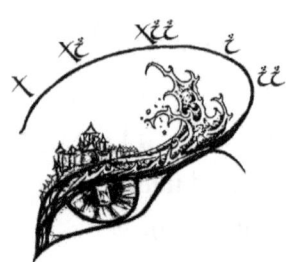

Parian opened his eyes with a groan and reached down to rub a raw ankle.

Not another dream-vision of those two!

For two months running, they'd plagued him, and the visions within visions were especially troubling. Because that had never happen before, he wasn't sure what it meant. He understood the theory of time stream jumping of course. All the seers did, but none of them had ever personally done it, not until he started doing it in his dreams, and even those jumps were different from what his mentor had taught him when he became a Seven. He was supposed to see the possibilities within the time stream once only, and then guide events towards the best possible outcome, not relive the possibilities for weeks on end.

He examined the long cut across his shin. *If this doesn't stop, my ankle will be as scar covered as Sarenka's.*

~*I've had another one,*~ he sent to the other Seven. ~*I'm going to them.*~

~*Not time-treading alone!*~ Pervasive horror flavored Airintia's thoughts.

~*No, I'm not a fool. Though if this really was The One, I'd be willing to do——*~

~*Parian!*~ Airintia interrupted. ~*Don't say that. Don't even think it.*~

His next thought was filled with dry amusement, ~*Cause you'll hear it.*~

A tickle of answering laughter brushed his mind.

~*Visit some pubs for me, brother, and keep us informed,*~ came Lanion's thoughts.

A wave of discomfort from Airintia interrupted anything else the man might have thought. Parian cut the connection, unwilling to get into the middle of another of their disagreements.

Without seeing it, he stared across his modest inn room for many a long minute. At last, thoughts in order, he stood to gather his meager belongings. His dream-self had no problem with jumping into the time stream alone, even if he knew better. Something had to be done about this. Neither D'trav nor Sarenka had shown any sign of the talent in his dreams, but they had to have at least some psychic abilities, or he wouldn't keep dream-visioning them.

And that last dream…

He shuddered.

If The One merged with the unliving…

What would happen?

The possibilities were endless, but he had to stop this course of events before they happened, and to do that he needed to arrive in Burmtin before Sarenka escaped the manor. He had watched their deaths a multitude of times over the last week. Rubbing tired eyes, he began packing an embossed leather satchel with all the tools he might need for trips through the time stream.

It was time for a trip to Burmtin.

The End…

Sort of…

Not really…

I'm about to ask you to feed me blood.

I know, that sounds weird, but read on…

I get asked all the time what it takes to write a book. A better question might be, what does it take to write a great book? And honestly, I do not believe I've written my masterpiece yet, but I can tell you what it takes to write a book that people want to read.

More than anything, it takes passion. First for the story and the characters, but also a passion for entertaining a specific group of people. Without the desire to entertain, stories are like grey, unflavored oatmeal that's been sitting on the table overnight. So essentially, what I'm saying is, a great story is written just for you. That's why the neighbor across the street prefers one book and you prefer another. That book was written for the neighbor, and the book you love is written for you.

But there is a secret part of writing great novels that you aren't supposed to know about. Not because we want to keep you in the dark, but because we want to keep the magic of reading alive. I'm going to tell you what it is though, because, in our instant gratification world, it is so often skipped. It takes time, hours and hours of careful editing and revising and networking with other authors.

When you look at this book, you see a story. You don't see the time, and that's good, as it would be a distraction from the story. You don't see all the days spent typing away, and the angst of deciding whether to kill off a character or give her blue skin. You don't see the hours a professional editor puts into making the book into something even better than the author could have done alone. Or the hours spent by a cover artist, putting together an image that fires the imagination without giving away too much of the story. Or the cold sweat that breaks out when an author has to write the back cover copy. (Okay, maybe only I do that.) You don't see the effort of the marketer who helped you find the book, or the time a manager spent coordinating all the above people. And you aren't supposed to. You see the magic of a girl who is trapped within an evil city and her struggle to survive. Which is exactly what we want you to see.

Now comes the blood part… Get ready for it… I need you to feed it to me, and if you liked Trapped, you owe it to yourself to do this. Honor the time that went into creating this book by enjoying it. Read it, share it, talk about it, buy it for your friends, post your reviews on sites, and write me. I need that. I need to know that you love, or even hate, a character. Your words are my life blood as an entertainer. They literally keep me writing.

This is how it works. If I get enough loves on a character then I write more about that character. For example: the Tahrek book I am writing is a direct result of all the people who told me how much they love Tahrek. Many of the online book sources will not allow a book in their system until it has enough reviews. And most of the algorithms (fancy mathematical term) at the online book stores only show their customers books that have a lot of reviews. If you have a blog and want to feature Trapped, please write me for a media kit. Or check my website at KyronsWorld.com for a downloadable media kit pdf.

That's it. Feed me the blood of reviews and letters and blog posts and I'll have the energy to continue. Pretty simple huh? It only takes a few minutes and your voice counts.

~~E. S. Tilton

I hope you've enjoyed this taste of Kyron's Worlde. If so, indulge in the rest of the saga.

For more about E.S. Tilton, Foretold, and the Kyron's Worlde books, visit us at:

www.KyronsWorld.com
www.facebook.com/elisabeth.tilton
www.facebook.com/ES.Tilton.Author
www.sexyfantasyfiction.com

Other books in the series include:
Foretold Betrayal
Foretold Seduction's Blade
Foretold Special Edition

Appendix

Kyron's Worlde

For those who, like myself, love all the little tidbits an author can throw your way, I've included the following descriptions of the people, places, and things of Kyron's Worlde. Most of them you have not encountered within the pages of this novel, but you will if you go on to read more of the series. Creating a glossary was not one of the simplest things I engaged in while writing the series, but it was well worth the effort if it brings enjoyment to you, the reader. My hope is that, like myself, you fall hopelessly in love with the people of Kyron's Worlde and come back to follow their stories.

The Races of Kyron's Worlde

All of the species standards are held up for comparison against the Humans of Earth.

Freni~Kyn

The people of this petite race, measuring no higher than 5'5", are born with varying degrees of personal illusion abilities. Their living hair, which is never cut, throws off gentle sparks of color, like a dandelion loosing its seeds upon the world. Their cat-like pupils enable them to see great distances, even in reduced lighting. Though their noses are not as sensitive as a Sharpra's, they are more sensitive to smell than all the other races. Their coloration is predominantly human in type, but there are some few individuals with a rare gene that produces blue, purple, or green skin. Their ears raise or lower, accordian fashion,— often in accordance with how interested they are in hearing something—and are pleated along the outside edges.

These fun loving entertainers, who used illusions to awe their audiences Before Betrayal, were nearly wiped out during the Rage Wars. This led to the restructuring of their entire society around their natural ability to cast personal illusions. The species became official camp followers, with bodies genetically manipulated for the job. This drastic shift— so that only those who excelled in this form of entertainment were allowed to mate or given political influence—caused their bodies to mutate with the passage of time.

Lacking emotional closeness with others, a driving need to fill this emptiness with unending sexual partners became prevalent. With birthrates climbing at an alarming rate, their council sought means to control who gave birth, and when. This led to more genetic manipulation and the curse of the Preral sickness, a mating cycle much like the heat of a common cat. One other unfortunate result of the mutation is a slight reduction of their lifespan and the early maturing of their children, which now occurs at the age of fifteen. While the uneducated believe this is a cultural decision, the Frevellian scholars have confirmed that it is indeed a medical condition. Due to both cultural interaction and the mutations, Freni-Kyns are the living physical standard of the People's preferred beauty.

FREVELL

This slim species, reaching a minimum of 6 feet tall, is well known for their intellect, though some scholars argue that this intelligence is due to living at least 150 years. After coming of age at 40ish, they take a turn as negotiators for the other races, using their superior knowledge to help them govern the lands. Their sensitive ears are long and pointed, between 4 and 6 inches, but remain close to the head. Skin tones run the gamut of normal human coloration but hair colors can include dark shades of blue or green. Their straight eyebrows slant upward at the outer edges, as do their elongated eyes.

Without the muscular stature to ensure their survival during the wars, the Frevells withdrew to distant secluded cities, securing them through both mechanical and magical devices, and dedicated themselves to regulating their own people. Over time, their laws multiplied, becoming so redundant as to be useless, a dagger to their own throats. While in the past they had been inventors, now, after exchanging creativity for law and order, they are lawyers.

It became impossible for them to accomplish anything of significance. Society stagnated, technology drew to a crawl and was lost, and a people once known for its ingenious conceptual inventions left off creating. With one exception: their knowledge of genetics played a heavy hand in the inbreeding techniques adopted by the M'hakru and Freni-Kyn.

GLIDARTH

Though the people of earth might be tempted to associate this species with that of angels or fairies, they are, in fact, closer to human, and the only known self-aware winged creatures of Kyron's Worlde. Their leathern wings are often enhanced with inked designs, both temporary and permanent, sometimes creating the visual illusion of colorful kites dipping and soaring in the breeze. The same feather-weight bone structure that helps them take flight was mistakenly thought to mean fragility early in the Rage Wars, however their bones are stronger than human standard.

Some of this species boast the rare gene that produces backward sweeping temple feathers, but this trait is seldom seen by the other races as those born with it are of noble birth. Like the Frevell, their ears are long and pointed but lay closer to the head, pointing backwards, rather than upwards towards the sky. Coloration for this group is that of normal Human standards with no known exceptions.

These free-spirited traders and metal-smiths refused to give metals to the other races after dismemberment of their wings became prevalent among the warring factions. Withdrawing to the fortified isolation of their mountaintop megatropolis, they turned in upon themselves. From the restriction of their freedom sprung such deep sorrow, that they sought fixated comfort in eating. Gluttony further restricted the use of their wings, leading, in turn, to overwhelming urges towards self-mutilation and suicide.

Despite childhood fairytales, often hailing from Before Betrayal, the typical modern Glidarthians is rotund, including the ones who retain the ability to fly. In the recent years of uneasy peace, when Glidarthians are seen, they are frequently in the capacity of messenger to the other races. Their tall jump-towers, at least 4-5 stories high, have sprung up across Llayentia, creating a safe network of places to launch into the air from, and are outfitted with a pulley elevator system. If there is a steampunk group of people in Kyron's Worlde, their love of gadgets, metal, and aviator style clothing would qualify the Glidarthians for that title more than any other race.

H'EJMANS

As their name implies, these are the Humans of Kyron's Worlde, with all of earth's variation in height, weight, and coloration. The spelling is an adaptation created by the M'hakru scholars who first discovered them.

They are the mutts of society, often hiding traces of other races, along with their various abilities, within their own bodies. After the Day of Betrayal, the H'eumans multiplied and warred and imbibed in the perversions infecting all the races, accepting every sordid atrocity, until their towns became as varied as the individual races.

Some few, outraged at the barbarism, left for isolated areas; creating pockets of strange ingrown societies based around the principles of science, religion, technology, or magic; each specialized group recklessly pursuing their field of interest without regard for the consequences. The alarming results of their experimentation can be seen throughout the lands, and it is not unusual for mutations to abound, and be revered, in these communities.

M'HAKRU

This species is of average to short human height, rarely reaching over 6 feet tall, with stout, muscular forms. Supernatural speed, their most predominant inborn trait, sets them apart from other races and was initially used for defensive purposes against animals.

At birth, their children's long pointed ears are surgically altered to point forward, beginning a lifetime of brutal body modification. As they mature, these same ears are often outfitted with metal sheaths and serve as close combat weapons.

Their coloration runs the gamut of a normal human but their eyes resemble birds of prey and their hands sport six fingers. Their goth-like preference for short or shaved hair, piercings, and lots of black leather straps and buckles, all serve a protective or defensive purpose in battle.

Once altruistic nature-lovers, this sturdy race turned to the art of war when their king was slain on the Day of Betrayal and their forest cities invaded during the Rage Wars. Because this is now all they know

and respect, they are almost obsessive in the meticulous care of their weapons and armor. The deliberate inbreeding as mercenaries had the unexpected liability of instilling cruelty into the bloodlines, leading to widespread physical abuse, even among their own people. In addition to their natural musk odor, which the other races find intrusive, most of this race refuses to bathe, believing that the stench adds to the fear factor during battle.

One other physical difference is worthy of note due to its effect on the history of Llayentia. The male's sexual organ is barbed and the female cannot be impregnated without that abrasion. Though to the M'hakru female this is not painful, a male of this race must trim his barbs in order to interact in a non-aggressive sexual manner with the other races. The use of their sexual organ as a weapon was outlawed by the M'hakru government when all the other races aligned against the M'hakru due to the atrocity of the rape war crimes.

During the early years of the Rage Wars, they wiped out all enemies in their path, including non-combative elders and children, earning a nickname they proudly wore, *The Death Bringers*. After years of warring, they began hiring out as mercenaries to the other races, waging their battles for them. Eventually, without the ability to do the most menial of labor, they turned to capturing their opponents as slaves; tying the very people they sought to eliminate to their survival.

SHARPRA

These shape-shifters share their ability with a few other creatures of Kyron's Worlde, but not with the werewolves of earth's lore. Wolf-like in their loyalty to each other and the pack, but not in appearance, they have complete control of when, where, and how they shift. Though born with shape-shifting abilities, that skill must be honed like any natural talent. Especially if they desire to imitate, and blend in with, other races or become spies. It is rumored that the male is endowed with two penises and the female a corresponding set of vaginas. But, due to their unwillingness to take mates outside of their own species, this fact is unconfirmed among the other races. Perhaps it is just as well that these facts are not commonly known, as there'd surely be a degree of penis envy.

Their bodies are Amazonian in stature and covered with a fine down of hair. A 3 inch long ruff of hair runs along the top of their shoulders and another ruff extends from the nape of their neck to the base of their spine, ending in a point. Their hair coloration is banded, or *ombré*, similar to a bear or wolf coat, with guard hairs often growing in darker than the rest of the hair. Among Sharpras, the more definition the banding has, the greater the desirability. Like some animals, they spend a portion of each year molting.

At the start of the Rage Wars, these shape-shifters—already natural hunters—became barbaric tribalists, warring amongst themselves as well as with anyone who dared approach their villages. After incessant in-fighting dangerously reduced their numbers, tribal leaders enacted laws to stop this spiraling, downward decline. They agreed to turn their warriors' aggression outwards, shape-shifting into similitudes of the other races in order to infiltrate the rest of the lands. Instead of warring with each other, they used stealth and deception to expose valuable information and use that information for the good of the whole Sharpra race.

The tribal leader's success in unifying the Sharpra and creating loyalty within the tribe was soon renowned among the lands. Now it is almost unknown for a Sharpra to aid another race, though they seem to move among them without malice when not engaged in active war. Loyalty to their own people has become the single most driving force in their behavior, causing supernatural ties with their mates. These ties are so strong that should a spouse die, the other falls into a coma, joining their mate within death's cold embrace mere days later.

WATRELK

This race is best known for its ability to spend extended lengths of time underwater. In fact, their lungs have the ability to filter oxygen from water for a half hour at a time, though few of Llayentia's scholars know this. Due to their affinity for water, both male and female Watrelk prefer loose flowing clothing while out of the water.

Their ears boast double points which they often decorate with water gleaned treasures; strands of pearls, coral, shaped shells. They have predominant, high cheekbones but this is not their most extraordinary facial feature.

Their eyes shift color according to their mood, as do the patterns surrounding their eyes. They have no control of this and it serves no known purpose, but some scholars speculate that it is used as a ward, or camouflage, underwater.

Their skin coloration is predominantly human-like, with some pale green, or light blue, but some few are born a brilliant chartreuse or fuchsia. The bright coloration is always accompanied by a keen psychic ability and is taken as a sign of Kyron's favor. This person is often given the ruling scepter, along with all the power that goes with it.

After the start of the Rage Wars, this reclusive water-dwelling people shut down the water lanes and their overseas trade, refusing passage to outsiders, and closing themselves off further from the other races. Their land-bound cities, abandoned for the safety of the ocean, became islands of interconnecting watercraft; a motley mass of boats, ships, and rafts. Eventually the other races built their own vessels, provoking a splintering within Watrelk society. Out of this disagreement, the Watrelk Pirates were birthed; a vicious group of killers, who, determined to jealously protect their seas from invasion, turned to trafficking in slavery and drugs, finding allies in the M'hakru and others of low honor.

GLOSSARY

PEOPLE

Airintia *air-e-awn-sha* – H'euman prophetess/ seer, one of the Seven.

Burk *berk* – H'euman middle rank Red Pelican Assassin.

Camille *cam-eel* – H'euman brothel owner, D'trav's lover.

Dick Charmer – H'euman gigalo that works for Camille. Randy's lover.

D'trav *duh-trahv* – H'euman guard.

Escrach *ezz-rock* – H'euman captive on the pirate ship.

Kyron *ky-rawn*– God – Creator of the world, Llayentia. Often used as slang in expression or exclamation.

Lance – H'euman member of the Red Pelican Assassin's Guild.

Lanion *lan-yun* – Glidarth prophet, seer, one of the Seven.

Lator *luh-tor* – Frevell, Red Pelican Assassins' Guild captain.

Parian *par-e-awn* – Freni-Kyn prophet/ seer.

Randy *ran-dee* – H'euman gigalo that works for Camille. Dick Charmer's lover.

R'kiax *ruh-ky-ax* – Sharpra assassin.

Sarenka *sah-reen-kah* – Young Freni-Kyn woman held captive by Burmtin.

Tahrek *tahr-ik* – Central dialect name used by everyone but the Sharpra people.

Tamika *tah-mee-kah* – H'euman leader of the washerwomen.

PLACES

Burmtin *berm-tin* – Southern city.

Claw Lake – A small lake named for an abundance of small clawed creatures, whose eyeballs are considered a delicacy in the southern reaches.

Crenach *cru-nosh* or *crin-osh* – Name of a province to the north.

Darkiorn *dark-ee-orn* – H'euman run city, near the Darkiorn mountain range.

Falksfall *falks-fall* – Tradesroad central city.

Istoarm Sea *is-storm* – Located along the Burmtin coast, southwest of the tri-arch.

Refuge – A village that is hardly more than an outpost. Located between Claw Lake and The Barrens, it is a favored place to rest up and obtain supplies by hunters of both animal and treasure.

THINGS

Airnelk *air-nelk* – Purple metal, more valuable than risen, less valuable than nighshk.

Alumoon tree *all-uh-moon* – A tree whose all-encompassing spring blossoms start out light peach, turn pale pink as the season extends, and finish off the season in a pink that borders on red. In some areas, the tree has spread to the point of becoming a nuisance tree, though none can deny the beauty of the areas when the blossoms cover the trees and ground with pink clouds of flowers. The tree produces a tiny, edible fruit which is not considered worth gathering by anyone but birds. Named after the second moon of Llayentia, Alum, which looks pink when in the sky alone.

Banish – The equivalent of triple strength coffee. Created from a variety of barks, beans, and spices. The most notable and highly questionable ingredient is Marnak dung. Although it is said to have been processed enough to remove all trace of the actual dung, many question its purported health benefits.

Breyt *breyet* – Blue metal, more valuable than gold, less valuable than riseen.

Carlt grapes – Striped grape named after the person who discovered them, Carlton. Though he is thought to have been a Frevell, little else is known about him.

Crenach apples *cru-nosh* or *crin-osh* – Sweet rare apple with a slight purple hue when ripe and a very short picking season. Used to create wine and other delicacies.

D'yroap – Primary coin of Llayentia. Nicknames include rings, loops, and o-links. Its origins are from Before Betrayal, a time when the seven races worked together towards the common good of all peoples. Records show that Frevellian artisans, working alongside Glidarthian blacksmiths, developed a monetary system based on a series of metal ovals. The metals, in order of increasing value, were copper, silver, gold, breyt, riseen, airnelk, nighshk.

The oval shaped rings of metal were further engraved with a symbol representing each race. Each loop had embossed upon its inner edge a symbolic design, chosen by the Glidarthian metalsmiths for the seven rulers. In the end, the oval shaped rings of metal were, in increasing value: copper star (Freni-Kyn), silver wave (Watrelk), gold arrow (Sharpra), riseen tree (M'hakru), breyt gavel (Frevell), airnelk wing (Glidarth), nighshk map (H'euman).

Currently, due to the weight of carrying massive amounts of d'yroaps for large purchases, gems are added to the ovals to make a higher value. A silver oval with a wave design might be worth a hundred copper stars, unless it is set with a ruby, in which case it might be worth more than a gold arrow. Though the system is complicated, it continues to be used to this day.

D'yroapbird – Bird named for its tendencies to sweep down and pluck d'yroaps from the hands of merchants. The merchants vowed revenge and began selling the birds' white feathers, nearly exterminating the species and causing the birds to become rare.

Foreveron Drug – A by-product of t'son barnacles accidentally discovered by pirates off the coast of the Istoarm Sea. Named after their ship Forever, meant to signify that that particular pirate band would rule the seas forever. Popular among slavers, it causes the person who takes it to become uninhibited and sex-crazed, to the point of bodily harm, while at the same time keeping the person from experiencing any form of sexual release.

Jeridite – A large and aggressive sea creature, sometimes measuring as long as 100 meters, which is primarily harvested for their massive shells. They are rumored to be magical, as none can explain how they stay afloat under the weight of the shell. Some parts of the shell are flexible, much like the bronze of earth, and can be beaten into shapes; therefore it is coveted as armor and adornment for the ordinary man.

Kyn *kin* – Slang for Freni-Kyn, one of the races of Llayentia.

Lenan spice *leh-nun* – Famous spice from the plants that grow around Lenan lake. Slightly bitter with a strong, sweet after-taste. Often used by aristocrats to clean teeth.

Llayentia – A continent of Kyron's world.

Loop or Loops – Slang for d'yroap, first used by the Freni-Kyn and sometimes adopted by the other races.

M'hakru push dagger – A blade created by the M'hakru because its small size can be easily concealed. The blade of this dagger can be made of any hard metal or stone and varies in length from two to four inches long. The hilt is placed at the top of the blade like a T, and therefore can be 'pushed' into someone with force.

Some elaborate M'hakru push daggers have multiple fold-out blades but require more skill and hence are less popular. These more complex daggers are carried in place of a shield during battle.

Vengeance – Another name for Memoryban, the equivalent of earth's moonshine or Everclear.

Nighshk *neyeshk* – Black metal, most valuable unamalgamated metal of Llayentia.

Oce-fel *os-uh-fel* – Horse sized cats, usually topping six feet, used as mounts. Originally named from a breed of cat called Ocelot. This was a fanciful name since the Ocelot cat proved to be too wild to be tamed for a mount. Because of a need to keep the creatures smart, friendly, and tame-able most Oce-fels look like huge common alley-cats; their genetics haven been taken from nearly every breed of cat. These are not to be confused with Hanirs, the large hunter cats used by warriors, hunters, and explorers.

Preral cycle pre-rawl – **or Preral time** – Refers to the cyclic time of a Freni-Kyn woman's life where her hormones drive her into an almost feral need to mate and with as many as possible or whoever is available.

Rings – Slang for d'yroap, used by Glidarths and barrenths.

Rinol-hide *righ-nol* – A herd animal raised in the Northeastern Lands primarily for its hide because its flesh is tough and difficult to chew. The hide is also tough, making it a popular choice for leather armor. There are, however, some culinary uses for the animals.

Riseen *reye-seen* – Green metal, more valuable than breyt, less valuable than airnelk.

Swamp cow – Large, slug-like mammalian creature that dwells in the Mystmirr; used by Sharpras to produce milk, cheese, and meat.

Tant tree *tawnt* – Large-thorned tree with wood so dense that it dulls the axes used to cut it within a few strokes. The roots are almost impossible to dig out and take years to break down.

Time-slave – This is a person who has chosen to sell themselves to another person as a slave for an agreed upon period of time. The deal is sealed with a tattoo, or ink, as the people of Llayentia call them. The tattoo must be placed in a prominent position, yet most people choose upper back and shoulder, as these areas can be covered by clothing more readily than a hand or wrist. The tattoo has the time period of the enslavement noted on it. When the time is up, most choose to have the tattoo removed or altered to make them disappear. Unless the removal is done by an expert, there will be a scar.

T'son barnacles – Barnacles that grow in the Istoarm Sea; source of the Foreveron drug.

Vapoor _vuh_-_poor_ – Venomous lizard whose dung is caustic enough to eat into stone.

Vespra-lanir _ves-pruh luh-neer_ – Small creature with razor-like teeth which hunts in packs. Their saliva holds bacteria which causes wounds to become infected, so that even if the prey escapes they can follow and take it out later after it has weakened.

Zaernut tree _zair-nut_ – This interesting tree grows in the Mystmirr swamp and is valued for its fruit, nut, and bark. While the health giving nut is odorous, the fruit that surrounds it is sweet scented and gathered for use in perfumes, as is the bark. The fruit is so bitter that the animals do not eat it and, given the degree of disagreeable taste, it is surprising that anyone discovered that the nut had nutritive value.

Acknowledgments

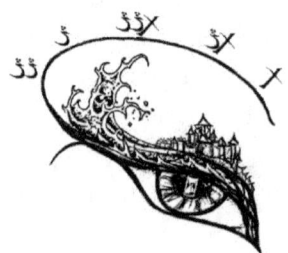

Many thanks to all the wonderful volunteer beta readers who have made Trapped possible, with special thanks to: Amanda Truax, Constance Epperson, Crystal Thompson, Harrison Brook, Heather Vaughan, James Taylor, Jennifer Thompson, Jenny Daugherty, Karen Swaty, Karin Rochelle, Katrina Pogue, Kellie Stone, Kim Franco, Lee Hunt, Matthew Wispinski, Nathan Thompson, Paula Biever, Rick Haga, Sandra Wolbert, Tiffany Corell, and Vickie Stephenson for your constructive criticism. I could never have done this without you. You kept me on track but, more importantly, expressed your love for the characters and concepts of Kyron's Worlde.

To Mark Hardman, a massive thanks for your work on this cover. How fortunate I have been to conspire with an artist of such marvelous caliber. You not only read my books but also understand the feel of Kyron's Worlde and its peoples.

For the help with creating the monetary system and realistic map distances, thank you to a very special friend, Tom Stiles. The intriguing array of odd information stored within that genius brain of yours fascinates me.

To Dr. Mike Meinhart, thank you for helping me keep the stab wounds and medical incidents realistic… for H'eumans at least.

To my editor, Jessica Westfield, comma conqueror extraordinaire; you are a true life saver! Thank you for helping me fine tune all the restructuring and being willing to discuss the merits of different decisions.

To Shelly Lazar, marketer and manager, thank you for all the late night marketing advice and encouraging my costume addiction. ;)

And finally to Samantha Zeiner, my proofreader; thank you so very much for your tolerance of all my oddities in formatting and for finding all the last minute oopsies.

E.S. TILTON

E.S. Tilton's hunger for all-things-fantasy was birthed at the age of eleven while reading *The Hobbit*. For the next 37 years she fed that craving with thousands of books. During that time she homeschooled three children, spent ten years making people's homes beautiful with paint, adopted more animals than she should have, and indulged in numerous role- playing games.

For most of her life she suffered from a writing phobia that made drafting even a simple letter an all day nightmare, yet through the use of EFT techniques and Holosync technologies, she overcame that fear. One perfectly normal morning in 2008, she awoke from sleep with a dream that haunted her, begging to be written. That dream is Kyron's Worlde. Step into her mind, where not everything is as it seems.

If you've enjoyed this book and would like to see more books from Kyron's Worlde, please review Trapped. Your voice is both the voice of encouragement for me, as well as the trumpet that calls in other readers. You can also friend me on Facebook or visit my webpage if you would like to give more feedback.

~~ E. S. Tilton

www.kyronsworld.com